Clement Mansfield Ingleby, Holcombe Ingleby

Essays

Clement Mansfield Ingleby, Holcombe Ingleby

Essays

ISBN/EAN: 9783741100017

Manufactured in Europe, USA, Canada, Australia, Japa

Cover: Foto ©Andreas Hilbeck / pixelio.de

Manufactured and distributed by brebook publishing software
(www.brebook.com)

Clement Mansfield Ingleby, Holcombe Ingleby

Essays

ESSAYS

BY THE LATE

CLEMENT MANSFIELD INGLEBY,
M.A., LL.D., V.P.R.S.L.

EDITED BY HIS SON.

LONDON:

TRÜBNER & CO., LUDGATE HILL.

1888.

Ballantyne Press
BALLANTYNE, HANSON AND CO.
EDINBURGH AND LONDON

PREFACE.

———×———

Of the essays included in this volume, four are now printed for the first time, viz.: 'A Dialogue on the Perception of Objects,' 'Law and Religion,' 'Romantic History,' and 'A Voice for the Mute Creation.' The first of these, though complete in itself, was intended to be only one of a series on the same subject. Five were actually written, but, on the advice of a friend, the late George Henry Lewes, who objected to the dialogue form, my father refrained from publishing them. What became of the complete MS. I do not know. In addition to what is here presented I have been able to find only a fragment of the second Dialogue.

The essay entitled 'A Voice for the Mute Creation' was delivered in the form of a lecture at the Reading-Room, Ilford: that 'On some Traces of the Authorship of the Works attributed to Shakespeare,' before the Royal Society of Literature: that on 'The Mutual Relations of Theory and Practice,' before the Birmingham Young Men's Mental Improvement and Mental Aid Association.

The essays on Bacon, Coleridge, and De Quincey appeared in the *British Controversialist* some years ago, having formed part of a series published in that magazine under the title of 'Many-Sided Minds.'

The essay entitled 'The Ideality of the Rainbow' appeared in the *Fortnightly Review*, 'An Estimate of Wordsworth' in *Hibernia*, a Dublin publication, and the essay on Henry Thomas Buckle in *The Church of our Saviour Magazine*, Birmingham.

I have to thank the proprietors of the above magazines for their courtesy in permitting the re-publication of these Essays.

HOLCOMBE INGLEBY.

VALENTINES, ILFORD,
        October 29, 1887.

CONTENTS.

I.

ON SOME TRACES OF THE AUTHORSHIP OF THE WORKS ATTRIBUTED TO SHAKESPEARE.

ONE does not look for popularity in the attempt to disturb a popular belief. One may, nevertheless, bespeak a favourable consideration for the most startling views if only they are supported by facts, and their advocacy is addressed to a competent tribunal.

An American essayist, who speaks from an intellectual eminence which justifies the speculation, asserts :—

"that what is best written or done by genius, in the world, was no man's work, but came by wide social labour, when a thousand wrought like one, sharing the same impulse." [1]

He points to the English Bible, the Anglican Ritual, and the Dramas of Shakespeare, as examples in point. He remembers, and so must we, that Shakespeare did not write for fame ; that he claimed no property in his published works, and did not assert their originality. If their whole merit has been assigned to him, it was by no act of his. They were produced for representation, not for literature, and their producer was rather a showman than an author.

[1] 'Representative Men,' by R. W. Emerson. A like passage occurs in his masterly *Essay on Compensation*, Essays, 1841, p. 108.

A

The time may come when every personal interest
about the man will be forgotten, when the schoolboys
of an American empire will confound the man with his
works, as schoolboys nowadays are said sometimes to
look upon Euclid as the name of a science.   When that
time comes, the reading public will be no more astonished
by the assertion that Lord Bacon wrote Shakespeare than
we are by the assertion that Babrius wrote Æsop.

But at present we have not wholly identified Shakespeare with "his booke," and when Mrs. Kitty, in
Garrick's farce, asks, "Who wrote Shakespeare?" and
my Lord Duke replies, "Ben Jonson," the humour is
still as fresh as the day when it was written.

Before entertaining Mrs. Kitty's question, we must
determine in what sense it is to be understood.   If the
inquiry be after some one man who originated, designed,
and executed the various dramas of the "booke," let us
consider whether such a requirement would be reasonable in the case of any great work of art.   Was
Tennyson the sole author of those Arthurian Romances
which have won for him a corner of Spenser's footstool?
Not at all.   The legends and materials were made to
his hand.   Yet, in the truest sense, Tennyson may be
called the author of the ' Idylls of the King,' for he re-
imagined and re-created them, without infringing the
rights of another.   In this sense, then, was the actor,
William Shakespeare, the author of ' The Merry Wives
of Windsor,' ' The Taming of the Shrew,' ' The Life and
Death of King John,' ' The Life of King Henry V.,' the
three parts of ' King Henry VI.,' ' The Life of King

Henry VIII.,' 'Titus Andronicus,' 'Romeo and Juliet,' 'Timon of Athens,' 'Hamlet,' and 'Pericles'? It seems not. You may suppose I have not selected those thirteen plays at random. The fact is, that not one of them is free from the suspicion that another hand has contributed to that fame which has been appropriated to Shakespeare alone.

We are here introduced into the thick of some of the most intricate problems of dramatic criticism, which I can only glance at now. Among the waifs which the wreck of the early Elizabethan drama has bequeathed to us are four plays bearing the following names:— 'The Troublesome Reigne of John, King of England,' 4to, 1591, 1611, 1622; 'The First Part of the Contention betwixt the Two Famous Houses of Yorke and Lancaster,' small 8vo, 1594, and 4to, 1600 and 1619; 'The True Tragedie of Richard, Duke of Yorke,' 4to, 1595, 1600, and 1619; and 'A Pleasant Conceited Historie called the Taming of a Shrew,' 4to, 1594, 1596, and 1607.

These respectively correspond to four of the plays attributed to Shakespeare, viz., 'The Life and Death of King John,' the second and third parts of 'King Henry VI.,' and 'The Taming of the Shrew.'

It is nearly certain that Shakespeare did not write a line of the old 'King John,' on which he constructed *his* play so named. It is equally certain that he had no hand whatever in the old 'Taming of a Shrew,' which we have every reason for believing to have been written by Christopher Marlow; but, on the other hand, he would be a "rash intruding fool" who should assert that Shakespeare had used this play in the composition of his own. Some day the knot will be untied; and then we shall see Mr. Charles Knight's conjecture established by the discovery of evidence that Marlow and Shakespeare used one and the same original in the composition of their dramas. I wish it were possible for us to see our way as clearly in dealing with 'The First Part of the Contention' and 'The True Tragedie.' They *seem* to have been originally the joint compositions of Marlow and Robert Greene, not improbably touched by Shakespeare subsequently, and exhibiting those touches in the edition of 1619; anyhow, Marlow's hand is unmistakably apparent in both plays. The following examples are adduced in support of this view by Mr. Halliwell in his edition of the 'First Sketches of II. and III. Henry VI.,' printed for the Shakespeare Society, 1843 :—

The wild O'Neile, my lord, is up in arms,
With troupes of Irish kernes, that uncontroul'd
Do plant themselves within the English pale.
First Part of the Contention.

The wild O'Neile, with swarms of Irish kernes,
Lives uncontroul'd within the English pale.
Marlow's Edward II.

This villain, being but captain of a pinnace, threatens more plagues than Abradas, the great Macedonian pirate. —*Ibid.*

I remember, Ismena, that Epicurus measured every man's dyet by his own principles, and Abradas, the great Macedonian pirat, thought every one had a letter of mart that bare sayles in the ocean.—*Green's Penelope's Web*, 1588.

What, will the aspiring blood of Lancaster
Sink into the ground ? I thought it would have mouuted.

True Tragedie.

But when the imperial lion's flesh is gored,
He rends and tears it with his wrathful paw,
And highly scorning, that the lowly earth
Should drink his blood, mounts up to the air.

Marlow's Edward II.

Stern Falconbridge commands the narrow seas.—*Ibid.*

The haughty Dane commands the narrow seas.—*Ibid.*

I am, however, far from sure that the argument founded on these and other similarities between the ' Contention' and the works of Marlow and of Greene would not go to prove that some of the very additions to the old plays, in II. and III. ' Henry VI.,' with which Shakespeare is credited, were the work of one or other of his contemporaries. I give one example to show what I mean. In II. ' Henry VI.,' i. 3, occurs the line :—

"She bears a duke's revenues on her back."

In the 4to, 1619, of the ' First Part of the Contention,' the line stands thus :—

" She bears a duke's whole revenues on her back ; "

but it is wholly wanting in the earlier editions ; and it is this edition of 1619 which Mr. Halliwell regards as an intermediate version, presenting Shakespeare's first draft of II. ' Henry VI.' Now this very addition is

almost wholly the property of Marlow, for in his
'Edward II.' we read—

"He wears a lord's revenue on his back."

Here then is an intricate problem. Was Marlow the
amender of the old play of the 'First Part of the Contention'? and was Shakespeare a purloiner from
Marlow? Perhaps neither.

In order to show in what manner Shakespeare availed
himself of the old plays of 'The First Part of the Contention' and 'The True Tragedie,' I will adduce five
passages from these plays, and place in juxtaposition
with them the corresponding passages in the second and
third parts of 'King Henry VI.' Further with a view
to afford the reader the means of appreciating the true
character of the quarto edition of 1619, which contains
both parts of the 'Contention,' I have added the corresponding passages in this edition, which Mr. Halliwell
regards as "an intermediate composition." I need only
add that, with the exception of a passage containing the
genealogy of the Duke of York, there is none other
which countenances, or at least supports, Mr. Halliwell's
view. The other variations are (as it seems to me) of
no greater significance than the general run of various
readings in the early quarto editions of Shakespeare,
and which assuredly have no source more respectable
than the blunders of printers and copyists, and the
tinkerings of players.

(1.) "*Humphrey.* This night when I was laid in bed, I dreampt
    that
        This my staffe mine Office badge in Court,

Was broke in two, and on the ends were plac'd,
The heads of the Cardinall of *Winchester*,
And *William de la Poule* first Duke of Suffolke."

The First Part of the Contention, 4to, 1594.

" This night when I was laid in bed, I dreamt
That this my staffe, mine office badge in Court,
Was broke in twaine, by whom I cannot gesse :
But as I thinke by the Cardinall.　What it bodes
God knowes ; and on the ends were plac'd
The heads of Edmund Duke of Somerset,
And William de la Pole first Duke of Suffolke."

Ibid., 4to, 1619.

" Methought this staff, mine office-badge in Court,
Was broke in twain ; by whom I have forgot,
But as I think, it was by the Cardinal ;
And on the pieces of the broken wand
Were placed the heads of Edmund Duke of Somerset,
And William de la Pole, first Duke of Suffolk.
This was my dream : what it doth bode, God knows."

II. Henry VI., folio, 1623.

(2.) " *Elnor.* Ile come after you, for I cannot go before,
But ere it be long, Ile go before them all,
Despight of all that seeke to crosse me thus."

The First Part of the Contention, 4to, 1594.

" Ile come after you, for I cannot go before,
As long as Gloster beares this base and humble minde :
Were I a man, and Protector as he is,
I'de reach to th' crowne, or make some hop headlesse.
And being but a woman, ile not be behinde
For playing of my part, in spite of all that seek to crosse
　me thus."

Ibid., 4to, 1619.

" Yes, my good lord, I'll follow presently.
Follow I must ; I cannot go before,
While Gloucester bears this base and humble mind.
Were I a man, a duke, and next of blood,

I would remove these tedious stumbling-blocks
And smooth my way upon their headless necks ;
And being a woman, I will not be slack
To play my part in Fortune's pageant."

II. Henry VI., folio, 1623.

(3.) " And his proud wife, high minded Elanor,'
That ruffles it with such a troupe of Ladies,
As strangers in the Court takes her for the Queene."

The First Part of the Contention, 4to, 1594.

" And his proud wife, high minded Elanor,
That ruffles it with such a troupe of Ladies,
As strangers in Court take her for the Queene ;
She beares a Dukes whole revennewes on her backe."

Ibid., 4to, 1619.

" Not all these lords do vex me half so much
As that proud dame, the lord protector's wife.
She sweeps it through the court with troops of ladies,
More like an empress than Duke Humphrey's wife :
Strangers in court do take her for the queen :
She bears a duke's revennues on her back," etc.

II. Henry VI., folio, 1623.

(4.) " I have seduste a headstrong Kentishman,
John Cade of Ashford,
Under the title of John Mortemer,
To raise commotion."

The First Part of the Contention, 4to, 1594.

" I have seduste a headstrong Kentish man,
John Cade of Ashford,
Under the title of Sir John Mortimer,
(For he is like him every kinde of way)
To raise commotion."

Ibid., 4to, 1619.

" I have seduced a headstrong Kentish man,
John Cade of Ashford,

To make commotion, as full well he can,
Under the title of John Mortimer."

II. Henry VI., folio, 1623.

(5.) " *Clarence* beware, thou keptst me from the light,
But I will sort a pitchie daie for thee.
For I will buz abroad such prophesies,
As *Edward* shall be fearefull of his life,
And then to purge his feare, Ile be thy death.
Henry and his sonne are gone, thou Clarence next,
And one by one I will dispatch the rest,
Counting my selfe but bad, till I be best.
Ile drag thy bodie in another roome,
And triumph *Henry* in thy daie of doome."

The True Tragedie, 1595.

" *Clarence* beware, thou keptst me from the light,
But I will sort a pitchie daie for thee.
For I will buz abroad such prophesies,
Under pretence of outward seeming ill,
As *Edward* shall be fearefull of his life,
And then to purge his feare, Ile be thy death.
King *Henry*, and the Prince his sonne are gone,
And *Clarence* thou art next to follow them,
So by one and one dispatching all the rest,
Counting my selfe but bad, till I be best.
Ile drag thy bodie in another roome,
And triumph *Henry* in thy daie of doom."

Ibid., 1619.

"Clarence, beware ; thou keep'st me from the light :
But I will sort a pitchy day for thee ;
For I will buz abroad such prophecies
That Edward shall be fearfull of his life,
And then, to purge his feare, I'll be his death.
King Henry and the prince his son are gone :
Clarence thy turn is next, and then the rest,
Counting myself but bad till I be best.
I'll throw thy body in another room
And triumph, Henry, in thy day of doom."

III. Henry VI., folio, 1623.

If Shakespeare had no hand in these two old plays,
it is demonstrable that more than four-sevenths of
those plays were borrowed, and appropriated *verbatim*
by Shakespeare, in the composition of the second and
third parts of ' King Henry VI.' Mr. Halliwell, however, thinks it not unlikely that they are both *rifaci-
menti* by Shakespeare of older plays ('The First Sketches
of II. and III. Henry VI.,' edited by Halliwell for the
Shakesp. Soc., 1843, introd. p. 19), a conjecture which
is unhappily unsupported by evidence, or it would
relieve Shakespeare from the charge of appropriation.
But we need not, I think, be very nice on that score,
when we consider the large levies he made on contemporary *prose* literature.[1] I ought to add that we know
of no old play corresponding to the first part of ' King
Henry VI.' This default, considered in conjunction
with the poverty of that performance, might incline
one to think that it owes as little to the genius of
Shakespeare as do ' The First Part of the Contention '
and 'The True Tragedie.'

These four (or five) plays form a class by themselves.
Into another class fall four other plays, which are
almost universally received and always cited as first
sketches by Shakespeare. These are as follows :—' An

---

[1] Compare, for example, Shakespeare's Roman plays with North's
'Plutarch :' take 'Coriolanus' as a sample : or better still, perhaps,
consult Florio's 'Montaigne,' and see how Shakespeare could appropriate a long and curious passage. In all such cases he made no
attempt to stamp his own originality on what he borrowed ; he simply
touched it up, so as to make it serviceable to his needs, and fall into
fair blank verse. In this art he certainly did not surpass Byron or
Coleridge.

excellent conceited Tragedie of Romeo and Juliet,' 4to, 1597; 'The Chronicle Historie of Henry the Fifth,' 4to, 1600, 1602, and 1608; 'A most pleasaunt and excellent conceited Comedie of Syr John Falstaffe, and the Merry Wives of Windsor,' 4to, 1602, and 1619; and 'The Tragicall Historie of Hamlet, Prince of Denmark,' 4to, 1603.

These respectively correspond to 'Romeo and Juliet,' 'The Life of King Henry V.,' 'The Merry Wives of Windsor,' and 'Hamlet,' of the folio collections. But though I have, for convenience, assigned these four sketches to one class, no two of them can be said to present common characteristics. In the first place, I find it hard to believe that Shakespeare had the lion's share in the composition of the old 'Romeo and Juliet,' and the old 'Hamlet' bears abundant internal evidence of having been printed from a manuscript copy, which had been fabricated out of the odds and ends furnished by an unskilled reporter. This play was entered on the books of the Stationers' Company in 1602, and so may have been acted some years before. It seems, however, not improbable that it was a *rifaci-mento* of an older play; that it was the older 'Hamlet' which was played at Henslow's theatre on June 9th, 1594, and that this was the play alluded to by Nash in his 'Epistle to the Gentlemen Students of the two Universities,' prefixed to Robert Greene's 'Arcadia,' and also by Lodge in that eccentric brochure, entitled 'Wit's Miserie, or the World's Madnesse,' 1596.[1] But

---

[1] Oxberry, the player, in his acting edition of Marlow's Dramatic

these are questions which it is impossible to discuss in the compass of this paper.

Into another class I must place the remaining four plays of those above cited, on which I will bestow but a passing remark. It is almost certain that John Fletcher wrote the greater part of 'The Life of King Henry VIII.' The author of 'Titus Andronicus' it is now impossible to determine. As far as I know, it has never been satisfactorily made out that Shakespeare wrote any part of it. It must be admitted that all the external evidences give him the sole authorship, as indeed they do in the case of several plays universally allowed to be spurious; but in this (as in those) the internal evidences wholly negative his claim. 'Timon of Athens' is a joint composition of which it is quite easy to determine the parts which were written by Shakespeare and those which were written by the older dramatist. As an example of this, take the two following speeches of Apemantus:—

> "Hoyday,
> What a sweep of vanity comes this way !
> They dance ! they are mad women.
> Like madness is the glory of this life,
> As this pomp shows to a little oil and root.

Works, 1818, asserts that in 'Richard II.' Shakespeare has borrowed largely, and to speak with candour, rather too largely, from Marlow's 'Edward II.' In support of this, he cites from 'Edward II.' the scene in which Edward is required by Leicester and others to give up his crown ; and the "looking-glass scene" from Richard II., viz., that in which Richard is required by Bolingbroke and Northumberland to do the like. The passages are too long for quotation here, and, in my opinion, do not support Oxberry's charge.

We make ourselves fools, to disport ourselves ;
And spend our flatteries, to drink those men,
Upon whose age we void it up again,
With poisonous spite and envy.
Who lives, that's not depraved, or depraves ?
Who dies, that bears not one spurn to their graves
Of their friend's gift ?
I should fear, those that dance before me now,
Would one day stamp upon me : it has been done :
Men shut their doors against a setting sun."

We may be quite sure that this is the older work.
It has not the ring of Shakespeare in any of his moods ;
and not only that, it has not a single feature, turn, or
style which suggests him. It is of the old, rude, dusty
school, dusty and rude enough ; evidently written by
one who bombasted it when Kyd and Marlow were in
their swaddling clothes. When Shakespeare conde-
scends to repair the old rubbish, see what sterling work
he makes of it. Here is Shakespeare's Apemantus :—

" What, think'st
That the bleak air, thy boisterous chamberlain,
Will put thy shirt on warm ? Will these moss'd trees,[1]
That have outlived the eagle, page thy heels,
And skip when thou point'st out ? Will the cold brook
Candied with ice, caudle thy morning taste,
To cure thy o'er-night's surfeit ? Call the creatures,
Whose naked natures live in all the spite
Of wreakful heaven ; whose bare unhoused trunks,
To the conflicting elements exposed,
Answer mere nature ; bid them flatter thee ;
O ! thou shalt find . . . . thou flatter'st misery."

Do we not here catch the rare old tones of him who
sang the outcast king in the storm, and the banished

---

[1] Moss'd trees. So Hammer's edition. The folios have *moist trees*.

duke in the forest of Ardenne? [1]   The study of ' Pericles' leads us to a similar conclusion, but the dissection is not so easy.

To these remarks I should add, that in ' The Life and Death of King Richard II.,' Shakespeare may have utilised an older play.   Anyhow, there was at least *one* old play on this subject.   Such a play was acted in 1601, and again in 1611.

In using up old materials, and grafting one play upon another, Shakespeare was merely conforming to an established usage.   We can hardly regret that he did so, even though the practice is to be reprehended, as likely to give currency to falsehood.   Be that as it may, we cannot but marvel at that magic skill which at the first touch endows the grub with wings, and then transmutes it into a lovely butterfly.   The material he used up seems generally to have been the livelier portions of the old theatric stock, which, like the bones in a dust-heap, become the property of the first person who takes the trouble to turn them to account.   He must, indeed, have wrought *ut magus* who made those dry bones live. [2]

---

[1] After making this selection, I observe that Mr. Charles Knight, in his 'Studies of Shakespeare,' 1851, p. 72, has selected the same speeches for comparison ; to these he adds two speeches of Flavius, the just steward, viz., that beginning, " What will this come to ?" and that beginning, "If you suspect my husbandry." These exhibit the double authorship almost as well as the former pair ; but, of course, the grander is the character, the more striking is the contrast.

[2] *Ut magus:* two words from Horace (Ep. l., lib. ii. l. 213) which surmount the noble portrait of Shakespeare, attributed to Cornelius Janson, the property of the Duke of Somerset.   It is instructive to

Justifiable or not, the practice was eminently advantageous; it not only effected a great economy in the playwright's mental resources and " midnight oil," but ensured for the audience the maintenance of their old interest in the story that was represented. I have elsewhere pointed out and established the low social status of the dramatist at this time.[1] Playwriting and acting were neither trades nor professions. When the Professor in ' The Water Babies ' caught Tom in his net, he called him an *eft*, but observing that he had no tail (so that he could not be an eft) and was to all appearance a land-baby (and therefore could not live under water), he let him go, and struck him out of the book of life. Like Tom, the Elizabethan players and dramatists fell "between two stools." Their patrons regarded them as persons *sans aveu*, and therefore statutable vagrants. Accordingly, it came to pass that where all was disreputable, no particular scandal arose from one dramatist *annexing* the lucubration or inspiration of another, unless, indeed, the preserve of one theatre were poached on by the playwright of another. In that event fired out the smouldering jealousy which maintained the standing quarrels of rival theatres; literally *rival* they sometimes were, being on opposite banks of the Thames. "It is an ill wind that blows nobody any good." To this wretched jealousy we are

compare this portrait with the mask in the possession of Professor Owen, and which is to be seen at the British Museum.

[1] I refer to a tract entitled, ' Was Thomas Lodge a player? An exposition touching the social status of the Dramatist in the reign of Elizabeth,' imp. 8vo, 1868.

indebted for a most curious piece of evidence, that
Shakespeare did more poaching at the Globe than ever
he did at Fulbrooke. I refer to the famous passage in
Greene's 'Groat'sworth of Wit bought with a Million
of Repentance,' 1592, to which I shall shortly revert.
Apropos of that, Mr. Halliwell quotes from a quarto
tract, dated 1594, called 'Greene's Funeralls,' by R.
B., Gent., the following lines :—

> " Nay, more the men that so eclipst his fame,
>   Purloynde his plumes ; can they deny the same ? "

Shakespeare was certainly one of the men censured
here.

I have called the more ancient Elizabethan plays waifs
from the general wreck of the older drama. In the
coming days of Macaulay's New Zealander, the grander
works of Shakespeare will remain to our posterity, not
like waifs that have drifted down by reason of their
lightness, but like the boulders which, by reason of
their solidity and weight, have escaped the general
denudation. Perhaps, too, in times to come, the
Apollyon power of criticism may reveal Shakespeare's
method of composition, by some subtle process of dis-
integration of which we now know nothing. I have
marked, on the sea beach at Filey, the work of destruction which the tide is ceaselessly waging among the
Oolitic rocks. The primeval sand had been amassed
by the ancient sea in the usual rippled form, and thus
became stratified. The sea is now silting out the less
solid particles from the rock, and breaking it up into

slabs, whose cleavage shows the old ripple-mark. "Nature," says Emerson, "can never keep a secret;" she never wholly erases her footprints, and we may be sure that the genius of Shakespeare was not more subtle or cunning than nature.

Putting aside the questions suggested by the plays, it is necessary, for the completion of our inquiry, to ascertain what contemporary testimony is extant, which by identifying William Shakespeare, the player, with the author of the plays, may prevent or rebut all rational doubt on the subject. Any difficulty which we may meet with here more or less infects all the poetical literature of that day. For instance, the beautiful epigram on "Sidney's sister, Pembroke's mother," which is No. 15 in Ben Jonson's 'Underwoods,' is also in a collection of poems by Jonson's friend, William Browne (Lansdowne Manuscripts, 777, first printed by Sir Egerton Brydges), with an additional verse. I suspect the second verse is all that belongs to Browne. The pastoral, "Come live with me and be my love," is assigned to Marlow in 'England's Helicon,' 1606; and the nymph's reply, "If love and all the world were young," is there given to Raleigh, under the pseudonym IGNOTO: yet the first of these, and the first verse of the second, constitute No. 20 in the collection of short pieces attributed to Shakespeare, printed in 1599, and senselessly called 'The Passionate Pilgrim.' No. 11 in the same collection, "Venus with young Adonis sitting by her," occurs in a volume called 'Fidessa, a collection of Sonnets,' by B. Griffin, 1596,

and Nos. 8 and 21, " If Music and sweet Poetry agree,"
and " As it fell upon a day," are included in Richard
Barnefield's 'Poems in divers Humors,' 1598. Who
is sufficient to solve *these* questions of authorship? and
those which relate to the drama are (for various reasons
inapplicable to minor poetry) infinitely more intricate
and perplexing.

There is a growing school who affect to disbelieve in
Shakespeare's authorship of the works attributed to him.
There were probably sceptics of this sort before 1852,
but the earliest attempt to impugn the prevalent belief,
as far as I know, was made in the number of *Chambers's
Edinburgh Journal* for August 7th in that year. The
spirit of the article is healthy enough. The scantiness
of our evidence is fairly pointed out; at the same time,
the two dedications to Lord Southampton, and the
testimony of Jonson, both in prose and verse, are
admitted to weigh heavily against the doubters. On
the other hand, the omission of Shakespeare's name from
the works of Raleigh and Bacon is indicated, but without the suggestion of their possible authorship of the
works attributed to Shakespeare. The game thus
started was hunted, by Miss Delia Bacon, I believe, in
Putnam's Monthly for January 1856 (vol. vii. p. 1).
It is here that the claims of Lord Bacon to the authorship of those works were first advanced. In 1856, an
original inquirer, Mr. William Henry Smith (then of
Brompton, now of Highgate), published a letter to the
first Lord Ellesmere, with the interrogative title, ' Was
Lord Bacon the author of Shakespeare's plays ? ' This

he followed up, in 1857, with a small volume on the same subject, entitled 'Bacon and Shakespeare.' In the same year was published the enormous volume (the composition of which cost Miss Delia Bacon her reason and her life), called 'The Philosophy of the Plays of Shakespeare unfolded.' In this book, the joint claims of Raleigh and Bacon are advocated with the faith and earnestness of a martyr. Lastly, in 1866 was published, in America, a large volume, entitled 'The Authorship of the Plays attributed to Shakespeare,' by Nathaniel Holmes, one of the Judges of the Supreme Court of the State of Missouri. This work is entirely devoted to the advocacy of Lord Bacon's authorship. Mr. Holmes having presented Mr. James Spedding, the editor of Bacon's works, with a copy of this book, and solicited his opinion thereupon, was so fortunate as to elicit an admirable criticism on the general question. This, together with other private letters which have passed between Messrs. W. H. Smith, Spedding, and Holmes, I have been permitted to read, but I am not at liberty to make known their very curious contents.

This remarkable controversy is not without its uses. It serves to call particular attention to the existence of a class of minds which, like Macadam's sieves, retain only those ingredients that are unsuited to the end in view. Mix up a quantity of matters relevant and irrelevant, and those minds will eliminate from the instrument of reasoning every point on which the reasoning ought to turn; and then proceed to exercise their constitutional perversity on the residue. This is the class of minds to

which Bishop Warburton belonged; so that what Thomas
De Quincey (Works, A. & C. Black, vol. vi. p. 259) writes
of that prelate will serve for a generic description :—

"The natural vegetation of his intellect tended to that kind of
fungus which is called 'crochet;' so much so that if he had a
just and powerful thought (as sometimes in germ he had), or a
wise and beautiful thought, yet by the mere perversity of his
tortuous brain, it was soon digested into a crochet."

The profession of the law (which at first was Warburton's) has (as De Quincey perceived) the inevitable
effect of fostering the native tendency of such minds.
For a fresh field of studying their idiosyncrasy we are
indebted to this controversy. It has also another use.
It incites us to look up our evidences for Shakespeare's
authorship; and we are reminded how few and meagre
they are.

The critic has the same interest in the works of Miss
Delia Bacon, Mr. W. H. Smith, and Judge Holmes, as
the physician has in morbid anatomy. He reads them,
not so much for the light which they throw on the
question of authorship, as for their interest as examples
of wrong-headedness. It is not at all a matter of moment
whether Bacon, Raleigh, or some mythical Mr. W. H.
be the favourite on whom the works are fathered; but
it is instructive to discover by what plausible process
the positive evidences of Shakespeare's authorship (scanty
as they are) are put out of court. As to Bacon as first
favourite, I suppose any one conversant with the life
and authentic works of that powerful but unamiable
character must agree with Mr. Spedding that, unless

he be the author of "Shakespeare," neither his life nor
his works give us any assurance that he could excel as
a dramatic poet. Of all men who have left their impress
on the reign of the first maiden Queen, not one can be
found who was so deficient in human sympathies as
Lord Bacon. As for such a man portraying a woman
in all her natural simplicity, purity, and grace, as to his
imagining and bodying forth in natural speech and
action such exquisite creations as Miranda, Perdita,
Cordelia, Desdemona, Marina—the supposition is the
height of absurdity. What, as it seems to me, has led
astray the few writers who have set up a claim for Lord
Bacon, is his admirable gift of language, scarcely
inferior to that of Shakespeare himself. This almost
unique endowment caused Bacon to manifest a kind of
likeness to Shakespeare in matters into which the
sympathies of the man and the training of the dramatic
poet do not enter. Hence it is easy to cull from the
works of these two great masters a considerable number
of curious parallels. I have looked over the collections
of Messrs. W. H. Smith and Holmes, and I must
confess I am astonished; but my astonishment has
not been provoked by the quantity or closeness of
the resemblances adduced, but by the spectacle of
educated men attempting to found such an edifice on
such a foundation. I could from my own reading add
to their collection some remarkable parallelisms which
they have overlooked.[1] But what of that? Is there

---

1 For instance, compare the following :—
"And because the breath of flowers is far sweeter in the air (where

anything singular in the case? Not at all. For if parallelisms can prove identity of authorship, what an array of anonymous plays ought to be put to Shakespeare's credit! For instance, the old play called 'Lust's Dominion' has no owner: in the course of its perusal I observed some very remarkable parallels between its text and that of Shakespeare. I will mention two by way of illustration. In Act I. Scene 1, the Moor, speaking of the multitude, asks the Queen-mother—

" Who arms this many-headed beast, but you ? "

Compare this with Coriolanus, Act IV. Scene 1—

> " The beast
> With many heads butts me away."

And with the chorus to Act II., ' Henry IV.'—

> "The blunt monster with uncounted heads."

Again, the Queen-mother, at the end of the play (Act V. Scene 3), when all her troubles are consummated, says—

> " I'll now repose myself in peaceful rest,
> And fly into some solitary residence, (?)
> Where I'll spin out the remnant of my life,
> In true contrition for my past offences."

---

it comes and goes, like the warbling of music) than in the hand," etc. Essay xlvi.

> " O, it came o'er my ear, like the sweet sound
> That breathes upon a bank of violets ;
> Stealing and giving odour."—*Twelfth Night,* i. 1.

Which reminds us of Paulina's last speech in ' A Winter's Tale,' somewhat as a flowered tea-tray reminds us of a garden.

How many of such resemblances between ' Lust's Dominion ' and Shakespeare would prove the right of that play to a place in the received collection ? My answer is that a large number of such cases would assuredly dispose of that claim, and a small number would go no way to prove it. It requires no minute acquaintance with Shakespeare's text to be struck with that inexhaustible pregnancy of language which rarely repeats an image once expressed without expressing it anew. In fact it is one argument against Shakespeare's authorship of ' The Two Noble Kinsmen,' which has his name, along with Fletcher's, on the title, that so many Shakespeareanisms occur in its text.

> " And I . . . .
> Doe here present this Machine, or this frame."
>
> *Two Nob. K.* iii. 6.

> " Thou mighty one, that with thy power has turn'd
> Green Neptune into purple."
>
> *Ibid.,* v. 1.

> PALAMON (*addressing* MARS).
>
> " Thou great decider
> Of dusty and old titles, that heal'st with blood
> The earth when it is sick, and cur'st the world
> O' the *pluresie* of people."
>
> *Ibid.,* v. 1.

And yet we are asked to believe that, because Bacon writes, " All was *inned* at last unto the King's barn," and " the cold becometh more *eager*," therefore he was the author of ' All's Well that Ends Well,' and ' Hamlet.'

Summarily disallowing, then, the claims set up on behalf of Bacon, I proceed to consider, with the utmost brevity, those evidences on which we are justified in attributing to Shakespeare the chief authorship of the dramas which have the passport of his name. I own at once that those evidences are scanty : not so scanty as Mr. W. H. Smith asserts, for he cites but four witnesses whose testimony was given in Shakespeare's lifetime, viz., Francis Meres (1598); William Basse (1599 ?); the anonymous author of 'The Return from Parnassus' (1606, said to have been written in 1602), who, however, does not connect the poems named with Shakespeare; and Ben Jonson. In fact, there are at least eleven besides; two of whom are among our chief witnesses.[1]

But so little weight do I attach to contemporary

---

[1] I do not count Spenser, for the oft-quoted line from his 'Teares of the Muses,'

> "Our pleasant Willy, ah ! is dead of late,"

unquestionably referred to Sir Philip Sidney, whose poetical *sobriquet* was Willy. Thus, in an eclogue signed A. W., in the 'Poetical Rhapsody' quoted by Mr. Collier, in his Introduction to 'Seven English Poetical Miscellanies,' 1867, occurs the following, in reference to Sidney's recent death :—

> "We deem'd our Willy aye should live,
> So sweet a sound his pipe could give ;
> But cruell death
> Hath stopt his breath :
> Dumb lies his pipe that wont so sweet to sound !"

Besides, as Mr. Halliwell has proved, Spenser's allusion could not be to Shakespeare ; for the 'Teares of the Muses' was written about 1580, and published ten years later. Shakespeare was but sixteen years old in 1580, and was not known in London *as a poet* till eight or nine years afterwards.

rumour as an evidence of authorship that I shall trouble
you with seven witnesses only. Of these, there are but
four who directly identify the man, or the actor, with
the writer of the plays and poems.

The first witness I shall call is John Harrison, the
publisher; though it is but little that he can tell us.
It was for him that 'Venus and Adonis' was printed in
1593, and 'The Rape of Lucrece' in 1594. No author's
name is on the title-page of either. But fortunately
he prefixed to each a dedication to Lord Southampton,
subscribed "William Shakespeare." It is to me quite
incredible that Harrison would have done this, unless
Shakespeare had written the dedications, or at least
had been a party to them. Now in dedicating the
first poem, the undersigned speaks of it as "my un-
polisht lines," and "the first heir of my invention,"
and he promises to honour his patron "with some
graver labour:" in dedicating the second poem he
speaks of it as "my untutored lines," and adds, "what
I have done is yours, what I have to do is yours, being
part in all I have, devoted yours."

So far, then, we have a tittle of evidence to prove
that one William Shakespeare was the author of both
these poems. Three or four years later a well-known
man of letters named Francis Meres speaks of Shakespeare as the author of 'Venus and Adonis,' 'Lucrece,'
sundry sonnets, and ten specified plays. Of these plays
nine are known to us and received as Shakespeare's.
Meres' testimony is given in seven pages of his book,
called 'Palladis Tamia—Wit's Commonwealth,' 1598;

but I have never seen quoted any of his remarks on Shakespeare's works, except the stock passages on folios 281 and 282, which one writer evidently borrows from another to save the trouble of consulting the original. It is especially noteworthy that on the first page of folio 280 Meres selects Sir Philip Sidney, Spenser, Daniel, Drayton, Warner, Shakespeare, Marlow, and Chapman, as the poets by whom the English tongue was "mightily enriched, and gorgeouslie invested in rare ornaments and resplendent abiliments;" and it is evident from subsequent remarks that he awarded the palm to the authors of the 'Faerie Queen' and the 'Arcadia.'

Robert Greene (the abler and better known of the two Elizabethan poets of that surname) wrote a number of plays in conjunction with Marlow, Lodge, Nash, and others, which had great popularity before the advent of Shakespeare. In his last publication, called 'A Groatsworth of Wit Bought with a Million of Repentance,' 1592, he addresses an admonition to three of his associates, exhorting them to abandon play-writing. These we may readily identify as Marlow, Lodge, and Peele. Then follow the words, so often quoted, which are for us the important testimony :—

"Base-minded men, all of you, if by my misery ye be not warned ; for unto none of you (like me) sought those burs to cleave: those puppets (I mean) that speak from our mouths, those antics garnished in our colours. . . . Yes, trust them not : for there is an upstart crow beautified with our feathers, that with his *tyger's heart, wrapt in a player's hide*, supposes he is as well able to bombast out a blank verse as the best of you."

So far it might be conjectured that Shakespeare is the man alluded to : providentially Greene adds these words, which convert that conjecture into a certainty :—

"and being an absolute Johannes *Fac totum,* is in his own conceit the only *Shakes-scene* in a country."

Burs, puppets, antics, crows in peacock's feathers— such are the hard words he gives the players ; and these he follows up with a second instalment of abusive epithets—*apes, rude grooms, buckram gentlemen, peasants,* and *painted monsters.* Why, this insolence out-Nashes Nash!

Now in turning this extract to account we must be more cautious than dramatic critics usually are to avoid reasoning in a circle. If we are fully satisfied that *Shake-scene* is a pun upon Shakespeare, independently of the verse (which, like *Shake-scene,* is in italics), we may infer, perhaps, that Greene, or one of the dramatists admonished by him, wrote the whole or a part of ' The True Tragedy of Richard, Duke of York,' and that Shakespeare pillaged his predecessor's work " to beautify " or rather to fabricate his third part of ' Henry VI.' Anyhow, the line quoted, or rather travestied, occurs in both the ' True Tragedy ' and III. ' Henry VI.'

The conclusion being reached that Shakespeare is the player assailed by Greene, the testimony of Henry Chettle, the editor of Greene's ' Groatsworth of Wit,' is invested with a curious and special interest. Immediately after the appearance of that book, Chettle published a work of fiction called ' Kind Hart's Dream.'

He here refers to the preceding work, and confesses to having expunged from the manuscripts some of Greene's hard words; but he protests that he added nothing to it. After remarking on the admonition to the three dramatists, he adds this sputter of solecisms :—

" The other, whom I did not spare so much, as since I wish I had, for that, I have moderated the hate of living writers, and might have used my own discretion (especially in such a case, the Author being dead), that I did not, I am as sorry as if the original fault had been my fault ; because myself have seen his demeanour no less civil, than he excellent in the quality he professes : besides diverse of worship have reported his uprightness of dealing, which argues his honesty and his facetious grace in writing that approves his art." [1]

This is indeed a singular apology. We may picture to our mind's eye the shadowless man, the tinker of old plays, the second-rate actor, who had already, like the hero of his masterpiece,

" bought
Golden opinions from all sorts of people,"

but who as yet had not become a man of worship, and an armiger in right of gentle blood, by the mere force of his unpretending frankness, his modesty, and his gentleness, disarming his contemptuous and jealous traducers ; insomuch that the respectable Henry Chettle, who had never been a motley and a vagrant, is induced to give the author of ' Hamlet ' an acceptable testimonial.

---

[1] Gabriel Harvey was even more complimentary to the upstart crow. " I speak generally to every springing wit, but more especially to a few : and, at this instant, singularly to one, whom I salute with a hundred blessings." Four letters especially touching Robert Green, and other parties by him abused, 1592 ; third letter dated Sept. 9, 1592.

Well, for my part, I honour Chettle for this tardy act of justice.

I suppose I must, in the next place, cite the ostensible editors of the first 'collection of Shakespeare's works; for they were none other than Heminge and Condell, two of the company of players which, at the accession of James the First, was under the joint management of Lawrence Fletcher and William Shakespeare. But unfortunately for their credit and our satisfaction their prefatory statement contains, or at least suggests, what they must have known to be false. They would lead us to believe that their edition was printed from Shakespeare's manuscripts.

"who, as he was a happie imitator of Nature, was a most gentle expresser of it. His mind and hand went together : And what he thought, he uttered with that easinesse, that wee haue scarse receiued from him a blot in his papers."

Now we have positive knowledge of a fact inconsistent with this excerpt. We know that the text of seven of the plays in that edition was printed from the quarto editions, which they denounce as stolen and surreptitious, "maimed, and deformed by the frauds and stealthes of injurious impostors," and which plays they now offer "cur'd and perfect of their limbes."

Nothwithstanding this, the testimony of Shakespeare's fellows must be allowed to have some weight in the question of authorship. It is to me incredible that they should in that matter have attempted a fraud which must have been transparent to the noble brothers who lent their patronage to the volume, and which must sooner or later have been exposed in the face of all England.

Our last and principal witness is Ben Jonson, though he is less communicative than might be expected considering the closeness of his friendship with Shakespeare. In what he writes of the man, he seems to take it for granted that we know all about him already, and the things he tells us are not those which we most want to know. There are the verses prefixed to the first folio of Shakespeare, and the remarks entitled, *De Shakespeare nostrati*, in his posthumous work called 'Timber or Discoveries.' These remarks must be read in connection with Heminge and Condell's preface to the first folio, and with the *Induction* to Ben Jonson's play, entitled 'The Staple of News.' In the latter, Expectation says to Prologue, " Sir, I can expect much." Prologue answers, " I fear too much, lady; and teach others to do the like." Expectation rejoins, " I can do that, too, if I have cause." To which Prologue says, " Cry you mercy, you never did wrong, but with just cause." Truly one would never have found any evidence for Shakespeare in that, but for the explanation which Ben vouchsafes in his 'Timber.' He writes :—

"I remember, the players have often mentioned it as an honour to Shakespeare that in his writing (whatsoever he penned) he never blotted out a line. My answer hath been, Would he had blotted a thousand. Which they thought a malevolent speech. I had not told posterity this, but for their ignorance, who chose that circumstance to commend their friend by, wherein he most faulted ; and to justify mine own candour : for I loved

the man, and do honour his memory, on this side idolatry, as
much as any. He was (indeed) honest, and of an open and free
nature ; had an excellent phantasy, brave notions, and gentle
expressions ; wherein he flowed with that facility, that sometimes
it was necessary he should be stopped : *Sufflaminandus erat*, as
Augustus says of Haterius. His wit was in his own power, would
the rule of it had been so too. Many times he fell into those
things, could not escape laughter : as when he said in the person
of Cæsar, one speaking to him, ' Cæsar, thou dost me wrong.' He
replied, ' Cæsar did never wrong but with just cause,' and such
like ; which were ridiculous. But he redeemed his vices with
his virtues. There was ever more in him to be praised than to be
pardoned."

This is direct testimony, not merely to the fact that
Shakespeare wrote the play of ' Julius Cæsar,' but that
Cæsar's reply to Metellus Cimber was—

> " Cæsar did never wrong but with just cause,
> Nor without cause will he be satisfied."

But of course the editors will not have it. It is proverbial that office is a potent perverter of the judgment.
It would seem as if a critic became blear-eyed as soon
as he turned editor.

We may, I think, unreservedly accept the whole of
Ben's testimony in *this* matter. The five couplets
which he wrote on Droeshout's engraved portrait of
Shakespeare, prefixed to the early folios, are, I am
afraid, merely complimentary : besides, they are little
more than a translation. Mr. J. Hain Friswell has
been so kind as to refer me to an old portrait (1588)
of Sir Thomas More, in the " Tres Thomæ " of Staple-
ton, under which are the following lines :—

> " Corporis effigiem dedit ænea lamina. At ô si
> Effigiem mentis sic daret iste liber."

Ben Jonson's lines—

> " O could he but have drawne his wit
> As well in brass as he hath hit
> His face, the print would then surpasse
> All that was ever wit in brass,"

are but an expansion of the Latin couplet, as Mr. Friswell says, " with a certain *back twist.*"

It is not, however, these lines on which we rely as an evidence of authorship, but the forty couplets which follow the preface to the Folio 1623, addressed by Ben " To the memory of my beloved, the author, Mr. William Shakespeare, and what he hath left us." These verses are a precious testimony both to the authorship of the plays and to Ben's friendly estimate of the author's genius. But forasmuch as they do not deal in specialities, I have no occasion to quote them at length. It is curious that one of the phrases of eulogy here employed is repeated by Ben almost *totidem verbis* in a note entitled " Scriptorum Catalogus," in his 'Timber;' but it is there applied to Lord Bacon. To Shakespeare he says—

> " O, when thy socks were on,
> Leave thee alone, for the comparison
> Of all, that insolent Greece, or haughtie Rome
> Sent forth," etc.

Of Bacon he writes,—

> " He who hath filled up all numbers, and performed that in our tongue which may be compared or preferred either to insolent Greece or haughty Rome."

Of course the heretics have not been slow to avail themselves of this resemblance. They are welcome to what it is worth.

The conclusion which I think we may safely draw from the evidences adduced is, that no other known name is entitled to the credit awarded by common consent to "William Shakespeare," unless we go back to the playwrights who preceded him, and are able to identify the authors of those plays on which Shakespeare founded so many of his. In this case a residual problem is presented to us of so great difficulty, that at present no approximation has been made to its solution; and though it is one which has a special interest for me, and comes within the scope of my subject, its treatment would require the monopoly of a separate paper.

Certain it is that in a considerable number (I think more than one-half) of the plays, Shakespeare's all-assimilating genius derives its *pabulum* from the clumsy productions of earlier writers. To get an adequate notion of Shakespeare's art in this sort of work, I would call attention to the play of 'King John,' in comparison with 'The Troublesome Reign,' and I shall be much surprised if the comparion does not create an entirely new notion of Shakespeare's dramatic talent.

If I might venture to express my own opinion on this difficult inquiry, I should say, that in all probability, several of the comedies (strictly so called), and of the tragedies, 'Macbeth,' 'Coriolanus,' and 'Julius Cæsar,' are not indebted to any older plays on the same subject; and that 'Antony and Cleopatra,' 'Troilus

C

and Cressida,' and the ' Tempest,' are, in the profoundest
sense, original compositions; the entire structure, as
well as the architecture of each play, being wholly due
to Shakespeare's incomparable art. Looking at those
three plays only, unless, indeed, my judgment has been
warped by force of habit, I there discern the figure of
a poet who was of a more "select and generous chief"
than any of the imaginative writers of Elizabeth's
reign. Hazlitt, who proclaimed Shakespeare's intellectual and æsthetic superiority to the men of that day,
qualified his verdict by saying that "it was a common
and a noble brood." With Mr. Alexander Dyce, let
me say that "falser remark was never made by critic."
That the times were curiously favourable to genius
may be allowed; and we may agree with Goethe's
opinion, that much of what the giants of those days
became and achieved was due to the "stimulating
atmosphere" in which they lived. None can say to
what forest trees the garden flowers of our day, such
as Tennyson and Browning, might have waxed, had
they been planted in an Elizabethan soil. But if so
much be due to a man's surroundings, we must also
admit with sorrow that the direction into which the
energies of Englishmen have been diverted is so unfavourable to artistic life, that an artist of Shakespeare's stamp will never more be possible among us ;
that we "ne'er shall look upon his like again."

II.

THE MUTUAL RELATIONS OF THEORY AND PRACTICE.

An eminent American essayist, in an essay on Compensation, gives us a striking instance of pregnant symbolism bought at the cost of good taste, if not of reverence: "There is," says he, "a crack in every work God has made." Now, without going out of my way to censure this aphorism, I propose to inquire whether it does not condense, as it were, in cipher, an almost universal truth, of which every branch of human knowledge furnishes a treasury of examples. It is not for us to inquire why it has pleased our Creator to make us as we are, or the world in which we live as it is. Let His sovereign pleasure suffice us. *Stet pro ratione voluntas.* Yet we may profitably and reverently scan the wonders of His hand, and take note of the various anomalies which meet us at every turn and impede us in every attempt to measure His works by our limited faculties.

In Psychology have we not the anomaly of the Fall of man? And is it not true that his every effort to practise the ideal even of his own religious instinct is fraught with failure as disheartening as it is shameful?

Then, in Theology, have we not the anomalous element
of miraculous agency which necessarily mars its scientific unity? In Moral Philosophy, too, we have certain
insoluble "cases of conscience," which casuistry has
essayed in vain; while in Jurisprudence we are presented with the so-called "cases of necessity and
equity," in which the sceptre of the lawgiver is broken
in his hand. Then, in the Painter's art, what have
we but anomaly? Does not it ever vibrate between
two scarcely discriminable points, so that, on the one
hand, it is in danger of bondage to the real, as the
diorama and the works of the Pre-Raphaelite school;
and, on the other hand, in danger of losing in propriety
and truth what it gains in exalted sentiment? In
Music we have "temperament," which may be popularly
explained to be an unscientific procedure, by which
those intervals called the "third" and the "fifth" are
reduced to a common measure with the "octave." Then,
to turn our thoughts to the exact sciences, I might
pause to explain how in every pure and applied science
we have difficulties absolutely insuperable, "impossible
problems," "failures," and "anomalous results," which,
however, I will do no more than mention.

It is a common saying, that such and such a thing
may be true in theory, but does not hold good in practice.
On this subject the great German philosopher, Immanuel
Kant, wrote an essay, with the view of correcting this
vulgar error. For myself, I conceive it is an error
rather in the use of words than in the thing signified.

In the vulgar use of the word "theory," there is

generally some confusion between it and "hypothesis;"
just as if it were not possible to have a theory consisting
of the relations of facts to one another, without involving
any hypothetical element whatever. I am not sure,
indeed I very much doubt, whether this confusion
between "theory" and "hypothesis" is always involved
in the ordinary use of the former word. However, it
will be safer to discriminate between the proper meaning of these two words before proceeding further. We
must understand, then, that a hypothesis is a supposed
fact, assumed for the purpose of accounting for some
known phenomenon. Thus, when Arago suggested
that falling stars and thunderbolts are fragmentary
planets, he simply propounded a hypothesis (on the
strength of some probabilities), which might be susceptible of disproof or confirmation by subsequent facts,
as the case might be. Or to take another example.
When M. Bomme (on the elements assigned by Mr. J.
Russell Hind) calculated the return of the great comet
of 1556, he did so on the assumption that it was the
same comet which had been observed in 1264. Now it
is just at the present time that this assumption is about
to be confirmed or disproved. The reappearance of this
great comet within the next year will convert the
hypothesis in question into a fact; while, on the other
hand, its non-appearance before the end of 1860 will
conversely disprove that hypothesis. Now let us observe,
that the assumption of the identity of the comets of
1264 and 1556, is the only hypothetical element among
the data upon which M. Bomme made those exceed-

ingly laborious calculations (of the comet's return) which would warrant us in regarding him as a champion, and almost a martyr, of science. With the exception of this assumption, all his data were facts, not hypotheses. His calculations in respect of them were theoretical, and as such need not have comprised a single hypothetical element.

To recapitulate, then, what we have said, theory is the introduction of organisation among the facts or data of science. Hypothesis is the underlaying of the phenomena with such imaginary data as appear capable of accounting for them. Henceforth let these two things be kept distinct in the mind, and we shall have made our first step towards an investigation of the question whether there be, or can be, an irreconcilability, or, at least, want of harmony, between the laws of theory and the results of observation and experiment; that is, between the so-called "facts of science" and the "facts of experience."

But it is not always practicable to avoid the risk of confounding theory and hypothesis: and even men of mark not uncommonly fail to discriminate exactly between them. However, we rarely meet with such an example of this mistake as the following, which is furnished by a work of the highest repute and desert.

Mr. John Stuart Mill ('Logic,' vol. ii. p. 28), after describing the Nebular Hypothesis of Laplace, writes thus: "The known law of gravitation would then cause them (i.e., the nebular zones) to agglomerate in masses which would assume the shape which our planets

actually exhibit, would acquire, each round its own axis,
a rotatory movement; and would in that state revolve
as the planets actually do about the sun in the same
direction with the sun's direction, but with less velocity,
and each of them in the same periodic time which the
sun's rotation occupied when his atmosphere extended
to that point; and this also M. Comte has, by the
necessary calculations, ascertained to be true within
certain small limits of error. There is thus, in Laplace's theory, nothing hypothetical: it is an example of
legitimate reasoning, from a present effect to its past
cause; it assumes nothing more than that objects which
really exist obey the laws which are known to be obeyed
by all terrestrial objects resembling them."[1]

In the first place let me correct Mr. Mill's estimate of
the value of Comte's calculations. Professor Sedgwick,
in the Introduction to his celebrated Discourse, has
pointed out that Comte has committed a *petitio principii*,
which is of so glaring a character that it could hardly
have deceived Mr. Mill if he had understood the question. Comte's calculations are based on the assumption
of the truth of Kepler's laws, which involve the whole
question at issue. The whole problem is one of the
expansion and condensation of a rotating fluid mass,
and this has been evaded by the great positivist. Mr.
Mill accordingly is on the horns of a dilemma. He
either understood Comte's argument, or he did not. If

---

[1] Mr. Mill, in his 'Examination of Sir W. Hamilton's Philosophy,'
1855, p. 544, asks, if ignorance is with any man a necessary condition
of wonder; can he find nothing to wonder at "in the probable former
extension of the solar substance beyond the orbit of Neptune"?

he understood it, he either perceived the fallacy, or he did not. Such a man could not have perceived the fallacy and have endorsed it. If he did not perceive it, he must have been either so obtuse or so careless as to be a very unsafe guide through the labyrinth of inductive philosophy. On the other hand, the supposition that he did not understand Comte's argument is equally damaging to the confidence of his readers.

But Mr. Mill has committed offences graver than this. Let us inquire how many of the fallacies enumerated by himself he has himself committed.

And, first, of "fallacies of observation." Mr. Mill has fallen into that which he describes (p. 387) as "non-observation," inasmuch as the evidence for the existence of pure nebulous matter is insufficient, as also the evidence for supposing that it resembles known matter; *i.e.*, supposing for the sake of argument that there be such a thing as pure nebulous matter. Every nebula, wholly or partially resolved into a star-cluster, diminishes the probability of the present existence of an essential nebulous fluid (*princeps limus*), and the non-resolution is but a negative evidence of the least conceivable weight.[1]

---

[1] A writer in the *Westminster and Foreign Quarterly Review* for July 1, 1858 (N. S., vol. xiv. p. 190), thus unsuccessfully labours to prove the existence of nebulous matter. "If we are to believe that one of these nebulæ is so remote that its hundred thousand stars look only like a milky spot, invisible to the naked eye, we must, at the same time, believe that there are single stars so enormous that though removed to this same distance they remain visible. If we accept the other alternative, and say that many nebulæ are no farther off than our own stars of the eighth magnitude, then it is requisite to believe that

The result of induction in reference to the nature of comets is that, with the possible exception of their nuclei, they are subject to laws of which we know nothing, and of which the whole series of terrestrial phenomena furnishes no type. That a material body should be as transparent as air, and yet should not refract light, and that it should augment instead of tone down the centres of light over which it passes, is inexplicable by the known laws of nature; and yet such are the properties of comets' tails which, with the Magellanic clouds, furnish the slight ground on which the hypothesis of pure nebulous matter has been reared.

On these grounds Mr. Mill stands convicted of several "fallacies of generalisation," viz. :—

1. That of "groundless generalisation" (p. 406) ; "such, for instance, as all inferences from the order of nature existing on the earth or in the solar system to that which may exist in remote parts of the universe."

at a distance not greater than that at which a single star is still faintly visible to the naked eye, there may exist a group of a hundred thousand stars which is invisible to the naked eye. Neither of these positions can be entertained. What then is the conclusion that remains ? This only ; that the nebulæ are not farther off from us than parts of our own sidereal system, of which they must be considered members ; and that when they are resolvable into discrete masses, these masses cannot be considered as stars in anything like the ordinary sense of that word."

Giving the writer credit (as we are bound) for logical consistency, and supplying the premises implied in the enthymemes, it becomes apparent that we are asked to assume that *unresolved* nebulæ are, on an average, no farther from us than *resolved* nebulæ ; and with the concession of this assumption, the writer securely puts us on the horns of a dilemma, unless we accept his conclusion. But why are we to grant him this ? Is it not *at least equally probable* that the nebulæ which are resolvable only by the higher powers of Lord Rosse's telescope are farther off than those which yield to a lower power ?

2. An attempt to resolve what may be radically different phenomena into the same.

3. "False analogy;" not to mention other offences against the canons of induction.

These remarks are not intended to disparage Laplace's theory, which has a high claim on our faith. But we must not lose sight of the fact that the theory in question contains several pure hypotheses, and, in fact, assumes that objects, not known to have ever existed, were yet subject to the laws which terrestrial objects (possibly wholly unlike them) obey. We have, then, the phenomenon of a writer on logic, of the highest intellectual endowments, lulled by the opium of French positivism into a fancied security in an induction against which his seven chapters on Fallacies are but one long, earnest protest.

After this example, it is right to call attention to the necessity under which all men lie of being furnished with a theory, before applying themselves to practice, unless they are content that what they do shall be ill done. There is a proverb, which I first heard from the lips of a mathematical Yorkshireman: "He lets his hand outrun his head." Practical power has been happily called, by Coleridge, "the brain in the hand." And these expressions do not imply merely a looking before you leap, but a diligent marshalling of all available facts in the case, and an investigation of their mutual relations; the character of such investigation and the method employed therein being determined by the practical object you have in view. This preliminary brain-work is called a *theory*, from the Greek θεωρία, which signifies, primarily, a *view* or *inspection*, secondarily, *science*.

By this procedure it is generally possible to attain the proposed end by the simplest and best means. Without some such procedure it is seldom, if ever, possible to attain the end at all. Nature rarely dictates the best manner of doing even that which she herself imposes. A man, in walking, naturally swings his arms: mechanical theory establishes the fact that, in fast walking, this motion of the arms is a hindrance. A man sitting in the stern of a wherry finds himself thrown back with each forward stroke of the waterman: theory shows that by a forcible resistance to this motion the rowing is made easier to the waterman than by yielding to it. Many such instances might be adduced.

It will be obvious by this time to all my readers that any complaint against theorising, or any objection to a man on the ground of his being a theorist, can have its origin only in the ignorance or thoughtlessness of the objector; and that if a theory have misled any one, the evil does not lie in his having trusted to the guidance of a theory, but in his having been really without a true theory; and he therefore stands in need of one.

When Lord Brougham, in his introduction to the publications of the Society for the Diffusion of Useful Knowledge, explained the law of terrestrial gravity to be that bodies were attracted by the earth in an inverse proportion to the square of their distances from it, so that a body four feet from the earth would weigh only

one-sixteenth what it would at the distance of one foot,
a critic waggishly replied—" We now see why a ticket
porter carries his burden on his back, instead of tying
it to his waist; and why the weights used by shop-
keepers are so generally found false in the scales : for
if one of them weigh a pound at one foot from the
ground, it is obvious, according to Lord Brougham, that
it can weigh little more than an ounce in the scales." [1]
The fact is, that Lord Brougham had, simply for want
of thought, ignored a distance of about 3982 miles (the
mean distance from the surface of the earth to its
centre); for the force of gravity of the earth upon a
body varies inversely as the square of the distance of
that body from their common centre of gravity—a point
really not far removed from the centre of the earth. In
comparison of such a distance as that, the variation of
a few hundred yards is a matter of small moment in the
calculation of a body's weight to the earth. Hence it
is always assumed (as it may be without sensible error)
that the force of gravity near the earth's surface is not a
varying, but an uniform force. Now, the practical man
who had been innocently misled by Lord Brougham's
statement would at once begin, in John Bull fashion,
to rail at theory and theoretical men. But it is easily
seen how unreasonable such a procedure would be ; for
of all men the person who could be so taken in stands
specially in need of a theory to direct him aright; in
point of fact, without some theory, even his weighing
operations would lead to no result.

[1] 'The Errors of Big Wig.' (I quote from memory.)

But say what one may, there will always be a disagreement between merely practical men and theoretical
men, be the latter ever so practical. An amusing instance of this occurred in my own professional practice.
A mining lease contained a provision for the indemni-
fication of the lessee against *faults* in a coal bed. A
fault in geological language is a discontinuity in the
bed in consequence of its dislocation, the fissure being
filled up with a foreign substance ; or otherwise, the
parts being not only dissevered but displaced. Now in
the instance in question the workings showed no *fault*
in the coal bed ; but, what was almost as bad for the
lessee's pocket, he did break into what miner's call a
"horse's back," which is an upheaving of the strata
which underlie the coal, so as to throw the latter out of
its normal, straight direction into a curve ; in geological
language a *contortion.* The lessee claimed the benefit of
his clause ; but that clause contained not a word about
horses' backs or *heaves,* or any such thing. So to law
the parties went. The scientific evidence for the lessor
went to prove that a horse's back is not a fault, while
the evidence of mine agents on the other side went to
prove that miners did call a horse's back a fault. In
this case common sense decided it against the geologists,
and the lessee got an award in his favour. Here the
geological theory was indisputably correct ; but the ter-
minology in which the theory was accurately enounced
had not obtained such currency as to induce the arbi-
trator to suppose that it had been strictly employed in
the mining lease.

Now let us inquire how far Kant and his commentator De Quincey are correct in their views on the subject before us. The latter, rightly expounding the views of the former, says—" Theory is no more than a system of laws abstracted from experience : consequently, if any apparent contradiction should exist between them, this could only argue that the theory had been *falsely* or *imperfectly* abstracted ; in which case the sensible inference would be, not a summons to forego theories, but a call for better and more enlarged theories."

In this view I cordially agree ; but I do so with this qualification, that the last theory thus arrived at will generally prove to be *false* and *imperfect*, either in consequence of the conditions under which, of necessity, the theory is arrived at, or in consequence of the nature of the subject matter investigated.

It may be of some use to set forth a systematic statement of the different kinds of theory, viewed solely in regard to the relation of the human mind to the objects of experience ; and to furnish with illustrative examples of each kind.

A theory may be *perfect* or *imperfect : practicable* or *impracticable : true* or *false*.

All *absolutely true* theories are *practicable* and *perfect*. All *approximately true* theories are *practicable* (whether *perfect* or *imperfect*) : but it is not a fact that all *perfect* theories are even *true*, much less *practicable*. These propositions I will proceed to explain.

And, first, as to an absolutely true theory, the theory of gravitation is such a one. It is universally practicable; and inasmuch as it is complete in itself, and needs no correction or readjustment, we call it a perfect theory. It is indeed true that, in practice, there may be found some very slight discrepancy between the calculation and the event; but this is always due either to the necessary imperfection of our instruments of measurement, or to the imperfection of some subsidiary theory employed in the application.

And, secondly, as to an approximately true theory, which is, first, *perfect;* and, secondly, *imperfect.*

The following is a simple example of a perfect theory taken from the science of plane geometry. If the sides containing the right angle of any right-angled triangle be respectively 3 and 4 inches, theory informs us that the third side, or hypothenuse, is *exactly* 5 inches. A careful admeasurement will go far to confirm this result; though, owing to the necessary breadth of actual lines (which theoretical ones have not), the experiment will not coincide with the theory, though there will be a close approximation to coincidence. If, however, any other proportions be selected for the lines including the right angle, the hypothenuse cannot be measured by any equal parts of either of those lines; in other words, it is *incommensurable* with either of them.

Now in this case, the theory, though still approximately true, is imperfect on account of the nature of the subject matter.

The theory of rectifying or squaring the circle is another example. It is well known that the circumference and diameter of a circle are incommensurable;

i.e., it is impossible to divide the one into such a number of equal parts that a certain number of those parts will make up the other exactly. In fact, the diameter is always to the circumference in the proportion of 1 to 3.1415926535589793 . . . . . . the series of decimals being interminable and non-recurrent. The content of a circle is 3.1415 . . . . × the square of the radius. Accordingly a square which has the same content as a circle has its side = the radius × $\sqrt{3.1415}$ . . . .= r × 1.77245385 . . . .[1] The side of such a square is therefore incommensurable in respect of the radius, and consequently the circle cannot be arithmetically squared. But we have already seen that a line which could not be numbered in units of two other given lines might nevertheless be accurately drawn by means of those two lines. In the particular case in which a right-angled triangle has each of its containing sides equal to 1 inch, the hypothenuse is as readily represented as in the case in which those sides are in the ratio of 3 : 4. But in the case supposed that hypothenuse is $\sqrt{2}$ = 1.4142135 . . . . . . (where the decimals are interminable and non-recurrent). So that the fact of a line being incommensurable in respect of another is no reason why it should not be actually drawn by means of that other.

For all, then, that we yet see to the contrary, a straight line of 1.77245385 . . . . inches long may be as readily represented as one of 1.4142135 . . . . inches long. But, in reality, such is not the case. In order

---

[1] r : side of square : : 100,000,000, : 177,245,385 nearly.

to draw a square, which shall be geometrically equal to a given circle, is required the aid of some other curve than the circle. With Euclid's allowance of means only —viz., the straight line and the circle—the geometrical quadrature of the circle is impossible. An approximation, however, may be effected to any extent that may be desired. The impossibility of an exact geometrical quadrature of the circle, *by the aid of the straight line and circle only*, is one of those points which self-educated and half-educated mathematicians find so difficult to believe. Accordingly not a year passes without the publication of some new demonstration of the quadrature of the circle, the writer of each tract having either altogether misunderstood the terms and conditions of the problem, or being himself altogether ignorant of geometrical processes. It is amazing that such an amount of brain power is constantly being sacrificed in so hopeless a pursuit. There was a time, indeed, when this problem had an interest for mathematicians, and many notable ones constructed curves, by the use of any one of which the circle might be accurately squared. But each of these curves required for its construction a process which is inadmissible in Euclid ; and in some—as the cycloid and trochoid—the rolling of a circle is employed for the construction. Now inasmuch as it is very easy to find a square equal to a given circle, *if only one is permitted to roll it along a straight line*, it is obvious that the employment of those curves for the purpose is something like taking Stafford on the road from Birmingham to Rugby. In

these days, however, when the problem can be solved
to any required degree of accuracy by analytical methods,
the question as to its solubility by the means of the
straight line and circle only is of no manner of consequence. The impossibility of so doing is another
problem, of which James Gregory, in 1668, published
a solution ; and this, while few mathematicians consider
it altogether satisfactory, no one has been able to gain-
say. The impossibility in question, however, is proved
by moral evidence of so conclusive a nature that it
behoves all young mathematicians to make themselves
familiar with the literature connected with this problem
before endangering their mental soundness by devoting
themselves to its solution.

Some, however, enter on this hopeless pursuit at the
instigation of avarice, under a belief that the Government or the Royal Society has offered a large reward
for its solution. This is an entire mistake ; though one
that may be found to have been occasionally committed
in print. A French Jesuit, however, did, in 1726, offer
a reward of three thousand livres to be paid to any one
who should *disprove his proof of the quadrature of the
circle;* and this is the only reward that, as far as I
can ascertain, was ever offered in connection with the
problem.[1]

Astronomy furnishes us with numberless instances of
an imperfect theory, which is practicable, but yet only
approximately true. Of such a character is the famous

---

[1] See several curious articles on this subject by Professor De Morgan,
in *Notes and Queries.*

"problem of three bodies." Given two bodies which gravitate towards one another, it is easy to prove that, under certain conditions, the one will describe a conic section about the other. But if a third body be introduced, the instruments of calculation which we already possess—viz., the Differential and Integral Calculus—in a certain sense fail us; for by the aid of the former we obtain an expression for which the latter has no finite equivalent, or "definite integral" as it is called. We are accordingly necessitated to express the value of that integral in an *infinite series*, which, however, in practice, enables us to attain any degree of exactitude that may be desired. That such an approximation may be attained as makes the imperfection of the theory unimportant in practice is abundantly evidenced by the calculation of the return of comets, which involves the mutual attraction of several planetary bodies on the comets and on each other.

Before giving examples, let me premise that known comets are divisible into two classes—those of short periods and those of long periods. Of the former, the majority have a period of less than seven years; of the latter, some have periods of some thousands of years. From the comets of short periods I select four—viz., those of Halley, Encke, Biela, and Faye.

Halley's comet performs its revolution about the sun in seventy-six years, or thereabouts, and has never been visible to us so long as ten months at a time. M. de Pontecoulant, of Paris, calculated the amount of perturbation due to the earth, Jupiter, Saturn, and Uranus

on this comet's motion, and announced to the world
that it would be nearest the sun at ten o'clock at night
on November 12. The comet actually attained that position at eleven o'clock on the morning of November 16;
the error of prediction being three and a half days in
upwards of seventy-six years.

Encke's comet has a period of three years and four
months, or thereabouts. Its return is regularly fore-
told within a very small fraction of a day.

Biela's comet has a period of six years and nine
months, or thereabouts. It was observed in 1832, from
which time no observations could be made on it till its
return in 1846; yet Professor Santini calculated its
return in that year to the position nearest the sun
within little more than nine hours!

Faye's comet has a period of about seven and a half
years. It was first discovered by that astronomer on
the 22nd of November 1843. M. Le Verrier, the since
renowned discoverer of the planet Neptune, calculated
the return of Faye's comet from the observations of
M. Faye, Professor Argelander, Dr. Goldschmidt, and
Professor Henderson, and announced that it would
attain its least distance from the sun on the 3rd of
April 1851, at midnight. The fact was—and it is one
that excites no kind of astonishment in the theoretical
astronomer—that the comet actually attained that
position at the very hour predicted.

These examples show that the deductions of an
imperfect theory may be relied on, notwithstanding its
imperfection. But imperfect as such theoretical results

are, they are often more exact than the result of observation by means of the finest astronomical instruments.

And thirdly, as to *perfect* theories, which are *untrue* and *impracticable*. The theory of "perpetual motion" is such a one. It is so because it ignores *friction* and *the resistance of the air*, both of which prevail in nature; and though both are fatal to the perpetuity of motion, neither can by any possibility be got rid of. It has always seemed to me that Cartwright's steam-engine affords theoretically the nearest approach to perpetual motion that has ever been arrived at; for the condensing apparatus is so contrived that there is no loss of water at all, except by accidental escapes of steam—and this can by no possible contrivance be obviated—and by the loss of such steam as escapes from the hot well when the air within it gets too much condensed to brook resistance. Dr. Lardner suggested working this engine by ardent spirits, which boil at so low a temperature that very little fuel would be required. Of course, if the requisite heat could be constantly supplied without waste—which cannot be done—the engine would yet, in time, wear out.

There can, as I have already said, be no true or practicable theory of a perpetual motion. The impossibility of such is demonstrable. Yet even in this absurd speculation men can be found to embark with a faith, a patience, and a devotion worthy of a true cause. No doubt, in some cases, avarice has its share among the motives which induce them to this self-sacrifice; but in this, as in the case of *the quadrature of the circle*, the expectation of reward is based on a popular tradition which has no foundation in fact. It is not improbable that these floating myths originated in a confusion in the popular mind of the two last-mentioned problems with that of *the longitude*, for the discovery of which a large sum of money was offered by Government; but the offer was long ago withdrawn.

I have now given examples from science in illustration of the three propositions with which I started. A due consideration of these established propositions must lead to the conclusion that only some—not all—practicable theories are perfect; and consequently that there are some practicable theories wherein there is, of necessity, not only " a want of harmony," but " an irreconcilability," between theory and experience. In point of fact, we may go farther than this, and affirm, without fear of contradiction from men of science, that this irreconcilability inheres in a vast majority of existing theories. And though the discrepancy between theory and experience is in many cases susceptible of diminution, we must not expect that the discrepancy will ever be eliminated. What can add to the perfection of a geometrical deduction? And yet one who denies the existence of discrepancy in this case is cast on one of the horns of a dilemma: *Lines have breadth, or they have not. If they have breadth, geometry is false. If they have no breadth, experience is impossible.*

Again, in theorising on the properties of force, we often assume bodies to be perfectly elastic, flexible, or rigid; to move in contact with one another without friction and in a vacuum: whereas we meet with no such conditions among terrestrial phenomena. To allow for imperfect elasticity, flexibility, or rigidity, or to introduce the element of friction, or that of the resistance of a medium, we have to deal with empirical elements which cannot be exactly measured, and which, consequently, instead of perfecting our theory, mar it. Kant, therefore, committed an error, at least in the use of words, when he called the introduction of these empirical elements "adding more theory."

Of all these empirical elements, friction is peculiarly difficult to theorise upon. Its amount varies with the kind of surface, the grain, and the hardness of the materials in contact. These being constant, it is proportional to the pressure. But when the pressure is excessive the amount of friction is practically incalculable. To this cause must be attributed the failure of Mr. Brunel to effect a launch of the *Great Eastern* steamship after an expenditure of some fifty thousand pounds. In this case the friction was produced by the attrition of iron on iron, under a pressure of somewhat less than five thousand tons. Every vessel of that burden will, for the future, be built in a dry dock.

The calculation of the resistance of the air is beset with difficulties as insuperable as that of friction. This retarding force varies with every change in the density of the atmosphere. This being constant, it is proportional to the moving force of the projectile. Lord Macaulay, in his celebrated essay on Lord Bacon, says: "William Tell would not have been one whit more likely to cleave the apple, if he had known that his arrow would describe a parabola under the influence of the attraction of the earth." Clearly not; but for reasons which Macaulay did not contemplate: for no point in the arrow would describe that curve, or anything like it. Of course a perfect theory of motion and force would prove that one point in the arrow, called *the centre of gravity*, would accurately describe that curve, provided that body did not penetrate a resisting medium. If, on the other hand, it moved through the air, the path of the centre of gravity would not be symmetrical with respect to the apex; but that point would dip more rapidly than it mounted, and reach the ground at a greater angle than that at which it left the bow.[1]

I might proceed to give illustrations from the elasticity, rigidity, and flexibility of bodies. Mechanical theory assumes, for instance, the existence of strings of perfect flexibility; but none such are possible. Dr. Whewell informs us, in what he intends for dignified prose, but which is in reality unintentional verse—

> " There is no force, however great,
>   Can stretch a cord, however fine,
>   Into a horizontal line
> Which is accurately straight."

In fact, whatever be the force applied, the line in reality hangs in a curve; but the nature of this curve is investigated by mathematicians on the assumption that the

---

[1] See De Morgan's 'Formal Logic,' chapter on Induction.

string is perfectly flexible. But as this is never the case, the calculated curve and the real curve are discrepant.

These indeterminate interlopers are repugnant to theory. Theory ignores them for the sake of its completeness, and recognises them for the sake of its truth. It is, however, little more than recognition that they can receive at the hands of theory; and when they are incorporated with theory, what is gained in truth is lost in scientific completeness.

It not unfrequently happens that a perfect theory is less practicable than an imperfect one, while the imperfection of the latter does not occasion any sensible discrepancy. The simplest examples of this are found in the science of mechanism, which regards the relations of the parts of a machine apart from any force that may be impressed upon it. One instance will suffice. When steam was used only on one side of the piston of the steam-engine, its up-and-down motion was converted into the angular motion of the beam by the simple means of attaching an arch-head to the beam, and connecting the piston-rod with the top of the arch by a chain passing over the arch-head. By this contrivance the piston-rod pulled down the beam, and the beam pulled up the piston-rod. But when Watt constructed a steam-engine in which steam was employed to effect the upward as well as the downward stroke, it became necessary to make the piston-rod lift the beam. Accordingly Watt contrived that system of levers called the " parallel motion," which gives the piston-rod an

almost perfectly rigid pushing as well as pulling power.
Now, in fact, if the lengths and normal positions of the
rods be discreetly chosen, the line described by the
motion of the point to which the piston-rod is riveted,
during the motion of the beam through an angle of 20°,
deviates so little from a straight line that it were
scarcely possible to construct a piston-rod of such
rigidity, or to joint it with such precision as to make
the deviation of the slightest importance. Now there
are many other devices by which the summit of the
piston-rod may be made to move in a line that is
theoretically straight; but all these involve the use of
cog-wheels, which, in the constant working of a steam-
engine, are found to be subject to such an amount of
wear and tear that they have been, to a great extent,
eschewed by engineers.

The saying that such and such a thing may be all
very well in theory, but it does not hold good in practice,
is, however, more commonly employed in respect of
political, social, and moral matters. Now, in this field, I
must confess that I think the saying worthy of respect:
for nothing is commoner than for men to theorise on
certain elements of the subject, while they, almost of
necessity, ignore others.

We have seen that, in physics, the marplots of theory
are certain empirical elements, about which we cannot
truly speculate, simply because they stand out of relation to the à priori conceptions of the understanding.
Doubtless extended knowledge about friction, elasticity,
&c., is possible, and for aught I see to the contrary,

extended knowledge may bring these aliens within the
legitimate sphere of speculation. But the case is different in politics and morals. Besides certain axiomatic
principles which prevail in one or other of these realms
of thought, there exist an immense number of elements,
all of them empirical, and of the majority we do not
possess that knowledge which can avail for their reduction to a scientific shape. I know of no topic which
can better illustrate my meaning than the currency.
Here we have the rival theories of Tooke, Ricardo,
Wilson, Lord Overstone, Attwood, &c. &c. Probably
in every one of these some important elements are
ignored; and the consequence is that a hypothetical
element is introduced into the theory. Thus, some
writers, in theorising on the causes of a glut or a drain
of gold in this country, altogether ignore the fact of
the Government having a fixed price of gold; not perceiving that it is a fruitful cause of both a glut and a
drain, according to the state of the gold market. The
simple fact is this: if a man take 1 oz. 2.62 gr., or
thereabouts, of 22 carat gold to the Mint, he receives
back four sovereigns, which contain nearly that same
amount of fine gold. The fact that the vendor of the
bullion receives from the Mint nearly as much fine gold
in the form of sovereigns as he takes to the Mint in the
form of dust or nuggets, is regarded by certain writers
as a proof of the equity of the transaction, not of there
being any price of gold fixed by the Government. Now
the real state of the case is this: the conversion of the
given amount of bullion into four sovereigns destroys

or suspends the value which that bullion would have in market-overt, and invests it with a purely *artificial value* or price: this is represented by eighty shillings in silver; and the fact is that 1 oz. 2.62 gr. is frequently worth more than eighty shillings in market-overt; not from any depreciation in the value of silver, but from the high market price of gold. The suppression of this fact introduces into the theory a hypothetical element, viz., that there is but one kind of value for gold; which is, as I have shown, a great blunder: for it has two incompatible values—the one as a precious metal, the other as a medium of circulation—the one intrinsic, and the other representative.

This is a fair sample of the kind of hypothesis which vitiates the majority of currency theories.[1] It is the confidence with which such theories are put forth that has brought the word "theory" into discredit with men of business; and these, not discerning the real difference between empirical and exact science, are apt to impute that discredit to physical theory, than which nothing can be more absurd or unjust.

Of the problems which defy the powers of the social speculator, how many are constantly meeting with a practical solution at the hands of a simple-minded worker, who, in love to Christ, and to those whom He came into the world to save, lay out their lives heartily in the work of converting sinners and evangelising

---

[1] I observe that something like this error is committed by my friend and fellow-townsman, Mr. W. L. Sargant, in his very able work, 'The Science of Social Opulence,' chap. xxiii.

the world! When duty speaks, we must not waste our days in speculating on the best mode of doing it. *Ars longa, vita brevis:* there are men specially endowed for the elaboration of theories. The practical man enters into their labours, and works with their instruments. But the more complex problems of social economy have not yet received any scientific solution. There is a work which is to be done; but how to do it we find not. So it is done, *quocunque modo,* as it may be; and thence spring the penalties of mistakes: for

> " Evil is wrought by want of thought,
> As well as by want of heart."

The fear of mistake, however, and of its consequences, is too often made the pretext of ignoble inaction. How many of us are given to murmur at the state of things among which we live, instead of manfully setting to work to do the little that in us lies for the well-being and advancement of our race! All of us have at one time or another reflected on the cause of an evil state of things, and said to ourselves "if that one circumstance had been otherwise, all this mischief might have been spared us." Is not this to credit ourselves with the foresight requisite for theorising on the circumstances that would be still left us, when we are, in all probability, entirely overlooking the fact that one circumstance cannot be thus eliminated in practice, without some new circumstance, which we cannot anticipate, taking the place of the one got rid of? I am speaking, not of what we can conceive, but of what is realised in the experience of life. The fact is that all such theorising is vain, because we are speculating with a portion only of the elements of the problem; and our result, though it may make us discontented, or possibly afford us consolation, as the case may be, is certain to be very wide of the truth. Such theories are simply false.

Social economy, however, is not a mere chimæra. It presents problems which can be solved perfectly and practicably. Thus, it is capable of demonstration that all expenditure of capital in the acquisition of those things which gratify and foster pride, vanity, malice, cupidity, or any other vicious propensity of our fallen nature, is an injury to society, and tends to the impoverishment of its wealth. For instance, the manufacture of fabrics which have no innate beauty, and which are yet the result of a labour disproportionate to quantity, is itself an evil. The manufacturers of all such goods, however, are "more sinned against than sinning." The sin, at least the great bulk of it, lies at the doors of the buyers, who, by expending their capital on such matters, direct the labours of the manufacturers into that channel, instead of distributing it so as to conserve and economise the capital employed.

In conclusion, I must call special attention to the relations which subsist between theory and art. *Theory* bears the same relation to *thought* that *art* does to *action*. Both are instruments more or less adequate. A theory of ideas (metaphysics) bears the same relation to a physical theory as a fine art bears to a mechanical art.

In both metaphysics and the fine arts there are nearly as many opinions as writers or workers. The cause of this lies too deep for discussion on the present occasion. However, it is consolatory to reflect that we can all of us do something towards training mankind in those habits of reverence and truth which cannot but conduce to the attainment of the desired unity of thought and sentiment. Whether the talents committed to a man's trust are such as fit him for speculation or realisation, he has still a work to accomplish by which alone those talents can be put out at interest for the good of his race.

> " Judge not which serves his mighty Master best,
>   Haply thou mightest be true worth's detractor ;
> For each obeys his nature's high behest—
>   The close-pent thinker, and the busy actor."

" Doubt not, but persist: say, 'It is in me, and shall out,'" is the advice of a transatlantic writer. Carlyle says the like : " Be no longer a chaos, but a world, or even a worldkin! Produce! Were it but the pitifullest infinitesimal fraction of a product, produce it in God's name. 'Tis the utmost thou hast in thee. Out with it then."

This is sound advice, but it needs qualification. Before we invest our powers in production let us first of all be sure that what we are about to produce is worth production, and if so, that it has not been already produced by some one else. The only safeguard against the waste of mental capital in repetition is a preliminary investment of it in mastering the history and literature of the speciality in the department of which the producer is about to labour. Coincidence in discovery cannot always be avoided. Newton and Leibnitz independently invented (or rather discovered) fluxions. James Watt and Lavoisier ought to divide the honour of discovering the constitution of water. Fox Talbot and Daguerre have equal credit in the discovery of photography. Adams and Leverrier contemporaneously discovered the planet Neptune by a purely theoretical process, though their methods were different. France, somehow, manages to divide the merit of discovery with England. Let us not grudge her that honour. But these are exceptional cases. Our first business, whether in theory or practice, is to become familiar with what has been done by the great who have lived before us or have wrought around us. When that labour is performed, we close the epoch of self-sufficiency and begin that of humility, which is the true pioneer of progress.

III.

A DIALOGUE ON THE PERCEPTION OF OBJECTS.

INTRODUCTION.

IT has been often observed that great events have sprung from trivial causes. "Si le nez de Cléopâtre eût été plus court, toute la face de la terre aurait changé." Thus Pascal sums up the general in the particular. How many instances of the remark does history afford! It is interesting to know that the career of a Cromwell or a Bonaparte was determined by an incident which at the time seemed fatal, or at least adverse to his advancement. If an Order in Council had not detained the ships in which Cromwell, Hampden, Pym, and others of their party had embarked for America, the history of our most notable rebellion would have been a blank, or the same great result would have been achieved later by other hands. If Sir Gilbert Elliott, when Governor-General of Corsica, had accepted the services of the young artillery officer, it is, to say the least, improbable that the Napoleonic Dynasty

E

would ever have been founded. Such a providence is there in the proportions of Cleopatra's nose!

What is thus true of universal history is true of biography. It was a toss-up whether Challis or Galle should have the credit of discovering or rather detecting the ultra-uranial planet, of which both Adams and Leverrier had assigned approximate elements. The seeming accident of a cloud passing across the field of the Cambridge equatorial decided the question in favour of Galle, though in fact Challis, like Adams, had the priority. Once more : Mr. Whymper, amid the dangers of the Matterhorn, owed his life to the chance of his staying to take a sketch of the panorama from the summit ; by his own neglect it was that a weak rope was used for the descent ; and if the Alpine Club rope had been used, as he intended, he and the two guides who actually escaped would inevitably have shared the awful and sublime fate of their less fortunate fellows.

The intellectual as well as the external history of many a man has been determined by an incident which seemed at the time of its occurrence insignificant, and which was but remotely associated with the revolution it inaugurated. The anecdote of Newton and the apple is proverbial, though probably a fable. For myself, I might have remained in life-long bondage to the school of Locke but for the train of thought originated by a rainbow. Thenceforth that commonest and most beautiful of meteors has stood to me as the historic clue of the whole visible universe. Nor did its uses end with my own advance in the philosophy of perception ;

but I availed myself of every favourable opportunity of
expounding to others the analytical lesson of the rainbow, and thus of guiding them in that " path of transit "
which had been vouchsafed to me. One occasion on
which I did so is distinguished from others by the
number of conversations in which I took part, and by
the mental characteristics of those with whom I maintained the discussion. I was staying at the country
seat of a friend, who, at a great disadvantage, had educated himself with no little success, and whose knowledge on a great variety of subjects was considerable.
Partly from living too secluded a life since he had
retired from active business, and partly from want of
quickness in perception, he had become somewhat
opinionated and hard to convince. At that time a well-
educated young man, some distant relative of his, was
residing with him, and the one was a foil to the other.
This lad, who might be anything from nineteen to one-
and-twenty, was intelligent, simple-minded, and in-
genuous. If I really made a convert of him, I am not
proud of the achievement, for he lacked both subtilty
and depth, and, like the sun-dial, took note of those
points only on which the light happened to fall. With
these two companions I daily took walks in a luxuriant
woodland country, which was now variegated by the
melancholy hues of autumn. Our pursuits and our discourse were mainly physical. The flower, the bird, the
woods and rocks, and the atmospheric effects of land and
sky, furnished ample materials for our employment and
pleasure. Philosophy in its highest sense was the last

thing either my host or his relative could have dreamed of: yet to that height were they conducted on the aerial pontifice of a rainbow.

In the following dialogue, of which I took copious notes at the time, I have designated my friend by the term *Dyspeistus*, his relative I have called *Euethes*, and myself *Scopus*.

THE DIALOGUE.

Scopus. Let us get under shelter. We shall have a smart shower.

Dyspcistus. A sunshine shower! It will soon be over.

Euethcs. What a magnificent rainbow! Did you ever see such vivid colours?

Dysp. Yes, I have; in the spectrum of a prism. But this is unusually bright for a rainbow.

Scop. What a remarkable coincidence!

Dysp. and Eue. What is?

Scop. Why, each of you sees a rainbow, and both rainbows are unusually bright.

Dysp. Both? You do not see a double rainbow, do you? For my part, I see but one. Let's see; it is the interior bow that has the red outside and the violet in; and the exterior reverses the order.

Scop. Yes; and I like you do not see the secondary bow.

Dysp. Then why do you speak of " both rainbows " ?

Scop. I mean by " both," the arch you see, and that

seen by Euethes. It struck me as a coincidence worth explaining, that both should be unusually bright.

Eue. I think I have heard or read that no two people either do or can see the same rainbow.

Scop. It is most certain: indeed if I am to speak according to knowledge, if I am to speak as well as think with the learned, I should say that the rainbow you see with one eye you cannot see with the other eye; and as you and Dyspeistus are using both eyes, I might have distinguished four rainbows which are seen among you.

Dysp. Well, I never heard such nonsense uttered so seriously.

Scop. I should say, then, that you have been very fortunate in your company, and ought to be thankful for the small mercy of "hearing some new thing." I have no doubt, however, that you will live to find that many of the serious judgments of common sense are both stale and false. Let me ask you what you take a rainbow for; you don't take it for a real thing, do you ?

Dysp. Most certainly I do. Have I any need to tell you what it is made of ?

Scop. I might guess, perhaps, what you will say it is made of; but my guess may be, for aught I know, as wrong as your belief. Which will you have—light or water ?

Dysp. It is made of drops of water, of course.

Scop. Then is it not remarkable that I do not see any drops of water in a rainbow ?

Dysp. On the contrary, I should think it miraculous, if at so great a distance, or indeed at any distance, you could distinguish such small objects moving so fast; to say nothing of the confusion of reflected and transmitted light, and its chromatism by refraction. But though we cannot distinguish the drops, it is the drops and nothing else that we see.

Scop. A very neat little paradox! The only thing we see in a rainbow is the very thing which for three sound reasons we cannot possibly see.

Dysp. Come, come, Scopus, that's not fair. I don't mind being refuted; but when you resort to the expedient of making me say what I did not say, it is not refutation you are bent upon, but mockery.

Scop. I beg your pardon; but what did you say, then?

Dysp. I purposely used the word "distinguish." I assert that we see the water in a rainbow, though we do not, cannot distinguish the drops. Let me illustrate this. I suppose you will allow that, in looking at a spoked wheel in rapid rotation, you see the wood, though you cannot distinguish the spokes.

Scop. You will oblige me by assuming nothing of the kind. I can brook no such abuse of language. If the spokes revolve so fast that I cannot see them distinctly, I cannot see them at all: still less can I be said to see the wood of which the spokes are made. You might as well assert that I see a sunken rock because I see a darker shade on the surface of the sea where the rock lies. If I am to use language without

abusing it, I must say that, if I do not see the spokes
of your wheel distinctly, I do not see them at all.

Dysp. That is, there is no vision but distinct vision.
A very neat little paradox!

Scop. Well hit! But I did not say anything equivalent to that. What I did say, at least implicitly, was
this—that of a distinct object there can be no vision
but distinct vision. When a definite body is moving
so fast that I cannot distinguish it, I still see something : in the case of your wheel I see, in fact, a phantom
which is produced in my imagination by the revolving
spokes reflecting light. Now, I see that phantom just
as distinctly as it is distinctly realised in my imagination, neither more nor less.

Dysp. But is not that phantom made up of the
spokes, and nothing else ?

Scop. It is not. The phantom is wholly the product
of sensations of colour and imagination. Of those sensations, I grant, the light reflected from the spokes is
the occasion, but I emphatically deny that I see the
spokes at all.

Eue. Would it not be more correct to say that we
see the light, and nothing else ?

Scop. It would not be correct at all. The eye,
indeed, affords us the sensation of light, but we feel
the sensation, we do not see it. To see is to perceive
by means of ocular sensations. I see the phantom
which is presented to my mind in imagination. If
nothing is so presented, I see nothing, and sensation
does not rise to the rank of perception. But so far

are we from seeing external light, that we are not conscious, even in the lowest and least significant form of sensation, of anything called light which is said to radiate from objects and to impinge on the retina of the eye. The light of which we are conscious as sensation is that which is excited in the optic nerve and brain. Popular usage, indeed, sanctions that employment of the verb *to see* against which I am protesting; but popular usage sanctions hundreds of such *idola fori* for no other conceivable reason than to evade the exertion of thought. Shakespeare, Milton, and other poets might be cited as a sanction for such a phrase as *the eye sees an object*, but only as a poetical figure. Even in poetry no correct writer would say that the eye, or even its owner, sees the sensation of light. He might say that the eye, or its owner, sees an object made visible by light, such as the phantom of the rotating wheel, the image in a mirror, or the fine solar meteor which is now fading out of the dark sky. The shower is over; let us continue our walk.

Dysp. With pleasure: though this fine terrestrial meteor—I mean the rain—has made the roads sloppy and the fields spongy. After all, then, it is a mere question of language whether we see material objects or the light which they reflect. I am not fond of splitting verbal hairs. What I meant to say was this: in looking at the rainbow I see a certain shining of the sun upon drops of water; so that the drops of water are the material thing in the phenomenon.

Scop. Doubtless the water and the light are the

joint physical causes of the phenomenon. I simply contend that in a strict sense of the verb *to see*, I see the rainbow, and not the drops of water or the light.

Eue. Just as in looking at the reflection of an object in a mirror one sees the reflected image, and not the glass or the light?

Scop. Just so; and as that image exists only to the mind perceiving it, so the rainbow exists not in the sunlight or the shower, but in the imagination, as it externalises the sensations presented to it.

Dysp. Do you seriously mean to assert that the rainbow we were just now looking at and admiring did not exist at a certain distance from us, nor occupy a definite *locus* in the rain-cloud?

Scop. I am perfectly serious in making that assertion; nay, more, I seriously maintain that not any one of the rainbows seen by us had any external existence whatever.

Eue. If, as I understand it, the rainbow is a reflected image, or rather a corona of reflected images, I think we must allow that it is as much related to the object imaged as the image in a mirror is to the thing reflected.

Scop. I grant you that; but our friend here was not contending that in looking at a rainbow he was looking at a circle of reflected suns, but at illuminated drops of water. Do you understand, Euethes, exactly how this truly sublime colour-band is formed?

Eue. I should be glad to hear you explain it.

Scop. Dyspeistus can do that as well as I can. Give us your version of the transaction.

Dysp. You must grant me an unclouded sun behind me and a rain-cloud in front of me. For convenience of exposition, conceive the drops of rain to be suspended at rest, forming a bed of small pellucid spheres on which the sunlight falls. It falls on all parts of the drops towards the sun ; so one small pencil falls on the upper parts of each drop, and this passes through the drop and falls on the opposite inner side. Some of this pencil passes out into the air, and some is reflected from the inner surface there, which falling on the lower parts, and issuing thence, proceeds towards the sun again, and enters the eye of an observer. Of course I am assuming that he is rightly placed, and that the light is not again intercepted. This light, then, has suffered two refractions and one reflexion at the surface of the drop, and like the light passing through a prism, is by refraction resolved into seven colours. The retina of an eye, situated in the straight line through which the issuing pencil travels, receives the image of a coloured spectrum, and—to speak by the card, the owner of that eye sees the seven primary colours—Scopus, I know, would have me say *feels* them.

Scop. I should not say that he feels the coloured light, unless he referred it to the retina, as in touch he refers roughness to the surface which is in immediate contact with the skin, and reciprocally to the skin itself.

Euc. But you spoke, Dyspeistus, of our seeing the

solar spectrum from one drop. Does the single drop, then, give us the segment of a rainbow?

Dysp. The single drop gives us a downward streak of light, the red at top, the violet at bottom. But inasmuch as the eye receives the spectra of drops of water in *all* available positions, the aggregation of such streaks becomes an arch.

Eue. But your raindrops are suspended at rest, and real ones are in rapid motion.

Dysp. True. If instead of the suspended layer of drops we conceive a constant succession of drops, the place of one being ever supplied by another, the conditions of the phenomenon are not materially altered, for the succession of drops now performs the same function as the stationary drops; for the eye, by a certain negative virtue it has, viz., a deficiency of sensibility, is so retentive of each impression, that its owner is unable to discriminate so rapid a substitution of one drop for another.

Scop. So far, Dyspeistus, I have nothing to except to in your explanation, which is careful and accurate. But there is one lesson I would draw from it, viz., that of "the permanent in the transitory." The Lee-cloud, which is not uncommonly seen on Alpine heights, like the rainbow, is a stable phenomenon, though its physical constituents are in swift motion. Transparent vapour is driven in a rapid current against the cold side or summit of a mountain. At the touch of the mountain the vapour is condensed, and minute drops of water are formed. But before they can be swept over the moun-

tain they are revaporised; and it is only about the point
of condensation that the water can maintain its state
as drops. So the gale sweeps it on again as invisible
vapour. But the place of every drop of water thus revaporised is supplied by the condensation of the vapour
rushing up behind it. The result is, that though the
huge body of invisible vapour is in violent transition,
and the condensed portion along with it, there is the
stable and permanent phenomenon of a motionless cloud
floating on the point of condensation. In fact the
stream of vapour flows through it, and no part is more
essential to its existence than any other. Now for the
moral of the story. We talk of the resurrection of the
body, and even of the flesh, in the once universal and
still prevalent belief that its material is proper to it
and necessary to its identity. But when once we have
ascertained the relation of material substance to organic
life, we find this doctrine wholly inconsistent with
facts. We now know that matter forms no constant part
of the bodily structure, but as it were uninterruptedly
flows through it, and the arrest of that flow we call
death. To reproduce the living organism, a resurrection
of the matter composing it at any time is not only unnecessary, but impertinent. The very condition on which
this doctrine rests is inconsistent with life. Matter,
then, has the same relation to the organism as the drops
or molecules of water have to the rainbow or Lee-cloud,
life being in the one case what light is in the other.

Dysp. It will be long before theologians will lay that
lesson to heart.

Scop. Naturally: for to hold to the natural fact means to abandon the superstition as a means of livelihood; and to teach the fact to ignorant men would, at first, give a violent shock to their hopes and aspirations: from both of which the professed theologian is sure to shrink. And here is a lesson for you, Dyspeistus: that which is permanent in the rainbow is not the raindrops. Those, indeed, are its physical constituents, but they are in a state of continual flux.

Dysp. I never doubted it: how could I with such instructive toys before me as Dr. Roget's gyroscope, Mr. Rose's photodrone, and M. Plateau's anorthoscope.

Eue. I thought Dr. Roget's invention was called the phenakistiscope.

Scop. So it was; but the gyroscope is essentially the same invention. I believe the French give the credit of that invention also to M. Plateau; but Roget had the priority by many years. It is a pity, however, that he gave it such a hideous name. Doubtless what we see in the instrument we see φενακιστικῶς, but *kinesiscope* or *phenakiscope* would have been a better formed and more euphonious name.

Eue. But to return to the rainbow, I have yet to learn why the spectrum is circular.

Dysp. That is a point which was never made clear to my mind in elementary treatises. I well remember when a boy wondering why the rainbow was circular; and on my asking my preceptor, who was a capital mathematician, to explain the circular shape of the rainbow, he gravely told me that it was due to the orbicular shape of the eye.

Scop. I think he must have seen some green in the eye of his pupil. I spare you the alternative.

Dysp. No good pun can turn on a mere verbal anti-thesis. But let us have your explanation of the circular shape of the spectrum.

Scop. It is circular, because the circle is the figure of symmetry. Sir David Brewster explains the rainbow by a pellucid globe held in the hand. Let the observer turn his back to the sun, and hold the globe above the height of his head in front of him, and he will see a horizontal spectrum of colours, the red at top, the violet at bottom; and all other positions of the globe may be found to the right and to the left in which the spectrum is seen, the inclination to the horizon of the spectrum varying for all the positions. It is plain that the phenomenon is not peculiar to one position of the globe; but that in every position in which the angle between the incident ray and the ray that comes to the eye is of the same magnitude as in any one of the observed cases, the incident ray always striking a similar part of the globe, the like phenomenon will be observed, the spectrum being at right angles to a plane in which are the centres of the globe, the sun, and the eye. All such positions clearly lie in the right transverse section of a cone of which the centre of the sun is the apex, and the axis is a line passing through the centres of the sun and of the eye. If then there be a series of glass globes in that section, a spectrum of colours will be seen in the form of a regular polygon. Whence it is easily seen that if the globes be very small, the arch closely approximates to the circular form; and what is true of glass globes is true of spherical drops of water.

Eue. Then the line joining the centres of the sun and the eye, if produced towards the rainbow, passes through the centre of the rainbow?

Scop. It does; and thus the rainbow lies symmetrically to the sun and the eye.

Dysp. Hardly, unless the observer, Ixion-like, be bound to a vertical wheel with his eye in the centre, and looking directly forwards, be made to revolve before the rainbow.

Scop. Your remark convinces me that your tutor was not such an ass after all. I have no doubt he meant to point this most important fact, that the orbicular form of the eye is a necessary co-efficient in the production of the circular arch. Evidently, but for that, some such a contrivance as you suggest would be essential to the symmetry. As it is constituted, the eyeball being nearly spherical, it is a matter of indifference whether its owner stand erect or lie on his side in observing any part of the rainbow.

Eue. You have hitherto been speaking of the primary or interior rainbow, such as we saw just now. Why did we not see the secondary or exterior rainbow?

Scop. For no other reason than the absence of rain-drops from the place where it should be seen, or, the drops being there, some other cloud intercepting the sunlight which would otherwise fall upon them.

Euc. I suppose an actual rainfall between those drops and the sun would hardly be sufficiently opaque to intercept all sunlight?

Scop. That depends: such a rainfall would probably divert too much light for the secondary bow to be visible. You must remember that such an intercepting rainfall would divert the light which strikes the drops, of which it consists, in various directions, so as to affect persons whose eyes are in position with primary and secondary bows, and so as to fulfil the conditions of conceivable tertiary and other bows. No, I do not think your secondary bow could be visible in the case suggested. In any case it is fainter than its primary, and therefore more liable to invisibility than the other.

Euc. Why is it fainter?

Scop. Because it is formed by the light which, striking the lower parts of the drop, enters it, and after two reflections issues from the upper parts, and thus reaches the observer's eye; so more light is lost in the transit than is the case with the light that makes the primary bow.

Euc. Is the tertiary bow ever seen?

Scop. Both the third and fourth bows fall near the sun, and are therefore rarely visible;[1] the fifth and sixth are indeed opposite the sun, but it is doubtful if they have ever been seen; so little light goes to their constitution.

---

[1] A tertiary segment seen by me, Oct. 27, 1868.

Dysp. It seems to me, Scopus, that the rainbow has always to contend with difficulties of this kind.

Scop. Yes; and it is therefore but seldom seen. If the sun is not too high, every rain-cloud passing from the sun would afford the conditions of a rainbow, but for the interception of the light.

Euc. That reminds me of a difficulty: if, as it seems, one corona of raindrops is sufficient and necessary to form a rainbow, say the primary bow, wherever that corona happens to lie in the bed of drops, there surely must be other drops either before or behind it capable of forming rainbows. Why do we never see a complication of rainbows overlapping and confounding one another?

Scop. Simply because, while you are looking at one primary bow, you are out of position for seeing others. Remember your eye must be in the axis of a cone of which the rainbow is the base, and the centre of the sun the apex, in order that the rainbow forming the base may be visible to you. Now if any other primary bow became visible to you, it would be exactly superposed on the other, the angle which the issuing ray makes with the incident ray being of constant magnitude. In fact, the image on the retina of the eye is of a constant size, both in radius and in breadth, and its reference to this or that part of space, and the consequent mental act or judgment by which it is seen as of this or that magnitude, are dependent on other and very different conditions. The study of the diminutive bow which spans the spray of a paddle wheel, a fountain, or a waterfall,

F

is very instructive in this particular, and for myself
I find no difficulty in reducing the ordinary rainbow to
very small dimensions, and I daresay I can teach you
to do the same.

Eue. How may one do that ?

Scop. By means of a sort of micrometer of two
intersecting stretched hairs. Look at the rainbow
through that, and shutting one eye look at the inter-
section of the hairs till you see them distinctly. To do
that you will involuntarily, or rather unconsciously, perform an adjustment of the crystalline lens, which will
make the rainbow very small and very distinct. You
may try the experiment with a page of large print
when we get home, and you will be surprised to see
how small it becomes.

Eue. Can you do the reverse—make a small-looking
object appear large ?

Scop. Not so well ; but it is possible. So you see our
sense of sight is remarkably elastic. By Dr. Roget's
and Mr. Rose's inventions you may see objects in
motion which are but drawings of fixed positions
successively presented to the eye, and by the photodrome you may see an object at rest which is really in
rapid motion. By the anorthoscope an unintelligible
confusion becomes the picture of a familiar object. And
now you have the receipt for altering the apparent size
of any object whatever. These experiments reveal but
an instalment of the entire debt which nature owes to
the percipient.

Dysp. Did you ever consider the *rationale* of the

apparently great size of the moon when near the horizon ?

Scop. Certainly; and I see no difficulty whatever in the phenomenon. Why do we see the rainbow so large, when after all we know it to be less than a section of the eyeball ?

Dysp. Do you mean to say you do not believe it to have any other objective existence than as a disturbance of the retina? If so, you will have to give up talking of seeing a rainbow, and speak of it as an extended sensation only.

Scop. Well, the fact is, we do see it, and see it as an object without us, and the size we assign to it depends on the relation to other external objects which we conceive it to have. If I see that the ends of the rainbow disappear behind some distant woods, or a distant range of hills, I unconsciously locate it at a definite distance from the eye—a distance of which my judgment can take cognisance; and I at once judge the rainbow to be very vast, since I see it spanning so great a belt of earth. So of the horizontal moon. If it seems to me to be a ball resting on the earth at the horizon, a matter of from five to fifty miles, suppose, I unconsciously make the inference of its great magnitude; just as if I were to conceive the ball rolling up to me, and looming larger and larger upon me as it approached. I once saw a rainbow in the Alps which opened out this question to me. It was at midday, in summer, when on the Wetterhorn I saw below me a double circular Iris, and in the centre of the concentric circles

I saw the shadow of my own head. The rain-cloud
which occasioned the phenomenon was so near that the
shadow of my head was pretty definite, and I suppose
I unconsciously judged from the size of the shadow
its distance from me, and referring the rainbow to the
shadow, I judged it to be much smaller than any one
I had ever seen. Further, I believe that if we could
see a circular Iris high in the heavens, so that it would
not be referred to any terrestrial objects, it would look
smaller still.

Eue. That is very wonderful.

Scop. It is so, because the explanation of the anomaly
is in the act of judgment, and is therefore purely mental.
We have here a case which demands metaphysics.
Mere physics is quite at fault—as indeed it is in all
ultimate issues.

Dysp. Then you really hold this meteor for a phantom,
a creation of the imagination and nothing else.

Scop. I do indeed ; but I do not base on that conclusion my assertion that no two people see the same
rainbow, and that there is a different rainbow for every
observing eye. Your own knowledge of the physics
of the rainbow ought to have secured you from calling
that statement "nonsense," as you did just now. You
cannot deny that every visible rainbow is the base of a
cone, of which the centre of the sun is the apex, that
rainbow being visible to a person whose eye is at a
certain point in the axis of the cone, and to no one
else. If two eyes cannot be at one and the same
moment in one and the same place, it follows that

the rainbow I see with my right eye alone is not the
rainbow I see with my left eye alone, unless I move
my head. In fact, each rainbow has its cone, and the
axes of those cones are not coincident, but inclined at a
very small angle.

Dysp. The angle is inappreciably small; it is for all
the purposes of the case, zero.

Scop. Not so; you forget we are dealing with very
minute spheres of water. But even if that angle were
zero, you will not say that, in the case of two persons
half a mile apart, looking at a rainbow, the angle is
inappreciably small. Even you cannot deny that these
people receive the light from a different corona of drops;
so that on your own assumption, that they are looking
at the drops, the rainbow seen by the one observer is
not identical with that seen by another observer.

Dysp. Why, you will soon be engaged in demon-
strating that no two eyes can see the same tree.

Scop. I cannot move so fast. In passing from a
phenomenon like the rainbow, which has no manner
of existence but to the perceiving mind—using its
organ of sight to such an object as a tree, which is
amenable to touch and feeling, as well as to sight and
other senses, we must see our way very clearly, lest
haply we should confound essentially different phenomena. Besides, we have not investigated the case of
vision with two eyes.

Dysp. Like Felix, I shall be happy to hear you on
another occasion. You may be sure I'll give you rope
enough. Though you may not hang yourself, you will

assuredly entangle yourself in a mesh of absurdities. Do you emulate the feats of those dialecticians, ancient and modern, who have opposed knowledge to belief, proportioned belief to improbability, or identified existence and nothing ?

Scop. I am not prepared to reject, much less deride, any of those famous paradoxes ; but at present it is out of my beat to meddle with them.

THE IDEALITY OF THE RAINBOW.

THIS familiar meteor, "the idol of children and men," was, as we all know, to the Hebrews the outward visible sign of a covenant made with them by Elohim (Gen. ix. 13–17). What the rainbow does say to all of us is, that the storm-cloud is past, and that the sunlight behind us is breaking on the diamond shower of the storm's departing skirt. What those old-world theists made it say to them was, that their Deity had unsuccessfully attempted to exterminate human wickedness by deluge; and, becoming convinced that the method was abortive, by reason of the wickedness being inherent in the race, pledged himself not to repeat the experiment. To the Greeks, Iris was the herald of Olympian Jove, and came, sometimes water-pot in hand, tripping down the vari-coloured arch that spanned the abyss between heaven and earth, on her errands of goodwill to men.

Great must have been the shock to religious prejudice while the true theory of earth's "rich scarf" was being, step by step, evolved by Kepler, De Dominis, Descartes,

and Newton.[1]   But there was, in fact, little cause for
fear.   Those who expected that the results of science
could make the slightest breach in the ancient citadel
of faith must have greatly mistaken the nature and mis-
calculated the strength of religious belief.   Here was a
phenomenon, declared by Holy Scripture to be miraculous, resolved into the very laws which paint external
objects alike on the retina of the eye and on the table

---

[1] Hallam's estimate of De Dominis' contribution to the optics of the
rainbow is too high ; and his account of Descartes' services is, in one
respect, erroneous ('History of the Literature of Europe,' 1843, vol. iii.
p. 203).   Most of the archbishop's discussion *de iride* amply justifies
Boscovich's sweeping censure.   Yet De Dominis clearly perceived that
the circular form of the arch was the result of symmetry, and so an
affair of geometry ; and that the phenomenon was an illusion.   "Osten-
sum est," he writes, " arcum illum primum ab oculo nostro determinari,
et nullum esse in nube arcum, quæ tota est colorata " (De radiis lucis,
&c., et iride, 1611, cap. xiv.) ; and what he here asserts of the primary,
he evidently applies to the secondary arch.   Happily for Descartes'
reputation, he did not attempt to prove that the pencil of light after
refraction, reflection, and emergence, is composed of parallel rays.   The
coloured pencil is convergent, as Descartes very well knew.

While speaking of Descartes, I may mention his incredulity as to
the production of a third exterior bow, under the ordinary conditions
of the other two.   "Quidam etiam mihi narrarunt, tertiam Iridem
duas ordinarias cingentem se aliquando vidisse, sed multo pallidiorem,
et tantum circiter a secunda remotam, quantum ab illa prima distat.
Quod vix accidisse arbitror, nisi forsan quædam grandinis grana,
maxime rotunda et pellucida, hinc pluviæ fuerint immixta," &c.   . .
('Meteora,' cap. viii. § 14).   Now, as to the matter of fact, I have seen
three concentric arches against Ben Nevis, where there was no water, and
that too in mild weather ; so that the third arch could not have arisen
from reflexion, nor from the presence of hail.   I ought to add that the
third arch was so faint that it was visible only where it was backed by
the dark mountain.   It was broader than the second arch, and more
distant from it than the second was from the first.   Surely it is easily
accounted for on the supposition that light falls on the lower parts of
the drops ; and after suffering *three* reflexions in the drops, emerges to
the observing eye.

of Porta's camera. But between a Divine revelation and a calculation of science there could be no competition. So the theology, unaffected by knowledge, held on its way—

> "And Science struck the thrones of Earth and Heaven,
> Which shook, but fell not."

Well, though I will not bid the old faith God-speed, small blame, I say, to those who cherish it; but as little to those who love the poetry of the Greeks more than the mythology of the Hebrews; who, gazing with discerning admiration on this richly invested product of natural laws, are still reminded of Iris and her aërial pontifice—

> "A midway station, given
> For happy spirits to alight
> Betwixt the earth and heaven."

But when religion, poetry, and science have had their say about the rainbow, there is yet an account to be rendered in its behalf by philosophy. We have it on the authority of men eminent in science that not only no two persons, but no two eyes, though paired in the head of Argus, can see one and the same rainbow; that, in fact, there are as many rainbows as there are eyes beholding. We shall soon see how this comes about. In the meanwhile let me say that this is not a doctrine borrowed from this or that school of idealism or scepticism, but is involved in the physical exposition of the meteor. Let the metaphysician make thereof what capital he may !

There are two sciences implicated in the rainbow : that of optics and that of geometry. The ordinary elementary treatises on dioptrics sufficiently expound the production of the two spectra, in converse orders of colours, when a pellucid sphere, held in two given positions in the sunlight, is observed by one who has his back to the sun. I will here assume the fact. An observer, with the sun at his back, views the globe in two *ascertained* vertical positions. In the upper position he sees a vertical spectrum of colours, violet at top and red at bottom ; in the lower position he sees a vertical spectrum of colours, red at top and violet at bottom ; the other colours, in both positions of the globe, being in the prismatic sequence. That is the optical fact. The rest is, for the most part, geometry. The essential point, for each arch, is that the sun, the eye, and the globe shall be so relatively placed, that light from the sun shall strike the globe at an ascertained angle ; and that every pencil of light of any given colour shall emerge from the globe to the stationary eye at an ascertained angle. These angles must be constant. But this condition being observed, it matters not where the globe is held, whether vertically or to the right or to the left. Evidently the imaginary plane passing through the centres of the sun, the eye, and the globe, may have *any* inclination to the line passing through those centres. Very well; then let it revolve round that line as its axis, carrying the globe with it, and the globe will continuously and successively assume every position in which the angles specified are of unchanged magnitude.

The circle, therefore, is what mathematicians call the *locus* of the centre of the globe which is moved under the given conditions. Hence a circular band will be the *locus* of the spectrum for each original position of the globe. That is, the observer would see the globe, starting from each of the two given positions, describe a circular coloured band, the colours being continuations of the spectra seen while the globe was at rest.

Accordingly, if instead of employing two rapidly revolving glass globes, I were to build an enormous wall of infinitely small solid transparent spheres, I should see *through it* (not on it) two concentric segments of circular prismatic arches, the centre of which would be in the same straight line with the centres of my eye and the sun. We thus find that each arch of the rainbow is the base of an imaginary cone, whose apex is the centre of the eye, and whose axis is the straight line passing through the centre of the arches, and those of the eye and the sun. For every position, then, of the eye in the axis there is a fresh cone; and for every position of the eye out of that axis there is a fresh axis and a fresh cone; so that having regard to the light alone, it is proved that for every position of the eye there is a rainbow of at least two concentric arches which cannot be seen in any other position; and therefore no two eyes can see one and the same rainbow.

What then happens when I look at a rainbow with both eyes at once? The same as happens when I look at my face in a glass. With the right eye alone I see a projection of my face which is invisible to the left eye, and *vice versâ*. But with both eyes I see an image of perfect stereoscopic relief, of which the two dissimilar projections are the co-determinants. In this case the axes of the eyeballs are converged to a point beyond the surface of the glass, so that a spot of dirt thereupon is seen double. If the axes are converged to that spot, then the spot is seen single, but my face is seen double. Now in the case of the rainbow, each eye has its image, and but for the great distance of the rain-bed, the act of coalescing the two images would, by the convergence of the optic axes, be very definitely determinate of distance. Such, indeed, is the case with the little prismatic arch which De Dominis tells us has been seen in the spray from the oars, and which I have seen against the paddle-boxes of steamers and over fountains. But owing to the great distance of the efficient drops in the case of the ordinary rainbow, the optic axes are approximately parallel; and the nearer they approach to parallelism the less significant they are of distance. Otherwise, we might, by the use of both eyes, be conscious of a phantom of a more determinate distance and position than we could possibly see with one eye; and we might conclude that the phantom seen with two eyes is not identical with that seen by either eye alone. However, this question of abstract identity is, as Berkeley found, one of considerable difficulty, and a fruitful source of paralogism.

If, instead of a wall of infinitely small transparent globules, we suppose a constant succession of globules in motion, as drops of water falling from a condensed

cloud, the place of each one being over supplied by
another, the conditions of the phenomenon are not
essentially varied : the succession of drops now effect
the same result as the stationary drops, since the eye
(even were the drops within the range of minute observation) is unable to discriminate so rapid a substitution
of one drop for another. In respect of the drops, then,
the phenomenon presents no identity even to a single
eye : nay, further, as Descartes perceived, for the
slightest change in the temperature of the drop, and for
the slightest change in its curvature (by reason of the
wind, or of its motion in the air), the luminous arch
varies, either in dimensions or in curvature. It is thus
found to be a physical fact that the rainbow, in every
objective particular, is an inconstant phenomenon : in
every *subjective* relation is, at any two consecutive
infinitesimal instants, an identical object, but one which
no other eye can see.

This meteor stands to the eye and mind of common
sense for an objective reality. What then is it made
of ? I much fear common sense will be divided on the
question : some holding, with Reid, that the thing seen
is the rain-bed ; some, with Hamilton, that it is the
light, and nothing else, that constitutes the objective
reality ; some, with Müller, that it is at bottom the
stimulated retina which is seen, and by which something else is, rightly or wrongly, inferred. Let us
examine these opinions, taking all possible care to avoid
sophistical reasoning, to which such questions are
peculiarly liable.

First then : Do we see the rain-drops at all? That they are sufficiently illuminated we may allow ; but, as it seems to me, there is a valid reason why we cannot see them. Without insisting on the fact of their remoteness (for that is not the case with the spray-bow), it is manifest that they are in too rapid motion to be discriminated, even were they in sufficient proximity for accurate inspection when at rest. Not to discriminate these drops is not to see them at all. For what are the constituents of any visible object, save its proper figure and colour? But the figure of any of these drops is invisible, and proper colour they have none ; or, if they have, it is overwhelmed in the play of accidental colour. Secondly: Do we see the light? It seems at first sight a very foolish question; and nine people out of ten would be tempted to reply with another question: "What else do we see?" But we must discriminate between seeing and feeling, or we shall soon be lost. We may and do obviously have a sensation of light whenever we open our eyes to the day, or to moonlight, or lamp-light; or excluding these occasions of vision, whenever by percussion, or a galvanic current, or otherwise, a luminous impression is excited in the retina. In all these cases, too, we may locate the construction which follows upon the sensation as a luminous object. But so far from seeing light (*i.e.*, as an object of sense), its objective reality is a mere hypothesis of the physicist. If there be an ethereal medium whose undulations evoke for us the sensation of light (primarily in the retina or optic nerve, and secondarily

in the mind), its reality is only an *ens rationis*, at most
believed in, not perceived ; and for all purposes of knowledge might be a *noumenon*. If there be any third
kind of light, besides the sensation and the dynamical
condition, I am unable to conceive it, and certainly
have never heard of it. If possessing the sensation (as
a merely subjective affection) we locate some construction ensuing upon it, or involved in it, as an object
without the eye, we are constituting an object expressly
fraught with the power of provoking that sensation.
But whether we locate it in the retina, or out of
the retina and in the organism, or wholly out of the
organism, the light is not the object constituted, but is
that which reveals the object: " for whatsoever doth
make manifest [and nothing else] is light." The infant's
visual perception is believed to be in this order : first,
the sensation of light ; secondly, a vague determination
of visible non-ego ; thirdly, a discrimination of two
kinds of visible non-ego—that which is not me but
my organism, and that which is neither me nor my
organism. In this third stage of perception the mind
not only judges an object to be non-ego, but extra-
organic ; that is, it not only says, "that is out of me,"
but "that is out of my eye," or "that is out of my
organism." This objecting and localising of a luminous
object is its constitution to the sight as an adequate
and intelligible condition of vision. It thus appears
that we never see light, but only that object which light
is understood to make manifest. But thirdly: Do we
see our own retina stimulated to the depicture of the

vari-coloured arch? Those who reply in the affirmative are bound to hold that in touch we do not feel the object touched, but the nervous extremity touching; in short, that we know nothing by the senses, but the nervous system, or, at most, the nervous and muscular systems. This is the doctrine expressly taught by Müller. ('Physiology,' by Baly, 1838, i. 766, ii. 1059, &c.) Could Berkeley ask anything more? If Müller can find assurance for inferring the existence of an external world of three dimensions, it by no means follows that the inference is valid—that it is not based on an illusion.[1] In point of fact, if the general consciousness of men testifies (though covertly) to the doctrine that in vision the only object is the stimulated retina, it follows that the external world of sight is a vision of the retinal impressions, and all objects, even the most distant, are all within the range of that stimulation. The retina, in fact, *is* the world without; and even the human body is in the retina, and the eye itself, as part of that body, is in the retina; and there is a complete introversion of the whole into a part! Berkeley, we may be sure, would make no account of the whole, as soon as he had reduced it to so small a

---

[1] It is worth a passing mention, that Hamilton ('Discussions,' 1852, p. 60) classed Berkeley with those who held that ideas are representative of things—what he called Cosmothetic Idealists; and this course is cited and not excepted to by Mr. J. S. Mill ('Examination of Sir W. Hamilton's Philosophy,' 1865, p. 161). A long and very familiar acquaintance with Berkeley's works justifies me in saying that there is no doctrine so constantly and obstinately confronted and contested by Berkeley as that imputed to him by Hamilton. Nor is it, by any means, a fair corollary from anything he taught.

compass; nor do I think any reasonable man would, after receiving the doctrine in question, have much compunction in going the whole way with him. But if, in seeing a rainbow, we see neither the rain-drops, nor the light, nor the retina, it becomes a question of some interest to determine what it is that constitutes the object seen. It is, at least, a phantom which obeys some, and some only, of the laws of what we call real objects; for instance, the rainbow, unlike most other objects of sight, becomes less the nearer we approach it. I would, for the nonce, call it a false object; and such are the phantoms produced by those beautiful toys—Dr. Roget's phenakistiscope[1] and Mr. Rose's photodrome, and that ingenious German contrivance for making the crooked straight, called the anorthoscope. In truth, all these artifices accomplish more than the rainbow. The rainbow, however, as a clue to a sound theory of visual perception, is, as it should be for that end, of the simpler kind. It is a phenomenon without a substance, presenting a plane geometrical figure at a certain distance from the eye. At this point, then, if at all, we pass over into idealism. But first, the question occurs whether we are justified in deducing a system of idealism from facts which involve the relation of objects to the sensitive organism. It might be said, and in effect has often been said . . . . You are bent on showing that this object is a creation of the mind. To do this you show that the efficient cause of vision is in

---

[1] This instrument was *re-invented* by Plateau. Why was it not called phenakiscope, simply, or kinesiscope?

the retina and nerves; in short, that what we experience is located there, and not outside at all. That is legitimate. But having done that, you have no right to build the doctrine of idealism on the fact that the retinal and other nervous affections involve the whole act of vision : for that very affection would not be at all but for the existence of an external object, by virtue of which light proceeds to the eye, and figures a photograph of that object on the retina. This is the case with all illusory phantoms, as well as visible objects. You cannot, then, be permitted, even in the case of the rainbow, to utilise one pole of the relation and ignore the other; to extract idealism out of the affection to which the organ and mind are subject; and then reduce to a nonentity the object by whose independent existence it was that the organ had that affection, and the mind (by virtue of that organ) had perception of the object. Now if the optical act be purely organic, and confined to the sphere of the organ affected, so be it; but it would not be at all if there were not an external object answering to it. . . . . Now I think this objection admits of the plea of "non relevat argumentum." The bearing of the objection is wholly on the correlation of object and eye, as manifested to a *second* percipient—*i.e.*, to an observer of *both*. The owner of the eye knows nothing of this objective character of the organ, save by an objecting process; he must see it by reflection, or see a fellow eye in the head of a second person. Shakespeare admirably expresses all this :—

"For the eye sees not itself,
But by reflection, by some other things."—*Julius Cæsar*, i. 2.

"Nor doth the eye itself
(That most pure spirit of sense) behold itself
Not going from itself ; but eye to eye opposed
Salutes each other with each other's form.
For speculation turns not to itself
Till it hath travell'd, and is married [1] there,
Where it may see itself."—*Troilus and Cressida*, iii. 3.

The relation of object to object is known only as represented to one who observes both *per sensus*. If, then,
one of the objects is an organ of sense to the observer,
it is plain that he can observe but one pole of the
represented relation. For the specified objection to be
allowed in bar of idealism, it must be assumed that a
relation between two objects which is represented to an
observer is also represented to him who owns one of
those objects as an organ of sense : that I, looking at a
tree, must find between my consciousness and the tree
the same relation which he finds who observes both my
organism and the tree, as two correlated objects. Now,
without dogmatically averring that there is not one
and the same relation subsisting for both me and that
observer, this I do emphatically maintain as a deliver-
ance of consciousness, that I, in perceiving that tree,
do not find any such relation, as that the tree as object
is the cause of the perception of the tree which I am
conscious of as object ; nay, rather the reverse ; but
for analogy I should never dream of such a relation.

---

[1] "Married," that is, *fellowed ; quasi* marrowed.

Analogy, however, leads me to believe that whatever relation subsists between a tree and the sense of another man (both objects being matters of my observation *per sensus*), that very relation also subsists between that tree and my senses. This is an intellectual speculation, not in the least drawn out of my consciousness of *my* relation to the tree. What, then, is that relation? It seems to me that it is the converse of the other: viz., that the visible tree is the effect of my act of vision, not the cause of it. In the act of seeing a phantom that has no substantial reality, such as the rainbow, I am introduced to this original objecting power of sense: I am thus led, at least, to entertain the doctrine of Kant's 'Transcendental Æsthetic,' and to attach some weight to his own views concerning the rainbow: viz., that "not only are the rain-drops [like the rainbow] a mere appearance (*eine blose Erscheinung*), but even their circular form [when visible], as well as the space they fall in, is nothing in itself (*an sich selbst*), but they are both a mere *modification* or groundwork of our sensuous *intuition* (*blose Modificationen oder Grundlagen unserer sinnlichen Auschauung*). (Kritik der reinen Vernunft. Tr. Æsth., § 8, Erste Auflage.)

But it occurs to me that another form of the objection already considered might be brought against the validity of this transit to idealism. I cannot express it better than in the words of Mr. Herbert Spencer, in the *Fortnightly Review* (vol. i. pp. 539, 540). Writing concerning idealism, he remarks: "Though the conclusion reached is that mind and ideas are the only

existences, yet the steps by which this conclusion is
reached take for granted that external objects have just
the kind of independent existence which is eventually
denied. If that extension, which the idealist contends
is merely an affection of consciousness, has nothing out
of consciousness answering to it, then in each of his
propositions concerning extension the word should
always mean an affection of consciousness, and nothing
else." I am unable to admit the conclusiveness of this
objection. I contend that there are two distinct stand-
points for speculation—(1) that of the physicist, whose
world are phenomena, and in which there is no subject
save the objective organism, and the relation of another
object to this (as the light-picture transmitted from the
former to the retina of the latter) is but one among
numberless physical relations which are amenable to
science; and (2) that of the conscious percipient, whose
world is mental and voluntary, and to which the
objects of sense are, in a manner, constructions serving
to accommodate the external universe to the understanding. Now I contend that between these two
there is no more discord than between two poles of the
same fact. To take Mr. Herbert Spencer's example of
extension: I may on the one hand say that extension
is learned piecemeal by experience: that is, on the
side of the physicist: and on the other hand I may
say that extension is given intuitively as a whole in
consciousness, and that its intuition underlies all
physical use of the senses: that is, on the side of the
percipient.

But in this place I do not intend to pursue further this difficult and intricate problem.   I do not here design a settlement of the question; but merely to open it up for further inquiry, and to turn the teaching of the rainbow to the account of psychology.

V

LAW AND RELIGION.

THE wise Emerson perceived that our self-consciousness
was no attribute of primeval man, but came to us at
the dawn of civilisation. Its discovery, he assures us,
is identical with the Fall of Man. Whether or not he
was right in that identification, the discovery entailed
momentous issues. Man was then first capable of the
sense of shame, of vanity and pride, of questionings as
to what he is, whither he is going, and why he exists
at all. Worst of all, man then became capable of
remorse and repentance. In a word, man then first
had a conscience. On a lower scale, every child treads
in the steps of this sad history. Almost every one in
childhood remembers to have experienced that painful
questioning which takes the shape of "Why am I
here?" and which usually follows close upon the dawn
of his self-consciousness.

Emerson was fond of comparing, or rather contrast-
ing, men with flowers, who know no past or future, and
"live ever in a new day;" and he saw no reason why
men should not revert to a life of less introspection and
greater trustfulness. He assured them that they had

no reason to mistrust God's spirit, as if it were incapable of reproducing the simplicity, innocence, and beauty of time past. Somehow he never seems to have boldly confronted and acknowledged the evils which lay around him, and doubtless also in him. He might have taken it for granted that every man would be only too glad to get rid of his conflicts, and to obey some simple law of his own nature. A dog, for instance, is, on his own level, supremely happy. He obeys his natural impulses without any of those embarrassments and hindrances which beset his less privileged masters. Situated as man is, he cannot help living a life of distrust and conflict; finding that his course is determined by an unending series of impulses and checks, he is forced to recognise the fact of a law without him, simply because it is manifestly not the law of his nature. This shows clearly what St. Paul meant when he said: "I find then a law in my members warring against the law in my mind, and bringing it into subjection to the law of sin." However this state of things may be described, whether, according to the Christian view, as a fall of humanity from a state of obedience and innocence to one of rebellion and remorse, or, according to Emerson, as a natural result, "unfortunate, but too late to be helped," it is, beyond cavil, to the last degree deplorable. It is abundantly clear that man has arrived at a point where he is "fallen between two stools," the one being instinctive obedience to a natural law, the other rational obedience to a spiritual law; and he can neither revert to the one, nor, by

taking thought, advance to the other. He has long
ceased to be like the flower or even the dog, for over-
whelming experience has established the fact that his
natural impulses, though possibly useful servants, are
the worst masters, bringing the man who is subject to
them not only to a condition below that of the brutes,
but to every conceivable misery.

The outcome of all this is the fact of a moral law and
the possibility of religion. It is at first somewhat
surprising to find St. Paul, who declares himself to be
" a Hebrew of the Hebrews," and " of the straightest
sect of the Pharisees," describing alike the law of Moses
and the law of the mind as of the greatest practical
inutility. He tells us the law can and does convince
man of sin, but that it is utterly incapable of delivering
him from it. It is like a man standing at the water's
edge crying to his drowning friend, " Come out of that
or you will perish." In truth, Emerson does give that
very advice to one who is living to the subversion of
moral rule, but, beyond uttering many wise and
scholarly aphorisms, delivered in a style of cold and
polished elegance, he affords him not the slightest help.
He simply stands by the law as one who, through some
power not disclosed, has been drawn over to habitual
obedience to its dictates. But St. Paul is undoubtedly
right: the law which teaches a man by transgression
is not only incapable of helping him, but capable of
driving him to despair, and it was with this conviction
that the apostle compares himself to a living man
chained to a dead body.

We have reached this point, then, that the moral law, and still more the ceremonial law, are utterly powerless to become the principle of a man's life. Hence arises, as has been said, the possibility of religion, understanding by that much-abused term a power or office capable of bringing a man into harmony with the rule of right. When we come to think of it, religion itself arises with the dawn of self-consciousness. But, by the nature of the case, we have no historic record of the earliest and rudest form of worship, and can only infer it from the material and linguistic relics of past races. The existing religions, professedly built on ancient documents, some of which belong to historic times, are but the artificial and comparatively recent products of civilisation.

The Christian religion without the Fall of Man has no *locus standi*. It requires as its very foundation that man should have been created in the image of God, a perfect and even divine being, and that he should of his own free will have thrown off his allegiance to his Creator by some act of disobedience. The scribe who relates the story of the temptation and fall in the Hebrew Scriptures is certainly not the author of the earlier story of the Creation. Apart from other evidences, the duality is established by there being two accounts of the creation of man and woman in the Book of Genesis. In the earlier account man, male and female, is the subject of a direct creation like that of the lower animals, and the Creator is designated the Elohim, commonly rendered *the Gods* or *God* indifferently. In the later narrative the Creator is called by the compound, Elohim-Jehovah, the Lord God, and proceeds to create *a* man out of the dust of the ground, with an evident reference to the operation of modelling in clay. Having accomplished this elemental work, he proceeds to endow his figure with life by breathing into its nostrils, and man thus became a living soul. Then follows what Professor Huxley admirably describes as a "preposterous fable"—preposterous, as putting the cart before the horse; and, in order to obtain a female exemplar of the same species, he renders the man insensible, and then deprives him of one of his ribs, with which he fashions a woman.

It is difficult to speak of this story with the reverence which is due to a sacred subject; but we are at once recalled to a more serious frame of mind by the reflection that while the first scribe is apparently narrating what he believes to be hard and fast fact, the second writer is veiling the most interesting fragments of an ancient philosophy in an allegory which, to modern notions, appears somewhat grotesque.

We have said that the earlier scribe is apparently dealing with fact. It is, at least, sufficiently obvious that the story of the Creation, even if a kind of philosophical poem, is not a pure allegory. It is an honest attempt to account for the existing state of things. Perhaps nothing in the history of philosophy gives us a keener sense of the advances made in modern times than the reflection that the old writer could fail to see that daylight proceeds from the sun, and that night and day are respectively due to the presence or absence of that luminary. Making all allowances, it is difficult to realise how any intelligent person, even at that early day, could have fancied he was simplifying the matter by first creating the light, secondly dividing the light from the darkness, and thirdly creating the sun to rule by day and the moon to rule by night. But perhaps it is even more astonishing that intelligent men of the present day should ask us to accept such " preposterous fables " as the dictates of inspiration.

What no doubt led this writer to the ascription of so fanciful a function to the sun, and of a co-ordinate one to the moon, was the superficial difficulty of accounting for the daylight or moonlight when the ruling luminary was wholly obscured. The view of the ancient scribe is just that of the little child who knows nothing of the diffusion of light by atmospheric refraction, and does not dream that the light of day or the darkness of night are phenomena due to the sun's illumination and the earth's rotation. We may suppose that this division of the light from the darkness was intended to cover the case of a luminary being totally obscured by clouds, and it is interesting in this connection to observe that reflective children, who are none the less ready (like other children) to see miracles in startling changes, are wont to refer the sudden withdrawal of light to an arbitrary will. I myself knew a child who manifested this peculiarity in an astonishing manner. In the early days of railways he accompanied his father on an excursion by train. When the train was entering the first tunnel, his father said, by way of preparation, "It's now going to be dark." Soon after emerging from the tunnel the child exclaimed, "Now, papa, do make it dark again;" and his father, a leading director of the railway company, not unwisely left him under the natural inference that the director had the absolute power of plunging the carriage in darkness whenever he chose. I have no doubt that the child made as absolute a division between the light and the darkness, as co-existing agencies, as the ancient scribe himself.

The later historian of the Creation apparently writes in ignorance of his predecessor's narrative. He is more minute and concrete in his treatment of those incidents which chiefly concern the fortunes of the human race, viz. (1) the production of two exemplars of the species, one of each sex; (2) the prohibition which was imposed upon them as a test of their allegiance to the Creator; and (3) the circumstances and consequences of their disobedience. The prohibition put them at once in a position of disadvantage; for, on the one hand, they were not shown its reasonableness, nor yet, on the other, were they warned of the subtle and persuasive enemy who was already a denizen of the garden. More-over, the weaker of the two was in no wise guarded against the danger to which, by her nature, she was peculiarly exposed. To compare great things with small, it was as if some children were enjoined by their father not to go near a certain spot around which were growing in tempting luxuriance the flowers they best loved. But what would be thought of him if he omitted to describe the danger peculiar to that favoured spot—namely, that the flowers which blossomed there concealed the mouth of a deep pitfall? Would not such neglect stamp the prohibition with injustice? And how much greater would be the unfairness towards them if their father knew that there was a person prowling about who had a mania for tempting children to the fatal spot, and, notwithstanding, failed to warn them of their special danger!

The Oriental treatment of the story of the temptation is suggestive of a satrap—a mere temporal ruler who lounges on his divan during the day, and strolls about his garden in the cool of the evening. But, as the basis of a theology, this Eastern potentate has to be taken to be the direct Creator and Divine Ruler of the universe; and conduct which might be thought culpable, or even criminal, in a human ruler, thus assumes a " monstrous bulk," too vast to be " covered by any size of words."

Whatever was the intention of the writer of this story, it is read by the Christian Church as an authentic account of the origin of sin. The man and woman who had been created innocent were subjected to a test of their allegiance; and we can well imagine a trial which would have been fair, because within that limit of strength and knowledge which had been given them. But, by the nature of the case, it was within the power of the Creator to subject them to a strain in excess of that limit, and, forasmuch as the man was the wiser and stronger, to impose the test upon the woman. In the case of a malignant deity, we could hardly give too

much praise to the craft by which he economised his
resources and placed the strain upon the weakest part;
what then are we to say when we find the Christian
Church imputing this policy to the Divine Being they
worship? Furthermore, the weaker vessel, having
yielded to a temptation beyond what she was constituted to bear, besides sharing her husband's banish-
ment, is subjected to a retribution exceeding in severity
that which is to fall on him. Nay, more, this very
penalty is made to perpetuate the curse throughout all
generations; and millions who have never participated
in the guilt of their first parents are judged guilty by
imputation, and made to bear the punishment. This
is what the Church designates "original sin," and it
is on this basis alone that the redemptive scheme of
Christianity finds its sole *raison d'être.*

It should be clearly understood that this indictment
does not touch the writer of the original story, whether
fable or allegory, but is against those who, by reading
it as an historical narrative, have drawn from it the
outlines of a dogma as incapable of facing the facts of
human life as of being reconciled with the attributes
of a wise, just, and holy God. In dealing with an
ancient record apparently professing to be a narrative
of fact, and as such bearing on the history of the human
race, it is of prime importance to determine whether
it is such. Clearly, a poem, a fiction, or an allegory
would not necessarily have that bearing. But granting that in such cases as those we have been considering
the writer (let him have been well or ill informed on

the relative matters) had an honest intention to record an event or tradition, other questions still remain to be solved. He may have been a bad observer, or an inaccurate or unscrupulous recorder; and in dealing with a tradition which he himself believed, he may have been utterly unable to discriminate the true from the false. Thus, in considering the claims of the first account of the Creation which the Christian Church asks us to accept as literal, or, at least, substantial history, we are bound to assure ourselves that there is nothing in the narrative which betrays the incompetence or untrustworthiness of the narrator. This would be more readily discovered in those portions where a man of common intelligence would be unlikely to err than in those which lie beyond the purview of his ordinary speculations. In a word we should apply to that narrative what is called the *argumentum a fortiori*. The less in this argument is taken to cover the greater, and a test which is found to fail when applied to the less has the power of discrediting the greater. Of course it might be argued on the other hand that a writer who was authorised by God to deal with facts which in the nature of the case were undiscoverable by human sagacity, might, with the divine sanction, record such matters faithfully and accurately, while he made the most puerile blunders in matters which lay within his own ken. But this is not only begging the question that this particular writer was divinely inspired, but, granting the fact of that inspiration, is arbitrarily limiting it to a certain range of subjects, and drawing a hard and fast line where, by the very nature of the case, no line need be drawn. Such an argument is so obvious a makeshift that it would be wasting words to refute it formally.

To elucidate our position, we may compare this case with one which has arisen in recent times. An important section of the Christian Church, composed entirely of educated persons, have accepted the teaching of Emanuel Swedenborg, and receive him as the apostle of interpretation. Now among the many demands which this industrious and productive writer makes upon our faith is one which is exceptionally staggering. He offers for our acceptance, in the most literal sense, a narrative of the visits he was permitted to make to the various bodies in the solar system. Up to the time of his death the planets which were recognised in the astronomy of the ancients were the only bodies known to circulate round the sun. A scientist, from whose voluminous works no branch of human knowledge was excluded, and who dealt with things both natural and divine in the most exhaustive way, could hardly have failed at least to speculate, as did Immanuel Kant, on the existence of extra-Saturnian planets. A seer, who was permitted by divine agency to visit the planets *seriatim*, might well be expected to discover the existence of a body or bodies beyond the orbit of Saturn? He does nothing of the sort. He finds no more than the five planets of the ancients. Now immediately after his death Sir William Herschel discovered Uranus, and in 1847 Adams and Leverrier

H

discovered Neptune. The natural inference is that Swedenborg did not visit the actual planets, and that the narrative is purely subjective.

In the same way we put the first narrator of the Creation to a test of his seership. We try him on matters which are within our own knowledge, and the test yields the same result. It is evident, on the face of the narrative, that this writer, who professes to know the greater, did not know the less. He tells us, for instance, that the sun was created after the Creator had divided the day from the night. From this point our interest in the sacred narrative becomes centred in the philosophy or the poetry, and we cease to value it as a revelation or record of fact. Like the visions of Swedenborg, it is mainly subjective.

The one remarkable feature in these old narratives is that all the events recorded are in the inverse order to that of nature. Astronomy assures us that the sun existed as the one great source of light and heat countless ages before the earth had become ripe to profit by those agencies, and that the alternation of day and night is the natural result of the rotation of the earth on her axis. Accordingly we should expect a divinely informed historian, who essayed the narration of the beginning of the present order of things, to relate first the formation of that stupendous body, without whose energy neither chemistry nor vitality would be manifested upon this earth. From this body, he would tell us, proceeded the light which first burst upon our void and formless planet. But the historian of the Creation

reverses this order, beginning with the heavens and
the earth, then proceeding to the creation of light, and
finally reaching that of the sun and moon as the pre-
siding luminaries of the day and night.

The later scribe, who relates the creation of man, also
reverses the natural order. This order is from spirit to
matter, as Spenser has it; "so doth the soul the body
make." The so-called matter of which alike divines
and physiologists tell us this universe is made, and on
which we are taught by sciolists that the laws of the
universe are impressed, has, sooth tó say, no possible
existence without those laws, and, what is more, without the coexistence of an immaterial energy in which
the great Schelling saw the poor remainder of an
extinct vitality. Let me repeat, the natural order,
established alike by philosophy and physics, is from
energy to materiality; and matter, whether in the form
of clay or dust, is simply a product or residue of life.
Accordingly a divinely informed historian would begin
with life and end with that organised body which is its
material envelope. But this old writer tells us that
the Creator moulded the first man out of the dust of
the ground, and, having completely formed him, endowed the image with vitality by breathing into his
nostrils the breath of life, whereby man became a living
soul. The scribe also reverses the natural order when
he comes to the production of a second exemplar of the
species. One imagines it would have been natural for
him to have obtained the first man from the first woman

in the manner described by the evangelist of the New Testament. But the most striking and serious of all these preposterities is that which is involved in the notions of the Fall of Man and original sin. It is true that science does not give us any absolute guarantee for believing that man is derived from a lower species of animal, but since the discoveries which have established against the theologians the antiquity of man, it is a matter of knowledge that man, as we know him, is a comparatively recent production derived from beings of a ruder and more animal type. The phenomena, then, which have led theologians to believe that man has fallen by wilful transgression from a divine and perfect state are simply due to his having grown into a state of self-consciousness, conscience, and reason. The very fact that reason shows us the law of a higher life with the promise of infinitely greater happiness and blessedness, and that experience proves that the law in our members—the animal and selfish propensities—is a great and often a fatal hindrance to the attainment of the higher life, should satisfy every cultivated mind that man is not a fallen but an ascending creature. It remains, then, to inquire what concern religion has with this new aspect of affairs. Is it possible, by reading between the lines, to make the records of Holy Scripture an instrument, not for convincing man of the good tidings of redemption, but of helping him to realise the better tidings of an accessible paradise from which he has never been excluded?

It behoves us before all things to realise in the fullest
and sharpest manner the tremendous issue at stake in
this conflict. Whatever be the value of the moral and
religious teachings of the sacred writings, it is hardly
too much to say that in their whole range there is not
an expression or image which exaggerates that momentous change implied in the words "repentance" and
"regeneration." The little we know of the inner life of
the more intelligent animals is derived from applying
to them the phenomena of our own consciousness; but
in that application we must be on our guard against
imputing to them those attributes which constitute the
differentiæ of humanity. In the case of subjection to
the animal impulses, a man so situated is tolerably safe
in reasoning from his own interior condition to that of
the dog; but even here he has to be on his guard against
imputing to the dog that attribute of will which is
peculiar to human nature. What we call the dog's
volition is doubtless analogous to the human will, but
that it is not a will is sufficiently evident from the fact
that it is by nature in subjection to animal impulses and
the corresponding mental associations. If the natural
resultant of these forces does not ensue, it is due to a
hindrance from without; and in the case of the dog this
hindrance is caused by the voluntary act of his master.
The process of crossing the natural bent of the dog is
called training, and it is just this training which elicits
from the mind of the animal an analogon to the human
will, viz., a volition which is capable of obedience to a

rule imposed on him from without. We have thus, in the case of the dog, an incomplete picture, on a lower level and on a smaller scale, of that stupendous education to which, as by a divine ordinance, human nature is submitted. But, after all, the difference is infinite; for the animal cannot resist, and the man can. It is just this power of spontaneous action which makes the human will what it is. It appears to be divinely constituted to do the work of obedience to a law above human nature; and though its actions are always determined by motives, it is to rational principles of action and not to mere blind impulses that man is called upon to yield implicit obedience. The resistance to these in any shape is called rebellion, which, according to a wise and notable saying of Scripture, is as the sin of witchcraft and idolatry; and nothing can be more fitly spoken than this concerning the evil motions of the human will. It is just this obedience or disobedience, this perceiving choice or blind rejection of the higher principles of life, that determines whether a man's course is to be upwards or downwards. And herein lies the justification of an exoteric religion. Be it as corrupt a religion as you please, it has always this merit—it demands implicit obedience. Now to the natural man there is nothing so galling as an external interference with his course of nature, and it is always at great cost that he thwarts his natural impulses in order to obey the dictates and injunctions of authority. The like merit belongs to the legislative and executive bodies of the state, who, whether they recognise it or not, are discharging a religious function. But the religion proper has this peculiar merit, that the sacrifice demanded is, at least indirectly, with the view of upholding and realising an ideal, and is therefore linked with a form of worship. It has often been a subject of debate whether Christianity has, from first to last, occasioned more good than harm to humanity. In my judgment it is paying the poorest religion the poorest compliment to acknowledge that it has done more good than harm.

It is assumed that the good of humanity is insured, not by multiplying and perfecting the comforts and conveniences of daily life, not by simplifying and economising the processes of human labour, in a word, not by increasing and developing the resources of the natural man, but by making each individual a good man in himself. What is the man? Is it his animal structure? Is it his intellect, or what? The concurrent answer of the great writers on Ethics is that man is his will, and that actions are simply the determinations of his will. The moral worth of those actions is just the moral worth of his determining motives, and these, as far as one can judge, can only work on him through his perceptions and affections, neither of which essentially constitute the man. It is only by these two avenues that religion can affect a man's actions. How far the traditional religion of any race or country promotes human advancement in these directions is a question demanding the most careful consideration ; and as no man, by taking thought, can create a religion any more than he can create a language, it is of the utmost importance to determine how far the Christianity of Western Europe can, without doing violence to established facts, be adjusted so as to discharge the function of a great moral regenerator.

VI

ROMANTIC HISTORY.

THERE is a game, which for want of a better name may be called *contes circulaires*, consisting of a short story (first committed to writing) repeated at second-hand by a person who received it orally from another who read it. The game may be prolonged at pleasure : the person hearing it so repeated at second-hand may repeat it to another, and so forth indefinitely. The last hearer must tell the tale to all the players, after which the original *raconteur* reads the story aloud, and the discrepancies always occasion surprise, and many of them are so absurd as to provoke great merriment. The game is not common, simply because it is troublesome ; but, if resorted to but once, it furnishes a most interesting example of the manner in which narrative is made to diverge, insensibly and involuntarily, from fact. The enormous difficulties of exact description, and the impossibility of perfect recollection, are thus strikingly made manifest. But this game exhibits only two out of many coefficients in the perversion of history from the facts originally experienced, or from the most faithful record of their occurrence. To complete the account, we must add to the causes at work in these *contes circulaires* every other source of error which lurks in the exercise of the senses, in the play of imagination and the emotions, in the state of bodily health, and in the many besetting temptations to untruthfulness in the use of the mental faculties.

The publication of M. Mortimer-Ternaux's five volumes on the Reign of Terror[1] once more impressed us with the fact, which had so often before been forced on our attention, that *history is a golden impossibility*, and that what usually arrogates to itself the name bears the same likeness to history that the scribble of a child bears to a geometrical figure. We are once again, and more strongly than ever, impressed with the fact that history at best is but an approximation to truth. The period of French history selected by M. Mortimer-Terneaux is rank with pseudo-historic details, which it has been reserved for him to confront with newly discovered contemporary records, and to brand with the name of *légende* or *mensonge*. Both the one and the other play an important part in the pseudo-history of this period, for which reason we propose to exemplify the general proposition above stated by a few of the more salient instances recorded by the historians of the French Revolution. In doing so we shall have occasion to signalise some very remarkable cases of "Romantic History" which are not turned to account in M. Mortimer-Terneaux's great

[1] *Histoire de la Terreur.* Michel Lévy, 1861-1866.

work; at the same time we shall extract some instances, not less important, from his pages.

But first let us consider with a little more accuracy how it comes to pass that written history is not a truthful representation of facts. The sources of un-truth, whether legendary or factitious, are *mainly* two—observation and narration. We all know the opinion of the criminal lawyer on the relative value of direct testimony and circumstantial evidence—καὶ τούτων ἐστὶν ἀγαθὸς κριτής—a question on which he ought to be the best judge. Such a man holds that in cases where the accused is convicted on the force of con-curring circumstances, there is, as a rule, less reason for doubt than where the conviction ensues on the mere testimony of an eye-witness. This at first seems strange and unreasonable, but we are disposed to believe that the professional opinion is sound. The ground of that opinion consists in this, that all ob-servation involves discrimination and valuation of the evidence of our fallible senses. Experience soon satisfies us, as in the case of the *contes circulaircs*, that testimony, where not wholly to be rejected, should always be received with suspicion. A very small per-centage of even honest, intelligent, and educated men are competent observers; and few have the slightest notion of the difficulties involved in the simplest observation. We remember a case in which three persons in a railway carriage concurred in the testi-mony that the fourth had given up his ticket to the collector; and all three were wrong. We call to mind

another case in which a well-known director of the
Bank of England believed himself to have given up his
ticket at Swindon, and told the collector so on his
being asked for it at Slough and again at Paddington.
He had it in his pocket all the while, and was un-
wittingly mingling a dream with his waking thoughts.
The fact is, prepossessions and assumptions are unconsciously mixed up with facts. What we look for we
are apt to imagine that we see, or to believe that we
have seen. In narration we are still more liable to
error. It is exceedingly hard to remember exactly
what we have seen and heard, and even harder to
describe or reproduce it. What we dream or read we
are prone to mix up with the memory of fact. What
we believe forms, almost of necessity, the *substratum*
of the language in which we describe what has been
presented to our senses; and too often, in the con-
catenation of events, *propter hoc* means nothing more
than *post hoc*.

The facts to which the observer is called upon to
attest are generally the identity of persons and things,
and the discrimination of events and actions. But how
difficult it is to connect the event with its cause, the
action with its motive. Equally difficult is it to avoid
a false *liaison*, and to separate an action from motives
which seem adequate to have occasioned it, but which
are not known to have so operated. We are also apt
to fancy that causes and motives are direct objects of
the senses, simply because we exercise observation
under the tacit assumption of this or that cause or

motive being a coefficient of the result. But a
judgment on cause is grounded on the reason, and a
judgment on motive is grounded on sympathy. Even
ignorance of a man's character or temperament, like
ignorance of facts, may determine a wrong valuation
of the actions witnessed, and lead to their being
described in terms which imply a knowledge of unknown motives. Further, by way of complicating what
is already inextricably involved, there may be special,
singular, and misleading features in the case which
defy that exact observation by which alone it is possible to elicit the clue to the motive of action: or
the witness, having observed well, may suffer from
some morbid freak of memory; or, what is still worse,
may wilfully and with evil forethought falsify the
facts which he happens to remember with sufficient
accuracy.

As Dr. Samuel Johnson well remarks (Life, by
Boswell, 1811, vol. iii. p. 250)—

"Nothing but experience could evince the frequency of false
information, or enable any man to conceive that so many groundless reports should be propagated, as every man of eminence may
hear of himself."

We know that Johnson's bearish manners gave offence
to persons who did not enjoy an intimate acquaintance
with him. The prepossession that he was bearish, joined
to the very common error of referring to indifference
what was really due to constitutional indolence, is quite
sufficient to account for the distortion of facts, and the
creation of fable in the following anecdote. Boswell

was assured by a friend (Life, by Boswell, 1811, vol. iii. p. 213)—

"That a gentleman who had lived in great intimacy with him [Johnson], shown him much kindness, and even relieved him from a sponging-house, having afterwards fallen into bad circumstances, was one day, when Johnson was at dinner with him, seized for debt, and carried to prison ; that Johnson sat still, undisturbed, and went on eating and drinking ; upon which the gentleman's sister, who was present, could not suppress her indignation : 'What, sir,' said she, 'are you so unfeeling as not even to offer to go to my brother in his distress ; you who have been so much obliged to him?' And that Johnson answered, 'Madam, I owe him no obligation ; what he did for me he would have done for a dog.'"

Now in this story the only facts are, that the person in question had done Johnson the particular service specified ; and that possibly Johnson may (as he admitted to Boswell) have described him as a man whose "generosity proceeded from no principle, but was part of his profusion ; he would do for a dog what he would do for a friend." It does not appear that this gentleman, who was so "full of the milk of human kindness," ever was in difficulties ; and we have Johnson's assurance that, in such an event, he "would have gone to the world's end to relieve him."

Such fables are being constantly forged and circulated of every man of mark. Thus they gain currency and credit, are repeated from mouth to mouth with frequent additions, omissions, and exaggeration of colour, till at length, in the case where their hero is a chief agent in the affairs which determine the fate of a kingdom, a church, or a people, they gain admission into history,

and poison the stream of national tradition. In order
to understand fully how this takes place, it is but
necessary to read Hume's 'History of England under
the Reign of Charles II.,' and then to verify the details
by reference to that wonderful *aubaine littéraire*, Pepys'
Diary. But the space at our command forbids us to
make any excursion in that direction. One of the
latest revelations of this kind has discomfited, not the
inaccurate Hume, but the accurate Macaulay. In the
first volume of his History (ed. 1849, pp. 500–502), we
have an eloquent description of the barbarous murders
of Margaret Maclachlan and Margaret Wilson, on May
11, 1685—"The former an aged widow, the latter a
maiden of eighteen."

It is a happy instance of Macaulay's descriptive rhetoric. His authority was Wodrow; and the narrative is
confirmed by the memorial to Margaret Wilson erected
in Wigtown Churchyard, which, for aught one sees, may
be as authentic as the Martyrs' Monument in Greyfriars
Churchyard at Edinburgh. But apparently Macaulay
quotes the epitaph, not from the stone, but from the
Cloud of Witnesses. As Mr. Emerson says on another
subject—"It is very unhappy, but too late to be helped,
the discovery we have made." It is now a matter
of certainty that neither of these poor women was
murdered, despite the monumental inscription and the
tradition. Sentenced to death they were, but that was
all. The Wigtown Session Books, which record their
sentence, also record their reprieve. How the memorial
came to be raised to Margaret Wilson "by Scottish

piety " is a problem that has yet to be solved; but as
it was not erected till some years after the alleged date
of the event it was intended to commemorate, it cannot
be allowed to weigh against the direct evidence of the
Session Books.

If such a fable as this can secure a footing in the
accredited History of Scotland, not in the years of her
tribulation, but long subsequently, what may we not
expect of the contemporary traditions and records of a
revolution which for violence and duration is without
parallel ?   At a time of popular tumult and excitement
it is evident that exact observation, if not impossible,
is peculiarly difficult.   This is the case, both in consequence of the extraordinary multiplicity of events to be
observed and of their complex relations, as well as by
reason of the perturbation of the mind and senses of
the observer.

We thus find any such historical question open to
various conflicting doubts.   We know that an observer
in such a case has a right to look for what is abnormal
and extreme ; but the very consciousness of that is
apt to make him see a swan in every goose.   On the
other hand, an observer, who, not considering that, is
exacting in his demand for proof in proportion as the
event is outrageous and difficult to observe, is apt to
make too great a discount upon "the attest of eyes and
ears ; " or otherwise to ignore what he seems to observe,
lest the record of the incredible should destroy his
credit.   In dealing, then, with the accumulated testi-
monies of the French Revolution, we are puzzled to

determine their just valuation. "In an age of miracles, such as the Reign of Terror," writes Carlyle (Misc. 1842, vol. v. p. 360), "one knows not at first view *what* is incredible." "But too often," says De Quincey on the other side (Works, Hogg, vol. x. pref. vi.), "writers who have been compelled to deal in ghastly horrors form a taste for such scenes; and oftentimes, as may be seen exemplified in those who record the French Reign of Terror, become angrily credulous and impatient of the slightest hesitation in going along with the maniacal excesses recorded." The latter remark has been completely borne out by the recent researches of MM. Michelet, Louis Blanc, and Mortimer-Terneaux.

In truth we can hardly be too cautious and hesitating in arbitrating upon the worth of evidence in such a circumstance as the Reign of Terror. We may be prepared, indeed, for "maniacal excesses;" but let it be remembered that among those excesses is the particular excess, so fatal to history, of colouring, whereby the already ensanguined aspect of affairs is heightened and falsified. If the actors are extravagant, the reporter is so too; and in proportion as they overstep the limits of probability, does he, in his amazement and revulsion, surpass the due proportions of the event.

To take one prominent and hitherto unchallenged episode of the *Terreur*, how shall any well-balanced mind, not agape and agog for horrors, receive the current story of the martyrdom of the fair and virtuous Princess de Lamballe? We are indeed confronted with a fulness of testimony—testimony of pretended eye-

I

witnesses—bearing on all, even the invisible, details of the monstrous tragedy. But to us some of the traditions are to the last degree incredible. That the unfortunate girl was struck down in the midst of the raging mob that beset the entrance of La Force is only too credible : would it were otherwise ! But the obscene indignities said to have been practised on her corpse, " which, " says Carlyle, " human nature would fain find incredible," should be henceforth dismissed as fiction—an infernal progeny begot between an intoxicated imagination and terror-stricken senses. Amid the ferment and confusion of unremitting carnage, and stunned by the roar and tumult of a multitude of raging fiends, what observer could be cool, calm, and collected ? What atrocities such a multitude may or may not have done on the body of the princess it is impossible for us to determine ; for it was impossible for any *unparticipating* spectator to observe. Speculate we may ; but speculation is not observation, and possibility is not history. We may be quite sure that no kind-hearted bystander, as our own countryman, Dr. Moore, regarding the scene of carnage from a necessary distance, his heart sickening and his head swimming at the bare possibilities of the case, could have discriminated any of those obscene details. He could well have seen *her already senseless and bleeding form* supported between two ruffians (Mortimer-Terneaux's *Histoire de la Terreur*, vol. iii. p. 270) on the elevated threshold of the black prison, far above the surging mob. He could well have noted her disappearance among the crashing pikes and flashing sabres; but more he could not see; and where testimony becomes impracticable, we have no call to eke out the narrative with speculations as to what might have happened then. We know it will cost the lovers of sensational history a pang to throw off the nightmare of their faith. Anxiously will they demand, " Where is all this uprooting to end?" Begin or end, it cannot much matter to you who demand not dear-bought truth and verisimilitude, but a narrative *teres atque rotundus*, heedless whether it be homogeneous, or whether the breaks and flaws of fact be concealed by the cement of fable and fiction.

For this same Revolution, with its crisis called Reign of Terror, but which was rather the chaos of elements which might reign, but were at this time without any reigning order,[1] there is indeed much that must be uprooted before we can find any trustworthy foundation for our faith. Even Carlyle's brief story, told in very questionable English, in three small volumes of large type, and with wearisome and utterly indigestible padding, concerning Windbags, Saraha-waltzes, Tophet, and what not, will bear a good deal of pruning and paring before human reason and faith can find a safe harbourage there. Happily in dealing with many of the current episodes of the Revolution we are not

---

[1] Madame de Staël will not allow that the rule of the Jacobin party was an anarchy; she maintains it to have been a despotism. A dominant and uncompromising *power* there was, but it was one which the leaders of the party themselves could not regulate, and which, accordingly, was as fatal to themselves as to their opponents. See ' Considerations on the French Revolution,' 1813, vol. ii. p. 120.

left to mere protests and expressions of doubt, but have relevant evidence of their falsehood. Poor Dr. Guillotin has enjoyed a species of immortality to which his name has little title, and which has been accorded to him at the expense of his philanthropy. Let us hear Carlyle's account of the Doctor's connection with the beheading machine :—

"And worthy Doctor *Guillotin*, whom we hoped to behold one other time ? If not here, the Doctor should be here, and we see him with the eye of prophecy : for indeed the Parisian Deputies are all a little late. Singular Guillotin, respectable practitioner ; doomed by a satiric destiny to the strangest immortal glory that ever kept obscure mortal from his resting-place, the bosom of oblivion ! Guillotin can improve the ventilation of the Hall ; in all cases of medical police and *hygiène* be a present aid : but, greater far, he can produce his 'Report on the Penal Code ;' and reveal therein a cunningly devised Beheading Machine, which shall become famous and world-famous. This is the product of Guillotin's endeavours, gained not without meditation and reading ; which product popular gratitude or levity christens by a feminine derivative name, as if it were his daughter, *La Guillotine!* 'With my machine, Messieurs, I whisk off your head (*vous fais sauter la tête*) in a twinkling, and you have no pain ;"— whereat they all laugh. Unfortunate Doctor ! For two-and-twenty years he, unguillotined, shall hear nothing but guillotine, see nothing but guillotine ; then dying, shall through long centuries wander, as it were, a disconsolate ghost, on the wrong side of Styx and Lethe ; his name like to outlive Cæsar's."—*French Revolution*, 1837, vol. i, p. 202 ; 1848, p. 173.

Carlyle's authority for the Doctor's speech is the *Moniteur* of Dec. 1, 1789, in the *Histoire Parlementaire*. It seems indisputable that Dr. Guillotin had an " Idea," as Carlyle elsewhere designates the design ; but whether that was the divine exemplar of the beheading machine which was named after him is doubtful.

Certain it is that the Bill proposed by him in the Constituent Assembly, and made law on Jan. 21, 1790, revealed no "cunningly devised Beheading Machine." That law simply enacted that "in all cases where the law pronounced the penalty of death, the punishment should be the same, whatever might be the nature of the crime;" and, moreover, that the criminal should be beheaded by means of a simple machine. What that machine should be, "cunningly devised" or otherwise, was a matter for subsequent discussion and arrangement. With anything beyond the *projet de loi* Dr. Guillotin appears to have had no concern. At this point his connection with the Penal Code and its instruments of death terminated.[1]

Granting that Dr. Guillotin had an "Idea," he does not appear to have had any opportunity of realising it. In September 1792, before the advent of the Convention, we find the Tribunal of the Commune commencing their operations on the aristocrats with a certain machine recommended by Dr. Louis, the perpetual secretary of the Academy of Surgery. After his name it was first

[1] To understand the admirable justice and humanity of the worthy Doctor's measure, we must remember that up to this epoch the nobles of France had enjoyed an exemption from many of the penalties attaching to offences committed by others. Among these was the mode of suffering the penalty of death, which in the case of the common people entailed various tortures and indignities from which the privilege of nobility secured a complete immunity. The law introduced by Guillotin destroyed this privilege, and insured for all capital offenders a merciful death. Surely, since Voltaire had, by his almost superhuman exertions, carried the measure, which rendered illegal the trial by torture for religious offences, no greater boon had ever been bestowed on the French nation.

called the *Louison*, or *Louisette*. The particular instrument used was constructed by a German named Schmitt,
a maker of harpsichords. It was this very machine
which was subsequently christened by the mob *La
Guillotine*, in grateful remembrance of the services which
"the worthy Doctor" had rendered to the cause of
humanity and justice.

Whatever Dr. Guillotin's "Idea" may have been,
neither its conception nor its execution could have
demanded any great exercise of invention. *La Guillotine*
did not materially differ from the *Manuaja* of Italy, or
the *Maiden* of Scotland. To the former fell the unhappy
Beatrice Cenci at Rome in 1605, and the Duke of
Montmorency at Toulouse in 1632; to the latter fell
the Regent Morton, who has the credit of having introduced the instrument into his native land.

On the whole, perhaps, the reader will be of opinion
that the error of Carlyle and the historians, and its
correction, are alike unimportant; still, as he more than
once elsewhere says, "universal history is not indif-
ferent." Besides, the current story is prejudicial to one
of the most humane and amiable men of the Constituent
Assembly. The genesis of the error is plain. Dr.
Guillotin had an "Idea" of a beheading machine.
Naturally enough, when Dr. Louis' recommendation was
carried out "in oak and iron" by the maker of harpsichords, the concrete machine was associated with the
first proposition, and so came to be christened after the
first proposer. Herr Schmitt's machine was no musical
instrument this time. Its utterances were clanking and

horribly discordant. No tuning, stringing, or buffing was ever needed by *La Guillotine* : a little cart-grease (*vieux oing*) was all she wanted to give despatch to her operations, and otherwise there was no fear of her rusting.

But let us pass on to the more turbulent and tragic times of the Reign of Terror; and first as to the great event of the tenth of August 1792. Let us hear M. Michelet :—

"I know of no event of ancient or modern times which has been more entirely distorted than that of the 10th August, more altered in its essential circumstances, or more charged and obscured by legendary or lying accessories. All parties, for envy, seem here to have conspired to exterminate history, to render it impossible, to inter and bury it, so that one cannot so much as find it any more. Sundry alluvial deposits of lies, of an astonishing thickness, have overlaid it. If you have seen the banks of the Loire, after the overflowings of late years, where the earth has been turned up or laid out, and the astonishing accumulations of ooze, sand, and pebbles, under which whole fields have disappeared, you will have some slight idea of the state in which the history of the 10th August still remains."

M. Mortimer-Terneaux writes:—

"If certain incidents of the 9th to the 10th August have been a hundred times recounted, we still remain in the most complete ignorance of the manner in which the Hôtel de Ville prepared and consummated the overthrow of the most ancient monarchy of modern Europe. The only documents historians have hitherto consulted have been truncated, mutilated, and falsified at pleasure ; and yet the lie has not been so well concocted but that the truth shows through the tissue, compressed [as it is] by the winding-sheet in which the conquerors would fain have shrouded it for ever."

It would occupy the space of several articles such as this to set forth in detail the various instances of exaggeration and distortion by historians both of England and of France in recounting the affairs of this critical period, and to confront them with the evidences discovered by M. Mortimer-Terneaux. He has unearthed and deciphered all sorts of seemingly worthless but really invaluable records, such as gaol-deliveries and reports of sections, which cast a flood of light on this obscure event of the 9th and 10th August. We select one instance as a sample of the rest, viz., *the assumed unanimity and co-operation of the Forty-eight Sections.* Let us hear Carlyle first:—

"Some new Twentieth of June we shall have ; only still more ineffectual? Or probably the Insurrection will not dare to rise at all? Mandat's Squadrons, Horse-Gendarmerie and Blue Guards march, clattering, tramping; Mandat's Cannoneers rumble. Under cloud of night, to the sound of his *générale,* which begins drumming when men should go to bed. It is the ninth night of August 1792. On the other hand, the Forty-eight Sections correspond by swift messengers ; are choosing each their 'three Delegates with full powers,'" &c.—*French Revolution,* vol. ii. p. 342.

This account, save as to the Forty-eight Sections, is probably as true as such English can ever be, where notes of interrogation do duty for semicolons, which have usurped the place of commas, and an adverbial parenthesis stands for a sentence without nominative or verb. But in this respect the extract we have just given is neither better nor worse than the general run of that quasi-primitive jargon in which, at so much pains, Carlyle attempts to give expression to his thoughts. It is true, of course, that *some* Sections did thus correspond. On this subject let us hear once more M. Mortimer-Terneaux :—

"We shall see that this unanimity of Sections, rising as a single
man to overthrow the constitutional monarchy, never had any
existence ; that this list of three hundred ' delegates of the people
in insurrection,' which has been so often spoken of, is false ; we
shall see how those full powers, 'committed by the people' into
the hands of its saviours, were obtained, and by whom they were
given ; and to those descriptions of giant contests, where we have
representations of thick masses heroically rushing to the assault
of the Tuileries, we shall oppose the net number of the dead and
wounded."

The very copious details which substantiate these
statements are perhaps a little too dry to interest general
readers, so we will not extract them, but pass on to
matters of more sensational attractions. For this char-
acteristic, what salient event of the *Terreur* is more
notable than the Massacres of the second of September
1792. After narrating on the authority of Félémhesi
and Dr. Moore the chief horrors of this red-letter day
in the French calendar, including the assassination of
the Princess de Lamballe, Carlyle writes as follows :—

"But it is more edifying to note what thrillings of affection,
what fragments of wild virtues turn up in this shaking asunder
of man's existence ; for of these too there is a proportion. Note
old Marquis Cazotte : he is doomed to die ; but his young
Daughter clasps him in her arms, with an inspiration of eloquence, with a love which is stronger than very death : the heart
of the killers themselves is touched by it ; the old man is spared.
Yet he was guilty, if plotting for his King is guilt : in ten days
more, a Court of Law condemned him, and he had to die elsewhere ; bequeathing his Daughter a lock of his old grey hair. Or
note old M. de Sombreuil, who also had a Daughter :—My Father
is not an Aristocrat : O good gentlemen, I will swear it, and
testify it, and in all ways prove it ; we are not ; we hate Aristocrats ! 'Wilt thou drink Aristocrats' blood ? ' The man lifts
blood (if universal Rumour can be credited) ; the poor maiden

does drink. 'This Sombreuil is innocent then!' Yes, indeed,
—and now note, most of all, how the bloody pikes, at this news,
do rattle to the ground; and the tiger yells become bursts of
jubilee over a brother saved; and the old man and his Daughter
are clasped to bloody bosoms, with hot tears; and borne home in
triumph of *Vive la Nation*, the killers refusing even money!"—
French Revolution, 1837, vol. iii. p. 42; 1848, p. 36.

The stories are substantially taken from Montgaillard,
vol. iii. p. 205, and are given on the authority of Dulaure.
More recently "the September ordeal of blood" has
been reproduced by M. Granier de Cassagnac, in his
Histoire des Girondins, in these words :—

"One of them took a glass, and poured into it some of the
blood that had issued from the head of M. de St. Mart, which
he mixed with wine and gunpowder, and told her [Mademoiselle
de Sombreuil] that if she drank *that* to the health of the nation,
she would save the life of her father."

How is it possible for any one henceforth to believe
such stories? The trick is too manifest. An imagination
more lively than representative is pressed into the
service of a mendacious book-maker, and in obedience
to the demand, the liquor is concocted for the ordeal of
the poor lady. Tradition gives blood as the only fit
libation; the historians variously season and spice the
horrible draught; but of all conceivable compounds that
the ingenuity of the romancist could pitch upon for
this purpose, this is the most atrocious. The wine,
however, is a *soupçon* of truth, as we shall shortly see;
but the act of drinking is the only particle of simple
truth in the anecdote.

Happily in this case, as in so many others, " Universal

Rumour," to which Carlyle pays the double homage
of capital initials and belief, is not to be credited henceforth. We have most fortunately the testimony of M. de
Sombreuil's daughter herself, given by her as Madame de
Villelume. It was recovered and published by M. Louis
Blanc (See *The Athenæum*, Sept. 26, 1863). The facts
are simple, and lie in a nutshell. The protestations and
entreaties of the daughter had touched the murderers,
and they granted her the life of her father. She then
fainted. When she returned to consciousness, she found
herself before the door of a *café*, supported by the very
men who had been massacring the prisoners of La Force.
One of them procured for her a glass of sugar and orange-
flower water, and made her drink ; but, she says, in
doing so,

" His fingers, stained with blood, had smeared the glass. My
first impulse, at the sight of the ensanguined hand stretched out to
me, was to turn away in horror ; whereupon one of those who
supported me whispered in my ear, ' Drink, *Citoyenne*, and think
of your father.' So I did, but ever since, whenever I see red
wine in a glass, I am seized with sickness."

Such an episode as this to the furious carnage of
the second of September would have pointed Carlyle's
remark on the " wild virtues that turn up in this
shaking asunder of man's existence " far more appositely
than the fable he has recorded. It is not difficult to
understand how this fable arose. An eye-witness may
very well have mistaken the gore-dropping glass for
an actual glass of blood. This single incident in the
course of frequent repetition might readily receive the

various additions which appear in the current story. A better example of the facility with which an eye-witness may receive a totally false impression of the events passing within the scope of his observation, and the fatality with which the perversion, when monstrous and unnatural, gathers about it an array of circumstances which render it intelligible, could not possibly be found.

Any account of the Romantic History of the *Terreur* would be incomplete without recording once more the famous case of the *Vengeur*, a frigate of the French fleet, which were vanquished by the English off Brest, on June 1st, 1794. Here is Carlyle's account of the affair :—

"War thunder from off the Brest waters : Villaret-Joyeuse and English Howe, after long manœuvring, have ranked themselves there ; and are belching fire. The enemies of human nature are on their own element ; cannot be conquered ; cannot be kept from conquering. Twelve hours of raging cannonade ; sun now sinking westward through the battle-smoke : six French Ships taken, the Battle lost ; what Ship soever can still sail, making off ! But how is it, then, with that *Vengeur* Ship, she neither strikes nor makes off ? She is lamed, she cannot make off ; strike she will not. Fire rakes her fore and aft from victorious enemies ; the *Vengeur* is sinking. Strong are ye, Tyrants of the Sea ; yet we also, are we weak ? Lo ! all flags, streamers, jacks, every rag of tricolor that will yet run on rope, fly rustling aloft : the whole crew crowds to the upper deck, and with universal soul-mad-dening yell, shouts *Vive la République*,—sinking, sinking. She staggers, she lurches, her last drunk whirl ; Ocean yawns abysmal : down rushes the *Vengeur*, carrying *Vive la République* along with her, unconquerable, into Eternity. Let foreign despots think of that. There is an Unconquerable in man, when he stands on his Rights of Man : let Despots and Slaves and all people know this, and only them that stand on the Wrongs of

Man tremble to know it.—So has History written, nothing doubt-
ing, of the sunk *Vengeur*."—*French Revolution*, 1837, vol. iii.
p. 335 ; 1848, p. 289.

To Carlyle himself is due the credit of thoroughly
investigating the facts of this case. He was, in fact,
the first to publish the evidence which invalidated his
own narrative. Rear-Admiral Griffiths, of the *Culloden*,
one of the British men-of-war in that action, was an
eye-witness of the behaviour of the *Vengeur* under the
English fire; and he answers and refutes Carlyle's
statements *seriatim* :—

"'The *Vengeur* neither strikes nor makes off.' She *did both*.
. . . 'Fire rakes her fore and aft from victorious enemies.' Wicked
. . . indeed would it have been to have fired into her, a sinking
ship with colours down ; and I can positively state that not *a*
gun was fired at her for an hour before she was taken possession
of. 'The *Vengeur* is sinking.' True. 'Lo ! all flags, streamers,
jacks, every rag of tricolor that will yet run on rope, fly rustling
aloft.' Not one mast standing, not *one rope* on which to hoist or
display a bit of tricolor, not one flag or streamer or ensign displayed. . . . 'The whole crew crowds the upper deck, and with
universa lsoul-maddening yell, shouts *Vive la République!*' . . .
Not one shout beyond that of horror and despair. At the moment
of her sinking we had *on board* the *Culloden*, and in our boats
then at the wreck, 127 of her crew, including the captain
[Renaudin, and his son]. The *Alfred* had many ; I *believe about*
100 : Lieutenant Winne, in command of a hired cutter, a
number, I *think* 49."

The source of this strange perversion of fact will be
found in the nationality and pride of the members of
the Convention. In their behalf the story was concocted
by Barrère : for them he was fain to give a lying version
of the sinking of the *Vengeur*, on the one hand to

aggrandise his *nation* and his *patrie;* on the other to conceal a mortifying defeat. He could not succeed in falsifying the fact that the *Vengeur* was utterly destroyed : so he did what seemed to him the next best thing : he invented and put in circulation a story, which, while it embalmed that fact, administered a sop to both the patriotism and the vanity of the French people. Perhaps also he thereby saved his own head.

This matter of refutation has been thoroughly well done by Carlyle ('Miscellanies,' 1847, vol. iv. p. 198). But having effected that refutation, it is astonishing to find him repeating his original version of the event in the third edition of his 'French Revolution' (1848). It is true that having set up his men he knocks them all down ; that he supplements the incomparable *boursoufflage* of the first and second editions with the comforting statement that " the *Vengeur,* after fighting bravely, did sink altogether, as other ships do," and that the " enormous inspiring feat, and rumour of ' sound most piercing,' " is " founded, like the world, upon *nothing.*" But in that case it strikes us as little better than a mock-swindle that the " billowy ecstasy of woe" of the old story should be inflicted on the reader, and that he should be drawn on towards the verge of distraction, to find his tempter, after all, grinning at him over the tragic mask.

The story of the *Vengeur,* substantially as Carlyle originally gave it, has in it, we fear, the seeds of immortality. It is all too good to be let slip, and no amount of evidence against it will be able to give it its

quietus. We have little doubt it will continue to walk
the earth for ages to come; and when the world at
large has become convinced that it was wholly the
invention of Barrère, the French will repeat and believe
it as they do at this present. Besides its own intrinsic
merits as a sublime piece of heroism, it is the one
dignifying incident among the disgraceful events of the
Terreur, and it is a case in which the glory of France
was earned *in despite of victory.* We much fear that
fables have more vitality than Carlyle is willing to
allow. He may give the myth a deadly wound; but
like the mystic living creature in the Apocalypse, that
"was wounded to death," its deadly wound has often a
wondrous power of healing; and the myth holds on its
way rejoicing against the truth.

The fifth volume of M. Mortimer-Terneaux's laborious
and well-written history adds its quota to the list
of myths surprised and branded. Among the many
false charges brought against the King and Queen
was that of having poisoned the locksmith Gamain,
in revenge for his having revealed the place in the
Tuileries in which the iron chest was secreted. This
story has recently received fresh currency by its admission, with credence, into M. Louis Blanc's *Histoire de
la Révolution.* Happily, M. Mortimer-Terneaux has
destroyed the only seeming evidence on which it rested,
and this *Mensonge de la Terreur* has received its death-
blow. How many more pieces of accredited history
will be banished to the wind on further searches being
made into the numerous archives of Paris it is of course

impossible to predict; but we may at least be sure of
this, that the True History of the French Revolution
has yet to be written, and that when it has at length
been "immutably fixed," it may be easily "comprised
in a few volumes," while the unauthorised incidents
which once formed the great bulk of the narrative will
have to be collected and edited by themselves, under
the title of *Légendes et Mensonges de la Révolution
Française,* as a standing warning to the historiographers
of the future.

VII.

FRANCIS BACON.[1]

PART I.

THERE are but two legitimate modes of studying a science: the historical and the systematic. There may, indeed, be a latent system in its historical development,

[1] The works of Francis Bacon, edited by J. Spedding, R. Leslie Ellis, and D. D. Heath. 1857, &c. Review of the above in the *Athenæum*, September 11 and 18, 1858. 'Francis Bacon of Verulam.' By Kuno Fischer. Translated from the German by John Oxenford. 1857. 'Bacon, sa Vie, son Temps, sa Philosophie.' By C. F. Remusat. Paris, 1857. 'Novum Organon Renovatum.' By W. Whewell. 1858. Chap. viii. § 2. 'On the Philosophy of Discovery.' By W. Whewell. 1860. Chap. xv., xvi., and xvii. 'On Bacon of Verulam and his Scientific Principles.' By Professor Lasson. 1860. 'On Francis Bacon of Verulam and the History of the Natural Sciences.' By Justus Liebig. 1863. 'Lord Bacon as Natural Philosopher.' By Baron Liebig. *Macmillan's Magazine*, July and August, 1863. Review of Baron Liebig's Discourse in the *Home and Foreign Review*. January 1864. A Reply to Baron Liebig's two Articles, in *Macmillan's Magazine*, by G. F. Rodwell. *The Reader*, June 2 and 9, 1866. 'The Correlation of the Physical Forces.' By W. R. Grove. Fifth edition. 1867. Pp. 8-10. 'Was Lord Bacon an Impostor?' *Fraser's Magazine*, December 1866. 'Was Lord Bacon an Impostor?' By Baron Liebig. *Fraser's Magazine*, April 1867. 'The Poems of Francis Bacon, Baron of Verulam.' For the first time collected and edited after the original texts by the Rev. Alex. B. Grosart, Blackburn. *Privately printed* in the Fuller Worthies' Library Miscellanies. 1870.

but that need not be identical with the system on
which the science may be best studied, and by which
it may be most readily taught. On the contrary, it is
the rule, not without exceptions, that the history of a
science is a history of error and its correction. The
quarry is run down after many faults and doubles,
instead of being picked off at a long range. Eminently
interesting and instructive is such a history; but it is
so in behalf of those who have acquired, with thorough
comprehension, at least the elements of the science.
Mutatis mutandis, but with far less force, may the same
be said of Philosophy; for at present its elements are
inextricably interwoven with its history. Of late years
some French writers have attempted to identify the
history of any branch of knowledge with the method on
which it can be best taught. It has been confidently
maintained that the only sound method of instruction
is "la méthode d'invention"—"la méthode suivie par
l'inventeur." If such be the fact in any case, it is so
exceptionally. The only sound method of instruction is
that which starts, not with the *locus standi* of the inventor, but with that of the learner, whose rude notions
and profound ignorance must be the very groundwork
of instruction. Ignoring both, and sublimely contem-
plating the architecture of the science to be imparted,
we may find that our foundations have been laid on a
morass or on a quicksand.

The history of a science, and therefore of science
in general, is for the initiated; and for such it has
almost the charm of a romance, at least of a romance

read backwards, like Froude's ' Lieutenant's Daughter.'
Fable, indeed, can hardly obtain a footing there, for
the results always exercise some check on the narrative
of those fictions and mistakes which the results have
overthrown. We know, at least, from the results what
could not have been observed or performed by the
physical philosopher during the epoch of discovery.
We know, for instance, that Bacon could not have
burnt a candle in the flame of spirit of wine; and that
Haüy's antimony could not have been rhombohedral.
We may thus with certainty determine what, among
alleged observations, were inventions or blunders, and
what, among alleged experiments, were performed in
fancy only, or not performed at all. We may indeed
err, through the insufficiency of evidence, in assigning
a discovery to one who was not first in making it, or
who did not discover it at all. This has been done in
the case of many notable additions to science, as the
composition of water, the polarisation of light, and the
doctrine of limiting ratios; in each of which there are
still contending claims, where some find it hard to give
the preference, while others administer a summary
justice or injustice.

There is a. small class of eminent men included in
the larger class of "many-sided minds," who became
distinguished by virtue of pursuits for which they had
received no special professional training. Such men were
Francis Bacon, Emanuel Swedenborg, and Johann Wolf-
gang Goethe. It may be remarked, however, in passing'
that these three men, presenting so many marked dif-

ferences, do also present some striking forms of agreement. All three were born to a position of eminence
or affluence : all were functionaries of the government
under which they lived, and rose to be eminent states-
men. All, by virtue of congenital powers and tastes,
became physical philosophers, equally rejecting ideas,
and working on nature by means of observation, experiment, and induction. The poet, however, is the only
one who can be credited with a positive and unequivocal
discovery in physical science. Between Bacon and
Swedenborg (quite irrespective of the spiritual experiences of the latter) it will be found that a remarkable
parallel subsists.

A sketch of Bacon's life is quite unnecessary here.
Mr. Hepworth Dixon, on the one side, and Messrs.
Jas. Spedding and J. T. Foard on the other, have com-
pletely exhausted the subject, and made the facts of
Bacon's life "familiar in our mouths as household
words." It is only with his philosophy that we are
concerned. Bacon was born at York House, Strand,
London, on January 22, 1560, O.S. (February 1, 1560,
N.S.), *i.e.*, four years and three months before Shake-
speare. He died at Highgate, at Lord Arundel's, on
April 9, 1626, having survived Shakespeare nearly ten
years.

Bacon's best philosophical works appear to have been
written in the seventeenth century; and the more
important of them were published in the last four
years of his life. Of the works by which this "many-
sided mind" became his country's glory the following

details may be found of interest to students of Bacon. In a letter written in 1623 or 1624, Bacon speaks of having composed an exposition of his philosophical method, to which he gave the title of *Temporis Partus Maximus*—'The Greatest Birth of Time.' One of his successors in the chancellorship, John, Lord Campbell, thinks this work was published, though copies of it are unknown to bibliographers. If such were the fact, this constitutes his first work, and must be referred to 1584. His 'Essays, Religious Meditations,' first appeared in type in 1597. There were originally only *ten* of them; in the second edition (1612) there were thirty-eight; and the latest edition published in his lifetime (1625) contained fifty-eight. In 1605 his 'Two Books of the Proficience and Advancement of Learning, Divine and Human,' were published. They, too, expanded and enlarged, were issued in Latin in 1623, with the title *De Augmentis Scientiarum*. In 1610 the *De Sapientia Veterum*, 'Concerning the Wisdom of the Ancients,' a fanciful, but wise and brilliant, book, gave evidence of his continued activity of mind. Having projected an 'Instauratio Magna,' or grand restoration of the sciences, he published in 1620, as the second part of it, his *Novum Organum Scientiarum*, or 'New Instrument of the Sciences.' In 1622, despite his fall from place and power, he published his 'History of the Reign of Henry VII.;' and in 1624 not only 'The Translation of Certaine Psalmes into English Verse' (recently reissued in 'The Fuller Worthies' Library Miscellanies' by the Rev.

A. B. Grosart), but also his 'Apophthegms, New and Old,' were published, having been produced during a fit of sickness, in that same year. To his political tracts, 'Miscellany Works,' the *Resuscitatio*, many fragmentary additions to his *Instauratio*, and some other writings, we are unable to assign any date. His 'New Atlantis,' or Solomon's House, in which he aimed at excelling Plato, as in his *Novum Organum* he had endeavoured to outdo Aristotle, as well as many other literary schemes, was left unfinished at his death. It will be seen from this mere mention of works written by this " Lord of Induction and of Verulam "— as Herbert calls him, in a most palpable anti-climax— that his authorship for the most part belongs to the seventeenth century, and that much of what he thought under the Tudors he wrote under the Stuarts. Of the illustrious Englishmen who lived in those times he is one of the most famed; and if we except Shakespeare under the former dynasty, and Milton under the latter, the entire literature of the age possesses no name equal to his own.

Above the fame of any discoverer in science is the glory of him who is believed to have furnished mankind with a certain if not a royal road to all physical knowledge : and such was once the lot of Francis Bacon. Hardly has such renown as his been associated with such a name. Think of the stupendous opposition to be overcome by poetic genius, before such names as Cottle and Tupper could act as a spell on men's imaginations. Philosophy had assuredly as hard a time of it with Bacon; and yet so intensely dazzling was the aureole that for two hundred years invested that unfortunate name that from thenceforth its contemptuous associations were consigned to deserved oblivion, and, even now that its almost Aristotelian tyranny has been broken, it acts as a spell on the imagination still.

The works of Lord Bacon belong to the history of philosophy rather than to the history of science, and to the latter rather than to science itself. In the study of geometry we necessarily encounter the constructions of Thales, Pythagoras, and Euclid, not to mention the more important contributions of Michel Chasles and the moderns. In algebra we as necessarily come upon the theorems of Newton, Euler, and Wallis, with those of very many other inventors. In physics we owe so much to particular discoverers that much of what we learn under that name is stamped with the peculiar genius of a few great men. Bacon is not one of these; nor yet is there a single physical discovery due to his industry or genius. The fact is certainly remarkable; for though he did not set up for a physical discoverer, he assuredly claimed to have constructed an organon, or instrument of universal discovery, which, accordingly, should have yielded some fruit in the hands of others. Some, indeed, have credited him with having discovered the relation of heat to friction. In point of fact, the correlation of heat and motion is found in Plato. In the *Theœtetus*, chap. 26, we read,—

Τὸ γὰρ θερμόν τε καὶ πῦρ, ὃ δὴ καὶ τἆλλα γεννᾷ καὶ ἐπιτροπεύει, αὐτὸ γεννᾶται ἐκ φορᾶς καὶ τρίψεως · τοῦτο δὲ κίνησις ἢ οὐχ αὗται γενέσεις πυρός ; that is—

"For heat and fire, which engenders and supports other things, is itself engendered by impact and friction, *but this is motion.* Are not these [? modes of motion] the origin of fire ?"

But we may find nearly the same thing in Heraclitus. I have no doubt whatever that Bacon did no more in this speciality than hundreds had done before him ; and it is certain that the theory of heat made no advance in consequence of his famous *Inquisitio in Naturam Calidi.* On the other hand, it is impossible, as I shall soon make manifest, to do justice to his unrivalled powers of mind without crediting him with a very remarkable *divination* as to the essential mode of sensible heat, which, in the hands of a practised experimenter, must have hastened the epoch of discovery in that science. But such was not the event. The conjecture perished like the seed that fell on stony ground. The Organon of Bacon has not, I say, been the *direct* agent in any physical discovery. This is the all but universal verdict of competent critics. A few, indeed, whose competency it would be invidious, if not presumptuous to call in question, contend that discoveries have been made on Bacon's method. Perhaps some new evidence in favour of that position may yet be adduced. But what is meant by the allegation is plain enough, when we find that able and elegant writer, Dugald Stewart, making this assertion :—

"I shall take this opportunity to remark that Newton had evidently studied Bacon's writings with care, and has followed

them (sometimes too implicitly) in his logical phraseology."—
Works, Ed. Hamilton. vol. iii., p. 236.

This is the inverted base of the pyramid, whose apex
is the solitary fact that Newton twice employs the word
" axiom "in the Baconian sense. But the pyramid will
not stand inverted; besides, I hardly think that fact
belongs to the pyramid; for Newton could not have
failed to get the word " axiom," in the sense of *general
expression*, from Peter Ramus, in the ordinary curriculum
of studies at the University of Cambridge. Others
assert that Newton employed Bacon's method, as in his
experiments on inertia : this, however, is a mistake.

But, allowing that no physical discovery has been
made directly by means of Bacon's Organon, the question still remains whether his works did not exercise
a very powerful indirect influence on the course of
physical science; and it is this question which has
been so hotly debated in late years. Certain it is that
never till Bacon wrote was the *corrupt* Aristotelian
method denounced and exposed with such trumpet-
tongued eloquence and with such studious and prophetic
iteration. None, till Bacon rose, had wearied the ears
of a generation with its eternal wail—*delenda est
Carthago*. Yet it is said, on the other hand, that the
labour was Quixotic, since the tyranny of Aristotle had
already received its *quietus*. Certain it is that never
till then had the keynote of induction—*well-digested
observations first, theory afterwards*—been sounded in
the van of a *Novum Organum*. Yet, on the other side,
it is asserted that a better method than Bacon's had

been actually employed with success before his great
work saw the light. Equally certain it is that the
publication of his work synchronised with the great
epoch of physical discovery, which was crowned by the
immortal speculations of Newton and Laplace. Yet,
the enemy has something to say against Bacon's influence on the science of his own day ; that he was not
the general but the herald of the victorious army ; and
that it was the blunder of a few enthusiastic followers
to attribute to him the splendour of a glory which
radiated from men of a very different order of mind.
In this view, Bacon was simply *felix opportunitate
vitæ.*

Coleridge, remarking on the necessity of amassing a
store of materials before constituting "a sound and
stable theory," thus indicates the special need of him
who would execute successfully the great work in which,
it is said, Bacon failed.

"All this, and much more, must be achieved before 'a sound
and stable theory' could be 'constituted ;'—which even then
(except as far as it might occasion the discovery of a law) might
possibly explain (*ex plicis plana reddere*), but never account for
the facts in question. But the most satisfactory comment on
these and similar assertions would be afforded by a matter-of-fact
history of the rise and progress, the accelerating and retarding
momenta, of science in the civilised world."—*The Friend,* 1844,
vol. iii., Essay 8.

It is just this need which has been so admirably
supplied by Dr. Whewell's 'History of the Inductive
Sciences,' his 'History of Scientific Ideas,' and the two
other of his works to which I have assigned a place at

the head of this paper. By the aid of these, and of Sir
John Herschel's 'Discourse on the Study of Natural
Philosophy,' and Mr. J. S. Mill's 'Logic,' we may very well
judge of the adequacy of Bacon's *Novum Organum*, as a
means of enlarging the borders of science; and allowing, with the mass of competent critics, the inadequacy,
or even failure, of that work, we shall, with these appli-
ances, be fully prepared to estimate the effect which
Bacon's writings had on the course of scientific discovery.

The time is not long past when Bacon's name enjoyed
the repute both of success in his great attempt and of
being the great regenerator of science. It was once the
universal belief that to Bacon's method was mainly due
the vast progress of science ever since the crystal spheres
of Purbach were shivered by the arrowy intellect of
Copernicus. Even Sir John Herschel once agreed with
this verdict.

"This important task was executed by Francis Bacon, Lord
Verulam, who will, therefore, justly be looked upon in all future
ages as the great reformer of philosophy."—*Discourse*, 1835,
p. 114.

This opinion ran out its course, and it is now generally looked upon as a mistake. It is curious that it
should have been combated by three distinct parties in
this criticism, whereof two are diametrically opposed to
each other. *First*, It was contested by those who held
that Bacon taught nothing but old truth; that his system
was as old as Aristotle, and that, though discoveries in
science, and any number of them, had been made by pur-

suing the method prescribed by Bacon, it was so only by virtue of the fact that Bacon's method was the method pursued by all physical discoverers, from the Stagirite downwards. *Second,* It was contested by those who held that Bacon's system was indeed a startling novelty, which neither Aristotle nor any one else, save its propounder, had ever dreamed of; but that unfortunately it was trifling and useless, and had about the same relation to science that a penny trumpet has to Spohr's 'Power of Sound.' Macaulay may be taken as the type of the former, and Lasson or Liebig as the type of the latter. *Third,* It was contested by a few, on the high *priori* ground, that his method was a *sell;* that the salt of Verulam could not be applied to the tail of the old bird called "Nature," till the bird was actually in the hand; or, to change the metaphor, that nature's cabinet, having a snap lock which had been shut *upon* the key, the locksmith of St. Albans would be glad to pick the lock, in order to get at the key. The most superficial view of the 'Advancement of Learning' suffices to show what Bacon was about; that he was proposing to himself a problem of the utmost difficulty, viz., to reduce the business of scientific discovery to a method which should be certain in its results, and, by its very perfection, be for the most part independent of private sagacity. His single aim was to invent an instrument of physical research which might be handled with thorough efficiency by average intellects, and which, being so handled, should constrain Nature to reveal her secret processes. Bacon never arrogated to himself the

title which has been awarded to him, viz., that of
Father of Induction; the actual claim he set up for
himself was that he was the inventor of a new and
infallible method of induction. As Mr. Leslie Ellis
well puts it—

"Ordinary induction is a tentative process, because we chase
our quarry over an open country : here it is confined within
definite limits, and these limits become, as we advance, continually narrower and narrower."—*General Preface to the Phil. Works,*
1857. I., p. 35.

Bacon, in fact, proposed to do for induction what
certain African Nimrods have done for hunting. Dr.
Livingstone tells us that the tribe of the Bakwains,
instead of hunting down the wild beasts in the jungle,
or over the open prairie, are accustomed to employ a
very ingenious device for snaring and destroying hundreds of head of game at once. They set up what they
call a *hopo,* which is a wattled fence in the form of a
V of vast dimensions, the angle of which is open, and
debouches on a long deep pit. The Bakwain hunters
send out scouts, who surround and drive their prey
from their retreats towards the wide mouth of the
hopo ; they are thus chased unawares into an area
which fatally narrows at every step, and ends in a
prison or a grave. Bacon proposed, I say, to do the
same by the universe and its "natures;" the *Novum
Organum* is his *hopo,* or at least a portion of it; and
it is yet the subject of fierce dispute whether, in the
event of the entire structure having been realised, it
would have been as successful as the African device.

Certain it is that the only quarry driven into it by its
inventor, viz., "the form of heat," had been marked
before it entered the *hopo*, and was hastily captured
by a secondary manœuvre before it reached the pit.
It was thus that the efficacy of the New Organon
remained untested.

Simple enumeration, or indiscriminate observation,
or chance experiment, is hunting the game, "over an
open country." Bacon's alternative was a *plan* of
observation and experiment, on which would sooner or
later arise a vast number of definite issues to be tried
by ulterior observation or experiment. From this
second batch of observations or experiments would crop
up a still smaller number of definite issues; and thus
the field of research is narrowed at each step of the
investigation, till at length the "natures," which are
the objects of the induction, are isolated and determined.
Such, in general terms, was the project. Nothing in
the nature of such an Organon had ever been proposed,
still less executed; yet it can hardly be maintained
that the end in view was a novelty, for it had been the
common practice of physicists to restrict the sphere of
observation and experiment by the adoption of some
plan of operation, though its application was restricted,
its name Legion, and *quot homines tot methodi*. No
one knew better than Bacon that Aristotle and Plato
taught induction, and that the former extensively
practised it. On this point see the *Novum Organum*,
book i., aph. 63 and 105. But whatever plans might
have been worked upon by the Stagirite, the only in-

duction *taught* by him was that "by simple enumeration," which, by its very form, is a barren process, and
that, moreover, is the only induction taught by modern
writers on logic, with a few notable exceptions, Mr. J.
S. Mill, the Archbishop of York, and Mr. S. Neil. Aristotle's example of this form of induction is as follows:
"Every man, horse, mule, is long-lived: whatever is
galless is man, horse, or mule; therefore whatever is
galless is long-lived." To sustain the validity of the
conclusion, says the Stagirite—

δεῖ νοεῖν τὸ Γ (*i.e.*, man, horse, mule, &c.) τὸ ἐξ ἁπάντων τῶν καθ'
ἕκαστον συγκείμενον . . . κ.τ.λ.—*Prior Analytics*, ii. 23.

That is, it is requisite that they be *full representatives*
of the class to which they are referred; so that the
class must be unwarrantably assumed, or else established by some more subtle process. Bacon not only
knew how barren was this form of induction, but also
that other inductive methods were practised with success; yet from so partial a study of causes, and one,
moreover, in which native wit and lucky accident had
so great a share, he augured ill for the restoration of
physical science, as a whole. Verulam, though from
the pressure of professional duties and the infirmity
of ill health he had been able to acquire but a comparatively small *répertoire* of natural facts, and these
not seldom very inaccurately noted, was as clear-sighted
and as far-sighted as an eagle. He saw that *induction,
however constituted, did extend knowledge;* whereas deduction could only serve as the handmaid of induction,

to disclose what was thought, however obscurely, in our general conceptions. He did not indeed anticipate Kant in his famous distinction of ampliative and explicative judgments; but he discriminated between the deductive syllogism and the inductive method with as much precision and rigour as Kant himself in his *Methodologie*.

It is not easy for us, standing on the eminence which inductive philosophy has raised for our speculation, to realise the actual state of the figment which passed for science at the time when Bacon wrought and wrote. It was not a fragmental discovery of Gilbert or Copernicus that can be shown as a sample of the methods then in vogue, or of the conclusions thereby arrived at. The human mind was under an incubus of physical speculations, handed down from the schoolmen, who had monstrously corrupted and deformed what they had received from Aristotle. It was in respect to science what it now is in respect to theology. The mass of educated persons were taught and made to believe in traditions, which, happily, while they had the effect of postponing the epoch of discovery, served to create the technical terms by which future discoveries were to be expressed. Bacon describes as truthfully as eloquently the state of things which then prevailed, and of which traces lingered in our universities long after the innovations of Newton's *Principia* had been somewhat grudgingly established. Scientific method was, for all purposes of instruction, wholly deductive, and its scheme consisted of logical *sorites* and *dilemmas*,

depending upon notions formed haphazard from a superficial, cursory, and inexact survey of the universe.
Such, indeed, are all our notions till we are educated
in observation; and they are therefore called *notiones
primæ*. Into the truth, generality, clearness, or fitness
of such notions to represent real things and their
qualities and relations, it was the business neither of
the teacher nor of the pupil to inquire. In playing
with such scholastic toys as were the instruments of
the dialectician, it was sufficient entertainment to
expound all that was connoted by the terms standing
for those notions; and thus it came to pass that it was
the subjective notion, and not the objective phenomenon, that was expounded or explained.

Bacon resolved to put a term to all such trifling:
but in his attempt to do so he was "wise in his generation." He knew the old fabric was doomed, though
men had grown so accustomed to its reprieve that they
almost adjudged it immortal. As it had awaited its
destruction for two thousand years, so my lord of
Verulam was well content that his great work should
bide its time in patience, if only he could get it written
and published before death arrested his labours (see
Proœmium). In the meanwhile he assured his readers
that he had no wish to overthrow at once the old
edifice; no, not even to win admiration for his own.
Note the irony and covered sarcasm of his protest:—

"For those who prefer the former, either from hurry or from
considerations of business, or for want of mental power to take
in and embrace the other (which must needs be most men's case),

L

I wish that they may succeed to their desire in what they are
about, and obtain what they are pursuing."—*Preface to 'Nov.
Org.'*

But all "true sons of knowledge" he invites to rally
round his standard : just as the more liberal among ourselves congratulate those who have thrown off the yoke
of an obsolete and effete theology, and in the same breath
protest that they have no wish to unsettle the faith of
timid and weak-minded persons, bidding them affectionately God-speed. They who pursue this course, if
they have not large hearts, have assuredly long heads.

It seems to me that Bacon addressed himself to his
task with no self-seeking, but with as honest a love of
truth, and with as earnest a resolve to pioneer for it, as
ever inspired Kepler or Galileo : and this point is to
be the more carefully noted, because, as we shall shortly
see, it has been bluntly impugned by one of Bacon's
later critics. Whatever be the fact, I must insist on
this, that it is grossly unfair to prejudge him a liar
because he conformed to the corrupt judicial customs
of his time, and to set down all he says as to the purity
of his ends and aim to the score of ambitious hypocrisy;
on the contrary, we are bound by the lowest principles
of humanity to presume that he speaks truth till he
be found a liar. As to this love of truth, then, let us
hear his own words :—

"For my own part at least, in obedience to the everlasting
love of truth, I have committed myself to the uncertainties and
difficulties and solitudes of the ways ; and, relying on the
Divine assistance, have upheld my mind, both against the shocks
and embattled ranks of opinion, and against my own private

and inward hesitations and scruples, and against the fogs and clouds of nature, and the phantoms flitting about on every side ; in the hope of providing at last for the present and future generations guidance more faithful and secure."—*Preface to the ' Inst. Mag.'*

Here he professes that his hope is the benefit of his race; but even this hope is secondary to his allegiance to the everlasting love of truth. Next, as to his humility, he adds :—

"Wherein if I have made any progress, the way has been opened to me by no other means than the true and legitimate humiliation of the human spirit. . . . And the same humility which I use in inventing I employ likewise in teaching."

Then in the first book of the *Novum Organum*, which was designed as the second treatise of the *Instauratio Magna* (the *De Augmentis Scientiarum* being a first sketch of the first treatise), he enumerates, in a strain of graceful rhetoric, the various grounds of hope for the realisation, at least by his successors, of his magnificent project. Among these is the following, which is pregnant with "true and legitimate humiliation of spirit : "—

"And this I say, not by way of boasting, but because it is useful to say it. If there be any that despond, let them look at me ; that, being of all men of my time the most busied in affairs of State, and a man of health not very strong (whereby much time is lost), and in this course altogether a pioneer, following no man's track nor sharing these counsels with any one, have nevertheless, by resolutely entering on the true road and submitting my mind to things, advanced these matters, as I suppose, some little way. And then let them consider what may be expected (after the way has been thus indicated) from men abounding in leisure, and from association of labours, and from successions of ages : the rather because it is not a way over which only one man can pass at a time (as is the case with that of reasoning), but one in which the labours and industries of men (especially as regards the collecting of experience) may with the best effect be first distributed and then combined. For then only all men begin to know their strength, when instead of great numbers doing all the same things, one shall take charge of one thing, and one of another."—*Aph.* 113.

In Bacon's scheme this collecting of instances was the *premier pas* which implicitly involved everything else. But they were to be collected on a definite plan of operation. From one class of such instances he was to obtain an *axiom*, or general expression of some relation or law. This was an axiom of the first order of generality; and this, like the axioms of Euclid, was to be made a basis of deduction forthwith. The conclusion thereby arrived at was to become the principle of a new class of observations or experiments, from which might be derived an *axiom* of the second order of generality: and so forth.—See *Nov. Org.*, book i., aph. 104. He says :—

"Hitherto the proceeding has been to fly at once from the sense to particulars, up to the most general propositions as certain fixed poles for the argument to turn upon, and from these to derive the rest by middle terms: a short way, no doubt, but precipitate, and one which will never lead to nature, though it offers an easy and ready way to disputation. Now my plan is to proceed regularly and gradually from one axiom to another, so that the most general are not reached till the last: but then, when you do come to them, you find them to be not empty notions, but well-defined, such as nature would really recognise as her first principles, and such as lie at the heart and marrow of things [talia quæ natura ut revera sibi notiora agnoscat, quæque rebus hæreant in medullis]."—*Nov. Org. Distributio Operis.*

"The one [way] begins at once by establishing certain abstract and useless generalities ; the other rises by gradual steps to that which is prior and better known in the order of nature [ad ea quæ revera naturæ sunt notiora]."—*Nov. Org.*, book i., aph. 22.

"Lastly, the true form is such that it deduces the given nature from some source of being which is inherent in more natures, and which is better known in the natural order of things than the form itself [notior est naturæ]."—*Nov. Org.*, book ii., aph. 4. *Cf. ibid.*, book i., aph. 43.

The contrast between *notio, prima aut prior,* and *id quod notior est naturæ* (it should rather be *naturâ*), though expressed in an obsolete and somewhat mistaken phraseology, is radical and thorough-going. Whatever be the method to follow, *the preamble is proved.* Be that method practicable or not, his philosophy has a valid foundation, which the subsequent course of inductive science has never disturbed. The inadequacy of first notions to deal with nature is further treated by Bacon under the head of *Idola Fori;* and he elsewhere declares the end of his labours to be "a true and lawful marriage between the empirical and the rational faculty, the unkind and ill-starred divorce and separation of which has thrown into confusion all the affairs of the human family." The term *form*, which plays so important a part in this philosophy, and is used in the third extract given above concerning first notions, is so utterly obsolete that it needs to be translated into modern technology, if that may be. Bacon contemplated the properties of matter as form-natures and sensible natures. The form was ideal; the sensible was real. The leading inquiry of the new philosophy was, how is the form of a given sensible nature to be determined from the various manifestations of that sensible nature? Hence we see, rudely at least, that the form-natures relate to our primary qualities, and the sensible natures to our secondary qualities of matter. This will become plainer as we proceed. But first, I must premise a few words more on the inutility of the old deductive method, which there are still critics to praise, both as being the method of Aristotle and as being the method employed by modern men of science.

It is plain that a notion, in order to serve as the middle term of a syllogism, must connote the predicate of the conclusion: so that, in fact, nothing can be got *out* of it but what is already thought *in* it. The very formula of deduction, then, is merely explicative, and cannot extend our knowledge of nature, though it may serve to force on our attention what we already know. It has, in truth, the same relation to induction that an analytical or explicative judgment has to a synthetical or ampliative judgment in Kant's philosophy. In fact, Kant's distinction involves the whole difference between deduction and induction; for, if there be no ampliative judgment in a syllogism, the procedure is barren, and the conclusion is a truism. If, then, the notion which is used as the middle term of a syllogism be not commensurate with nature—be neither precise, clear, nor appropriate—and such is the case with all *notiones primæ*—the syllogism is not merely incompetent to enlarge the borders of science, but its explicative power is thrown away by dealing with the con-

tents of a notion which is utterly worthless. Against
the dominion, then, of this alliance between *notiones
primæ* and the syllogism Bacon waged war; and I am
satisfied that he did not—

> " Come in the rearward of a conquered *foe*,
> But in the onset."

In his attempt to substitute an unfailing inductive
method for the old scholastic trifling he claimed the
credit of a reformer, and proclaimed the novelty of the
attempt. " Sunt certe prorsus nova," &c. These
words occur in his dedication to James I., which is
singularly free from the usual servility and sycophancy
of such compositions. It is here, too, that he makes a
request in simple and dignified language, that the king,
who resembled Solomon in so many things, would
further follow that wise man's example "in taking
order for the collecting and perfecting of a natural
and experimental history, true and severe, such as
philosophy might be built upon." Here we have the
keynote of his Organon, and he is never wearied with
sounding it. Now, James did not grant Bacon's
request. The work was not set in order by the king,
nor undertaken by others. Well might he utter his
old complaint,—

> " I have at length become a mere labourer and hod-carrier, there
> being many things necessary for completing the design, which
> others, from an innate pride, have avoided."—*De Augmentis*,
> book vii., chap. i.

By some means or other the work of collecting
instances must be first accomplished. He might well

insist on this preliminary; for *he had gone a little too
far* in discrediting hypothesis as the initiative of
experiment. At one time he *seems* to have thought
it practicable to make such collections exhaustive.
Probably we must not take his statements quite au
pied de la lettre. He writes:—

"Moreover, since there is so great a number and army of
particulars, and that army so scattered and dispersed as to dis-
tract and confound the understanding, little is to be hoped for
from the skirmishings and slight attacks and desultory movements of the intellect, unless all the particulars which pertain
to the subject of inquiry shall, by means of tables of discovery,
apt, well-arranged, and as it were, animate, be drawn up and
marshalled; and the mind be set to work upon the helps duly
prepared and digested which these tables supply."—*Nov. Org.*,
book i., aph. 102.

And in aph. 103 he speaks of the time when "all
the experiments of all the arts shall have been collected
and digested, and brought within one man's knowledge
and judgment." Truly it has been said, "C'est le
premier pas qui coute;" and it may well be asked,
"Who is sufficient for these things?" Some suspicion
of the impracticability of realising this stupendous preliminary must have crossed Bacon's mind; and it was
probably this which moved him to *allow* the inductive
philosopher to proceed from time to time to provisional
vindemiations, as an "indulgence of the understanding." Still, the method of Bacon demands, to say the
least of it, a provision of vast collections of instances in
each department of research, before the actual work of
induction in each can begin. How are these collec-

tions to be made? What are their guiding principles? The observers find themselves committed to a task of Briarean multifariousness. "The world is all before them *what* to choose." Even after the universe is parcelled out into special fields of research, the possible instances of any one department are practically infinite, and the energies of the experimenter are paralysed by the vastness of his resources.

Accordingly, it follows that he must work on some principle of selection. In our days the principle is furnished by intelligent hypothesis, and there is always a definite issue (that Bacon called a *crucial* case) to be tried. But Bacon's object was to perfect an organon which should be theoretically independent of individual sagacity; and it is from individual sagacity that intelligent hypothesis arises. To this question, then, of the principle of selection, the method according to which the observer could always select the most promising and suggestive instances for his collection, Bacon now addressed himself. As a principle of selection, and a method of classification of instances, Bacon propounded his doctrine of prerogatives, the nature and plan of which, in the Baconian induction, we shall consider in the second part of this paper.

VIII

FRANCIS BACON.

PART II.

SIR JOHN HERSCHEL thus defines prerogative instances:—

"Phenomena selected by the investigator on account of some peculiarly forcible way in which they strike the reason, and impress us with a kind of sense of causation, or a peculiar aptitude for generalisation."—*Discourse*, 1835, p. 182.

Bacon discusses these under the classes of *solitary, migratory, glaring, clandestine, constitutive, crucial,* and many other heads.

The collections of prerogative instances being thus made up in tables, the business which devolves on the philosopher is to construct from them four kinds of tables. 1. Tables in which the presence of the given nature is shown. 2. Tables in which the given nature is not presented at all. 3. Tables in which the instances presenting the given nature are graduated, according to the degree in which that nature appears. 4. Tables of rejections of instances.

Having arrived at this point, Bacon allows the philosopher to frame a *hypothesis*, which, for purposes of verification, he has to treat as if it were an ascertained *axiom*. This hypothesis is the first vindemiation, or first vintage. The *Athenæum* review, writing in depreciation of Bacon's method, says:—

"Wrong hypotheses rightly worked from have produced more useful results than unguided observation. But this is not the Baconian plan."—*Athenæum*, September 18, 1858.

Now, curiously enough, this is a mere paraphrase of Bacon, who assigns as his reason for allowing the use of hypothesis as a basis of deduction, that "truth will sooner come out from error than from confusion."—*Nov. Org.*, book ii., aph. 20. The result of this verification, if it do not lead to the most general axiom, will assuredly enable the observers and experimenters to restrict the field of their research. (See *Nov. Org.*, book i., aph. 106.)

I have given Sir John Herschel's definition of prerogative instances; I will now add his opinion of their value:—

"It has always appeared to us, we must confess, that the help which the classification of instances under the different titles of prerogative affords to inductions, however just such classification may be in itself, is yet more apparent than real. The force of the instance must be felt in the mind, before it can be referred to its place in the system ; and before it can be either referred or appreciated, it must be known ; and when it *is* appreciated, we are ready enough to interweave it in our web of induction, without greatly troubling ourselves with inquiring whence it derives the weight we acknowledge it to have in our decisions."—*Discourse*, 1835, p. 183.

This opinion comes to us with the highest possible authority. Of course we are not prepared to regard it as conclusive ; indeed, the utmost care must be taken to view Bacon's doctrine in every light, and so to do the utmost justice to it ; for we must bear in mind that the doctrine of prerogatives is cardinal. If the proposed classification is useless as an economic of research, the question may be asked in vain, " What other means are proposed by Bacon as a principle of direction for the collector of instances ? " Let us now hear Whewell's opinion on the matter,—

"Such a classification is much of the same nature as if, having to teach the art of building, we were to describe tools with reference to the amount and place of the work which they must do, instead of pointing out their construction and use :—as if we were to inform the pupil that we must have tools for lifting a stone up, tools for moving it sideways, tools for laying it square, tools for cementing it firmly. Such an enumeration of ends would convey little instruction as to the means."—*Philosophy of Discovery,* 1860, p. 140.

This metaphor is less happy than Sir John Herschel's, for the instance *is* a woof in the web of induction, a constituent part of the entire method ; but it is not a tool for accomplishing the work. The real tool *is* the Organon, and its constituent parts are no more like building-tools than are the stones and bricks of which the house is built. But letting the metaphor pass, it hardly tells against Bacon's prerogatives. For if a large chest of building and other tools were placed at the disposal of a man who knew nothing of the builder's art, the bare description of the kind of work usually done by the requisite tools would be *some* guide to him in his attempt to select them from the *omnium gatherum* of the tool-chest. In another place Whewell attacks Bacon's " classes of instances " from another point.

"But we may remark that instances, classed and treated as Bacon recommends in those parts of his work, could hardly lead to scientific truth. His processes are vitiated by his proposing to himself the *form* or *cause* of the property before him, as the object of his inquiry ; instead of being content to obtain, in the first place, the law of *phenomena."—Nov. Org. Renovatum*, 1858, p. 225.

And, in continuation of the penultimate extract, he says :—

"Moreover, many of Bacon's classes of instances are vitiated by the assumption that the 'form,' that is, the general law or cause of the property which is the subject of investigation, is to be looked for directly in the instances ; which, as we have seen in his inquiry concerning heat, is a fundamental error."— *Philosophy of Discovery*, 1860, p. 141.

And elsewhere, in reference to the *Inquisitio in Formam Calidi*, Whewell says :—

"One main ground of Bacon's ill-fortune in this undertaking appears to be, that he was not aware of an important maxim of inductive science, that we must first obtain the *measure* and ascertain the *laws* of phenomena, before we endeavour to discover their causes."—*Philosophy of Discovery*, 1860, p. 137.

It is curious to find Whewell correcting Bacon almost in his own words. Thus, in the penultimate extract Bacon is charged with the vice of looking for the cause directly in the instances. Now Bacon, in his 70th aph., book i., says,—"For no one successfully investigates the nature of a thing in the thing itself." And as to the next extract, Whewell might have been well assured of Bacon's acquaintance with the "important maxim," for in his 98th aph., book i., he complains of the natural history of his own day, for that "nothing [was] duly investigated, nothing counted, nothing weighed or measured." Bacon may indeed have neglected all this in his own collections; but it can hardly be said that his "ill-fortune" in his *Inquisitio in Formam Calidi*, was due to his ignorance of the maxim.

To these objections Whewell adds Bacon's attempt to dispense with private sagacity. To this it is sufficient to reply that Bacon does not, as some have asserted, propose to supersede all use of sagacity. As to this, see the Preface to the *Instauratio Magna* and the *Novum Organum*, book i., aph. 61 and 91 ; and book ii., aph. 27. So far from this being the case, he looks to sagacity for aid in the investigation of "physical conformities and similarities," which play so important a part in the formation of tentative and provisional vintages, as well as in the selection of prerogative instances.

Leslie Ellis, in his character of editor of Bacon's Philosophical Works, may be expected to rate Bacon's merits as an inductive philosopher at their highest, yet even he finds himself obliged to indicate two essential defects in Bacon's method. The chief of these must receive our best attention. This, without directly invalidating the doctrine of prerogatives, does in effect establish its utter insufficiency. The physical discoverer is supposed to be master of the operations which precede induction. He has, we will suppose, an army of observers, experimenters, collectors, marshals, and recorders under him, whom he directs like a centurion, and who obey him with the promptitude and precision of Roman soldiers. If the collections could but be adequately made, Bacon's method, in Mr. Ellis's opinion, "leads to certainty, and may be employed with nearly

equal success by all men who are equally diligent."
But the collections cannot be adequately made; for
not only is the prerogative, the only aid to collection
vouchsafed by Bacon, utterly insufficient, but *no such
aid can be given.* Hear Mr. Ellis's own words :—

"We may, perhaps, be permitted to believe that, so far as
relates to the subject of which we are now speaking, Bacon
never, even in idea, completed the method which he proposed.
For of all parts of the process of scientific discovery, the formation of conceptions is the one with respect to which it is the
most difficult to lay down general rules. The process of establishing axioms Bacon had succeeded, at least apparently, in reducing to the semblance of a mechanical operation ; that of the
formation of conceptions does not admit of any similar reduction.
Yet these two processes are in Bacon's system of co-ordinate
importance. All commonly received general scientific conceptions Bacon condemns as utterly worthless. A complete change
is therefore required ; yet of the way in which induction is to
be employed in order to produce this change he has said nothing.
The omission is doubtless connected with the kind of realism
which runs through Bacon's system, and which renders it practically useless. For that his method is impracticable cannot, I
think, be denied, if we reflect not only that it never has produced any result, but also that the process by which scientific
truths have been established, cannot be so presented as even to
appear to be in accordance with it. In all cases this process
involves an element to which nothing corresponds in the tables
of comparance and exclusion ; namely, the application to the facts
of observation of a principle of arrangement, an idea existing in
the mind of the discoverer antecedently to the act of induction."
—*General Preface to the Philosophical Works,* 1857, p. 38.

On the other hand, let us hear Mr. Spedding, who
was partner with the late Mr. Leslie Ellis in the production of his admirable trade edition of Bacon's works.
He says :—

"One man may be used to make a rough and general collection, what we call an *omnium gatherum.* Another must be em-

ployed to reduce the confused mass into some order fit for
reference. A third to clear it of superfluities and rubbish. A
fourth must be taught to classify and arrange what remains.
And here I cannot but think that Bacon's arrangement of instances according to what he calls their prerogatives, or some
better arrangement of the same kind which experience ought to
suggest, would be found to be of great value ; especially when
it is proposed to make, through all the regions of nature, separate
collections of this kind, such as may combine into one general
collection."—*Preface to the Parasceue Works*, vol. i., 1857, p. 379.

Mr. Spedding wrote these remarks in 1847. He
submitted them to Mr. Ellis, with the context, which
certainly should be read with them, though space fails
me for presenting it here. Mr. Ellis's judgment on
the question is so important that I subjoin it.

" That it is impossible to sever the business of experiment and
observation from that of theorising, it would, perhaps, be rash
to affirm. But it seems to me that such a severance could hardly
be effected. A transcript of nature, if I may so express myself
—that is, such a collection of observed phenomena, as would
serve as the basis and materials of a system of natural philosophy—would be like nature itself, infinite in extent and variety.
No such collection could be formed ; and were it formed, general
laws and principles would be as much hidden in a mass of details
as they are in the world of phenomena. The marshalling idea,
teaching the philosopher what observations he is to make, what
experiments to try, seems necessary in order to deliver him from
this difficulty. Can we conceive that such experiments as those
of Faraday could have preceded the formation of any hypothesis ?
You allude, I think, to what has been done in the way of
systematic observation with reference to terrestrial magnetism.
And beyond all doubt the division of labour is possible and
necessary in many scientific inquiries. But then this separating
of the observer from the theoriser is only possible (at least in
such a case as that of magnetism) when the latter can tell his
'bajulus' what experiments he is to make, and how they are
to be made. As a matter of fact, the memoirs of Gauss, which

have done so much to encourage systematic observation of terrestrial magnetism, contain many results of theory directly bearing on observation, *e.g.* the method of determining the absolute measure of magnetism."—*Ibid.*, p. 386.

Mr. Spedding accepts this judgment "as perfectly sound and just." But he thinks that, without aiming at the completeness contemplated by Bacon, and admitting "that the collection of natural history could not have been used *in the way Bacon proposed* unless it were more complete than it ever could have been made," yet much might be done in that direction which has been hitherto unattempted.

My old friend, now, alas! no more, James Walker, C.E., when a young man, formed one of a deputation to wait on James Watt, who, sinking under bodily infirmities, was then living in retirement near the north bank of the Thames (I think in Surrey Street), in order to ascertain his opinion on the projected scheme of steam-locomotion. The veteran engineer shook his grey head in doubt as to its practicability; yet, after all, said, " I think it's worth a trial." Mr. Spedding seems to be more confident of success in his attempt to realise, to some extent, the project of Bacon, than James Watt was of the success of steam-locomotion. For myself, I must confess I think Mr. Spedding's scheme may be " worth a trial," though I fear the trial would be very costly. Three sciences have already been conducted in the manner proposed ; and, as to two of them, with very encouraging results. Not to speak now of Brahe, or of Flamsteed and his staff of observers,

M

or of Gauss and his staff of observers, let us consider the single case of meteorology. As opinions differ, let us hear what Herschel, Whewell, the *Athenæum* reviewer, and Mr. Spedding have to say on the prospects of this science. My extracts shall be as brief as possible. Herschel shall speak first :—

"Meteorology, one of the most complicated but important branches of science, is at the same time one in which any person who will attend to plain rules and bestow the necessary degree of attention may do effectual service."—*Discourse*, 1835, p. 133.

"Occasional observations apply to occasional and remarkable phenomena, and are by no means to be neglected : but it is to the regular meteorological register, steadily and perseveringly kept throughout the whole of every voyage, that we must look for the development of the great laws of this science."—*Manual of Scientific Inquiry*, p. 281.

Mr. Spedding, who quotes the last extract, with its context, adds :—

"Between the officers of her majesty's navy registering the readings of their instruments in all latitudes and longitudes, and the man of science in his study deducing laws of meteorology from a comparison of the results, the division of labour is surely as complete as Bacon would have desired."—*Preface to Parascene Works*, vol. i., p. 389.

But have their labours, distinct but co-operating, been as fruitful as Bacon would have expected, or are they likely to be so? Have *any* such laws been deduced? On this let us hear the *Athenæum* reviewer :—

"There is an attempt at induction going on, which·has yielded little or no fruit, the observations made in meteorological observatories. This attempt is carried on in a manner which would have caused Bacon to dance for joy ; for he lived in a time when Chancellors did dance. Russia, says M. Biot, is covered by an army of meteorographs, with generals, high officers, subalterns, and privates, with fixed and defined duties of observation. And what has come of it ? Nothing, says M. Biot ; and nothing will ever come of it."—*Athenæum*, Sept. 18, 1858.

Whewell allows the record to have a certain value, but adds :—

"Observations of the weather, made and recorded for many years, have not led to any general truths forming a science of meteorology ; and, although great numerical precision has been given to such observations by means of barometers, thermometers, and other instruments, still no general laws regulating the cycles of change of such phenomena have yet [*i.e.* up to 1858] been discovered."—*Nov. Org. Renovatum*, 1858, p. 57.

I suppose by "general laws," &c., Whewell did not include such a fact as "the diurnal oscillations of the barometer ;" for he knew of it, and uses it as an illustration of "the method of means" (*Nov. Org. Ren.*, 1858, p. 214). The same might be said of Osler's law of "the rotation of the wind," discovered by a reduction of the continuous record of his anemometer ; though that discovery was made since Whewell's lamented death.

It must be owned that the prospects of meteorology are not very bright : yet I think we may hope for a better state of things than at present exists by the improvement of the means of observation and registration, and by the substitution of *continuous* for *periodic* observation. To effect this, without the costly use of photography, Mr. Alfred King, of Liverpool, has perfected an instrument which he calls the Floating

Barograph, which self registers, by means of clockwork, the curve of atmospheric pressure. A description of this most ingenious instrument, with illustrations, is given in the *Report of the Astronomer to the Marine Committee, Mersey Docks and Harbour Board*, December 1865. The instrument itself may be seen at work in the Liverpool Observatory.

In the various critical remarks on Bacon's system which I have brought together in this paper, there is but little agreement. One might be disposed to argue from this that the critics have not all understood their author. If I might hazard an opinion on this point, I should say that Sir John Herschel and Mr. Leslie Ellis are the only two clear-headed and understanding critics among them. Of the rest, the *Athenæum* reviewer is the most flippant, and his remarks are tinged with the genuine German spleen. Still that writer, as well as Sir J. Herschel and Whewell, has the merit of insisting on the immense debt under which inductive science lies to mathematics. Hypothesis, suggested by facts, made the basis of mathematical analysis, whose outcome has to be tested, and, if possible, verified or falsified by express experiment, has been the most fruitful source of inductive science. But while it is fair enough to hold up this method as distinguishable from Bacon's, it is not correct to assert that Bacon's method is that of modern meteorologists. So far from Bacon dancing for joy at being made aware of a network of meteorological observatories over Europe and America, with their legions of

observers and their voluminous records, I make no
doubt that he would have frowned upon, if he could
not have frowned down, the whole proceeding as blind
and objectless. For two or three narrow-minded men
to be pottering over and pondering the same kind
of observation of the same kind of fact excited his
ridicule and scorn. That whole armies of intelligent
beings should be engaged on this sort of work, at an
enormous cost, would assuredly have filled him with
despair.

The almost uniform failure of meteorological enter-
prise is not, I apprehend, far to seek. Compare this
embryonic science with the tidal theory, which has
made but little more way. Determine, which it is
easy to do, why that theory has been so unfruitful,
and you have the opposite reason for the meteorological
failure.

"In all other departments of astronomy, as, for instance, in
the cases of the moon and the planets, the leading features of the
phenomena had been made out empirically before the theory
explained them. The course which analogy would have recommended for the cultivation of our knowledge of the tides would
have been to ascertain by an analysis of long series of observations
the effect of changes in the time of transit, parallax, and declina-
tion of the moon, and thus to obtain the laws of phenomena ;
and then to proceed to investigate the laws of causation."—
History of the Inductive Sciences, 1857, vol. ii., p. 191.

Conversely, the failure of meteorology has been due
to the fact that hitherto there has been no mathematical theory; there have been observations, and
nothing else. In truth, the theories of the dynamics
of fluids, of electricity, and of heat (not to mention

others) are in their infancy. When they advance, meteorology will not long remain an all but barren record.

Bacon's mathematical attainments were unquestionably small; and, to judge by the slight and almost slighting manner in which he occasionally speaks of mathematics, as well as by their occupying no conspicuous place in his method, we must conclude that he was far from anticipating the dominant power which they now exercise on the course of inductive science. To speak plainly, Bacon, like Goethe, was not only non-mathematical, but was somewhat jealous of mathematicians. The likeness holds, too, in many other respects. Just as Bacon wished to emancipate astronomy from the dominion of mathematics (*Nov. Org.*, book i., aph. 96), so did Goethe endeavour, at great cost of experiment and theory, to accomplish a like emancipation for optics.

Both had an innate contempt for theology and priestcraft; both were courtiers, and did homage to rank; and both were selfish. Great differences there were, undoubtedly: for though Bacon's system is pervaded by a strong realistic leaven, yet he was eminently the philosopher, as Goethe was the poet. Even here, however, there was likeness; for, while both mistrusted the ideal, both, in fact, derived their excellences from the ideal. If we look carefully into the matter, it is not on the prescribed method of Bacon that his fame was built. It was the power of divination in the man which made him great and influential. Let us see

how the matter stands in respect to his famous judgment on the form of heat. Concerning this, Professor
Tyndall's evidence is important: for he it is who has
wrought with such remarkable success in perfecting
the theory of "Heat considered as a mode of motion;"
and this great authority, in the first of his course of
lectures so named, gives the credit of this magnificent
discovery to Bacon. It derogates no whit from his
credit that he had been, in some degree, anticipated.
Bacon, it appears, was very near discovering the law of
the correlation of the physical forces. In the *Novum
Organum*, book ii., aph. 4, he lays down with minute
accuracy the relation of the form-nature (as the special
configuration and motion of molecules) to the sensible
nature (as heat, colour, sound, &c.). But, perhaps by
the accident of his scholastic training, he places the
form only in the relation of cause, and the sensible
quality only in the relation of effect. Still his use of
the word "convertible" is eminently suggestive of the
actual correlation. He writes :—

"For a true and perfect rule of operation, then, the direction
will be *that it be certain, free, and disposing or leading to action.*
And this is the same thing with the discovery of the true form.
For the form of a nature is such that, given the form, the nature
infallibly follows. Therefore it is always present when the
nature is present, and universally implies it, and is constantly
inherent in it. Again : the form is such, that, if it be taken away,
the nature infallibly vanishes. Therefore it is always absent
when the nature is absent, and implies its absence and inheres in
nothing else. Lastly, the true form is such that it deduces the
given nature from some source of being which is inherent in
more natures, and which is better known in the natural order of
things than the form itself. For a true and perfect axiom of

knowledge, then, the direction and precept will be, *that another nature be discovered which is convertible with the given nature, and yet is a limitation of a more general nature, as of a true and real genus."*

His favourite examples are latent *motion* and latent *configuration:* as in the *Novum Organum,* book ii., aph. 1, and *Valerius Terminus,* book ii., chap. 1. Taking Bacon's *form* as a departure from the term of the schoolmen, *i.e.*, as the scholastic form with a realistic element, we may readily perceive that in Bacon's works it is *our idea of a specially conditioned primary quality.* Bacon's experiments soon taught him that latent motion of some sort was the form of heat, and latent configuration the form of colour; and, armed with these most sagacious divinations, his business was to determine how, by his own method of philosophising, these axioms could be evolved from experiment. Like Dr. Whewell, I accept the view of Mr. Ellis :—

" If it were affirmed that Bacon, after having had a glimpse of the truth suggested by some obvious phenomena, had then recourse, as he himself expresses it, to certain ' differentiæ inanes' in order to save the phenomena, I think it would be hard to dispute the truth of the censure."—*Footnote to ' Nov. Org.,'* book ii., aph. 20.

In any view of the method of Bacon, it must be allowed that his attempt to exhibit the operation of that method in the inductive determination of the form of heat is a miserable failure. If Mr. Ellis's statement is correct, " that the process by which scientific truths have been established cannot be so presented as even to appear to be in accordance with Bacon's method," it is not unreasonable to suppose that its inventor would have found it as little answerable to his expectations as it has proved to be comformable to any *actual* process of discovery. But granting that, it by no means follows that Bacon, in his attempt to apply it, even to a foregone insight, would have been reduced to the miserable shift of bolstering it up by such trifling and absurd "instances" as he has pressed into its service. In fact, a greater contrast cannot be found or conceived than that between the masterly grasp, as well as eloquence, displayed in the first book of the *Novum Organum*, and the imbecile and worse than childish trifling which pervades the whole of the *Inquisitio in Formam Calidi* of the second book.

Such is the general result of modern English criticism on the Baconian philosophy. It is, in all conscience, sufficiently adverse to the actual claim of its author, without reinforcing it with the unfair and spiteful attacks of German critics: yet it is necessary to glance at these before our survey is at all complete. We will take Professor Lasson and Baron Liebig, the invidious champions or rather ringleaders in the anti-Bacon revolt, as a sample of the band to which they belong. Liebig, indeed, has been exceeding well answered by Mr. G. F. Rodwell in the *Reader* for June 2nd and 9th, 1866; and a writer in *Fraser's Magazine* for December 1866, and April 1867, has attempted to discharge the same task, but with far less ability, and, I regret to say, with no manner of fairness. He has fought Liebig with his own weapons; and the result is, to say the least, unsatisfactory. Of Professor

Lasson, one of the most celebrated men in Europe, this writer is so bold as to say that "his name is unfortunately unknown in this country." It is, indeed, possible that the writer had never heard of him; though "not to know *him* argues himself unknown." In this matter at least I beg to assure Professor Lasson, if he should happen to encounter and be so good as to read *this* article, that the paper "Was Lord Bacon an Impostor?" is no representative of the knowledge which Englishmen have of illustrious foreigners.

In the first place, both Professor Lasson and Baron Liebig fall into a number of positive mistakes concerning Bacon's philosophy; and, unfortunately, *all* their mistakes are to Bacon's prejudice. I am not disposed, for my part, to rate Bacon's moral character very high. He was unsympathetic, unamiable, unscrupulous, and sensual ; a lover of power and rank, a hater of women. Yet, for all that, I believe that, in the single scope of physical discovery, Bacon was a lover of truth, and an investigator for truth's sake, as well as for that of utility. Small blame to him if he did combine both motives in all he attempted to do and all he accomplished. Small blame to him if, when advancing under the spur of "the eternal love of truth," he found his energies provoked and his industry sustained by the reflection that "man is born to trouble as the sparks fly upwards ;" that the very elements are, as in Blake's masterly sketches, arraigned against him; and that the "tyrants, giants, and monsters" of the world, man's miseries and necessities" (*Valerius Terminus*, book ii.,

chap. 11) are so often triumphant over the only defenceless and reasonable creature in it. In that direction
the truth-seeker had a touch—only a touch I own—of
that kindly sympathy which "makes the whole world
kin."

Just to show the sort of error into which these
German critics have fallen, I will take an example from
each, and place, side by side with the extract, the words
of Bacon himself. First: Professor Lasson writes:—

"*To Bacon, perceptions of sense and memory are sufficient :* the
task of reason begins only when the experiment is performed."—
Baco von Verulam. 1860.

"Those who have handled sciences have been either men of
experiment or men of dogmas. The men of experiment are like
the ant ; they only collect and use : the reasoners resemble spiders,
who make cobwebs out of their own substance. But the bee
takes a middle course ; it gathers its material from the flowers
of the garden and of the field, but transforms and digests it by a
power of its own. Not unlike this is the true business of philosophy ; for it neither relies solely or chiefly on the power of the
mind, nor does it take the matter which it gathers from natural
history and mechanical experiments, *and lay it up in the memory
as it finds it;* but lays it up in the understanding altered and
digested."—*Novum Organum,* book i., aph. 96.

Secondly, let us hear Baron Liebig:—

"In all his investigations Bacon sets great value on experiments. Of their meaning, however, he knows nothing. . . .
But in science all investigation is deductive, or *à priori.*"—Second
article in *Fraser's Magazine.*

"But my course and method, as I have often clearly stated and
would wish to state again, is this,—not to extract works from
works or experiments from experiments (as an empiric), *but from
works and experiments to extract causes and axioms ; and again,
from these causes and axioms, new works and experiments,* as a
legitimate interpreter of nature."—*Nov. Org.,* book i., aph. 117.

What is this but the method of verification by deduction, which is denied to Bacon alike by Baron Liebig and by the writer of the review in the *Athenæum?* It is in this same aphorism that Bacon points out the inadequacy of his own collection of natural history (the *Sylva Sylvarum*) "to serve the purposes of a legitimate interpretation:" yet a great part of Professor Liebig's censure is devoted to extracts from this very work, which he quietly assumes to have been destined to occupy the place of book ii. in the *Novum Organum*, and to have been intended to serve the very end for which, as we have seen, Bacon says it is wholly inadequate. I can hardly think the Baron had read the 117th aphorism; and, if he ignored that, other aphorisms may have shared the same fate. Such mistakes as these are fundamental, and are only acceptable to a reviewer on the ground that a critique which is infested with them can hardly be worth detailed review. But Baron Liebig's articles are rendered worthless by another fault, viz., personal invective. Bacon, according to this would-be censor, "shows like a quack doctor;" in whose vocabulary "the word *truth*, as we understand it, which is the sole aim of science, is not to be found;" whose "experiment to cheat the world has succeeded;" who "approached nature with a lie in his mouth;" and whose intellect "had only receptivity for the false, no feeling for the true;" and so forth. When we find the Baron indulging in this reckless slander of a man who has been three centuries in his grave, we can hardly help

believing that he attacked Bacon with a sinister motive,
and intended to wound others through his sides.   If
this production has been received in Germany with
respect, we are satisfied that time will reverse the
judgment; and if Bacon's countrymen have given the
Baron a fair hearing, he must none the less expect
that his discourse will be speedily consigned to that
oblivion, which such a combination of perversity and
malignity deserves.

IX.

SAMUEL TAYLOR COLERIDGE—
THE POET.[1]

THE founder of the distinguished family of Coleridge
was John Coleridge, the son of a woollen trader at
South Molton, Devon.   John Coleridge was born in

[1] Whatever may be thought of the outcome embodied in these
pages, the sources whence it has been drawn are numerous and voluminous ; in fact, I have spared no pains to discover all that has been
written *about* Coleridge ; and with very few exceptions I have made
myself acquainted with every work recorded in the subjoined biblio-
graphy.   In addition to these published sources of knowledge (some of
which, however, as 5 and 33, are grossly inaccurate), I have had the
benefit of personal communication with the Rev. Derwent Coleridge
(the poet's second and only surviving son), the late Herbert Coleridge
(grandson of the poet), and Mr. Arthur Duke Coleridge.   I am also
indebted for some facts to the Registrar of the University of Cambridge,
the University Librarian, and the Vice-Provost of King's College,
Cambridge.

1. Alsop, Thomas.—'Letters, Conversations, and Recollections of
   S. T. Coleridge' (extending over the period 1818-1832), 2 vols.,
   1836.
   Anonymous Writings relating to S. T. Coleridge.
2. 'College Reminiscences,' *Gentleman's Magazine*, December 1834.
3. 'Conversations from Cambridge,' 1836. (There is a section
   relating to "S. T. Coleridge at Trinity.")
4. 'Poets, Preachers, and Politicians' [*circa* 1847,] (describing a
   conversation with Coleridge).
5. Obituary Notice, *Gentleman's Magazine*, vol. ii., N.S., p. 544.
6. Obituary Notice, *Quarterly Review*, vol. lii., August 1834, p. 291.

1719. Nothing is known of his early life. He
matriculated at Sidney Sussex College, Cambridge, on
March 18th, 1748; and, having graduated there, became Vicar of Ottery St. Mary, Devon, and Master of
the Free Grammar or King's School in that town,
founded by Henry VIII. He was the author of three
works, viz., 'Miscellaneous Dissertations on the Seventeenth and Eighteenth Chapters of the Book of Judges,'

7. Review of 'Christabel,' 'Kubla Khan,' and the 'Pains of Sleep.'
   —*Edinburgh Review*, vol. xxvii., September 1816, p. 58.
8. Review of Statesman Manual, and Lay Sermons.—*Ibid.*, p. 444.
9. Review of 'Table-Talk,' *Edinburgh Review*, vol. lxi., April 1835
   p. 129.
10. Review of Poetical Works (by Prof. John Wilson), *Blackwood's
    Magazine*, October 1834.
11. College Reminiscences of S. T. Coleridge, *Gentleman's Magazine*,
    December 1834.
12. Review of Cottle's Early Recollections, *Quarterly Review*, vol.
    lix., July 1837, p. 25.
13. Review of Poetical Works, *ibid.*, vol. lii., August 1834, p. 1.
14. 'A Century of Great Poets. No. IV.—Samuel Taylor Coleridge.'
    —*Blackwood's Magazine*, November 1871, p. 552 (said to be by
    Mrs. Oliphant).

The list of reviews might have been almost indefinitely augmented:
the foregoing appear to me to be the most noteworthy. The last is the
most recent contribution to Coleridgeana, and is a most interesting sketch
of Coleridge's life and poetry. It contains, however, eight lines of un-
mitigated nonsense, p. 553, col. 2. I postponed the perusal of the larger
and biographical portion till I had written my own biographical sketch.

15. Carlyle, Thomas.—'Life of Sterling' (with account of Coleridge
    at Highgate, chap. viii., pp. 46–54 of People's Edition).
16. Carlyon, Dr.—'Early Years and Late Reflections.'
17. Coleridge, Henry Nelson.—'Biographical Supplement to the
    Biographia Literaria,' 1847, vol. ii., pp. 311–447. See under
    Stuart, Letter in *Gentleman's Magazine*.
18. Coleridge, John Taylor.—Letter appended to Coleridge's 'Table-
    Talk.'

1768; ' A Critical Latin Grammar,' 1772 ; and a Latin exercise book, entitled *Sententiæ Excerptæ*. He also printed a sermon, and contributed many papers to the *Gentleman's Magazine* from 1745 to 1780. He was said by the poet (his youngest child) to have been reputed " a profound Hebraist," and in life and character to have been " a perfect Parson Adams." He married (secondly) Ann Bowdon, and by all accounts had ten

19. Coleridge, Sara.—Introduction to the *Biographia Literaria*, 1847.
20.   ,,   Chapters V. and VII. added to the *Biographia Literaria*, 1847.
21. Coleridge, Samuel Taylor.—Satyrane's Letters appended to the *Biographia Literaria*, 1847, vol. ii., pp. 187-254.
22. Cottle, Joseph.—'Early Recollections, chiefly relating to the late Samuel Taylor Coleridge,' 2 vols., 1837.
23. De Quincey, Thomas.—'Coleridge and Opium-Eating.' *Tait's Magazine*, September, October, and November, 1834.
24.   ,,   'Autobiographic Sketches.' Samuel Taylor Coleridge—'Grave and Gay,' vol. ii., chap. 4, 1854.
25. Dibdin, Thomas Frogden.—'Reminiscences of a Literary Life,' vol. i., p. 253; and *Gentleman's Magazine*, vol. vi., N.S., p. 255.
26. Emerson, Ralph Waldo.—'English Traits ' (with account of a visit to Coleridge at Highgate).
27. Ferrier, Prof.—'The Plagiarisms of S. T. Coleridge,' *Blackwood's Magazine*, March 1840, p. 287.
28. Gillman, James.—'Life of Coleridge,' 1838. (Only one volume published : this stops at 1819.)
29. Hamilton, Sir William [Stirling].—Edition of Reid's Works, Appendix p. 890, *note*.
30. Hare, Julius Charles.—'S. T. Coleridge and the English Opium Eater,' *British Magazine*, January 1835, No. 37, p. 15.
31. Hazlitt, William.—'Spirit of the Age ; or, Contemporary Portraits,' 1825. ('Mr. Coleridge,' p. 55.)
32. Hort, Fenton John Anthony.—'Cambridge Essays,' 1856.
33. Howitt, William.—' Northern Heights of London,' 1869, 'Coleridge,' p. 300 (*circa*).

children, of whom the subject of this sketch was the tenth. He died at Plymouth, October 4, 1781.

Henry Nelson Coleridge mentions ten children of John Coleridge, but names only nine.[1] According to Coleridge himself, the omitted child was one named William, who died in infancy;[2] and the tablet at Ottery St. Mary follows Coleridge. John Coleridge's children, then, were—

---

34. Ingleby, Clement Mansfield.—On the 'Unpublished Manuscripts of Samuel Taylor Coleridge,' 'Transactions of the Royal Society of Literature,' vol. ix. New Series, 1867.

35.   „   'On Some Points connected with the Philosophy of Coleridge,' 'Transactions of the Royal Society of Literature,' vol. x., New Series, 1869.

36. Jerdan, William.—'Men I have Known,' 1866, 'Coleridge, p. 119.

37. Lamb, Charles.—'Recollections of Christ's Hospital,' 118.

38.   „   'Essays of Elia,' 1823. Essay entitled 'Christ's Hospital Five-and-thirty Years ago.''

39. Robinson, Henry Crabb.—'Diary and Correspondence,' *passim*.

40. Stirling, James Hutchison.—'De Quincey and Coleridge upon Kant,' *Fortnightly Review*, July 1, 1867.

41. Stuart, Daniel.—'Anecdotes of the Poet Coleridge,' *Gentleman's Magazine*, May 1838, p. 485.

42.   „   'Newspaper Writings of the poet Coleridge,' *ibid.*, June 1838, p. 577.

43.   „   Copies of Letters from Mr. Coleridge to Mr. Stuart, *ibid*, p. 580.

44.   „   Letter of Mr. H. N. Coleridge to, and Mr. Stuart's Reply, *ibid.*, July 1838, pp. 22 and 23.

45.   „   'The late Mr. Coleridge, the Poet,' *ibid.*, August 1838, p. 124.

Mill, John Stuart.—'Dissertations and Discussions' (Samuel Taylor Coleridge, vol. i. p. 392).

[1] 17.   [2] 28, p. 9.

N

1. John : a captain in H.E.I.C.S.; died in India in 1786, aged 31.

2. William : died an infant.

3. James: a colonel of Militia; married a Miss Duke, and was the founder of a distinguished branch of the family; died 1836, aged seventy-five.

4. William : said to have been of Pembroke College, Oxford, certainly of Wadham College; graduated B.A. 17th March 1779 ; died 1780, aged twenty-three.

5. Edward : a notable wit, of Pembroke College, Oxford; graduated B.A. 25th May 1780 ; a clergyman; died March 15, 1843, aged eighty-two.

6. George : a most learned divine, of Pembroke College, Oxford; graduated B.A. 9th June 1784, and succeeded his father as Vicar of Ottery St. Mary, Devon; died 1828, aged sixty-four.

7. Luke Herman : a surgeon; died 1790.

8. Ann : died at the age of twenty-three, in 1790.

9. Francis Syndercombe: a midshipman, afterwards an officer in H.E.I.C.S.; died in 1792, at the age of twenty-two, a lieutenant, after the siege of Seringapatam. He was called " the handsome Coleridge."

10. Samuel Taylor.

A word or two as to the next generation.

The children of Colonel James Coleridge were—

1. James Duke, D.D.: Prebendary of Exeter.

2. Frederic Bernard : a midshipman; killed by a fall from the top to the deck.

3. John Taylor : now the Right Hon. Sir John Taylor Coleridge, late Justice of the Q.B. He is the

father of Sir John Duke Coleridge, the present Attorney-General.

4. Francis George, a solicitor at Ottery : he was the father of Arthur Duke Coleridge, Barrister-at-law, translator of Goethe's " Egmont," and author of a " Life of Franz Schubert."

5. Henry Nelson Coleridge: late Fellow of King's College, Cambridge. He married Sara Coleridge, the Poet's only daughter. The late Herbert Coleridge was their only son.

6. Edward : Fellow of Eton College.

7. Frances Duke : she is the relict of Sir John Patteson, late Justice of the Q.B., and mother of the unfortunate Bishop of Melanesia.

George Coleridge, the Vicar of Ottery, had only one son, the Rev. George May Coleridge, M.A., Vicar of St. Mary Church, Devon.

Luke Herman Coleridge had one son, the Right Rev. William Hart Coleridge, late Bishop of Barbadoes and the Leeward Islands, and subsequently Warden of St. Augustine's College, Canterbury.

Samuel Taylor Coleridge was born at Ottery St. Mary on October 21, 1772, " about eleven o'clock in the forenoon." He was christened Samuel Taylor after a godfather of that name. At two years old he went to an infants' school kept by a woman of the name of Key, who was said to be nearly related to Sir Joshua Reynolds.[1] At six, or soon after, he entered his father's school, but his pupilage was cut short in 1781 by the

[1] 17, pp. 311–318.

old man's death; and in the spring of the following year he removed to London, where he lived for ten weeks with his uncle Bowdon.[1] Mr. Justice Buller, who had been educated by old John Coleridge, obtained for Samuel Taylor Coleridge a presentation to Christ's Hospital.[2] He was entered on the books on July 8, 1782, and at once went to reside in the junior school at Hertford. In the following September he returned to London, and was placed in the second ward of the Under Grammar School.

These ten years of his childhood had borne witness to that abnormal and precocious sensibility which was repeated many years after in his eldest son. Coleridge relates that shortly before the death of his father, through the jealousies infused into his brother Francis's mind by Molly, the nurse, he was driven to isolation, and his mind was forced in upon itself. Let me quote from his own touching narrative:—

"I never played except by myself, and then only acting over what I had been reading or fancying, or half one, half the other, with a stick cutting down weeds and nettles as one of the seven champions of Christendom. Alas! I had all the simplicity, all the docility of the little child, but none of the child's habits. I never thought as a child, never had the language of a child. I forget whether it was in my fifth or sixth year, but I believe the latter, in consequence of some quarrel between me and my brother, in the first week in October, I ran away from fear of being whipped, and passed the whole night, a night of rain and storm, on the bleak side of a hill on the Otter, and was there found at daybreak, without the power of using my limbs, about six yards from the naked bank of the river."[3]

---

[1] 17, p. 352.   [2] 25, p. 11.   [3] 28, pp. 10, 11.

Another account—which, however, presents ample evidence of inaccuracy and embellishment—contains the very natural incident that " a waggoner, proceeding along at four in the morning, thought he heard a child's voice. He stopped and listened. He now heard the voice cry out, ' Betty, Betty, I can't pull up the clothes.' "[1] For "four" we may read *six*; and for " Betty," *Molly*: while many of the recorded incidents are utterly at variance with the poet's own narrative. This anecdote is significant, if we bear in mind that fourteen years later he once more turned himself adrift, and was discovered by accident, not asleep on the banks of the Otter, but on duty in a military hospital.

One's heart sickens when one reflects on the sufferings of this poor child, endowed by nature with such exquisite sensibility, when he found himself face to face with the unsympathetic and Procrustean world of a public school. What Coleridge might have achieved under the plastic power of a more kindly culture we may imagine, but we shall never know. In my view, the case of Coleridge is that of a man of rare and priceless genius, marred and ruined by an insane and monstrous system of education. Let us fancy what a Samson or a Hercules would turn out if forced to grow awry in a dark and pestilential dungeon, or in the *res angusta* of what our ancestors called a " Little-Ease," and we shall be able to realise in some degree how much of Coleridge's errors and failures were due to the

[1] 22, vol. i., p. 248.

perverse and inappropriate machinery by which his opening faculties were directed and trained.

At the time to which I am referring, Christ's Hospital was presided over by a fiend of the name of James Boyer (or Bowyer), a pedagogue of the Parr type, who professed but one principle of action in the education of a boy,—"Flog him!" Lamb[1] has given us a "full, true, and particular account" of the proceedings of this great school under the iron sway and remorseless discipline of Boyer.

Boyer, of course, had his likes and dislikes; and among other objects of aversion he particularly disliked ugliness and awkwardness in a child, for which I do not hold him to be very blameworthy. But the *gravamen* of the charge against Boyer is that he regulated his punishments, to a great extent, by his likes and dislikes. Lamb records one instance which speaks volumes, and which, at the risk of disproportionate illustration (no small sin in a biography), I will adduce with some severity of abbreviation. Boyer detested a certain long, dark, ugly boy; but, forasmuch as the boy was industrious and well-conducted, he could find no pretext for subjecting him to any extraordinary punishment. Caned he was every day of his life, and many times a day, but such fleabites were wholly inadequate to allay the Boyer rage. Fortunately for his peace of mind, the class in which was his *bete-noire* was reported to him for some breach of rules. The master advanced to the class, and pulling out his watch, said, "Gentle-

[1] 37 and 38.

men, I have not time to flog all the class; you must
draw lots for two." The lot did not fall on the intended
victim. Thereupon Boyer, unwilling to be balked of
his prey, once more took out his watch and said,
"Gentlemen, I find I have time to flog the class, *and I
shall begin with you, sir.*" The ugly boy was forthwith
conducted into the retirement of Boyer's *sanctum.* In
a quarter of an hour boy and master returned into
school—the former in abject and sorry plight, the
latter appeased and radiant. Once more taking out
his watch, the miserable ogre, addressing the class,
said, "Gentlemen, I find I have not time to flog the rest
of the class; you are discharged." Such was the fiend
under whose ferule and birch the most sensitive child
in the land was doomed for years to suffer. Coleridge
was eight or nine years of age when one of the "Deputy
Grecians," named Middleton (afterwards Bishop of
Calcutta), found him in playtime, with his points
untrussed and his shoes down at heel, reading Virgil
for amusement. Middleton reported the fact to Boyer,
and Boyer at once sent for the master of the lower
school, from whom he learnt that Coleridge was a dunce,
who could not be got to repeat a single rule of syntax.
This report brought the boy before the dreaded head-
master; who, on being found sufficiently advanced in
Latin, was promoted to the upper school. Coleridge,
who was the kindest of beings, was always ready in
after life to make the best of his old master's character
and scholarship; but even he was obliged to allow that,
when he was flogged, Boyer gave him an extra cut

saying, " You are such an ugly fellow ! " [1] We have
Samuel Johnson's *coup d'essai* in versification, in his
' Epitaph on a Duck.' I will not take upon myself to
omit Coleridge's first attempt, which seems to have been
made while he was suffering under an irritating application to his skin. It runs thus :—

> " O Lord, have mercy on me !
>   For I am very sad ;
> For why, good Lord ? I've got the itch,
>   And eke I've got the tad,"

tad being the school-name for ringworm.[2] The verse
for humour promises much, but it is remarkable that
Coleridge's serious poetical efforts in early life contain
no prophecy of that wondrous poetic power which
broke forth into song in his twenty-fifth year.

It was about the same time that he was made free of
a circulating library. What a redeeming " touch of
nature " is that quality which we self-flatteringly call
humanity! How many men walking the Strand at
that or any other time would have turned to so good an
account the accident of a boy catching at his coat ?
Coleridge was acting one of his day-dreams in the
Strand—just as he used to play the Seven Champions
of Christendom in the fields of Ottery. He fancied
himself Leander swimming the Hellespont, when his
hand committed the alleged offence. The story, as told
by Gillman, is simply incredible, by which assertion it
is not very strongly differentiated from the majority
of stories in his book.[2] No gentleman would suspect a

[1] 2S, p. 20.   [2] 2S, p. 17.

Blue-coat boy of picking his pocket. Be that as it
may, the gentleman with whom Coleridge came in contact was both kind and discerning. God bless him!
say I, for being both, since his kindness and discern-
ment concurred in placing at the boy's disposal a very
treasury of book-lore.

Henceforth, barring a little mechanical drudgery at
Greek, the circulating library in King Street, Cheap-
side, was Coleridge's school.[1] His own account runs
thus:—

"I read *through* the catalogue, folios and all, whether
I understood them, or did not understand them, running all risks in skulking out to get the two volumes
which I was entitled to have daily; conceive what I
must have been at fourteen. I was in a continual low
fever. My whole being was, with eyes closed to every
object of present sense, to crumple myself up in a
sunny corner, and read, read, read: fancy myself on
Robinson Crusoe's island, finding a mountain of plum-
cake, and eating a room for myself, and then eating
it into the shapes of tables and chairs—hunger and
fancy!"

Such a course of life was fatal to his bodily health.
Just as in the case of De Quincey, Coleridge contracted
at school a morbid affection of the stomach—partly
caused by want of bodily exercise and partly by want
of food—which became the bane of his mature years.
He himself tells us that, "what with jaundice, and
what with rheumatic fever, full half the time from

[1] 17, p. 329.

seventeen to eighteen was passed in the sick ward of Christ's Hospital."

The incidents of his youth, many of them so significant of his future life, seem to grow upon me as I write; and it is with great unwillingness that, in view of that future life, and the limits of this article, I pass over so much that ought to be taken into account in estimating his character. I have already forestalled one romantic incident in his after-life, viz., that the Cambridge student abandoned the academic shades of Jesus College for a barrack. Just so did the Blue-coat boy of fifteen deliberately resolve, with as little regard to his position and scholarship, as for the judgment of his masters and his friends, to be apprenticed to a shoemaker! He, and a cobbler keeping shop hard by, conspired to carry this resolve into effect; and Coleridge instructed the old man how to broach the matter to Boyer, preparing him for the head-master's inevitable anger. It is told by Gillman that Boyer once threatened to flog a girl who had come to beg a half-holiday for her brother. On the occasion of the shoemaker's application, Boyer held out threats, but followed up the exclamation of "Od's my life, man! what d'ye mean?" by so furious a demonstration of physical force, that the old shoemaker found discretion the wiser part of valour.[1] So the shoemaking was abandoned, and Coleridge remained at school till he had attained the dignity of a Grecian. He left Christ's Hospital in September 1790, and was entered at Jesus College,

---

[1] 28, p. 21.

Cambridge, on the 5th of the following February. He was then nineteen years of age.[1]

We must hurry over his Cambridge career. In the following year he gained Sir William Browne's medal for a Greek ode on "the Slave Trade." It is a specimen of average scholarship, but in no way remarkable. He wrote for the Porson prize what he called his "finest Greek poem," but was unsuccessful. He continued in residence at Jesus College till November 1793, when moved by some disappointment, academical or other, he left Cambridge without an *excat*, for London, where on December 3rd he enlisted in the 15th Light Dragoons under the name of Silas Titus Comberbacke (Cottle gives the name as Silas Tomken Cumberbatch, but he blunders after his fashion). It is said that the surname was taken from a shop in Lincoln's Inn Fields or the Temple; and it is not impossible (though I have never met with the suggestion) that the first Christian name was suggested to Coleridge by Aubrey's "Captain Silas Taylor." The story of his life in barracks is too well known to need repetition here; let it suffice to say that his Latin and Greek betrayed his grade. He was at length discovered by some of his family or friends as he was doing duty in the infirmary of the barracks at Hounslow, and was bought off and discharged on April 10, 1794. He seems to have returned to Cambridge the same month, and to have become a Unitarian in religion. In the following June, Coleridge visited Oxford, where he made the acquaintance of Robert

[1] 28, p. 38.   [2] 19, vol. i. p. 253.

Southey, who was then at Balliol College. The friendship thus formed between these two poets and men of letters lasted till Coleridge's death, with one brief interruption arising from some act or default of Southey's as editor of the *Quarterly Review.* In August or September Coleridge went by appointment to meet Southey at Bristol. Southey's mother lived at Bath, but it does not appear that Coleridge stayed there. The object of this meeting was to organise a society whose members were forthwith to embark for America, and to found a Communist colony on the banks of the Susquehannah. This society at the time in question consisted of four male members, and was called a Pantisocracy, *i.e.*, one in which all had common rights and equal powers. Coleridge was the founder; the rest were Southey, Robert Lovell (a young Quaker poet), and George Burnet, son of a Somersetshire farmer, and, like Southey, an Oxonian.[1] To Burnet was confided the agricultural department, and on the requisite funds being raised he was to purchase the implements. What the others were to do it is hard to say, unless they were to write poetry and preach to one another. I suppose, too, that Burnet was to be "without encumbrance;" for Lovell was already committed to matrimony, having married Mary Fricker, one of three sisters who resided with their mother at Bristol; which was on the whole a considerate proceeding, as it left one sister for each of

---

[1] Lovell died about July 1795 ; and Burnet, at the age of thirty-two, in 1807. So says Gillman.

his brother poets. Coleridge, indeed, once more returned to Cambridge in September, where he published a poem called "The Fall of Robespierre." But in February 1795 he was again with Southey in Bristol, where both gave themselves to public lecturing, and Coleridge to Unitarian preaching; and at private gatherings Pantisocracy was an inexhaustible theme of conversation and dispute.

On October 4, Coleridge married Sarah Fricker, and six weeks afterwards her Sister Edith became the wife of Southey.[1] Doubtless marriage was in a sort a condition of colonial success; but in default of the necessary capital it was an absolute bar to the realisation of the project; and so it fell out that Pantisocracy was tacitly abandoned, though it was all the more eagerly pursued in speech. Southey was the first seceder; his nuptial knot had no sooner been tied than he sailed for Portugal to earn the means of keeping a wife. Doubtless it would have been more regular (and for matter of fact more prudent also) if he had done the earning first and the marrying afterwards. But he was the very soul of honour; so he redeemed his promise out of hand, and he extended to Edith Fricker the protection of a husband's name while he began his life of honourable toil in a distant land. Coleridge, on the contrary, found "love in a cottage" at Clevedon; and after enjoying his honeymoon, and celebrating it in very sweet verses, set forth alone on a visit to friends in Worcester, Birmingham, Derby, Sheffield, Man-

[1] 17, p. 347.

chester, and Liverpool. His ostensible object was to obtain subscribers to a periodical to be written by himself, and entitled *The Watchman*. On this tour he made acquaintance with Joseph Strutt, the father of Lord Belper, Dr. Darwin (who from the testimony of Mrs. Schimmelpenninck seems to have combined the four characteristics of naturalist, poet, atheist, and glutton), Charles Lloyd, a brainsick young poet; James Montgomery, the poet, and others. During his absence his forgotten bride found the *ennui* of the cottage insupportable, and returned to her mother's house on Redcliff Hill, Bristol, and there fell sick. Coleridge was summoned from Liverpool to her bedside. The double misery of sickness and poverty which was thenceforth to poison their matrimonial life had now commenced with a vengeance; and the biographer, who is determined to do his duty by his hero's wife and children, as well as by the hero himself, finds himself obliged to allow that the peculiar training of the juvenile poet had proved a very insufficient discipline for the correction of the bosom vice of selfishness. It is very hard to hold the balance fairly between Coleridge and his wife. It always is hard to be just to both parties in an ill-assorted marriage. For myself I decline the task, believing that the time has not yet arrived—if arrive ever it will—for passing an objective judgment on this remarkable being.

> " Then at the balance let's be mute,
> We never can adjust it;
> What's *done* we partly may compute,
> But know not what's *resisted*."

However, once for all, let me say that, except for brief
and uncertain intervals, Coleridge never did maintain
either wife or children. At one time Southey, poor as
a church rat, but industrious as a bee, with a wife and
children of his own to provide for, kept Coleridge's wife
and children too. The story is pitiable; perhaps of
all the parties involved in Coleridge's seeming self-
indulgent life, Southey and his poor wife are most to
be pitied and most to be loved. How matters could
have turned out better it is hard to say : for assuredly
Coleridge was wholly unfit for any other kind of
work than that he actually accomplished ; and with
that work posterity seems to be very well satisfied ;
so we may allow that in some inscrutable way "it's
all for the best."

The *Watchman*, like almost everything Coleridge
attempted, proved a miserable failure. The first number
was published on March 1, 1796, and it expired with
the tenth number, viz., that of May 13. In March,
Mr. and Mrs. Coleridge removed from Redcliff Hill to
Oxford Street, Kingsdown. He drew his maintenance
from Cottle, the Bristol bookseller, doing, it must be
owned, very scant work for very liberal pay. Cottle
published Coleridge's first volume of poems early in
April. According to the poet's own view, his ' Religious Musings ' were a certificate of high merit. In
each of two letters to a friend, Mr. Thomas Poole, of
Nether Stowey (dated April 1st and 11th), he says,
" I rest all my poetical credit on the ' Religious
Musings.' "

Coleridge now bethought him of the necessity of keeping the wolf from the door by his own personal exertions. Three schemes were soon on foot, of which the one entailing the least exertion on his part was actually realised. In July, Mr. and Mrs. Coleridge visited Darley, near Derby, where a negotiation was opened for Coleridge to undertake the education of the sons of a Mrs. Evans. It came to nothing. After visiting Oakover, Ilam, and Dovedale, they left Darley, to stay at the house of a Mr. Thomas Hawkes, of Moseley, near Birmingham, at which town Coleridge preached on Faith to a Unitarian congregation. Here he again met Charles Lloyd.

In September, Coleridge, leaving his wife at Kingsdown, once more visited Birmingham. He seems to have stayed with the Lloyds of Bingley Hall, with a view to Charles Lloyd—who was a young man of fine poetic genius, but in extremely delicate health—being domesticated with him at Kingsdown.

While here the news arrived that Mrs. Coleridge had, on September 19th, presented him with a son. He hurried back to Bristol, taking Charles Lloyd with him. Matters had changed in his absence: Southey had returned from Portugal to claim his bride; and the ideal pantisocratic colony had received the addition of one who was to inherit no little of Coleridge's poetic genius, and a great deal of his weakness. This child was christened David Hartley, after the famous author of the "Observations on Man," who at that time, jointly with Bishop Berkeley and the poet Bowles, shared the bulk of Coleridge's hero-worship.[1]

Soon after we find Mr. and Mrs. Coleridge, with their child and Charles Lloyd, residing at a cottage taken for them at Nether Stowey by Mr. Thomas Poole of that place.[2] As Coleridge rarely dated a letter, and when he did do so contented himself with the year or the week-day only, it is difficult to fix with nicety the time of his entering on this new residence. However, he was there in November 1796, preparing a second edition of his poems, which was published by Cottle in the summer of 1797.

The more distressing effects of Coleridge's life at Christ's Hospital seem to have become chronic before his marriage. Early in 1795 (if I may infer a date for an undated note to Cottle[3]) he complains that "a very devil has got possession of my left temple, eye, cheek, jaw, throat, and shoulder." It is unquestionable that it was about this time that he first had recourse to opium to allay his sufferings. On the 1st November 1796, he was seized with violent neuralgia,[4] and took laudanum, evidently not for the first time. Assuredly

---

[1] Coleridge's other children, whose names occur seldom or never in the published biographies, were Sara, born at Bristol: and Derwent, born at Keswick. The former married Henry Nelson Coleridge, and was the accomplished author of 'Phantasmion,' Pickering, 1837. The latter alone survives. He was Principal of St. Mark's Training College, and is now Rector of Hanwell; and he has been for many years one of H. M.'s Inspectors of Schools. He edited his brother Hartley's 'Remains' with a short biography, and has contributed important papers to the London Philological Society.

[2] 22, vol. i., p. 187; 17, p. 391.

[3] 22, vol. i., p. 54   [4] 17, p. 330.

he had not the slightest suspicion that he was contract-
ing a habit of body which would render a periodical
supply of the narcotic a positive necessity. He records,
under date 1826, " I wrote a few stanzas three-and-
twenty years ago, soon after my eyes had been opened
to the true nature of the habit into which I had been
ignorantly deluded by the seeming magic effects of
opium," &c., which is to say, that his eyes were not
opened till about 1803, *i.e.*, seven or eight years after
he first took laudanum. In the same paper his bondage to opium is attributed to Kendal's Black Drop,
which he took experimentally on the recommendation
of a medical review, and which "worked miracles;
the swellings [in the knees] disappeared, the pains
vanished." But here was a mistake, or a self-delusion,
for the habit had been already formed from the occasional use of laudanum. He continues, "Alas! it is
with a bitter smile, a laugh of gall and bitterness, that
I recall this period of unsuspecting delusion, and how
I first became aware of the maelström, the fatal whirl-
pool to which I was drawing just when the current
was beyond my strength to stem. . . . God knows that
from that moment I was the victim of pain and terror,
nor had I at any time taken the flattering poison as a
stimulus, or for any craving after pleasurable sensations.
I needed none; and oh! with what unutterable sorrow
did I read the 'Confessions of an Opium-Eater,' in
which the writer, with morbid vanity, makes a boast of
what was my misfortune, for he had been faithfully and
with an agony of zeal warned of the gulf, and yet wil-

fully struck into the current! Heaven be merciful to him!—April, 1826."[1] De Quincey amply avenged himself for this;[2] and Sara Coleridge gently replied to De Quincey;[3] but I have no space for the consideration of this controversy now. I note *en passant* that William Wilberforce, Robert Hall, Coleridge, De Quincey, and J. P. Nichol, the astronomer, were all consumers of opium. All of these, except poor Robert Hall, took it inordinately; and for them that drug had irresistible fascinations. With Wilberforce, Coleridge, and Nichol, the consequential mischief was found to be so serious as to render expedient a lengthened residence in the house of a medical man, with a view to the discontinuance of the habit. In all these cases, as in that of De Quincey, it was found impossible to permanently accustom the nervous system to the enforced abstinence; and in the event the narcotic resumed, if it ever relaxed, its baneful sway.

At Nether Stowey Coleridge wrote his tragedy of 'Osorio,' which he afterwards altered and printed under the name of 'The Remorse.' It was completed up to the middle of Act V. by September 6th, 1797,[4] and was brought out at Drury Lane (by favour of Lord Byron) nineteen years after it was composed, when Rae took the chief part. This year (1797) has been called Coleridge's *annus mirabilis;* for in the course of it he produced an unusually large number of poems; among which we count the first part of 'Christabel,' 'Genevieve,'

---

[1] 28, pp. 246–248.   [2] 20.   [3] 19.
[4] 22, vol. i., p. 234.

and the 'Hymn before Sunrise in the Vale of Chamouni,' and a considerable part of 'The Ancient Mariner.' This famous ballad was completed in February 1798, and published with Wordsworth's 'Lyrical Ballads' in the following June. At this time, too, he met at Mr. Poole's, Thomas and Josiah Wedgewood,[1] who introduced him by letter to Mr. Daniel Stuart, and he began to contribute to the *Morning Post*. He must have returned with the Wedgewoods to Cote House, and stayed there till the end of the year.[2] In that month of February he made another attempt to obtain a preachership. His success at Birmingham had been small; the Unitarians, fresh from the school of Priestley, found Coleridge's doctrines too pronouncedly metaphysical, and also probably tinged with orthodoxy. He had not succeeded better at Sheffield. At the chapel of Mr. Jardine, at Bristol, Coleridge had made a lamentable failure. He now went to Shrewsbury, as candidate in succession to the Rev. Mr. Rowe. Whatever may have been his design, he withdrew his candidature on learning that the Messrs. Wedgewood had settled on him a pension of £150 a year.[3]

On September 16, 1798, Coleridge, Wordsworth, and Miss Wordsworth sailed from Yarmouth for Hamburg. They landed on the 19th, at four o'clock p.m., and the following day the two poets were introduced to the brother of the poet Klopstock, and to Ebeling. A few days later they made the acquaintance of the greater

---

[1] 22, vol. i., pp. 250, 305, and 307.   [2] 41, p. 486.
[3] 17, p. 389 ; 22, vol. i., p. 308.

Klopstock, with whom, however, they were much disappointed. Doubtless Klopstock had a reputation
vastly in excess of his merits; but much of the disappointment must have been owing to the want of an
adequate medium of communication. Wordsworth left
for England on September 27; but Coleridge remained
in Germany for the purpose of acquiring the language,
and of extending his acquaintance with German cele-
brities.

In my opinion De Quincey has exaggerated Coleridge's
acquaintance with German. During the year and two
months of his residence in Germany a hard-working
student might have obtained a passable acquaintance
with the language; but Coleridge, after his first year
at college, was never a hard-working student; and at
this time he was physically incapable of the exertion
necessary to so vast an acquirement. His version of
Schiller's 'Wallenstein' teems with mistakes of translation, though it is a treasury of fine original poetry.
I suspect he knew no foreign language so well as Latin;
but he had acquired sufficient French and Italian to
read (doubtless with more or less difficulty) the classics
of France and Italy.

Coleridge returned to England on November 27, 1799.[1]
The months of July and October, 1800, he passed at
Keswick as the guest of Southey, who then resided at
Greta Hall.[2] In this year he composed his fine but
inaccurate version of the 'Piccolomini,' and 'The

---

[1] 21, *passim*, and 17, p. 230.
[2] 17, p. 393; and 41, p. 489.

Death of Wallenstein,' which it is said he wrote in six
weeks. It was published immediately, but few copies
were ever sold, and at length the large remainder was
disposed of as waste paper.[1]   He now composed the
second part of 'Christabel.' Soon after this period,
with the exception of some short pieces, he discon-
tinued writing poetry.

In the preface to the second part of 'Christabel,'
written early in 1800, he observes, "Till very lately
my poetic powers have been in a state of suspended
animation." I cannot make out that he wrote any
poetry after this time but 'Zapolya.' 'Kubla Khan,'
and 'The Pains of Sleep,' whensoever written, were
published in the same volume with 'Christabel,' in
1816. 'Sibylline Leaves' and 'Zapolya' appeared
in that year also.

In October 1803, Coleridge, in company with Wordsworth, visited the Highlands. The scenery of Scotland,
which inspired Wordsworth, and made his genius productive, had but little effect on Coleridge. In truth,
the poetical period of his life was rapidly rounding to
a close. We may consider it closed by 1804, when he
sailed for Malta. We may well credit the assertion that
Coleridge *the poet* died there, but Gillman's assertion
has no such qualification. He says, "He seemed at
this time [*i.e.*, while in Malta], in addition to his
rheumatism, to have been oppressed in his breathing,
which oppression crept on him imperceptibly to himself without suspicion of its cause: yet so obvious was

[1] 28, p. 281.

it, that it was noticed by others 'as laborious;' *and continuing to increase, though with little apparent advancement, at length terminated in death.*" [1]

Happily, however, he came to life again in England —not indeed as a poet, but as a religious philosopher. As I have recorded that Coleridge became a Unitarian in religion about the spring or summer of 1794, let me add that he had outgrown his Unitarianism by the time he left Malta, and was an outspoken defender of the Holy Trinity by the year 1807. It is the more important to note this, since Mr. Wm. Howitt[2] appears to attribute Coleridge's Unitarianism to his study of the German philosophers, and distinctly states that " towards the close of his life he even disclaimed them, and returned a strict Trinitarian to the bosom of the Church of England." This extraordinary perversion I have elsewhere exposed.[3]

We learn from Lamb that Coleridge's talk, while at Christ's Hospital, acted like a spell on chance visitors. " How have I seen the casual passer through the cloisters stand still, entranced with admiration!" &c.[4] It was just the same at Jesus' College and at Hounslow Barracks. Students and soldiers alike could not resist the fascination, but on the cessation of his diatribe, like Adam after the angel's discourse (' Paradise Lost,' xii.)., must often have—

" Thought him still speaking, still stood fixed to hear."

This gift of speech was in full perfection in 1797, and

[1] 28, p. 167.   [2] 33, p. 315.
[3] 35, pp. 27-30.   [4] 38.

we are indebted to Mr. D. Stuart for the fact that it did Coleridge a disservice in the Christmas of that year. He was an inmate of Cote House, where a large party, including James Mackintosh, were assembled, and "so riveted by his discourse the attention of the gentlemen, particularly of Mr. Thomas Wedgewood," and "so prevented general conversation, that several of the party wished him out of the house." The result was that "Mackintosh, at the instance of some of the inmates, attacked Coleridge on all subjects—politics, poetry, religion, ethics, &c. Mackintosh was by far the most [*i.e.*, more] dexterous disputer. Coleridge . . . was speedily confused and subdued. He felt himself lowered in the eyes of the Wedgewoods," and incontinently left the house, *a sadder*, if not *a wiser man !* "[1]

Of Coleridge's extraordinary gift of consecutive talking, which Madame De Stael called *le monologue*, as distinguished from *le dialogue*, we have several trustworthy accounts. I take Dr. Dibdin's, which is certainly *not* overcharged :—

" The orator rolled himself up in his chair, and gave the most unrestrained indulgence to his speech ; and how fraught with acuteness and originality was that speech, and in what copious and eloquent periods did it flow ! . . . For nearly two hours he spoke with unhesitating and uninterrupted fluency. . . . The manner of Coleridge was rather emphatic than dogmatic, and thus he was generally and satisfactorily listened to. It might be said of Coleridge, as Cowper has so happily said of Sir Philip Sidney, that he was 'the warbler of poetic prose.' . . .

[1] 41, p. 485.

Coleridge was eminently simple in his manner. Thinking and speaking were his delight ; and he would sometimes seem, during the more fervid movements of discourse, to be abstracted from all and everything around him, and to be basking in the sunny warmth of his own radiant imagination." [1]

Lamb used to tell an amusing and wholly incredible story of Coleridge's abstraction when he was once engaged in the evolution of discourse. Coleridge met him (so the story runs) as he was on his way to his place of business, the India House, in Leadenhall Street. Coleridge stopped him, and opened upon him the floodgates of his eloquence. To avoid the interruption and observation of passers-by, Coleridge drew Lamb into an entry, and was soon absorbed in his spoken day-dream. Lamb had no time to spare, so he slipped out of the entry, apparently unobserved by the rapt talker. Six hours later—the India House times were from ten till four—Lamb was on his way home, and happening to pass the entry of the morning's exploit, he observed Coleridge still standing there, holding forth, with impassioned eloquence, to an imaginary listener. Well, the story is rather hard to swallow, but the *six* hours' talk is quite credible. The present Bishop of St. David's has given me the particulars of a similar display in his rooms at Cambridge, when he was a tutor of Trinity College. He says :—

" I remember very distinctly that we dined at the early hour of four, for the purpose of allowing the longer time for conver-

---

[1] 25, vol. i., p. 253.

sation in the evening, when several who were not of the dinner party joined our company. At this distance of time I could not be sure as to the precise hour at which Coleridge began his monologue or ended it. But I feel quite certain that it did not occupy much less than six hours, if it did not last longer ; for I think we did not break up before midnight."

The Bishop assured me that during this time no one interrupted the monologue ; indeed, it would have been impracticable to have drawn the speaker from his magic circle without positive rudeness; and that, but for the necessary interruptions of sleep and meals, there seemed to be no reason why Coleridge should not have realised the classical description of a river,—

> "at ille
> Labitur et labetur in omne volubilis ævum."

Coleridge's early poetical efforts gave, as I have said, little or no promise of his future excellence. Perhaps the earliest examples of his marvellous poetic genius are found in the lines 'To Sara,' and those 'To a friend who had declared his intention of writing no more poetry.' From the latter I select a dozen lines which might have been written by the author of 'A Midsummer Night's Dream,' or the author of 'Comus :'—

> " On a bleak rock, midway the Aonian Mount,
>   There stands a lone and melancholy tree,
>   Whose aged branches to the midnight blast
>   Make solemn music : pluck its darkest bough,
>   Ere yet the unwholesome night dew be exhaled,
>   And weeping, wreathe it round thy poet's tomb :
>   Then, in the outskirts where pollutions grow,
>   Pick stinking henbane, and the dusky flowers

Of nightshade, or its red and tempting fruit;
These with stopped nostril and glove-guarded hand
Knit in nice intertexture, so to twine
The illustrious brow of Scotch nobility!"—

i.e., the brow of that nobility which, with so exquisite a sense of propriety, made an exciseman of their national poet. Of course these lines, like all worthy poetry, must be read aloud: the anastomosis, which is here so masterly, would otherwise be lost. The writer of the able critique in *Blackwood*[1] quotes from Coleridge the following remarks:—"The sudden charm which accidents of light and shade, which moonlight or sunlight, diffused over a familiar landscape, appeared to represent the practicability of combining both powers;" viz., "the power of exciting the sympathy of the reader by a faithful adherence to the truth of nature, and the power of giving the interest of novelty by the modifying colours of imagination." "These are the poetry of nature. The thought suggested itself (to which of us I do not recollect), [*i.e.*, himself or Wordsworth,] that a series of poems might be composed of two sorts. In the one, the incidents and agents were to be, in part at least, supernatural; for the second class subjects were to be chosen from ordinary life." He was thus led to make the experiment of a poem belonging to the former class. The first result was 'The Ancient Mariner,' the second was 'Christabel.'

These two masterpieces belong to the same class

[1] 14.

as the immortal romances of La Motte Fouqué. 'The
Ancient Mariner' and 'Christabel' are to poetry
exactly what 'Undine' and 'Sintram' are to prose
literature. If it be allowed that neither of those
poems is comparable, as a romance, to 'Undine,'
Coleridge must nevertheless be credited with having
clothed his thoughts in a far nobler investiture of
words.

Those who would attribute the production of such
poems to the influence of opium, or laudanum, should
consider that of the thousands who have habitually
eaten opium or drunk laudanum, only one has given
us an 'Ancient Mariner' and a 'Christabel.'

On these two poems, and on 'Genevieve,' rests
the splendid reputation of Coleridge as a poet. His
own claim to originality, on the score of rhythm,
must be disallowed. In the Preface to 'Christabel'
he enumerates his "new principle, namely, that of
counting the accents, not the syllables. Though the
latter may vary from seven to twelve, yet in each line
the accents will be found to be only four." Thus—

> " Is the night chilly and dárk?
> The night is chilly but nót dárk."

Coleridge would claim for the seven syllables of the
one, and the eight of the other line, but four accents.
All the same, it can hardly be doubted that both
lines are indistinguishable from prose, in which respect
they may be likened to many in the 'Paradise
Regained.'

Hazlitt delivers himself of this brief but emphatic praise of 'Christabel,'—"In 'Christabel' there is one splendid passage on divided friendship."[1] As if a great poem could be judged by its "beauties," or a carcanet by its gems! However, speaking of such incidents, Hazlitt is right. The passage is singularly splendid :—

> "Alas ! they had been friends in youth ;
> But whispering tongues can poison truth ;
> And constancy lives in realms above ;
> And life is thorny ; and youth is vain ;
> And to be wroth with one we love
> Doth work like madness in the brain.
> And thus it chanced, as I divine,
> With Roland and Sir Leoline.
> Each spake words of high disdain
> And insult to his heart's best brother :
> They parted—ne'er to meet again !
> But never either found another
> To free the hollow heart from paining—
> They stood aloof, the scars remaining,
> Like cliffs which had been rent asunder.
> A dreary sea now flows between ;
> But neither heat, nor frost, nor thunder,
> Shall wholly do away, I ween,
> The marks of that which once hath been."

To understand the nature (not at all the secret) of Coleridge's poetry we must picture him to our minds as a *seer*, one who has inward vision of the inner world, the vision of which is simply provoked by the outward sight of outer objects. Unhappily, this aphorism is all I have to say in the nature of

[1] 31, p. 69.

criticism: *To every seer the outer is but a means of suggesting the inner.* To the simple-hearted and profound-souled Böhme, the auroral redness was fraught with spiritual regeneration; to Tennyson (in the ' Vision of Sin '), it was instinct with divine vengeance.

William Blake used to say that when he looked at the sun he saw angels and archangels around the throne of God. Tennyson, with appropriate insight, assigns to Merlin (in ' Vivien ') a similar confession respecting the nebula in the sword of Orion :—

> "A single misty star,
> Which is the second in a line of stars
> That seem a sword beneath a belt of three ;
> I never gazed upon it but I dreamt
> Of some vast charm concluded in that star
> To make fame nothing."

Coleridge was fully conscious of his seership. He says, "In looking at objects of nature, while I am thinking, as at yonder moon dim glimmering through the dewy window-pane, I seem rather to be seeking, as it were *asking*, a symbolical language for something within me that already and for ever exists, than observing anything new. Even when that latter is the case, yet still I have always an obscure feeling, as if that new phenomenon were the dim awakening of a forgotten or hidden truth of my inner nature." [1] *The greatness of Coleridge as a poet consisted in his*

[1] 28, p. 311.

possession of this seership, his fidelity to it, and his extraordinary wealth of language for giving it utterance. It is just such an inner vision, inseparably linked to or mingled with the world of sense, that he strove to express, in 'The Ancient Mariner' and in 'Christabel;' neither story has a real end, and the latter, by its very nature, is a fragment. These poems are criticised in a genial and appreciative spirit by the author of 'A Century of Great Poets, No. IV.' Especially am I rejoiced to find in that paper a corroboration of my own judgment on 'Genevieve.' "For our own part, we are afraid to say all that we think of its perfection, lest our words should seem inflated and unreal." Just so. I, too, hold it to be the most perfect poem in the English language. It is a lesson and a warning to young poets. The brevity of a poem precludes all excuse for shortcoming or imperfection. A brief poem should be faultless and perfect, or it had better have remained unwritten. The faults we tolerate in a building are intolerable in a statue. 'Genevieve' is brief; but it has such unparalleled perfection of structure and language, of story and sentiment (just a tale within a tale, as 'Kubla Khan' is a dream within a dream), that its author, had he written nothing else, would for ever have taken his place in the roll of great poets. After all talk about Coleridge being incapable of sustained effort, of his inability to accomplish a voluminous poem like 'Paradise Lost,' let us remember what Henry Taylor, in one of his 'Essays on Books,' has said so well, that

a long poem is always, in truth, a connected series
of short poems, and that Coleridge, if he wrote but
little, wrote that little with consummate excellence. [1]

[1] Copy of the slab in the church of Ottery St. Mary, commemorating
the Coleridge family :—

IN MEMORY OF

Rev. John Coleridge, who died A.D. 1781, aged 63.

Of Ann, his wife, who died A.D. 1809, aged 83.

And of their children.

John died in the East Indies, A.D. 1786, aged 31.

William an infant.

William, at Hackney, A.D. 1780, aged 23.

Luke Herman, at Thorverton, A.D. 1790, aged 24.

Ann, at Ottery, A.D. 1791, aged 23.

Francis, in the East Indies, A.D. 1792, aged 22.

George, at Ottery, A.D. 1828, aged 64.

Samuel Taylor, at Highgate, A.D. 1834, aged 62.

James, at Ottery, A.D. 1836, aged 75.

Rev. Edward Coleridge, B.A., who died March 15th, 1843, in the 83rd
year of his age.

X.

SAMUEL TAYLOR COLERIDGE— THE DIVINE.

ONE of two grave charges brought against Coleridge in several of the writings recorded in my bibliographical list,[1] and in particular in 35 and 40, is, in short, this: that as a philosopher, he professed so much and performed so little. Of course, the *so much* and *so little* are correlative; for assuredly, compared with many other men of genius, Coleridge accomplished a great deal. It would be hopeless to contest the truth of either clause in that charge. A few words to exemplify this will suffice. In the *Biographia Literaria*,[2] he writes:—

"In the third treatise of my *Logosophia* . . . I shall give (*Deo volente*) the demonstrations and constructions of the Dynamic Philosophy scientifically arranged."

---

[1] Prefixed to the preceding essay. Here (as there) I refer to those writings under their numbers in the list. I am convinced that many must have eluded my search. I am told that Mrs. Oliphant's 'Life of Edward Irving' contains interesting reference to Coleridge. I forgot to include Mr. J. S. Mill's 'Dissertations and Discussions,' 1859, with whose paper on Coleridge, vol. i. p. 392, I was acquainted. I ought also to have included a Review of Coleridge's Poetical Works (by Prof. John Wilson) in *Blackwood's Magazine*, October 1834, in the list of "Anonymous Writings." We will call this 46, and Mr. Mill's paper 47.

I must add, that I omitted the mention of Coleridge's son, Berkeley, who died an infant in 1799.

[2] 1847. Vol. i., p. 267, footnote.

That is to say, in the *third* treatise of a work whereof
no *first* nor *second* treatise ever existed! This *Logosophia* is the "great work" which is so often alluded
to and even described in his Letters;[1] and it was this
work which *was* (but was *not* destined) to contain the
boasted Coleridgean "system," characterised in such
very general terms in the 'Table Talk.'[2] What this
system actually was, as existing only in the brain of
Coleridge, is an open question, on which there may be
quot homines tot sententiæ, i.e. *homines* who may care to
speculate on the nature of a nonentity! This much is
certain—that no *systematic* treatment of any *strictly*
metaphysical doctrine (on its theoretical side, at least)
is to be found amongst Coleridge's published works.
What it was believed to be (though, again, mainly on
the practical side) by the late Joseph Henry Green we
know from his two volumes (edited by Dr. J. Simon)
on 'Spiritual Philosophy,' recently reviewed in the
columns of the *British Controversialist*. So fully was
the Coleridge-Green system considered in that paper,
and so largely was it exemplified by extracts from
Green's work, that it is unnecessary for me to expound or discuss that system here. I wish it to
be clearly understood, however, 'that the conclusions
I have arrived at, after a long and careful study of
Coleridge's works, are unfavourable to his pretensions.
I believe he made certain German philosophers his
"thinking-ground" (in particular, Lessing and Schel-

---

[1] *E.g.*, 1, vol. i., pp. 7, 154–156, 161, &c.
[2] Ed. 1851, pp. 146 and 329.

ling, and, in a far less degree, Kant, Maasz, and some others), deliberately intending to utilise their work, to stand on their shoulders, to make their germs fructify in his own mind, to scale the philosophic heights with their ladders, or (to employ a phrase of the late Prof. Ferrier) to swim in the philosophic depths with their bladders; and having scaled the one, or (if you will) *approfondi* the other, to kick down the ladders, or puncture the bladders, and thenceforth to set up as climber-in-chief, or swimmer -in-chief, or, to combine both metaphors, as the great explorer of the unknown in *meta*physical geography. This was the *rôle* of a man of great parts; who possessed sublime powers of imagination, and whose intellect, in his chosen walk, was not contemptible, but who was, nevertheless, by defect of constitution or of discipline, *incapable* of excogitating *proprio marte* a philosophy for himself. I believe, then, that Coleridge had no *original* philosophical system, but only the fragments of a system borrowed, without due understanding, and without original elaboration, from some earlier works of Schelling; and that, as a theoretical philosopher, it will henceforth for ever be impossible to reinflate Coleridge's collapsed reputation. Some English philosophers there are, I am quite aware, who are not prepared for the reception of this verdict. They will "for time, times, and half a time," work as if for their very lives at patching up the hole; but the reinflation will be postponed *sine die*.

But there is also a practical philosophy closely allied

to religion. Now in this field I conceive Coleridge's industry to have borne notable fruit; and to this special industry I attribute the remarkable influence which I hold his works to have had on the course of religious thought in England and America. Admitting the shortcomings of Coleridge, and deploring the enormous disproportion which his performance bears to his promise, I still think *this* fault admits of complete explanation without any very disastrous imputation on his morals. In the 'Table Talk'[1] we find him speaking of himself thus:—

"Hamlet's character is the prevalence of the abstract and generalising habit over the practical. He does not want courage, skill, will, opportunity; but every incident sets him thinking: and it is curious, and at the same time strictly natural that Hamlet, who all through the play seems reason itself, should be impelled at last by mere accident to effect his object. *I have a smack of Hamlet myself, if I may say so.*"

This may, perhaps, serve as a key to unlock the problem of Coleridge's stupendous failure. But as a critique on *Hamlet* it is surely at fault. "He does not want will," says Coleridge. Why that's the very thing he does want; else he would not need to be "impelled at last by mere accident to effect his object." I strongly suspect that disease, in the first place, must be credited with Coleridge's indolence and desultoriness of study, producing an idiosyncrasy which opium (such is its perilously subtle influence) only served to strengthen and to disguise; and that, in the second

[1] Ed. 1851, p. 40.

place, the evil is due to the elevation from which he viewed his own relation to the great problems of life. The present Regius Professor of Divinity at Oxford, the Rev. J. B. Mozley, a man of such admirable power and attainment in his faculty, that he has been called "the modern Butler," expresses in the most appropriate terms what I am seeking to convey. He wrote,[1]—

"Persons of the greatest capacity are often those who for this reason do the least ; for, surveying themselves from the highest point of view, amidst the infinite variety of the universe, their own share in it seems trifling, and scarce worth a thought, and they prefer the contemplation of all that is, or has been, or can be, to the making a coil about doing what, when done, is no better than vanity. It is hard to concentrate all our attention and efforts on one pursuit, except from ignorance of others ; and without this concentration of our faculties, no great progress can be made in any one thing. It is not merely that the mind is not capable of the effort ; it does not think the effort worth making."

Here we have both the causes (co-operating with bodily sickness and the somewhat fraudulent habit of mind, which the habitual use of opium unfailingly engenders or confirms) which I conceive to have concurred in rendering Coleridge's intellectual powers so much less productive than they ought to have been, and his actual achievements so disproportionate to his pretensions,

"not answering the aim,
And that unbodied figure of the thought,"

of which he is so often found speaking and writing as of a *fait accompli*. That he could have done better

1 *Christian Remembrancer*, Jan. 1842.

philosophical work than almost any Englishman of his own time I do not deny; but the sort of work he could have done, and I think would have done with a narrower range of tastes, and less self-consciousness, would have borne no proportion to what had been accomplished by the great Germans.

Coleridge's fourteen months' residence in Germany was for him an opening of the eyes. Fancy a poetic Rasselas, who had lived so long in his "happy valley" that he knew and loved every tree within its rocky bourn, till he could interpret the murmured language of its mountain runlets, and felt a yearning towards every little island which was lovingly embraced by the gliding river, or overwhelmed by the swollen torrent. Fancy such a man being taken for the first time to the summit of a glacier-bound Alp, and beholding thence "the kingdoms of the world and the glory of them." Is it wonderful that his heart should sink within him, when he finds how insignificant he is in the midst of creation, how little he can do, and how unsatisfactory it is when done? Is it wonderful that his will should fall before the work which he is invited to accomplish, and that after all the work should be left undone? Is not this a picture of Coleridge the poet growing into Coleridge the philosopher?

Such thoughts were suggested to me on attempting to trace Coleridge's career after his return to England from Malta in the year 1806. In 1807 I find him residing alternately at Nether Stowey with Mr. Thomas

Poole (at whose house he made the acquaintance of
De Quincey), and at Bristol, probably with Cottle.[1]
I have been unable to follow his footsteps in the next
two years, except that he delivered a course of lectures
on Shakespeare at the Royal Institution in 1808,[2] and
that in 1809, on June 8th, the first number of *The
Friend* was published. This we may regard as his
first essay in philosophy. The twenty-seventh and
last number was issued on March 15, 1810.[3] This
work will assuredly live, though its political economy
has been condemned by Mr. J. S. Mill[4] in terms
which I conceive applicable to its metaphysics.[5] To
my mind, the most curious thing in it is the story of
Maria Schöning in the second volume; for I am convinced, on internal evidence, that it contains scarcely
a sentence of Coleridge's writing.[6] In 1810 I find him
residing with Southey at Greta Hall, Keswick,[7] and
then with Basil Montagu. His irregular habits at
Montagu's were so disturbing to that quiet household,
that the host found it expedient to remonstrate with
his eccentric guest, which led to a rupture. The result was, that Coleridge left in dudgeon and removed
to lodgings at Hammersmith; thence he went by
invitation to reside with a Mr. Morgan at Calne. In
this grateful retirement he wrote his *Biographia
Literaria*, and composed, or perhaps I should say
completed his *latest* and *last* poetical work of any pre-

---

[1] 22, vol. ii., pp. 74 and 134.   [2] 28, p. 333.
[3] 28, pp. 187 and 190.   [4] 47, p. 452.   [5] 35, p. 9.
      [6] 34, p. 7.   [7] 28, p. 261.

tensions, viz., 'Zapolya.' These, as I said, were
published six or seven years later.

I have stated what is to me the most curious thing
in *The Friend*. I will now notify what is to me the most
curious thing in the *Biographia Literaria*: it is the
enormously long letter which almost constitutes Chapter
XIII., and is put there as the moving cause why that
chapter was not written! This letter purports to be
addressed to the poet by "a friend whose practical
judgment," says Coleridge, "I have had ample reason
to estimate [? esteem] and revere, and whose taste and
sensibility," &c., in reply to one from the poet asking
that friend's opinion on the expediency of the proposed
chapter. If the chapter was not written, how could
this friend give any opinion upon it, *à fortiori*, such an
elaborate and detailed opinion as he does give? That
would be a *crux* indeed but for the fact that the friend
knew intuitively what that chapter was (not) to be;
for he was none other than Coleridge himself—his own
best friend; like Mr. Noah Claypole's "number one,"
in 'Oliver Twist.' The simple fact is this: Coleridge
was not prepared to write a chapter on such a subject
as that announced at the head of Chapter XIII.; and
he wrote this letter to serve as a plausible excuse for
not doing so, and a means of making his readers believe
that he had written and withdrawn it. To make this
the more plausible, he refers them to a "detailed
prospectus" of the chapter which is to be given at the
end of the second volume. This was "going rayther too
far," as Mr. Weller, senior, expresses it; for Coleridge's

incapacity to write the chapter was gross and total, and even *teetotal*, embracing an inability to furnish the prospectus : which accordingly is as much a nonentity as the chapter "on the imagination or esemplastic faculty."

During the period from 1810 to 1816, I have not been able to follow Coleridge with any constancy or detail. In 1811–12[1] he delivered a course of twelve lectures on Shakespeare and Milton, at the Scottish Corporation Hall, Crane Court, Fleet Street. These are the lectures which Mr. J. P. Collier professed to have taken down in shorthand, of which notes the volume published by him in 1856 professes to contain *verbatim* copies. But the whole thing was exploded by Mr. A. E. Brae, of Leeds, in a pamphlet, entitled 'Collier, Coleridge, and Shakespeare,' in which he proves that the lectures published by Mr. Collier are fabrications ; and the late Mr. Herbert Coleridge told me that he regarded them as "apocryphal."[2] In the year 1811, too, Coleridge delivered a course on the same subject to the London Philosophical Society, the first of which was on November 18.[3] In 1814 he lectured at Bristol,[4] and at the Surrey Institution in London. During these six years, too, I gather that Coleridge's consumption of laudanum was excessive ; in fact, his health began to suffer so much alternately from the abuse of

[1] 28, p. 262.
[2] It is unfortunate that Mr. Hort, in 32, adduces one of these spurious lectures as the sufficient evidence of an important date,
[3] 28, p. 352 ; 15, p. 52 ; 1, vol. ii., p. 220.
[4] *Quarterly Review*, vol. cvii., p. 480.

laudanum and from his efforts to discontinue the practice, that he called in Dr. Adams, by whose introduction he made the acquaintance of Mr. James Gillman.

In the month of April 1816, Coleridge called upon Gillman, who resided in the Grove, Highgate, and made a proposal for his being domiciled there, in order that he might be restrained from the excessive use of opium. He warned Gillman that though prior habits had rendered it out of his power to tell an untruth, he dared not promise that he "should not, with regard to this detested poison, be capable of acting one." On Monday, April 15th, 1816, he became an inmate of Gillman's house; and, with the exception of somewhat rare visits to Ramsgate, Cambridge, and some other places, the Grove was his constant residence till death. Up to a few years since, many a stranger has made a pilgrimage to this spot, and been shown Coleridge's study, religiously preserved in exactly the same state as it was in his lifetime. But all that is changed now. Even the old-fashioned dormer-windows in the top story have given place to an execrable modern structure of sashes: and but for the specific instructions which were given me by another Highgate celebrity (now no longer resident there) I should never have dreamed that this hideous, staring, topheavy piece of cockneyism was the shrine of that Ancient Mariner, who, in De Quincey's words, had "cruised on the broad Atlantic of Kant and Schelling."

From the time of Coleridge's removal to Highgate, his life was uneventful. In 1817 he delivered his

second course of Lectures on Shakespeare at the Royal
Institution;[1] and some time later, a single lecture
to the London Philosophical Society, 'On the Growth
of the Individual Mind,' the subject of which seems
to have been chosen for him immediately before the
lecture was spoken.[2] In 1818 he delivered three courses
—one on the 'Choice of Books,' in Fleur-de-Lis Court,
Fetter Lane;[3] one elsewhere on the 'History of Philosophy,' 'Works,' vol. xiii., as well as Charles Lamb's
exquisite squib, 'Letter to an Old Gentleman whose
Education has been neglected,' and one on the 'English
Dramatists' at the Crown and Anchor. Other courses
he delivered later, at Willis's Rooms, and at the Russell
Institution.

It was on January 26, 1818, after delivering one of
the lectures on the English Dramatists, that a young
man among the audience stepped forth and requested
his advice on the best means of remedying the faults of
a neglected education. This was Mr. Thomas Alsop.
Coleridge's kindness to the stranger emboldened Mr.
Alsop to write to him the next day, with a present of
game; and thus began that strange and eventful intimacy between them which gave us the two remarkable
volumes of 'Letters' and 'Table-Talk,' standing at the
head of my biographical list, and also, I think, the
'Letters to a Young Man,' &c., by De Quincey.

Coleridge's habits and health were now such as to
preclude him from really hard work: besides it was, in

---

[1] *Quarterly Review*, vol. cvii. p. 480.   [2] 28, p. 354.

[3] 1, vol. ii., p. 80

any case, too late for him to make up lee-way. It is not surprising that during the sixteen years of life which remained to him, he did not redeem the magnificent promise which he was always holding forth to his disciples and friends, and which he ratified even in his published works. Fragments of a philosophical system, indeed, are found in *The Friend*, the *Biographia Literaria*, and the 'Theory of Life:' but they are little else than translations from Schelling.

Those sixteen years, however, were not wasted. He dictated to the late Mr. Joseph Henry Green one large volume on 'The Dynamic Philosophy;' to Mr. Seth B. Watson the essay on 'The Theory of Life;' to the late Mr. Stutfield, a fragment on Logic, which is still in the possession of that gentleman's widow. Finally he dictated some portions of a 'History of Philosophy' to the late eminent scholar and poet, the Right Hon. John Hookham Frere, who took them down in shorthand. This manuscript and the volume on the Dynamic Philosophy are, I believe, at present at Hadley, near Barnet, in the custody of Mrs. Green. Both were adjudged by Mr. Green, as Coleridge's sole executor, to be unfitted for publication. We know that as to the latter Coleridge thought differently. He tells Mr. Alsop that it was dictated to Mr. Green "so as to exist fit for the press." [1] Be that as it may, he invested Mr. Green, by his will, with absolute discretion as to the publication of his manuscripts; so that Mr. Green's verdict can be impeached only on the ground of his

[1] I, vol. i., p. 156.

want of judgment. But for one thing I hold him to have been not free from blame—that he used the materials of the manuscript volume for the purpose of completing his own 'Spiritual Philosophy.' His reason for doing this was, I think, a conscientious desire to give Coleridge's "system" a logical consistency, so that the public mind might be prepared for the disclosure (inevitable in course of time) of the fragmentary views contained in the unpublished manuscripts. Here, however, his sanguine temperament led him astray; for there never was any prospect of his own work attaining that popularity which even the name of Coleridge (so potent a spell in the promotion of his kinsfolk)[1] has failed to do for the 'Theory of Life.'

Other works more directly bearing on Divinity were written or dictated by Coleridge during this period. The more important of these were 'Two Lay Sermons,' 'Aids to Reflection,' 'Constitution of Church and State,' and 'Confessions of an Inquiring Spirit.' The last was a posthumous publication, edited by Mr. Green.

It was most unfortunate that Gillman did not write the second volume of his 'Life of Coleridge' before the first; or that he did not live to accomplish the former, and complete his work; for with the exception of the last few pages, his solitary Volume I. is of very little value; for the materials were necessarily taken at second-hand, and are presented in a singularly slipshod manner; besides which the anecdotes are mere

[1] I, vol. i., p. 225.

travesties, and many of the particulars inaccurate. Whereas the materials for his Volume II. would have been the record of his own experiences of the last eighteen years of Coleridge's life, and would therefore, despite the faults of authorship, have had an abiding value. As it is, of those years we have no record whatever. What the late Henry Nelson Coleridge might have done to supply the defect we know nothing; for he died after writing a mere fragment of the biography he was attempting, and which is printed at the end of the second volume of the *Biographia Literaria.*[1] The additional chapters added by his accomplished and admirable wife, Sara (the poet's only daughter), afford but few biographical facts.[2] In truth the somewhat sudden death of all those who, among Coleridge's relatives and friends, could have completed his biography, leave us at the mercy of mere "anecdotage," which too often is found dispensing with the first two syllables.

This is my all-sufficient apology for the meagreness of my own account. I can venture on the allegation of only one fact more in Coleridge's life; viz. that he attended the meeting of the British Association at Cambridge in June 1833; and that this was the occasion of the remarkable monoloquial display described by the Bishop of St. David's in the preceding essay.[3] He died July 25th, 1834.

Pursuing my prescribed plan, I proceed to a brief

---

[1] 17.   [2] 19.

[3] 3, p. 1. The correct title is, 'Conversations *at* Cambridge.'

consideration of some of the work performed by Coleridge during the period of his domestication with the Gillmans. I considered him in the preceding essay as the Poet; in *this*, as the Divine. According to my judgment, what he wrote in that capacity has had an enormous influence on religious belief, and possesses an abiding value. It was provoked under two impulses; (1) to satisfy the legitimate wants of his own moral nature, sorely tried and even broken down as it was by his own repeated backslidings, and his inability to emancipate himself from the bondage of a vicious habit; (2) to supply a grave and pressing intellectual want common to all thoughtful men of his own times, viz., the means of holding to certain religious verities and facts in man's nature, while questioning alleged facts in sacred history, and inferences therefrom inconsistent with our primary ethical notions.

As to (1)—I remark that Gillman protests against the justice of Coleridge's designation of his opium-habits as a vice; asserting that his moral weakness was the result of disease, which made the craving too strong for him to resist. We are thus plunged at once into the vexing and vexed question[1] of moral guilt, in cases where habits inconsiderately, if not innocently established, or strong inherited tendencies, have subjugated the moral will. I am disposed to admit the justice of Coleridge's designation. His habit was a *vice* in two senses. It was a physical vice in the same

---

[1] *Quæstio vexata* is a question that has been much tossed about or canvassed. The phrase is often greatly misapplied.

sense in which we speak of the vice of a malicious or nervous horse. Any physical fact which carries a man beyond self-control is a *vice*, even though it were unjust to impute to him a corresponding degree of guilt. Coleridge's habit was also a moral vice. He was fully alive to the mischief of the submission of his will to the physical demand, and to the consequential injury to his bodily, mental, and moral health. Moreover, being very sensitive and contemplative, he had the advantage, such as it is, of stating to himself the whole nature and scope of the evil, and was able to devise the most likely means of procuring his liberation. In the face of all which he would stoop to the grossest deception, and resort to the meanest artifices, in order to procure a supply of that "detested poison" which he had solemnly and prayerfully resolved to adjure. Such an experience may be common; I believe it is. But surely it argues the utmost moral devastation in him who is self-abandoned to the Dantean hell of fierce extremes, throbbing for ever between both, without power of rest or means of extrication.

As to (2)—The doctrines of Christianity, as they were usually expounded, not only in Coleridge's day, but centuries before, were open to many rational objections; not the captious cavils of evil or crotchety persons, but the reasoned objections of those who set the highest value on intellectual and moral truth. In fact, the objections to which I refer grew out of the great ideal of a personal God, out of the moral principle itself, and out of its supporting emotions of benevolence and self-respect. Coleridge's faith had once been shaken by these very considerations. He had renounced the Tri-unity of the Godhead, the Atonement of Christ, and the use of Prayer. But he grew out of these objections, lived them down and reasoned them down, and found at length that it was not the Bible that was at fault, but the foregone conclusion set forth by divines as.to its peculiar origin and nature, and the strained and literal interpretations which they had put upon its utterances. Accordingly he addressed himself to the work of destroying certain mischievous dogmas, and vindicating anew the impeached doctrines of the New Testament. In his own words (borrowed from Holy Scripture) he endeavoured not so much to destroy as to fulfil. He was, in fact, the great pioneer in that work which has been carried on by so many divines since his time ; among which we reckon J. C. Hare, Dr. Arnold, Bunsen, Dean Stanley, and others as great and good as they were.

Coleridge attempted to perform this delicate task by demanding a secure position between those of the *literalising* and *allegorising* divines. This he found in the great doctrine of the *symbol*, as being alike distinct from the *fact* and the *metaphor*. He thus established the *tautegory*, as the correlate of the *allegory*. The allegory is so named because it finds a superficial and often illusory resemblance between two facts or events of different genera : then the tautegory would be an *essential likeness*, a *substantial identity* between two

Q

distinct and differing facts or events that are of one genus. It is by this fundamental distinction between allegorical and tautegorical figures, that he expounds the chief doctrines of Christianity, certain of them, as regeneration, being figured tautegorically; others, as the redemptive work of Christ, being figured allegorically. I will briefly consider the latter, as a sample of Coleridge's work.

He contends that when Christ's work is described in Holy Scripture as a *sacrifice for committed sin, an atonement or reconciliation between man and God, a redemption of the soul from the bondage of original sin, a liquidation of an infinite debt due from man to God,* or as a washing of the sinner's conscience from moral taint, or even as a penalty inflicted on Christ for man's violation of the law, and imputed to man—these descriptions (which are not only various and discrepant, but *incompossible,* and quite inconsistent with one another) are mere allegories or metaphors, intended to convey to man some notion of the consequential benefit he receives by virtue of Christ's life and death, and not at all substantive figures or tautegories, whereby man may learn the nature of the act itself, which is efficient in bringing upon man that benefit. Of course such an interpretation sweeps away at a blow the whole machinery of (so-called) *evangelical* exegesis, together with the point, so often insisted on, that Christ's death was a veritable oblation offered up to, and accepted by the Father, and also a penalty inflicted on him by the Father for our sakes.

This particular "aid to reflection" must prove at least of great negative advantage to Christian faith. Evangelical divines have fastened on Christ's "work" such absurd, incongruous, and repulsive features, for which Holy Scripture gives no countenance whatever, that it must be felt as a great relief when we find that those features are a travesty of a mere allegory, one among many employed by the apostles, with the aim of enforcing the *inestimable value* of that "work,"

"Whose worth's unknown, although his height be taken." [1]

Thus it is said that "the blood of Jesus Christ cleanseth us from all sin;" that He "washed us from our sins in His own blood;" and that the souls of the saved had "washed their robes and made them white in the blood of the Lamb." Divines of the school referred to have not hesitated to take these phrases as veritable symbols, good to the minutest detail for a representation of Christ's "work." Accordingly, they are never tired of insisting on the cleansing power of Christ's blood. The majority, however, mean by this no more than a Jew would understand by the sprinkling of sacrificial blood for purification; but even this would be to take the figure as tautegorical, instead of being, what all such figures must necessarily be (since the redemptive work transcends all understanding), a mere allegory. [2]

---

[1] Shakespeare's Sonnet çxvi.

[2] Some have gone the length of insisting on the appropriateness of an image which is not to be found in the whole length and breadth of the Bible, viz., that the soul is *to be* plunged into the stream or fountain

A ludicrous sophism fastened upon Professor Fawcett in Ruskin's periodical work, *Fors Clavigera*, is called by that writer "the position of William." In imitation of Ruskin, I will call an illustration adduced by Coleridge, in refutation of the literal interpretation of any of those figures, "the position of James." Coleridge says :—

"A sum of £1000 is owing from James to Peter, for which James had given a bond in judgment. He is insolvent, and the bond is on the point of being carried into effect, to James's certain ruin. At this moment Matthew steps in, pays Peter the £1000, and discharges the bond. In this case no man would hesitate to admit that a complete *satisfaction* had been made to Peter." [He then puts the case that James had been guilty of the basest and most hard-hearted ingratitude to a most worthy and affectionate mother, &c. He then supposes a friend to step in and discharge all the offices of a son to her ; saying,] "Now I trust you are appeased, and will be henceforth reconciled to James. I have satisfied all your claims on him : I have paid his debt in full ; and you are too just to require the same debt to be paid twice over. You will therefore regard him with the same

of Christ's blood in order to be cleansed from sin ! So sang poor Cowper, when residing at Olney, under the influence of John Newton :—

> "There is a fountain filled with blood
>   Drawn from Immanuel's veins ;
> And sinners plunged beneath the flood
>   Are washed from all their stains."

We read in Holy Scripture of a water-baptism, of a Spirit-baptism, and of a fire-baptism, but not of a blood-baptism ; which is so revolting an image that one would have thought, apart from its unscriptural nature, it would have always provoked more loathing than liking. Besides, the language is open to grave exception : for a "fountain" is the spring or source ; and of that one may not say that it is full or empty, but that it flows or fails. Strange as it may appear, this shocking hymn, breathing of Cowper's unhappy malady, has been admitted into most of the collections used in Anglican churches.

complacency, and receive him into your presence with the same love as if there had been no difference between him and you. For I have *made it up*."

Coleridge draws hence the grand distinction between things and persons in respect to *satisfaction*, and demands that when "the position of James," in the *latter* case, is called one of indebtedness, that shall be taken as a metaphor or allegory borrowed from the *former*, but possessing no features of essential likeness. In the first edition (1825) of the 'Aids to Reflection,' appended to pages 323-325 (where the point is argued at length), is a long footnote, detailing the case of Angelini, who offered his own life in lieu of Fontleroy's when the latter was sentenced to be hanged for forgery. It seems that the Lord Mayor, to whom Angelini addressed his singular request, told him that "it was contrary to all justice that the life of an *innocent* person should be taken to save that of one who was guilty, even if the innocent man chose to devote himself." But when Angelini adduced, in refutation of this argument, the example of our Saviour, he was told that it could not be so, because he (Angelini) was not *absolutely innocent*. The Lord Mayor of that day did not see that his surrejoinder destroyed his replication. But he had the excuse that he had not mastered "the position of James," *i.e.*, if excuse be needed; for it seems to me that the contradiction is merely verbal. I have called attention to this curious footnote, because it bears on the question of editorship; for it has been bodily omitted from all editions published since

Coleridge's death, and it is not stated, by any of the editors, on what authority, or on what ground, the omission was made.

Such was Coleridge's doctrine of the symbol. Its value is unquestionable; but evidently its reach is restricted to the enunciations of doctrine. But the greater part of scriptural difficulties spring out of an apparent (if not real) clash between the Book and either ethics or science (physical or historical), and evidently all such difficulties involve the question of the authority of Holy Scripture. To this question Coleridge addressed himself in his 'Confessions of an Inquiring Spirit,' being six letters on the inspiration of the Scriptures. In the fourth letter he addresses an imaginary friend in these remarkable words:—

"Friend! the truth revealed through Christ has its evidence in itself, and the proof of its divine authority in [? is] its fitness to our nature and needs;—the clearness and cogency of this proof being proportionate to the degree of self-knowledge in each individual hearer. Christianity has likewise its historical evidences, and these as strong as is [*sic*] compatible with the nature of history, and with the aims and objects of a religious dispensation. And to all these Christianity itself, as an existing power in the world, and Christendom as an existing fact, with the no less evident fact of a progressive expansion, give a force of moral demonstration that almost supersedes particular testimony. These proofs and evidences would remain unshaken, even though the sum of our religion were to be drawn from the theologians of each successive century on the principle of receiving that only as divine which should be found in all,—*quod semper, quod ubique, quod ab omnibus*. Be only, my friend, as orthodox a believer as you would have abundant reason to be, though from some accident of birth, country, or education, the precious boon of the Bible, with its additional evidence, had up to this moment been

concealed from you; and then read its contents with only the
same piety which you freely accord on other occasions to the
writings of men, considered the best and wisest of their several
ages! What you find therein coincident with your pre-estab-
lished convictions you will of course recognise as the Revealed
Word, while as you read the recorded workings of the Word and
the Spirit in the minds, lives, and hearts of spiritual men, the
influence of the same Spirit on your own being, and the conflicts
of grace and infirmity in your own soul, will enable you to
discern and to know in and by what spirit they spake and acted,
—as far at least as shall be needful for you, and in the times of
your need.

" Thenceforward, therefore, your doubts will be confined to such
parts or passages of the received canon as seem to you irreconcil-
able with known truths, and at variance with the tests given in
the Scriptures themselves, and as shall continue so to appear
after you have examined each in reference to the circumstances
of the Writer or Speaker, the dispensation under which he lived,
the purpose of the particular passage, and the intent and object
of the Scriptures at large. Respecting these, decide for yourself : and fear not for the result. . . . [The apparent
exceptions to the fidelity of the Canon] will be found neither
more nor greater than may well be supposed requisite, on the
one hand, to prevent us from sinking into a habit of slothful,
undiscriminating acquiescence, and, on the other, to provide a
check against those presumptuous fanatics who would . . .
frame oracles by private divination from each letter of each
disjointed gem, uninterpreted by the priest, and deserted by the
Spirit which shines in the parts only as it pervades and irradiates
the whole." [1]

---

[1] This looks like a tacit allusion to the text of 2 Pet. i. 20, 21, where
undoubtedly the words translated "private interpretation" present a
great difficulty. The context suggests that the expression should be
private divination; and a learned friend points out to me, while I am
writing this paper, that not improbably ἐπιλύσεως is an error for
ἐπηλύσεως. This conjecture is felicitous, for επηλυσίη in the Homeric
hymns, &c., means *enchantment;* while the confusion between η and ι
in late Greek is the commonest of mistakes. It is now beyond the
shadow of a doubt that in the somewhat similar passage in 2 Tim. iii.
16, the conjunction copulative καὶ has no business there.

All this is a careful feeling after the principle which Coleridge enunciates and supports at length in the sixth letter, viz., " that it is the spirit of the Bible, and not the detached words and sentences, that is infallible and absolute," a principle which implicitly disallows a plenary or verbal inspiration, and is consistent with the admission of various degrees of value in the various parts of the canon, as, for instance, that Jael could not have been blessed in her deed of treachery, and that it is of little or no importance to us to know that St. Paul left his cloak at Troas.

There is, indeed, nothing at all profound in these letters, nothing whatever to make one believe that the writer was a great philosopher; but they present an agreeable association of sound sense and eloquent language. The really important distinction indicated by Coleridge is that between *private divination*, or, perhaps, personal illumination, which may endlessly differ with different 'minds, and that catholic inspiration of God's Spirit which is one and the same for all inspired writers. The former is subjective, the latter objective. If we can but once for all be sure that the objects and purposes of that inspiration are the regeneration and conversion of man as a moral and responsible being, the foothold which Coleridge offers for faith seems sure enough; for then it matters not if the Scriptures are repugnant to each other in historical points, or that they are antagonistic to the results of physical science, for in his view those are matters on which the sacred penman need not have been inspired. I am far from asserting that this is a satisfactory conclusion, or that it is free from difficulty. I ought to add that from first to last Coleridge is opposed to that worship of the letter of the Bible which he was the first to call *bibliolatry*.

Space now fails me for the further illustration of his services to the cause of sound religious faith. For these sketches of Coleridge the poet, and Coleridge the divine, I must solicit the largest indulgence. It is not easy to trace Coleridge through the later years of his life; and it is a task of prodigious difficulty to epitomise the character and genius of so eccentric a being. It is a common saying, thirty or forty years after an eminent man is dead, that "he has been vastly overrated." It is said of Johnson, of Goethe, of Scott, of Coleridge, and many others. Will time bring about its revenges? It is curious that the larger number of men of mark do not attain an adequate popularity, nor to any just appreciation, till they have been many years dead. But there is a minority, consisting of men who were illustrious in their lifetime, each of whom lived to see his lustre culminate, and left behind him the waning track of an exploded meteor. Of such was Coleridge. I have done my little best to estimate his worth as poet, and as philosopher. I have rated him very high in the one character, and very low in the other: at the same time I have allowed the influence of his religious writings on his own generation, and on that which succeeded him. If I have ever found it hard to determine with firmness his moral worth, I have never doubted the intensity of his human sympathy. He had certainly a warm heart as well as an aspiring intellect. Whenever I read his letter to Lamb on the tragedy which embittered Lamb's life, yet moulded to highest excellence his character, it is "borne on my mind" that Coleridge was a good man ; and that clear verdict I have now no temptation to qualify by the faintest echo of doubt. In conclusion, I will apply to Coleridge his own words :—

"Take him in his whole—his head, his heart, his wishes, his innocence of all selfish crime—and . . . what will be the result ? The good—were it but a single volume that made truth more visible, and goodness more lovely, and pleasure at once more akin to virtue, and, self-doubled, more pleasurable !—and the evil,—while he lived, it injured none but himself; and where is it now ? In his grave. Follow it not thither."

[1] Lit. Rem., vol. i., p. 368.

XI

AN ESTIMATE OF WORDSWORTH.

WORDSWORTH has been dead thirty-two years; for upwards of fifty, during a lifetime of fourscore years, he wrote poetry, the great bulk of which was, so far as we know, fondly cherished by its author, and printed, and reprinted with more or less anxious emendation, in the innumerable editions of his poems. We know, however, that verses written by him very late in life, and probably others that he composed in early youth, have never been included in his published works, though printed to serve an occasional purpose. It is scarcely disputed that much of what he so included has been a detriment to his reputation; yet, notwithstanding that drawback, his fame has been steadily on the increase during those thirty-two years; and at the present time, both in England and America, he has been placed upon an eminence which to many thoughtful critics seems invidious and unjust. By the late Professor Henry Reed and Mr. Matthew Arnold he is placed above Byron. Mr. Reed's judgment was probably biassed by the unhealthy tone of much that proceeded from Byron's genius: indeed he carries his

abhorrence of that profanity, which dares to consecrate
in poesy its rebellious aspirations—to desecrate poesy
thereby, he would say—that he bodily excludes Shelley
from the roll of British poets! It is well to be grateful for the smallest favours; and assuredly, after seeing
in what fashion he drags Byron before his own private
court martial, where (as Hood says of the 'Last Man,')
" He was judge and jury and all," we were thankful
that Mr. Reed ignored Shelley's existence altogether.
It was in good taste, at least, to spare that "bright
but ineffectual angel." On the contrary, Mr. Matthew
Arnold's sympathies are with every honest rebel
against " Anarch Custom; " and if he is ever drawn
aside from the golden line of justice to give Wordsworth more than his due, the kindly aberration is
prompted by the enthusiasm of private feelings. To
have associated with Wordsworth in his home, and
among the solitudes of Rydal woods and mountains,
could hardly have failed to prejudice in his favour the
mind and feelings of the younger poet; and we more
often find ourselves in disagreement with Mr. Arnold's
deliverances when they praise, than when they blame
the compositions of Wordsworth.

The establishment of Professor Knight's " Wordsworth Society," and the more recent estimates of those
compositions by Mr. Matthew Arnold, and by a writer
in the last *Quarterly Review*, invite us to a renewed
study of what has proved so fertile a subject of criticism
and controversy. The greatness of Wordsworth may
be taken for granted; for it would be easy to select

from the abounding results of his industry, a considerable quantity of poetry, which should incontestably prove him to be one of the greatest poets of the century. Perhaps his 'Lines composed a few miles above Tintern Abbey' is at once the most exquisite and the most representative of all; to that may be added the somewhat artificial, but still superb, 'Ode on the Intimations of Immortality in Early Childhood;' and the still more artificial and more ambitious poem called 'Laodamia;' that simple and finely balanced narrative of 'The Leech Gatherer,' and, though in our judgment somewhat inferior, 'Michael;' and of the shorter pieces, 'To a Highland Girl,' 'She was a phantom of delight,' 'Three years she grew,' 'I wander'd lonely as a cloud,' 'Elegiac Stanzas on Peele Castle,' 'Yew Trees,' and 'Nutting;' all intensely beautiful: to which some still slighter pieces might be added, as 'To the Cuckoo,' 'The Longest Day,' 'The Solitary Reaper,' 'Lucy Gray,' and the verses 'To the Nightingale,' and 'On the Skylark' (the shorter of the two so named), and others of less, but still of decided merit. To read and appreciate those poems only, is to concur in the verdict which has placed Wordsworth upon one of the very few thrones reserved for English poets of the nineteenth century.

Doubtless, in order to present Wordsworth fairly to a reader who comes fresh to the study of his works, a much larger number of his poems should be selected than the seventeen we have adduced; but in our view, the danger in making a representative selection is not that of too great restriction, but of including poems of small merit, whose presence can only mar the effect of the rest, and dim the glory of the poet.

It is perhaps true that no critic, however able, is competent to make a selection for another—which is another way of saying, that at present the critics have not arrived at an objective judgment. We agree with the writer in the *Quarterly Review* that Mr. Arnold's selection from Wordsworth is insufficiently select, and that we should be the gainers by the omission of much that he has included. Perhaps, too, we should add several poems and extracts which are not given in his volume. The justification of large omissions lies in a fact which is almost peculiar to Wordsworth, as one of the great poets, namely, the astounding inequality of his workmanship. Mr. Arnold thus remarks upon it in the 'Introduction' to his selection (pp. xii.–xiii.) :

"His best work is in his shorter pieces, and many indeed are there of these which are of first-rate excellence. But in his seven volumes, the pieces of high merit are mingled with a mass of pieces very inferior to them ; so inferior to them, that it seems wonderful how the same poet could have produced both. . . . Work altogether inferior, work quite uninspired, flat and dull, is produced by him with evident unconsciousness of its defects, and he presents it to us with the same faith and seriousness as his best work. In reading Wordsworth, the impression made by one of his fine pieces is too often dulled and spoiled by a very inferior piece coming after it."

This is indeed quite true; and is a reason for re-arrangement, rather than for such a selection as Mr. Arnold has given us. We except to one phrase, "His

best work is *in* his shorter pieces." This may mean
either of two things: but, not to be hypercritical, we
will say that we find much of Wordsworth's best work
in what we understand by his longer pieces, and some
of his worst *in* certain of his shorter pieces. Further,
admitting the stern necessity of liberal exclusion if
ever the general reader is to appreciate the consummate
greatness of Wordsworth, we must say that the reason
adduced fails to account for the presence of no small
number of inferior pieces in Mr. Arnold's volume.
Such inferior work, as 'Anecdote for Fathers,' 'The
Childless Father,' 'The Power of Music,' 'The Star-
gazers,' and some others, could hardly be excused in
any collection: for these stand on a very different footing from 'Goody Blake and Harry Gill,' 'The Idiot
Boy,' and 'Peter Bell.' Wordsworth usually writes
with absolute fidelity and decorum. Many of his
subjects, indeed, are (in our view at least) utterly
unsuitable for poetical treatment. We will shortly
illustrate this remark in the example of 'Goody Blake
and Harry Gill.' Mean or poor thoughts are expressed
in mean or poor language: dignified or exalted thoughts,
in dignified or exalted language; and so dear was
nature to this poet, that he never touches her, be it ever
so gently (see last two lines of 'Nutting'), slightly, or
incidentally, but his verse becomes instinct with natural
beauty, and is fraught with a subtle power to call up
in us the gladness, melancholy, or reverence which she
occasioned in him. This is as it should be. A reader
is always quite safe in dismissing from serious considera-

tion a piece expressed in prosaic or puerile language;
for whenever the treatment is prosaic or puerile, the
subject is so too, and it may " go by the board." But
when all this truly inferior work is omitted (as it is in
Mr. Arnold's selection), there still remains much work
worse than inferior (in Mr. Arnold's sense), downright
bad work, which unhappily confronts us in his ' Select
Poems of Wordsworth,' side by side with the best, and
we seem driven to apply to the critic the remark he
makes on the poet, that he is unconscious of the *enormous*
difference between the downright bad and the absolutely
good.   In fact, the ' Select Poems ' presents on a smaller
scale the offensive and injurious contrast which Mr.
Arnold complains of in Wordsworth's seven volumes.
But this complaint, which doubtless justifies the omission of such nursery verses as ' Goody Blake and Harry
Gill,' is not the worst that can be said on the subject
of Wordsworth's *inequality*.   Seeing that he mixes up
in a hopelessly confusing fashion his earlier and his
later poems, it is scarcely worth remark, that " pieces
of high merit " are mingled with " inferior work," except
for the purpose of recommending such an edition of
Wordsworth as, we understand, Professor Knight is at
present engaged upon, namely, one that shall present
the poems in chronological order.   The one fact really
worth considering in this matter of *inequality* is, that
in one and the same piece, where the workmanship is
generally inferior, a single verse in the middle or at the
end, or perhaps only a single line, may be found in
splendid contrast or relief, like a cloud glowing in full

sunlight, while the rest of the cloud-world is in deepest shade; and in such cases we cannot help inferring that the author is unconscious of the astounding inequality, or rather of the disproportion, between the inspired verse and the prevailing insipid, dull, and puerile verbiage which constitutes the tissue of the poem. The writer in the *Quarterly Review* incidentally points out one instance of this peculiarity in 'The Song at the Feast of Brougham Castle,' of which the prevailing language is "equally poor and unpoetical," but which contains this verse of solitary beauty :

> " Love had he found in huts where poor men lie ;
> His daily teachers had been woods and rills,
> The silence that is in the starry sky,
> The sleep that is among the lonely hills,"

of which the third line recalls one of the loveliest lines in Byron—

> "To mingle with the quiet of her sky."

Again, in 'The Idiot Boy,' in the midst of such twaddle as the following :

> " And Susan's growing worse and worse,
> And Betty's in a sad *quandary* ;
> And then there's nobody to say
> If she must go, or she must stay !
> She's in a sad *quandary*."

—in fact, embedded in a morass of eighty-nine of such stanzas, we come upon this gem :

> " By this the stars were almost gone,
> The moon was setting on the hill,

R

> So pale you scarcely looked at her :
> The little birds began to stir,
> Though yet their tongues were still."

Surely, no poet ever wrote a more simple, graceful,
and touching description of the edge of night—on the
side towards daybreak. Not more stirring, if more
numerous, are the poetical oases in ' Peter Bell ; ' " that
sandy desert of verse," for which its creator had a
profound admiration, as well as fatherly affection ; for
which he claimed, in the preface, a permanent place
in English literature, and which he actually defended
from critical assault in a sonnet. In this waste, at
last we come upon the following stanzas of startling
beauty ; the hero

> " reach'd
> A spot where in a sheltering cove,
> A little chapel stands alone,
> With greenest ivy overgrown,
> And tufted with an ivy grove ;
> Dying insensibly away
> From human thoughts and purposes
> It seem'd—wall, window, roof, and tower—
> To bow to some transforming power,
> And blend with the surrounding trees."

Can anything be more poetical in conception and
expression ? Still later we find another gem : the
hero now is

> " taught to feel
> That man's heart is a holy thing ;
> And Nature, through a world of Death,
> Breathes into him a second breath,
> More searching than the breath of Spring."

Surely no poet ever wrote more worthily !

But last—whether least or not—we take 'Goody Blake and Harry Gill.' We hold 'The Idiot Boy' and 'Peter Bell' self-condemned on the ground of the subject. We devoutly believe that the great poet did all that poet could do for such subjects : indeed he seems to have almost glorified 'Peter Bell,' by occasional touches of natural beauty, and chiefly the lovely stanzas we have quoted. We do not wonder that Mr. Matthew Arnold can read it "with pleasure and edification" (the two last words were first added in the reprint of the *Macmillan* article, July 1879, where we find "with pleasure," only). We should rather wonder if any poet could read 'Peter Bell' without being profoundly touched by what is so lovely and affecting in some of the stanzas—alas! too few, "like angels' visits." But when we come to 'Goody Blake and Harry Gill,' we are not solicitous to inquire whether Mr. Arnold obtained either pleasure or edification there. Here is an early verse, which we commend to the extreme clique of Wordsworthians :

> "In March, December, and in July,
>   'Tis all the same with Harry Gill ;
>   The neighbours tell, and tell you truly,
>   His teeth they chatter, chatter still.
>   At night, at morning, and at noon,
>   'Tis all the same with Harry Gill,
>   Beneath the sun, beneath the moon,
>   His teeth they chatter, chatter still !"

"Delightful iteration!" we can imagine that clique to ejaculate. We, on our part, are content to leave the stanza to speak for itself; merely remarking that

Wordsworth was quite sane when he wrote it; and that at that very time he was quite capable of writing good poetry. He chose a subject utterly unsuitable for poetic treatment, and he treated it *as such* in unpoetic (*i.e.*, in prosaic and puerile) language, even to the confusion of accent and quantity. When he does come upon a touch of nature, he is thoroughly himself, as in this stanza:

> "Remote from shelter'd village green,
> On a hill's northern side she dwelt,
> Where from sea-blasts the hawthorns lean,
> And hoary dews are slow to melt."

And again, in this:

> "The moon was full and shining clearly,
> And crisp with frost the stubble land,"

either of which gives us a perfect and beautiful picture.

The story of 'Goody Blake and Harry Gill' is unsuitable for serious poetic treatment, because its interest is mean and vulgar, and its critical situations humorous and funny. Even in the homely and serious drapery with which Wordsworth has clothed it, it is provocative of irreverent feelings, and the fun is none the slower for the attempt to convey a moral of very questionable value. There can be scarcely a farmer, who has not had at one time or another to chastise persons of either sex, for converting his fences into a store of firewood, and for destroying them *fasciatim*. Evidently no farm could prosper if every needy person were to be allowed

to carry off the wood of the fences, night after night, for
fuel; and we must candidly say we sympathise more
with Mr. Gill than with Mrs. Blake, despite all the
poet has done to enlist our feelings on her side. The
critical situation emerges on the night when, after
several unsuccessful night-watchings, Mr. Gill, already
chilled to the marrow of his bones by repeated exposure
to frost and snow, discovers and pounces upon his prey.
We have then the picture of these two persons con-
fronting each other; a young farmer and an old woman
of the labouring class, both as cold as frost and snow
could make them. Then the woman kneels down on
her sticks (or rather *his* sticks), and prays to God that
the man may never more be warm. Well, for matter
of that, Mr. Gill's case has already become more serious
than Mrs. Blake's; for he had contracted a chronic
rigor from his repeated night-watchings; and so there
was small need for the woman's curse. But it is just
the curse that the poet lays most stress on, and to it
he appears to attribute the illness of the farmer; the
moral being—"Farmers, let poor women burn your
fences, lest they curse you, and your teeth chatter like
Harry Gill's."

It is quite another question how Wordsworth came
to choose such a subject for a narrative poem. Its
adoption was probably due to his obstinate adherence,
in the face of provocative criticism, to the letter of the
rules enunciated by him in his prefaces. Indeed, we
cannot but think there was just a touch of spite in the
employment of such violations of poetic propriety as

"July" and "quandary," and in the choice of the most offensively proper names for the characters of his narratives.

But it is not merely in such "inferior work" that Wordsworth's inequality comes out. We see it quite as distinctly in smaller pieces of better workmanship. In the lines 'To Hartley Coleridge, six years old,' the only bit of really fine work is in the last seven lines :

> "Thou art a dewdrop which the morn brings forth,
> Ill fitted to sustain unkindly shocks ;
> Or to be trailed along the soiling earth ;
> A gem that glitters while it lives,
> And no forewarning gives ;
> But at the touch of wrong, without a strife
> Slips in a moment out of life."

A passage of great beauty, distantly recalling the concluding stanza of Mrs. Barbauld's Life, though of very different import. Again, the lines on 'Memory,' which are excluded by Mr. Arnold, has one verse, the last, conceived in the purest spirit of imaginative beauty ; it describes the contentment and serenity of the good, in the retirement of age :—

> "With thoughts as calm as lakes that sleep
> In frosty moonlight glistening,
> Or mountain rivers where they creep
> Along a channel smooth and deep,
> To their own far off murmurs listening."

We have observed a passage of similar imagery in the first chapter of 'Ann of Geierstein ;' but neither is borrowed from the other. On the other hand some of the finest of his shorter pieces are just a little dashed with bits of prose or bathos, or even damaged by some awkwardness of construction or expression. To take a few examples, 'She was a phantom of delight' has that unfortunate couplet :—

> "A creature not too wise or good
> For human nature's daily food."

The second piece, 'To a Skylark,' is marred by the middle verse. Its awkwardness in that place is accounted for by the fact that it was inserted by an afterthought. Mr. Arnold praises 'The Highland Reaper,' a piece which in all the editions we have seen is entitled 'The Solitary Reaper.' But the last verse was (and in some editions is) not a little marred by the line,

> "I listened *till* I had my *fill*,"

The inference that the Laureate was unconscious of the fault in such case, is disproved by the fact that in this last, and many others, he reconstructed the line or verse, and removed the blemish. Accordingly, the last verse of 'The Solitary Reaper' now stands :—

> "I listen'd motionless and still,[1]
> And as I mounted up the hill
> The music in my heart I bore,
> Long after it was heard no more."

---

[1] It should be remarked that "motionless and still" is not a pleonasm. We lately read a critique of a performance of Handel's 'Messiah,' in which it is said that "when the band had ceased, a death-like silence prevailed, and it was not until after some minutes had elapsed that a foot was moved—a word spoken:" that is, the audience were *motionless* and *still*. No doubt Wordsworth liked the familiar concrete imagery, involved in "human nature's daily food," and "till I had my fill"—but a refined taste will always rise against it.

It is curious that the *Quarterly Review* not only praises this piece—" perhaps the best of any, certainly one as good as any," but, following Mr. Arnold, quoted it with the objectionable and superseded line. We are without evidence how far the consciousness of the blemish in any poem of Wordsworth's was brought to him by the criticism of some judicious friend. We do know, however, that his attention was called to blemishes of the kind, by Coleridge and his daughter, by Lamb, and others. According to his own theory of poetry, nothing was too homely, nothing too common, to be embalmed in poetry; and that whatever was to be so embalmed should be treated with the utmost simplicity, and without the affectation of fine writing. He wrote an address to Mr. Wilkinson's spade, and he called a spade a spade. A writer in the *Spectator* of June 3, attempts to account for Wordsworth's occasional lapses into bathos and the intrusion of "gritty " bits into his otherwise well-fused poetry, by an assertion which is utterly at variance with the facts. "All that is external, and the outward dress of poetry, is more difficult to Wordsworth than it has probably been to any great poet before or since." But Professor Masson was right when he asserted that Wordsworth must have possessed an " easy and perfect mastery over the elements of language and a natural gift of rich and exuberant expression; but it is equally evident that he must have, at a very early period, submitted this natural exuberance to a careful and classic training, and also that he must have bestowed his last pains in finishing,

according to his own ideas of correctness, all his compositions individually." It is in the words we give
in italics that may be found the reason for much that
offends us in his versification. It was the natural
outcome of a theory of composition, according to
which the language should be that of common life,
freed from its vulgarisms and solecisms, and that
it should differ from prose only in its metrical construction. Even Wordsworth did not slavishly carry
this theory into practice. But it is self-evident, that
however liberally he applied his own principles, they
would certainly lead him into prosaic expressions, of
which he could not fail to be conscious, and to
which he would, on revision, be likely to apply
some remedy. It is remarkable that, in one of the
worst of such cases, in which, in deference to the
judgment of his friends, he twice re-wrote that part
of the poem in which the offence lay, his preference
for the original verses remained unshaken. The piece
to which we refer is, 'The Blind Highland Boy,' and
the cancelled verses ran thus:—

> "Strong is the current : but be mild
> Ye waves, and spare the helpless child !
> If ye in danger fret or chafe,
> A bee-hive would be ship as safe
> As that in which he sails.
>
> But say, what was it? thought of fear !
> Well may ye tremble when ye hear !—
> A household Tub, like one of those
> Which women use to wash their clothes—
> This carried the blind boy.

Close to the water he had found
This vessel, pushed it from dry ground,
Went into it ; and without dread,
Following the fancies in his head,
He paddled up and down."

Sara Coleridge ventured to suggest to the poet a
change in the Washing-Tub couplet. It was a tub
that the real boy embarked in, so a tub let it be, only
let it not be called a washing-tub ; there was really no
need to associate the utensil with so unpoetical a subject as the laundry. So she proposed as a substitute :

" A tub of common form and size,
    Such as each rustic home supplies."

Coleridge's accomplished daughter must have been
down in the lowest depths of bathos when she proposed
that ultra-prosaic couplet. Why, it reminds one of
another tub : " a small tub," into which Professor Tyndall's copious libation of goat's milk was poured for his
accommodation, and which he tells us he emptied in
three draughts, by the process of raising it in his
two hands, and " giving it the necessary inclination : "
and of both these tub episodes, " the effect was
astonishing." But Wordsworth's stomach rose against
Sara Coleridge's tub : for the very indefiniteness of the
characterisation (" of common form and size ") was
against one of the poet's canons ; for the description no
more brought before the mind's eye the utensil actually
employed by the blind boy, than the size of an object
can be conveyed by saying that it is " as big as a lump
of chalk." In the event the poet wearied, we dare say,

by the adverse criticism of friends and foes, sent the refractory tub to limbo ; and substituted for it a turtle-shell. But now emerged another difficulty. Turtle-shells are not found " close to the water," unless the turtles are on duty inside them ; in which case, the blind boy could not play the part of the hedgehog in the old fable, and turn out the rightful occupant. The objections of the turtle would be too great, and the blind boy would never have a chance of being saved from a watery grave. So the poet had to account for the possession of this very uncommon article by the young navigator ; and this involved a radical change of conception. So he cancelled all three verses—thus wiping out every trace of the tub (washing or other), and wrote four stanzas instead ; which are certainly quite up to Wordsworth's average. Of these he was ultimately induced to cancel two, and substitute others, which we agree with the late Archdeacon Hare in judging to be utterly unsuited to the poem, and in regard to the context much inferior to those they supplanted. But, why rake up this old story? some will be disposed to ask. Because we see in Wordsworth's " Household Tub" the key to the situation. When we see clearly why he adopted it, why he displaced it, and why he regretted it, we shall see clearly why he admitted so many prosaic, puerile, or inharmonious passages (" gritty bits," if we prefer the crystalline metaphor), into his poems ; and why he made so unfortu-nate a selection of incidents for them, and of names for his *dramatis personœ*. His was a prodigious genius trained by self-imposed restrictions into obedience to a subjective theory of poetry. He had an abounding and versatile faculty of speech. There is such a thing as having that faculty in excess : a fault imputed by Ben Jonson to Shakespeare. Posterity has reversed Jonson's judgment. We have now in our midst two respectable poets of the same name, whose works bear witness to their authors' possession of a power of expression greater than that of Wordsworth ; yet in the whole body of their voluminous writings, there is not a passage which would have passed the ordeal of Wordsworth's judgment. One salutary effect they have had on us : they have made us gentle towards the great poet's faults, and respectful towards the modesty which led him to revise what he had deliberately written.

The conclusion we have reached is certainly unfavourable to Wordsworth's great reputation. We attribute most of his faults, not so much to a defect in the poet, such as want of knowledge, taste, wit, or humour, as to the hampering effect of certain canons of verse composition, which he had adopted in early youth, and from which, owing to the retired and contemplative life he led, he was never able entirely to extricate himself. Why he adopted them is not far to seek. It was as a recoil or revolt of his genius against the debased and artificial poetry of the eighteenth century, and an expression of adhesion to the naturalistic school of Cowper and Crabbe.

With such results before us, it is almost unnecessary to add that Wordsworth's theory is untenable. That so costly an experiment has been made by so great a poet, and has, in the main, failed, should be a warning to all who, attracted by the exceeding beauty of much that Wordsworth wrote, may dream of following his lead. Let us, by all means, have " a new departure."

XII

THOMAS DE QUINCEY.

" O genius of good sense, keep any child of mine from ever sacrificing his intellectual health to such a life of showy emptiness, of pretence, of noise, and of words."—*De Quincey.*

THE Rev. Sydney Smith, one of the wittiest and wisest of his cloth, addressing an assembly of students, gave them this advice :—

" There is a piece of foppery which is to be cautiously guarded against, the foppery of universality—of knowing all sciences, and excelling in all arts, chemistry, algebra, mathematics, dancing, history, reasoning, riding, fencing, low Dutch, high Dutch, and natural philosophy ! In short, the modern precept of education very often is, ' Take the Admirable Crichton for your model : I would have you ignorant of nothing.' Now my advice, on the contrary, is, to have the courage to be ignorant of a great number of things, in order that you may avoid the calamity of being ignorant of everything."

Very similar to this is the counsel of Hegel (quoted by Dr. J. H. Stirling, at the end of an admirable article contributed by him to the *Fortnightly Review*, October 1, 1867 :—

" He who wills something great must, as Goethe says, know how to restrict himself. He who, on the other hand, wills all, wills in effect nothing, and brings it to nothing. There is a number of interesting things in the world : Spanish, poetry, chemistry, politics, music ; this is all very interesting, and we cannot take it ill of any one who occupies himself with these. In order, however, as an individual in a prescribed position, to bring something about, he must hold by what is definite, and not split up his strength in many directions." [1]

Even Hegel was—perhaps not contentedly—ignorant of the physico-mathematics ; and it is a remarkable instance of the large demand which philosophy makes upon human knowledge, that this ignorance was detrimental to his philosophy in its ultimate issues, and fatal to its reception in England.

Good as this advice is, it does not necessarily follow that its neglect is fatal to success in life. Kant, Hegel, Goethe, Alexander von Humboldt (to which roll might well be added the living Helmholtz), and many other Germans, are proofs to the contrary :—all of whom not only achieved the most distinguished success in their several specialities, but rendered their names historical. With Englishmen and Frenchmen the case is somewhat different. The names of Frederick Schlegel, Brougham, Whewell, and Michelet, occur to me as instances of the sort of success attainable by those who have made the Admirable Crichton their model. A few of those who dare to attempt to know everything may, notwithstanding such unwise temerity, attain to considerable eminence ; but their names are never found in the first rank. With men of less mental and

---

[1] Compare with the above the Second Proposition in Père Buffier's "*Examen des Préjugés Vulgaires*," "Que la science ne consiste point à savoir beaucoup" (That science does not consist in knowing much.)

bodily strength the attempt is simply fatal. The *physique* of Brougham and Whewell was of extraordinary tenacity, and their natural abilities were excellent, insomuch that it is difficult to say to what perfection and power of intellect they might not have reached, had each devoted himself to the cultivation of a single set of faculties, or to the acquisition of a single branch of knowledge. Virgil's advice to the vinegrower (in which he reiterates the counsel of Hesiod) may be figuratively applied to the student :—

> "Laudato ingentia rura,
> Exiguum colito:"

i.e., admire large vineyards, but cultivate a small one. Equivalent to the counsel of Sydney Smith, Hegel, Buffier, Hesiod, and Virgil, is the old proverb,— "Whatever is worth doing is worth doing well," for few indeed have the mental endowments and physical endurance necessary to the attainment of great excellence in many distinct subjects of study. Since the establishment of the Classical Tripos at Cambridge, it has never once happened that the Senior Classic had been Senior Wrangler. The nearest approach to this occurred in the year 1835 (which was what is called a weak mathematical year), when Mr. Goulburn, the only and highly gifted son of the late ex-Chancellor of the Exchequer, was second Wrangler and Senior Classic ; and he paid for this double honour with his life.

The application, however, of the above-quoted maxim varies with different orders of mental endow-

ments. The subject of this sketch was fond of sub-
tilising (as he and Tennyson call it), and his favourite
distinctions were between imagination and fancy,
between power and knowledge, and between genius
and talent.

"Walking Stewart," says De Quincey, "was a man
of very extraordinary genius;" but he was utterly
devoid of talent, and, as a natural result, produced
nothing. Many years ago, I knew a gentleman
named James Arthur Davies, who might well have
been called "the admirable Davies." He appeared to
me to possess every conceivable talent, and, up to the
limits of his brain-power, to have turned all his talents
to account; but, as I surmise, for want of some touch
of true genius, he produced nothing, and did not
achieve even a moderate success in life.[1]

Now to the man of genius, with or without these
special gifts, and to the man of many talents, with or

[1] After Davies' death his MSS. were placed at my disposal. They
weighed almost exactly a hundredweight : and they may fairly be
described as *de omnibus rebus et quibusdam aliis*. My first examination
of them revealed such versatility of talent, painstaking industry, and
wide erudition, that I was prepared for the discovery of some works of
the highest value. Something like half of the MSS. were written in
Latin, a language which Davies spoke fluently; but I also found in
them a good sprinkling of Greek and Hebrew, as well as French,
German, and Italian. Of the last language Davies had acquired the
most perfect mastery ; but he ordinarily conversed in English or French.
My expectation was disappointed. The MSS. proved to be little more
than digested collections. A few original pieces in which he appeared
to have worked wholly on his own mental resources were but elaborate
failures. I have arranged seven volumes of his Lectures and Treatises
on Music for presentation to his and my college—Trinity College,
Cambridge.

S

without some touch of the Promethean fire, the foregoing protest against versatility in mental culture must not be taken too literally; for there are cases in which an exemption may be claimed. The subject of this essay was, in the best sense, a man of genius, and possessed all the talents requisite and sufficient for the accomplished philosopher. Metaphysics was his hobby, and the work which he constantly kept before him, as the one thing for him to do, was a treatise *De Emendatione Humani Intellectûs;* yet that book was never written, perhaps not attempted. The bent and powers of his mind carried him to philosophy, and his early training had thoroughly fitted him for the study of any philosophical works in Latin, Greek, or German. He read Plato with appreciation, and subsequently applied himself to the mastery of Kant's 'Critic of Pure Reason.' His various notices, both of Kant and of his philosophy, are hopelessly discrepant. In one place he brands Kant as a liar, and in another calls him "the most sincere, honourable, and truthful of human beings." At one time he imputes Atheism to Kant, and at another he conceded to him the character of a Christian; and his remarks on the philosophy are equally contradictory. The key to all this is easily found. De Quincey wrote flippantly and dogmatically on these subjects before he had acquired any real acquaintance with them at first hand. Having once devoted himself to the study of the 'Critic,' his remarks are just and genial. Henceforth he proclaimed this book to be the Alpha and Omega of philosophy, and hurled great scorn at the troop of unhappy impostors who had hitherto encumbered with their help such English students as dreamed of cracking this huge cocoa-nut. And that was all: no help in that direction was ever vouchsafed by De Quincey himself.

We cannot be far wrong in attributing this unfortunate result to the fact that, instead of concentrating his faculties on some one subject, such as fiction, criticism, history, in any of which he might have taken the first rank, or on philosophy, the successful prosecution of which would have called into healthy action every faculty of his mind, he divided his forces, and lost the vantage of their co-operation. A glance at the tremendous index appended to the fifteenth volume of Messrs. Black's edition of his minor works is sufficient to show that philosophy necessarily shared the fate of all the other subjects which occupied his versatile mind, and about which he delighted to pour forth his voluble, but often most eloquent gossip.

Thomas Quincey, the father of the author, was a West Indian merchant, carrying on business in Market Street Lane, Manchester. All we know about him is, that he had four sons and four daughters: that, growing genteel, he declined the retail trade from the beginning of 1783, and that he died at Greenhays, Manchester, on July 11th, 1793. His son Thomas (the fourth child) was born at Greenhays, on August 15th, 1785. He was instructed in the rudiments of the classics by the Rev. Samuel Hall, Incumbent of

St. Peter's. Three years after the death of his father, the widow removed with her family to Bath, and for the following three years "young Thomas" continued his education at the grammar school there, and at a private school in Wiltshire. He was then removed to the grammar school at Manchester, in the expectation of being able to obtain an exhibition for Oxford. Mr. Lawson, the head-master, placed him at once in the first class. The system pursued at this school was such that no boy of delicate health could conform to it without serious detriment to his constitution. To this cause De Quincey (as he called himself) attributed that fatal derangement of the stomach which first led to his having recourse to opium. Whatever may have been the effect of the school discipline on his bodily health, it is certain that to it he owed that mastery over Latin and Greek composition which, in early years, made him so great a name.

At the end of three years he would have been entitled to stand for an exhibition, and his pre-eminent classical attainments would have insured his success; but his failing health, and the impatience and irritability resulting therefrom, rendered school restraints insufferable, so that in his eighteenth month he clandestinely left the town, and for two years abandoned himself to a wandering life, being found in Chester, North Wales, London, and other parts of England. At length, on December 17th, 1803, he matriculated at Worcester College, Oxford; but, like Shelley, Landor, and the late Lord Derby (to which list we might add

Coleridge [at Cambridge], and some other distinguished
poets), he left without taking a degree. At this time
he had acquired so extensive and accurate a knowledge
of the classics that he would certainly have attained
the distinction of a first class, had he merely kept up
his reading. His Greek scholarship is reputed to have
been prodigious, and he himself professes that, before
he went to Oxford, Attic Greek was to him almost as
familiar a medium of conversation as his native tongue.
The reason for his abandoning the university course
lies in one fatal word—*Opium*. The excess to which
he indulged in this delusive and pernicious drug,
turned his life into a voluptuous dream. His habits
were, in all respects, inconsistent with the ordinary
life of his fellow-creatures, food, sleep, and study being
resorted to according to the fit that was on him, and
without the least regard to times and places. For such
a man university discipline was simply torture.

It is most difficult to trace De Quincey's erratic
course from the time he left Oxford. His ' Confessions and Autobiographic Sketches ' are chiefly personal revelations, designed, in all probability, to set
forth their eccentric author as a psychological curiosity.
They must be read *in extenso* to be appreciated, so
that our space will not be occupied by any extracts
from them. We find De Quincey residing at Grasmere
in 1817, in which year, on February 15, he married
Miss Margaret Simpson, by whom he had several
children. One of these, a daughter, is now living at
Greenhays, St. Leonard's-on-Sea. De Quincey now

enjoyed constant intercourse with the so-called *Lakists*, Wordsworth, Coleridge, Southey, Wilson, and others of that distinguished *coterie*.

He seems to have left Grasmere in 1819, and to have once more betaken himself to a shifting life. In 1822–24 he was one of the chief contributors to the *London Magazine*, edited by John Scott. As soon as *Blackwood's Magazine* came under the influence of Professor John Wilson, De Quincey's services were put into requisition in its behalf; but he also contributed to *Tait's Magazine*, the *Edinburgh* and *North British Reviews*, the *Encyclopædia Britannica*, and *Hogg's Weekly Instructor*. Later in life he wrote for the *Titan* and several other periodicals.

In 1843 his wanderings (which we believe never extended far beyond his native land) came to an end, and he settled, with his family, in the beautiful village of Lasswade, in the neighbourhood of Edinburgh, and became *the Coleridge of the North*, in both the characters of Talker and Opium-eater. He might be described as a sort of soliloquising Plato. He did for Lasswade what Socrates did for Athens, Johnson for London, and Goethe for Weimar. There he constantly associated with Sir William S. Hamilton, Professor John Wilson, Samuel Browne, Professor J. P. Nichol (also an opium-eater), Professor J. F. Ferrier, Blackie, &c., and, for a time, J. W. Semple, the erratic and learned translator of Kant. He died December 8th, 1859, and was buried in the Churchyard of St. Cuthbert, Edinburgh.

De Quincey's head was a splendid study for the phrenologist, presenting a wonderful combination of the reflective and perceptive types. His portrait, prefixed to either the first or the last volume of the English editions, represents a man advanced in life, the face pale and emaciated, and the dress slovenly. The face and head suggest a strange compound of opposite and usually incompatible qualities. There is infinite power and wealth in the massive cliff-like head, and the utmost weakness and poverty are expressed by the nose and mouth. How to interpret that weird, good-natured, and suffering expression of the decrepit face? It is truthful yet sinister, earnest yet satirical; the sinister and the satirical blending in a dream-like insipidity. The upper lip is treacherous, the lower jaw sensual; but the face is so drawn with suffering or age as to complicate or obliterate the usual landmarks of physiognomy.

De Quincey unquestionably belongs to the class of minds called by the Germans *mannichseitig*, or many-sided. He is, perhaps, best known to the world as an opium-eater, and therefore, despite all he said or could say in praise of opium, in a disreputable character. I will say no more on this infirmity or vice, whichever it may have been : it is best lost sight of altogether, or at least kept in the background. *We* will resolve henceforth not to know him in that character. From which of his many sides, then, shall we approach him? We have called him scholar, philosopher, theologian, economist, humorist, romancer, historian, biographer, and critic. He was all these, and more. Those who have read the fifteen volumes of his minor works agree, on the whole, to praise him as a stylist. Truly he must rank *very high* in this regard. Passages in his autobiographic sketches, his memoir of Charles Lamb, his monograph on the 'Knocking at the Gate in Macbeth'[1] (not to specify *many* other *opuscula*) are unrivalled for simple and natural beauty. But it is his *matter* rather than his *style* that shall now engage our attention; and it is as a critic on the obscure problems of ancient records that we shall approach the study of his versatile and voluminous writings.

De Quincey, while resting his claim to the favour of posterity on that section of his writings which may be called *Dream Literature*, still set a high value on the results of his critical labours; in fact, he went so far as to assert that, till his advent as a critic, there was "no rational criticism on Greek literature; nor, indeed, to say the truth, much criticism which teaches anything, or solves anything, upon any literature."— (Ed. A. and C. Black, vol. xiii., p. 59.) The critics, he held, "had one and all been deluded by the seeming force of certain foregone conclusions respecting the intellectual and moral status of the ancients."

---

[1] The 'Cambridge Editors' of Shakespeare, in the edition of 'Macbeth' which forms part of the 'Clarendon Press Series' (p. 109), declare their opinion that the Porter's speech (act ii., sc. 3) "seems strangely out of place," &c. That opinion argues an ignorance on their part of De Quincey's criticism. This goes far to justify the seeming incongruity, but does so indirectly.

It would be impossible to do justice to De Quincey's views on the entire subject within the limits at our disposal; and as it behoves us to follow our own counsel, and to do a little thoroughly rather than much superficially, we shall restrict our remarks to one single point of the general question, viz., *the Antagonism between Paganism and Christianity.*

De Quincey tells us that it was from his conversations with Wordsworth that he was led to draw the first and fundamental distinction in the functions of books, *literæ humaniores,*—the literature which confers power, and which alone deserves to be called literature—being contrasted with *literæ didacticæ,* the literature which confers knowledge. From this distinction emerge the only two possible modes of human culture, the one which *instructs* and the other which *informs.* By the one the faculties of the *mind* are fed and quickened; by the other the potential forms of *feeling* are actualised, and elevated into consciousness. Now it is with literature proper that criticism is mainly concerned.

In the third of the 'Letters to a Young Man whose Education has been neglected' (vol. xiii., pp. 53–60), (which, by the way, were written some years before they were published) De Quincey broaches this most interesting subject, but his allusion to it is tangential. In fact, he simply throws out this hint, "that the antique or Pagan literature is a polar antagonist to the modern or Christian literature; that each is an evolution from a distinct principle, . . . and that they are to be criticised from different stations and points of view." He adds that he attempted to develop this thought in a series of "reveries." To what *limbo* are they consigned? Little, it is to be feared, is the chance of their discovery; a remark which applies to some other writings of De Quincey, the titles of which are given in a note at the end of this essay.

The conclusions he arrived at will be found in four essays, viz., 'Christianity as an Organ of Political Movement,' 'The Pagan Oracles,' 'The Theban Sphinx,' and one in 'The Autobiographic Sketches.'

The following extracts will furnish the reader with a convenient summary of the chief of those con-clusions :—

"What is a Religion ? To Christians it means, over and above a mode of worship, a dogmatic (that is, a doctrinal) system ; a great body of doctrinal truths, moral and spiritual. But to the ancients (to the Greeks and Romans, for instance) it meant nothing of the kind. A religion was simply a *cultus :* a mode of ritual worship, in which there might be two differences, viz. : 1. As to the particular deity who furnished the motive to the worship. 2. As to the ceremonial, or mode of conducting the worship. But in no case was there so much as a pretence of communicating any religious truths, far less any moral truths. The obstinate error rooted in modern minds is that, doubtless, the moral instruction was bad, as being heathen ; but that still it was as good as heathen opportunities allowed it to be. No mistake can be greater. Moral instruction had no existence even in the plan or intention of the religious service. The Pagan priest, or flamen, never dreamed of any function like that of *teaching* as in any way connected with his office. He no more undertook to teach morals than to teach geography or cookery. He taught nothing. What he undertook was simply to *do*, viz. : to present authoritatively (that is, authorised and supported by some civil community, Corinth, or Athens, or Rome, which he represented) the homage and gratitude of that community to the particular deity adored. As to morals, or just opinions upon the relations to man of the several divinities, all this was resigned to the teaching of nature, and for any polemic functions the teaching was resigned to the professional philosophers, academic, peripatetic, stoic, &c. By religion it was utterly ignored."— *Autobiographic Sketches, Works,* vol. xiv., p. 413.

"The reader must understand, upon our authority, *nostro periculo,* and in defiance of all the false translations spread through books, that the ancients (meaning the Greeks and Romans, before the time of Christianity) had no idea, not by the faintest vestige, of what, in the scriptural system, is called *sin;* that neither one word nor the other has any such meaning in writers belonging to the pure classical period. When baptized into new meanings through their adoption by Christianity, these words, in common with many others, transmigrated into new and philosophic functions. But originally they tended towards no such acceptations, nor *could* have done so, seeing that the ancients had no avenue opened to them through which the profound idea of *sin* would have been even dimly intelligible. Plato, 400 years before Christ, or Cicero, more than 300 years later, was fully equal to the idea of *guilt* through all its gamut ; but no more equal to the idea of *sin* than a sagacious hound to the idea of gravitation, or of central forces. It is the tremendous postulate upon which this idea reposes that constitutes the initial moment of that revelation which is common to Judaism and to Christianity. We have no intention of wandering into any discussion upon this question. It will suffice for the service of the occasion if we say that guilt, in all its mortifications, implies only a defect or a wound in the individual. Sin, on the other hand, the most mysterious and the most sorrowful of all ideas, implies a taint, not in the individual but in the race—*that* is the distinction ; or a taint in the individual, not through any local disease of his own, but through a scrofula equally diffused through the infinite family of man. We are not speaking controversially, either as teachers of theology or of philosophy ; and we are careless of the particular construction by which the reader interprets to himself this profound idea. What we affirm is, that this idea was utterly and exquisitely inappreciable by Pagan Greece and Rome ; that various translations from Pindar, from Aristophanes, and from the Greek tragedians, embodying at intervals this word *sin*, are more extravagant than would be the word *category*, or the *synthetic unity of consciousness*, introduced into the harangue of an Indian sachem amongst the Cherokees ; and finally, that the very nearest approach to the abysmal idea which we Christians attach to the word sin (an approach but to that which never can be touched, a writing as of palmistry upon each man's hand, but a writing which "no man can read,") lies in the Pagan idea of *piacularity*, which is an idea thus far like hereditary sin, that it expresses an evil to which the party affected has not consciously occurred ; which is thus far *not* like hereditary sin, that it expresses an evil personal to the individual, and not extending itself to the race."—*The Theban Sphinx, Works*, vol. ix., p. 239.

Copernicus, finding that he could not read the heavens upon the time-honoured assumption of a firmament of stars revolving around a stationary earth, tried what would come of assuming the earth to be itself revolving in a firmament at rest. This happy expedient was imitated by Kant in the world of philosophy, and he tried the experiment of reversing Locke's hypothesis, and assuming that the *phenomena* revealed to the senses were conformed to the perceptive faculty of the observer. De Quincey was profoundly struck by the success of both experiments, and (perhaps without any conscious intention of doing so) applied the Copernican expedient to theology ; and this he did in two ways, and for these two purposes : to explain the prerequisite of Christian regeneration, as embodied in the command *metanoeite ;* and to explain the apparently irregular or retrograde movements of Christianity in generations long after the preaching of the Baptist.

De Quincey's remarkable speculations on this subject

will be found in four volumes of his collected works, viz., vol. xiv., pp. 410–418; vol. xi., p. 234 *et seq.*, vol. vii., p. 165 *et seq.*, and vol. ix., pp. 339–341, from which last I have given one quotation. In the first of these four references we have his exposition of μετάνοια (alluded to in a footnote to vol. vi., p. 310, and vol. xi., p. 247). He says:—

"*Metanoeite* was the cry from the wilderness: wheel into a new centre your moral system ; *geocentric* has that system been up to this hour—that is, having earth and the earthly for its starting-point; henceforth make it *heliocentric, i.e.,* with the sun, or the heavenly, for its principle of motion."

And this exposition is followed by a statement of the distinction between the ritual worship of Paganism and that of Christianity. At the second of those four references he essays the application of the Copernican expedient to defend Christianity from the assaults or objections of men like the poet Shelley and General Jacob; "minds of the highest order," who, not referring the movements of Christianity to its true centre, "have arraigned it as a curse to man, and have fought against it, even upon Christian impulses, impulses of benignity that could not have had a birth except in Christianity:" and he says at length that, though we may discern the fact that its apparently irregular or retrograde motions are really regular and progressive, yet that "no finite intellect will ever retrace the total curve upon which Christianity has moved, any more than eyes that are incarnate will ever see God."

The key to this position is the distinction between

Paganism and Christianity, in their nature, their ends, and their effects. . . .

De Quincey enforces the position that Paganism was a mere *cultus*, or ritual worship, teaching nothing, and accomplishing (positively) nothing for the advance of man. This *cultus* was founded on the assumption that man, *as a person*, was not in any reciprocal relation to the gods ; that he was not in any sense the object of their solicitude ; and that he could not by any means make them actively or positively friendly to him. The utmost that was proposed by this *cultus* was, by costly sacrifices, to propitiate the gods and, so far, to protect defenceless man from the selfish or passionate ravages of malignant beings invested with irresponsible power.

Christianity, on the contrary, afforded a ritual worship, which was in close connection with a system of ethics and philosophy. It was founded on the enlightened assumption that God was not only friendly to man, but had Himself incurred the most costly sacrifice for man's regeneration and promotion. Accordingly, the end of the Christian *cultus* was to bring him within a *positive* spiritual influence for his own good, making him better, wiser, and happier, both in fruition and in expectancy ; making possible for him the possession of good, though also as a result of self-denial in this world, and the reversion of eternal good after death.

The elements of Christianity are stated by De Quincey to be—1. A *cultus*. 2. A new idea of God. 3. An idea of the relation of man to God, " breathing

household laws." 4. A doctrinal part, ethical and
mystical. Of these elements, Paganism had but the
first. It was a *cultus*. Now a *cultus*, in the Christian
system, has four parts : (*a*) an act of praise, (*b*) an act
of thanksgiving, (*c*) an act of confession, (*d*) an act of
prayer. Of these the first and the last *appear* present
in Paganism. Pagans glorified and invoked their
deities. But how ? " You read of *preces*, of αραι, &c.,
and you are desirous to believe the Pagan suppli-
cations were not *always* corrupt." But, "vainly you
come before the altars with empty hands. 'But *my*
hands are pure.' Pure, indeed ! would reply the scoff-
ing god ; let me see what they contain." *Do ut des* (*i.c.*,
I give thee that thou mayest give me), or *quid pro
quo*, was the maxim. *Do* or *quo* was either a costly
gift or a banquet (*cœna*) dedicated to the god : to the
oracle it was a gift ; to the altar it was a feast. But
neither advice nor aid (even from a tutelary deity,
could be had gratis. Even the magnificent choric
prayer to Onca and the rest, in the 'Seven against Thebes,'
is backed up by reminding them that the sacrifices
had been paid. Such was Pagan prayer ; and Pagan
praise was often the exaggerated imputation of the
grossest vices. But from this *cultus* thanksgiving and
confession were absent by the nature of the case ; for
thanks could not be due where every advance was paid
for beforehand ; and what were the poor Pagans to
confess ? Their sins ? How could that be ? for, first,
they did not regard their vices as sinful, else were their
gods the gravest of sinners ; and, not regarding them

as sinful, how could they feel remorse for them? Penitence they had none. *Pœnitentia* meant regret, vexation. Μετάνοια meant either second thoughts, or afterthought, as being too late to be of any avail. Neither αμαρτια nor *peccatum* meant sin; the nearest approach to sin was *piacularity*. No personal transgression was contemplated, but simply an offence against the idiosyncrasy of the god, and in such an offence the devotee was as often as not involved by the act of others, while he himself was wholly innocent of it. But not the less did the vengeance of the god fasten on him unless he could propitiate him; and such was precisely the case of Œdipus. On his devoted head were poured the vials of wrath for the committal of three unconscious crimes—regicide, parricide, and incest; not for slaying a man on the king's highway, not for marrying the king's widow—acts which he had done with his eyes open, but, for crimes involved in these acts, but which were wholly hidden from his knowledge, he met with that pariah fate, which in its mysteriousness and its pathos is a likeness, and for its despair and misery is a contrast, to the fabled doom of our King Arthur. For this reason it is that De Quincey takes Œdipus as the type of the child of wrath according to the Pagan scheme.

It must be allowed that, even if De Quincey's theory is a little too *prononcé*, it is pregnant with a truth which is of great value to the Christianity of our own day. It is incident to any religious development from a new centre that it should adopt and resuscitate the words that did duty for the religious system which it supplanted; and thus it must happen that in after ages a grave risk will be run of reflecting back on the words of ancient usage a sense and power which they did not then have. If this danger be not avoided, there is the consequent risk of mistaking the actual freshness and originality of the religious ideas of the latest development, and of arguing that all its peculiar doctrines are borrowed from the supplanted system. In this way it is that many are now, let us hope in ignorance, assailing the originality of the special characteristics of Christianity; and it was against this stupendous blunder that De Quincey devoted his best powers and his ripest learning.

But it must be confessed that these views as a whole are chargeable with inconsistency. The Baptist's *Metanoeite* was addressed to Jews: the mainstay of the theory that the Jewish sect of the Essenes was a secret society of early Christians is, that on any other assumption there must have been a Christianity before Christ. The drift of De Quincey's remarks on these questions seems to be that Judaism, in a less degree than Paganism, but still in a great degree, had a distinct centre of evolution, and that a change in the point of reference, and an intellectual and moral revolution, were demanded in the one as in the other. But when brought face to face with this fact, De Quincey wards off the inevitable conclusion by the following note:—"Once for all, to save the trouble of continual repetitions, understand Judaism to be

T

commemorated jointly with Christianity — the dark root together with the golden fruitage—*whenever the nature of the case does not presume a contradistinction of the one to the other*" (vol. xi., p. 241). But the only question between Judaism and Christianity is just this—in what respect are they to be contradistinguished? in what respect was the "New Commandment" opposed to the old? And the answer to this, if searching and true, must go far to reduce Judaism to a rank with which Christianity had nothing in common save the doctrines of monotheism and original sin.[1]

---

[1] In the course of De Quincey's works mention is occasionally made of other of his writings, which are not known to have been published. Such as *Suspiria de Profundis* (twenty to twenty-five sketches, of which 'The Daughter of Lebanon' and (a) one other piece are all that have been published), mentioned in vol. i., preface, xiv. *De Emendatione Humani Intellectus*, mentioned in vol. i., p. 254. 'Prolegomena to all Future Systems of Political Economy' (possibly the same as 'The Logic of Political Economy'), mentioned in vol. i., p. 256. 'Reveries on the Evolution of Pagan and Christian Literatures,' mentioned in vol. xiii., p. 60. And a work citing the 'Antigone,' mentioned in vol. xiii., p. 204.

Besides these, there are various papers by De Quincey scattered about our periodical literature, which have never yet been gathered in. Foremost is the admirable article on 'Kant in his Miscellaneous Essays,' published in *Blackwood's Magazine*, August 1830, included, I believe, with some other papers unknown in England, in Messrs. Ticknor & Field's American edition of De Quincey's works. There is also the paper above mentioned to which (a) is prefixed, which I read in some English periodical *circa* 1850–1855. De Quincey mentions (vol. vi., p. 267) a paper by himself on 'Freemasonry,' published in a London journal about 1823 or 1824; and (vol. xiv., p. 71, note) another on 'The Prevalence of Danish Names of Places in England,' published in a provincial newspaper. These are possibly only a few of the monographs of this gifted and voluminous writer yet to be garnered. One is loath to lose a line which fell from

that inspired penman. These references are to Black's reissue of
Hogg's edition. Neither of the English editions, nor the American
edition, nor the combination of all these, includes those of his works
which had been published separately, viz., 'The Logic of Political
Economy,' 1844 ; 'Walladmor,' &c.

XIII.

HENRY THOMAS BUCKLE.

LITERATURE has sustained a severe loss in the untimely death of Mr. Buckle. He leaves the work, to which he had devoted his life, unfinished, and none is found worthy to complete it for him. Not a line, I understand, has been written beyond what has been printed, save his numerous and copious common-place books; these, indeed, bear superfluous witness to the almost unexampled extent and selectness of his reading; but it is a grave question, which his executor has not yet resolved, whether it is expedient, either for the reputation of their author, or the benefit of his nation, to give them publicity.

Having had some personal acquaintance with the illustrious deceased, having conversed with him on some of the most interesting and momentous questions of the day and of all time, having seen his common-place books, and been with him when he was writing the MS. of the second volume of his great work, it may be interesting if I give a short sketch of the life, writings, *personnel*, and character of the historian of civilisation.

Henry Thomas Buckle was born at Lee, on November 24, 1821 [the *Times* of June 9th says 1822, which I believe to be an error]. His father was a wine merchant, and gained considerable wealth by his calling. His extensive library is an evidence that he, too, was a reading man. His son did not enjoy the advantages of a public school, or of a university. He was educated in the private academy of Dr. James Thomas Holloway, at Gordon House, Kentish Town, and it is evident that this circumstance of his private education gave a peculiar colour to his future career. On his father's death, in 1840, Henry succeeded to the library, and a part only, I believe, of his father's fortune, as his widow may be supposed to have had a life interest in a portion of the property. The early life of Henry was dedicated to letters and chess. By dint of constant practice in that game, he became the best English amateur chess-player of his day; and he eminently distinguished himself in the Chess Congress of 1851. He does not appear to have subsequently cultivated that laborious "game," all his time being sedulously devoted to his great work, 'The History of Civilisation in England,' which he calculated would fill seventeen thick octavo volumes, whereof he lived to write but two.

The first volume, dedicated to his mother, was published, at his own expense, in 1857. It at once made an immense sensation, and a second imprint was demanded and published within the year. Buckle rose, *per saltum*, to a pinnacle of fame. He became one of the "lions" of the London season of 1858. Now he had never once opened his lips in public. On March 19 he delivered a brilliant oration on "The Influence of Women on the Progress of Society," before a crowded and fashionable audience, at the Royal Institution. He made but little preparation for this formidable ordeal. He took into the lecture theatre a small card containing the heads of his discourse; but, finding that he spoke with perfect fluency and exactness, and with a full retention of his prescribed order of thought, he had no occasion to consult his notes at all. His hearers, even the physical science men who were so shocked at his heterodoxy on the subject of Induction, one and all testify to the lecturer's extraordinary eloquence, despite the natural unmelodiousness of his voice. Happily the address was taken down in shorthand: and when written out, it was corrected by Buckle himself, and published in *Fraser's Magazine*, vol. lvii. p. 325.[1]

Buckle's next publication was another contribution to *Fraser's Magazine*, vol. lix. p. 509. It is an article entitled 'Mill, on Liberty,' and consists of a review of Mr. J. Stuart Mill's work on that subject. This was Buckle's "great sensation article," and how it ever came to be inserted in *Fraser* is to me a mystery. In it he righteously fell foul of everybody concerned in the prosecution of Thomas Pooley, a labourer, of Liskeard, in

---

[1] In the copy of that volume in the library of the Athenæum Club, the leaves of the address are almost worn out of the binding with the constant use to which it has been subjected, and the type is, in places, partly worn out: facts which, standing alone, furnish no inconsiderable proof of the extent to which the address has been read and studied in town.

Cornwall, who, in 1857, was committed for trial on a charge of blasphemy, and was afterwards sentenced by Mr. Justice Coleridge to a long term of imprisonment. The incarceration of the unhappy man was, in fact, cut short by an outbreak of insanity : the actual fact being that he had been of unsound mind for years. Most religious lunatics believe themselves apostles of Christianity, and not a few conceive themselves to be Jesus Christ Himself, and to be charged with the mission of redeeming a fallen world. Pooley's madness was of a less frequent kind, but one not without its instances. He believed Jesus Christ to be a scoundrel, and himself to be commissioned to publish that fact, and put down the Redeemer. I hardly know if this be a more shocking delusion than the other. Perhaps it is. No conclusive evidence of Pooley's insanity was tendered for his defence : indeed he was undefended. So the jury did not find Pooley insane, and he was left to the religious prejudices of an otherwise admirable judge. Coleridge did not spare Pooley ; and Buckle did not spare Coleridge ; he calls him bad names—" that stonyhearted man," &c., and congratulates himself on having " done something towards dragging the criminal from his court, and letting in on him the full light of day ! " Hard words : but *very venial*. While one hopes that they did not injure the judge, one feels sure that they will be of use to protect some future Pooley from the judicial persecution of men who may be as conscientious as Hale, and yet as culpably ignorant. This attack drew forth an indignant reply from the

judge's son, Mr. John Duke Coleridge, Q.C., who was
counsel for the prosecution of Pooley. This learned
gentleman retaliated on Buckle with as little mercy as
Buckle had shown his father (see same vol. p. 635).
The poor editor of *Fraser* found that what with the
heterodoxy of Buckle's opinions on "Liberty," and what
with the fiery indignation of Coleridge's partizans, he
had, by the insertion of Buckle's article, got a hornet's
nest about his head. He made a most undignified dis-
claimer of Buckle's views, and subjected them to the
earnest and persuasive pen of that genial, if not powerful, contributor who writes under the initials A.K.H.B.,
but whose name is well enough known. This writer
came down with a review on a work anonymously published, entitled ' Man and his Dwelling-place.' [1]

In this contribution A.K.H.B. attempted to circulate
the antidote to Buckle's bane: and the attempt is a
model of Christian courtesy combined with deadly conflict. Buckle never wrote another line in *Fraser*. His
friends said he sadly wanted discretion. But discretion
was no part of Buckle's policy. It was his design,
with a firm, relentless hand, to pluck from the poor
weak eyes of justice her conventional bandage of rose-
tinted or red-taped propriety.

The second volume of the ' History of Civilisation in
England ' appeared in 1861. In the meanwhile his
mother died, to whom he was most devotedly attached,

---

[1] W. Parker & Son: 1859. The work is by Mr. Hinton, and I
must confess, despite the ability it displays, I never saw so little said
in so many words.

and owing to whose illness the completion of that
volume had been delayed for some months. It was
"consecrated" to her memory. At the conclusion of
chapter iv., Buckle enters a timely confession that he
had projected a work too vast for the labour of one life,
(pp. 325–329), and announces his intention of deviat-
ing materially from his original design, by curtailing
the remainder of his programme. Poor fellow! He
little thought that death would effectually save him
that trouble. He tells us that imperfection in the
evidence on which the solution of the problems of
civilisation depend is henceforth an essential part of
his plan. " It is essential, because I despair of supplying those deficiencies in my knowledge, of which I grow
more sensible in proportion as my views become more
extensive. It is also essential, because after a fair
estimate of my own strength, of the probable duration
of my life, and of the limits to which industry can
safely be pushed, I have been driven to the conclusion,
that this introduction, which I had projected as a solid
foundation on which the history of England might subsequently be raised, must either be greatly curtailed, and
consequently shorn of its force, or that, if not curtailed,
there will hardly be a chance of my being able to
narrate with the amplitude and fulness of detail which
they richly deserve, the deeds of that great and splendid
nation with which I am best acquainted, and of which
it is my pride to count myself a member." Even here
Buckle overrated his physical powers. He had had
one warning. He had suddenly fallen to the ground ;

and though he recovered his consciousness immediately, and was able to rise without assistance, his friends feared that the attack was of an apoplectic nature. As soon as the second volume of his gigantic work was a *fait accompli*, he went to Filey for the benefit of the sea breezes: and ultimately arranged to spend the winter and spring in Egypt and Palestine. He left England last autumn, in company with two young friends. In his last letter to a cousin, resident in town, he speaks of his health having been completely re-established, and says that he was never better in his life. He announced his intention of going to Cyprus, and sailing thence for England, in order to avoid the physical inconveniences of an overland tour in the heat of summer. Unfortunately he was taken ill with typhus fever, at Beyrout, and with his constitutional headstrong temper, intensified by his sickness, insisted, while the fever was approaching its height, and delirium was imminent, on being carried in a litter over the mountains to Damascus. He arrived there utterly exhausted, and soon fell a prey to the malady which would, in all probability, have yielded to careful nursing, and due medical treatment. He died at Damascus, on May 26th last, in the 41st year of his age.

This is not the time to form an estimate of the results of Buckle's natural powers and acquirements. Of the vast extent of his researches we may form some notion from the fact that he had some access to the literature of twenty-four languages, and made a laborious use of his linguistic attainments. He could read sixteen languages with scholarly precision, and in four or five he could converse. He was widely read in the literature of physical, political, and physiological science. He was deeply versed in all the Metaphysical Schools, and in an amount of Theology which it is sickening to contemplate, and which he himself regarded as the most arid tract of mind that he had to traverse. As an example of the accuracy and extent of his knowledge of German Metaphysics, I may cite the fact that he removed from my mind a misapprehension as to the evidences of the reality of *phenomena* and *noumena*, according to the critical philosophy; and gave me *ex tempore* the required proof that Kant held those two evidences to be of the same degree, but of different kinds, by citing, in German, a passage from one of Kant's letters: thus evincing his familiar knowledge, not merely of the great works of Kant, but of his minor writings. In a similar exact and off-hand manner Buckle settled the question, which was much mooted two years ago, as to the discoverer of the Polarisation of Light. I have his own assurance that he had read every English drama that had been printed up to the Georgian epoch. If I were called upon to say in what particular department of knowledge Buckle was fundamentally deficient, I should indicate *Mathematics*. There is a proof of it in vol. i. of his history. At p. 28 Buckle makes an analogical use of "the Parallelogram of Forces," which he enunciates as if the demonstration depended on two parallelograms. I took the liberty of pointing out to him this error shortly before he left England. There is also a grave misstatement of the principles of geometrical deduction, at p. 435 of vol. ii. Notwithstanding Buckle's headstrong tendencies, great intellectual power, and huge stock of knowledge, I never knew a man who more gracefully, though cautiously, submitted to correction. In his discourse at the Royal Institution he had spoken of the late Sir W. Hamilton, and Professor De Morgan, as the orginators of the doctrine of "the quantified predicate." I found no difficulty in convincing him that neither of those able men had any title to the distinction assigned to them; but he was not satisfied till I had pointed out to him an enunciation of the doctrine in question in the works of Laurentius Valla. He has been called dogmatic and crotchety: whatever he may have been, I never found him otherwise than ardent and conscientious in the pursuit of truth. So that he got at the truth he cared little whether he had to correct another or to submit to correction himself.

In morals he was a firm necessitarian: in religion he was a positivist, sympathising, however, with the Broad Church party. In both he was jealous of the claims of tradition as superseding or limiting positive science. I never was able to determine whether any private dislikes had whet his trenchant criticism on the Scottish clergy. I am inclined to think that the virulence with which he assailed *them* would have been extended to any other party who used a powerful theological influence to the detriment of civilisation.

In personal appearance Buckle was tall and spare, of fair complexion, with mild yet penetrating eyes, light hair, a nose like a hawk's bill, a large mouth, and huge under-jaw. His head was handsome, his forehead massive and expanded. His voice was somewhat loud and dissonant, and his accent was broad and unmusical. He had a hesitating manner of talking, as if he were forcibly restraining the current of speech until his thoughts were clearly ordered, and he had a very disagreeable way of emphasising the word *and* and some other monosyllables. Yet the expression of his face, and his manner generally were pleasing. They were significant of earnest and vigorous thought, and indomitable firmness. He had little sense of the humorous, and made little allowance for the absurd. With all his vehemence and animosity, and his vast overbearing intellect, he had a genial equability of temper and a generous sympathy which made him the friend of men who had little in common with him. *He had no conceit or vanity in his composition,* and he could not understand it in others. They who have charged him with this vice have foully libelled him. I never knew a man to whom such a vice was so impossible; yet he had a thorough appreciation of his own great powers, and kept himself and his aims so constantly before him, that he might, in the French signification of the term, be called an egotist. This brief and imperfect sketch of Buckle's life and character must be taken with due allowance for probable error. It must be borne in mind that at present but little is known of the last few months of his life; and that though I had occasional opportunities of intercourse with him before the publication of his second volume, I was by no means his intimate friend. He always treated me with the most perfect candour and thorough sincerity, and though I disagreed with much in his philosophical systems, I deeply respected and admired him. He was indeed a man of mark; and I know of no man whose intellect and training fit him to succeed Buckle in his immortal labours.

XIV

A VOICE FOR THE MUTE CREATION.

THERE are, in my opinion, many moral questions as to which the Old Testament is favourably contrasted with the New. In moral precepts the former is scarcely less rich than the latter. In the duty of sincerity and purity of heart, as in that of recognising the equality of all men, according to the famous Terentian *dictum ;* in the duty of consideration towards strangers, as in those of restraining the tongue from lying, slandering, and evil-speaking, the two Testaments are co-ordinate, and the New sometimes borrows of the Old.

But further, there is, I think, one point upon which the Old Testament has a *decided* superiority over the New : viz., in respect to the conduct of man towards his less richly gifted associates in Creation. I do not intend to impute the slightest blame to the writers of the New Testament for their omission to enjoin kindness towards the brutes : nor for their still more remarkable silence respecting a " peculiar institution." They were probably not directly called upon to pronounce upon any questions of those kinds. Whatever may be the explanation of their omission respecting our treatment of the brutes—and I doubt not a sufficient one existed—we must still say that for all moral purposes the Old Testament is here better than the New.

Let us briefly inquire what is enjoined in the Old Testament on the subject before us. We shall not find much; but what there is, is pointed and significant. In the Book of Exodus (xxiii. 12) we shall find an ordinance for the observance of the Sabbath based on a most merciful consideration. "Six days shalt thou do thy work, and on the seventh day shalt thou rest:" and one of the reasons assigned for this rest is, "that thine ox and thine ass may rest." In the Book of Numbers (xxii. 28–33) we hear the Divine Voice lifted up on behalf of an ill-used ass. "What have I done unto thee, that thou has smitten me these three times? . . . Am not I thine ass, upon which thou has ridden ever since I was thine unto this day? was I ever wont to do so unto thee?" (i.e., to fall down under him). So spake the Lord by the mouth of an ass. And what saith the angel? "Wherefore hast thou smitten thine ass these three times? behold I went out to withstand thee, because thy way is perverse before me: and the ass saw me, and turned from me these three times: unless she had turned from me, surely now also I had slain thee, and saved her alive." Never did ass do a man such "yeoman service" as this, except perhaps when Samson slew his thousands with the jaw-bone of that animal. Now, I question whether I am far from wrong if I aver that, if any man

were guilty of cruelty towards a harmless and defenceless creature, he might, if he listened with his inward
sense, hear both the plaintive remonstrance of the
animal, and the denunciation of the Angel of God.
"In reason's ear" I am sure both voices will be loud
enough. How much do we not lose by shutting up
that avenue of perception against whose closed door the
hand of God is never wearied with knocking! What
heavenly precepts and persuasions, what Divine har-
monies of righteousness and truth might we not catch,
as the shy breathings of a far-off Æolian lute, if we did
but stand and listen! Sad, indeed, is it to think how
many of that patient, toiling, hard-lived race have
suffered at man's hand since Balaam in anger smote
his ass three times. Let us at least hope that God
tempers the strokes we inflict by the endowment of a
less sensitive structure than is possessed by creatures
of a higher class. How many of our best writers have
"stooped to enlogise an ass!" a noble band, headed
by God's own angel, with Sterne, Wordsworth, and
Coleridge for followers, whose words shall live as long
as the angel's rebuke can find utterance in the English
language.

We have another just and merciful precept in the
Book of Deuteronomy (xxv. 4), which forbidst he use
of the customary head-gear for oxen, when it is not
needed for guidance and control. "Thou shalt not
muzzle the ox when he treadeth out the corn." And
this prohibition is remarkable as being the only one
having reference to our treatment of the lower animals

U

which is found in the New Testament, and it is
there repeated twice (1 Cor. ix. 9; 1 Tim. v. 18). In
another part of the Book of Exodus (xxxiv. 26) we
find an injunction conceived in a singularly quaint yet
kindly spirit. It appears a second time in Deuteronomy
(xiv. 21); and though we may perhaps look upon it as
an over-refinement upon considerate kindness, border-
ing on the romantic, we cannot fail to perceive that it
is profoundly significant of the importance which the
Israelitish Lawgiver attached to the duty we are considering. He says, "Thou shalt not seethe a kid in
his mother's milk." Later in Deuteronomy (xxii. 6-7)
is an equally quaint instance of the kindness he incul-
cated towards birds: but to our modern and doubtless
better feelings the precepts seem strangely one-sided.
"If a bird's nest chance to be before thee in the way in
any tree, or on the ground, whether they be young ones
or eggs, and the dam sitting upon the young, or upon
the eggs, thou shalt not take the dam with the young:
but thou shalt in any wise let the dam go, and take the
young to thee; that it may be well with thee, and that
thou mayest prolong thy days." What a capital excuse
have we here for the young gentlemen to whose depre-
dations, according to Virgil, we are indebted for the
"doleful ditty" of the widowed nightingale. Let
Jehovah be deemed if you will a harsh and severe God
towards men; but who will deny that by the mouth
of Moses he is a kind and merciful God towards His
lower and more defenceless creatures? The numerous
instances which appear to contradict this judgment

are all explicable by considering the supreme importance of sacrificial institutions, and the duty of implicit obedience to the commands of the Israelitish
prophets.

Such is the morality of the Old Testament in respect
to our treatment of the lower animals. Under the
influence of the Christian teaching we have attained
to much higher and more exhaustive maxims than any
we can cull out of the Old Testament. I am not going
to recite a code of morality concerning the subject we
are considering. Let us look to our practice in these
enlightened days. Does it bear any proportion to our
enlightenment? I fear not. Unfortunately, civilisation, while it gives increased opportunities and better
means of moral training, also furnishes us with more
refined instruments for the perpetration of wickedness.
We may now sin with perfect good taste, and without
discomfort to our sensitive feelings. Let me lay bare
this sore of civilised society. Great is the temptation
to divorce "might" from "right." The exercise of
power is pleasant for its own sake: and where the
creature upon which it is exercised can be thereby
made to subserve the profit or pleasure of the exerciser,
there is a secondary and consequential temptation to
use it in disregard of the obligations which its possession entails. The preservation of life is a first motive
with most men, and it is instinctively and rightly so.
The fact that animal food conduces to its preservation
as well as to sensual enjoyment blinds most of us to
the horrors of the shambles and the slaughterhouse.

The fact that neither the business of life could be conducted nor some of its pleasures enjoyed without the use of horses, blinds most of us to the sufferings and sorrows of that truly noble animal. If any of us are sufficiently alive to these hard facts, the very difficulty which we experience in self-discipline and self-denial, as well as the very limited influence which we necessarily have in modifying the iron usages of society, and thus in mitigating the sufferings of our mute fellows in Creation, . . . these are circumstances which ought to make us gentle towards those who do not feel as we feel, or do not see the relations of man to brute in the same light as ourselves. Let us ever remember that men commonly act cruelly from the want of moral culture —that discipline, which fosters the kindly feelings of a man, enlightens his conscience, and trains him in habits of considerate forbearance and willing self-denial.

It is proverbial that children are cruel by nature, and in this, according to my experience, they are not slandered. They are cruel partly from "want of thought," and partly from "want of heart," *i.e.*, from a barbarous pleasure taken in the infliction of suffering, as a wanton exercise of blind power on that which cannot resist. A highly educated lady of station, who was driven by sudden adversity to get her living as a governess, and whose breeding and accomplishments obtained for her a situation in the family of a well-known marquis, confessed to me that she could not endure to associate with her young charges because they were "addicted to torturing frogs."

My own childish experiences afford me, on this point, a sufficiently bitter retrospect: yet I was not so cruel as many other children of my own age, and moreover I was always, as I am now, morbidly sensitive to pain endured by man or beast. I sometimes think I suffer more from seeing an act of cruelty which I cannot prevent than is endured by the creature on whom it is inflicted; and I always pay a heavy penalty if I forego an opportunity of intercession in the animal's favour, even where I know that my interference will be unavailing. Unavailing it too often is, from the apathy of the bystanders, who, as a rule, if you interfere, will look upon the inflictor as the injured party, and will side with him against you.

The simple fact is that it requires maturity of mind to be thoroughly conscious of the heinous sin of cruelty. Individually we learn this lesson by slow degrees. Immanuel Kant teaches that the wanton destruction of an organism of inanimate beauty—as a shoot, or a blossom—is sin ('Metaph. of Eth. Elementology,' book i. sec. 17). And though this is not cruelty, it is closely allied to it. But the little pleasure, either immediate or consequential, derivable from such an act (except, indeed, in the way of retaliation for an injury received) is necessarily so small that but little culture is required for the eradication of this despicable and childish practice.[1]

---

[1] In the year 1814 Edward Pollo was hanged at the new gaol, Chelmsford, for cutting down a cherry-tree, in a plantation at Kelvedon, in Essex, the property of a Mr. Brewer. Mr. Justice Heath, who tried him, told him that "a man that would wilfully cut down a young cherry-tree would take away a man's life!"

But not only is the lesson of kindness to "the mute creation" (as Lord Erskine called the lower animals) slowly and gradually learned by the individual, but it is slowly and gradually learned by the race or tribe of which that individual is a unit. We English were once notably cruel on principle both to man and to beast. Sir Thomas Elyote was a popular writer of the sixteenth century; and it will excite surprise to learn that he found no better way of extolling the blameless habits of the Roman Emperor Alexander, than by setting forth his keen relish of diversions which we count among the most cruel. He writes ('The Image of Governaunce,' 1549, p. 15): "In feasts or bankettyng he neuer wolde haue any wanton pastime. *His pleasure was to behold byrdes fightyng together.* And therefore he had in his gardein, places, where birdes of sundry kyndes were inclosed and kepte, wherein he toke singular pleasure." Indeed both cock-fighting and bull-baiting were not only commonly practised in England for a century after the time of Sir Thomas Elyote, but they were regarded as respectable and innocent diversions, and, as such, were frequented by the best educated of both sexes.

Now I am not prepared to say that the sports of the field are as cruel as cock-fighting and bull-baiting; at least the cruelty in the one case is not so barbarous as in the other. In the case of field sports the infliction of cruelty is incidental, not essential, to the pleasure. It usually forms no part of the sportsman's enjoyment. His delight is not in the terrors or anguish of a deer at bay, or, what is often worse, of an over-ridden horse, but in "the glory of motion," the excitement of pursuit, and the not too formidable dangers of the fence and brook. He takes no pleasure in the torments endured by a winged partridge or a limping hare, but in the exercise of the trained eye and arm, and the athletic morning walk. Yet be these manly exercises as exhilarating and invigorating as they may, the sportsman should not allow his feelings to become callous to the sufferings which "the mute creation" pay as the extorted price of his pleasure. None but the sportsman can accurately know what amount or kind of suffering is usually inflicted in the course of a day's hunt; and as he does not trouble his head about the feelings of a terror-stricken fox, or the toils of a dead-beat horse, these silent sufferers get little sympathy either in the field or in the hall. Yet how often have I heard of a sportsman breaking his horse's back in training or in the hunt. One of the best riders I ever knew set his horse at a high double fence, which he refused. Again and again, under the stimulus of whip and spur, did he repeat the experiment, and each time the sagacious animal, from instinctive knowledge of his own inability, refused the leap. The rider at last came off victorious, and the horse broke his back. I had the privilege of travelling with a first-rate sportsman in the month of October 1860, and I now rejoice that I was prompted by the character of his conversation to take some of it down. It was addressed to a sporting friend who sat opposite him: so I shall indicate the sportsman by the letter A. and his friend by B.

A. Ah! the hardest run we ever had was one day last year from Ingatestone. To my knowledge *eight* horses died after the hunt! I was prepared against emergencies, and sent on a second horse to be in readiness; but he did not come up in time, so I had to ride one poor devil all day; and he died the next morning. Bless you! at last he could hardly draw his hindquarters out of the loam.

B. Good G——! and I suppose others were injured for life?

A. Why, yes; *five* of the survivors to my knowledge were good for nothing afterwards.

B. That's thirteen: out of how many?

A. Out of fifteen or thereabouts. Some fifteen only were left at the end of the day. Let me give you a bit of advice. It's of no use to keep a horse that has gone through such a day as that. And mind you this, *one palpitation of the heart is enough for one horse.* My advice is, " Sell him."

B. I dare say you are in the right there.

A. And if your horse takes to bleeding at the nose, lose no time, sell him as soon as you have him in condition, you'll get more for him then than ever afterwards.

Here I closed my note-book. I had got a faithful photograph of an Essex sportsman, and "a right-down good fellow" into the bargain: and I was satisfied. However, I made this mental comment on the sportsman's sound advice. "And as for the purchaser of the damaged horse, I suppose he must take care of himself. *Caveat emptor.* He will doubtless find out when it is too late that his newly purchased hunter is worth a trifle more to the knacker than to the huntsman. And thus the iniquity of cruelty is capped by the iniquity of fraud."

And yet I dare say this fox-hunter was not in other respects a bad man. He is probably an excellent landlord, and, as times go, a judicious magistrate. Habitual cruelty is unfortunately an abstraction, or I should say that it must bear the blame of much that is faulty in the worthy gentleman's character. We may say of it, as Angell James said of the sin of indifference, "It rots the heart," or as Burns said of illicit love—

> "It hardens a' within,
> And petrifies the feeling."

Call it a case of putrefaction or petrifaction—it is all one in metaphorical language.

Do you suppose Assheton Smith was a bad man? Not at all. If we may believe the united testimony of all who knew him, he was a fine, manly old English gentleman. But his virtues could not make that right which is wrong: nor ought his high character to blind any reader of his biography to the fact that he devoted a long and vigorous life to the prosecution of *a pastime which is inseparably connected with cruelty.* Wise is that advice of Zimmerman: "Put this restriction on your pleasures: be cautious that they injure no being which has life."

After these examples of inhumanity, I will say, perhaps excusable inhumanity, how delightful it is to read the confession of a brave soldier and an able general, who early resolved—whatever may have been his motive—

> " Never to blend his pleasures or his pride
> With sorrow of the meanest thing that lives."

I allude to the late Sir Charles James Napier. He writes thus of his illustrious family :—

> " We are all a hot violent crew ; to do us justice, with the milk of human kindness, though. We were all fond of hunting, fishing and shooting ; yet all gave them up when young men, because we had no pleasure in killing little animals. George and I were bold riders. . . . We, however, always found it pain, not pleasure, to worry poor animals. Lately, in camp, a little hare got up, the greyhounds pursued, and the men shouted to aid the dogs. My sorrow was great, and I rode away ; yet at dinner I ate a poor fowl ! It is not principle, therefore, on which we act ; it is a painful feeling. As to cat-hunting and dog-fighting, feeling and principle unite to condemn : a domestic animal confides in you and is at your mercy ; a wild animal has some fair play, a domestic one none. Cat-hunters and dog-fighters are, therefore, not only cruel, but traitors : no polished gentleman does these things."—*Life of Sir C. J. Napier*, 1857, vol. ii. p. 291.

Let us take another example of the man, who, according to the wise king, " doeth good to his own soul " (Prov. xi. 17).

When Beckford of Fonthill built the high wall round his estate, society, who are never at a loss to imagine a bad motive where a good one is not known, would have it that he built it " to cut himself off from mankind." But he had a good reason for doing so, as he tells us :

"I built the wall because I would not be intruded upon by sportsmen. In vain were they warned off. Your country gentleman will transport a pauper for taking a few twigs from a hedge while they break it down without ceremony themselves. They will take no denial when they go hunting in their red jackets to excruciate to death a poor hare. I found remonstrance vain, and so I built the wall to exclude them. I never suffer an animal to be killed but through necessity. In early life I gave up shooting because I consider that we have no right to murder animals for sport. I am fond of animals. The birds in the plantations of Fonthill seem to know me : they continued their songs as I rode close to them. It was exactly what I wished."
—*Memoirs of William Beckford,* 1859, p. 259.

This is to me a green spot in the life of Beckford ; and with me his kindness to his birds and game shall cover a multitude of sins.

Cruel as are the most innocent of English field sports, I must admit that they fall short, in cruelty, of some which prevail in other lands, whether of the field or of the arena. I wish, however, I could believe that England furnished no parallel to the cruelties of German deer-stalking. But I much fear the following incident might have happened as well in Scotland as in Germany. It must be premised that a stag had been hit in the hind leg, and was lost. Two keepers with a bloodhound and a turnspit fast to their waists by a leathern thong, took to the track of the wounded animal. The dogs were at last let loose ; then came the *dénouement* of the tragedy, which I give in the words of an eyewitness.

"The stag, as was expected, came down to the meadow, and he emerged from the trees, limping forward very fast, *with one dog hanging on to his nose and the rest to his heels and sides*. Down he came to a little brook into which he threw himself, and at last, turned at bay. The hound hanging to his nose kept a firm grip of him, even when the stag, holding his head down, tried to drown him in the stream; at the same time the stag butted violently with his horns in every direction, making the dogs cautious. Then tired out, he fairly lay down in the stream, and at this moment a shot from the Duke's rifle struck him, and a huntsman running up plunged his dagger into the expiring animal's heart."—*All the Year Round*, No. 85.

I would ask, what more could these wretches have done had they been dealing with a leopard or a tiger, instead of a poor deer? And, if the animal was to be killed, why did not "the Duke's rifle" put him out of his miseries when he first emerged from the trees? If the first shot fails to arrest the stag, is it necessary to wait till he is at bay before you deal with him? I do not profess to understand the ceremonies of the chase. But it seems to me as if one part of the diversion consisted in aggravating the dying agonies of the prey. In this I hope I do his serene highness an injustice. At all events, if this be deer-stalking, it is a most barbarous sport.

I am sore afraid it is only too easy to blunt the kindly feelings of those that have any. The excitement of the field or the arena soon overwhelm the emotions of humanity; there is an excellent example of this in the 'Confessions' of St. Augustine (book vi. c. 8, translation revised by Dr. Pusey). It is stated that one Alypius, though "utterly averse to and detesting" the spectacles of the gladiators—*i.e.*, from report only, was induced at last to enter the Amphitheatre protesting all the while, "though you take my body to that place, and there sit me, can you force me also to turn my mind or my eyes to those shows? I shall then be absent while present, and so shall overcome both you and them." The result is thus told :—

"So soon as he saw that blood, he therewith drank down savageness ; nor turned away, but fixed his eye drinking in pleasure unawares, and was delighted with that guilty fight, and intoxicated with the bloody pastime ; nor was he now the man he came, but one of the throng he came unto, yea a true associate of theirs that brought him thither."

It is thus that the humanest person in Spain soon learns the terrible fascination of the bull-fight. Here, as in the gladiatorial spectacle of ancient Rome, the danger encountered by the assailants might seem to redeem the pastime from that contemptible meanness which marks at least one of our athletic and most of our field sports. But, in point of fact, there are circumstances in both the former which degrade them to the level of the ring and the chase. Indeed I am not sure that I am not wronging the shows of the gladiators in classing the bull-fight with them. In the latter, there are acts which deserve to be ranked with what Sir C. J. Napier called "traitorous cruelty."[1] In the first place the

---

[1] The persons who take part in a bull-fight are called generically toreadors.

   1. Alguaciles (officers).

   2. Picadores—on horseback.

   3. Banderilleros and Chulos—on foot.

bull, if shy, is often urged to the contest by the most revolting acts of torture; it is the business of the banderilleros to insert in the flanks of the unhappy creature barbed darts and hand-rockets, which goad him to fury or madness. In the next place, the animals used to protect the picador are selected from among the aged beasts of burden; with the merciful among us those horses who have faithfully worked out a long term of service are rewarded with the grateful repose of the meadow or the moor for the rest of their declining years. Now, in Spain, it is just from this class that horses are chosen to encounter the dying agonies of the arena, which thus becomes a dreadful substitute for the knacker's yard. Then again, though the picador and matador run great risks, often encountering a dreadful death, yet the spectators and proprietors, they for whose enjoyment and profit the spectacle is maintained, are well and securely protected from reaping that recompense of their wicked folly which is meet. Bevies of well-dressed ladies and their gallants look on unmoved except by fierce exultation, while sometimes bulls, horses, and occasionally men are involved in one common destruction.[1]

4. Matadores or Espadas—on foot; whose business it is to slaughter the bull.

5. Mæstros; and

6. Attendants with mules.

[1] The *Times* (during the month of October 1862) reported a bull-fight at Saragossa, in which the first bull, after having two fireworks stuck into his shoulder, became so furious that the President advised the use of the demilune—which is an instrument used for mowing off the legs of the bulls. The matador, in this case, refused the offer, and accordingly engaged the bull, when he was so badly thrown and gored that

I am afraid that the callousness which I have
pointed out and explained in the frequenter of the bull-
fight and the chase is very generally diffused among
ordinary men. However, I am both surprised and disappointed when I find men of high intellectual culture,
and who are not professed sportsmen, devoid of kindly
feelings towards our domestic animals. How few men
care how much the driver "punishes" his horse.[1] For
my part I generally put a summary stop to the castigation
of horses; and I can assure those who do not do so,
that there is no slight instruction and amusement in
the excuses cabmen make when reprimanded for their
cruelty. One driver said to me, " Well, I can assure you
that most of the gentlemen I carry insist on my putting
my horse to the top of his speed, and keeping him
there." Another driver, whom I corrected for repeated
applications of the whip in the course of a short drive,

he was removed in a hopeless state. The demilune was then brought
into play, and the bull fought on his hind legs and two stumps : but
he was still so formidable that he *had to be* reduced to four stumps,
before he received the *coup-de-grace.*

In the month of September 1862 the Emperor and Empress of
the French witnessed a bull-fight at Bayonne. "A bull-fight" is,
however, rather a misnomer—a double misnomer : for there was no
genuine fighting, and such as it was there were *six* fights. Six fine
bulls were slaughtered on the occasion.

[1] Hear the most sensible and the most devout savan of the reign of
George II. "When I am on my way," said Johnson, "to dine with
a friend, and, finding it late, have bid the coachman make haste, if I
happen to attend when he whips his horses, I may feel unpleasantly
that the animals are put to pain, but I do not wish him to desist. No,
sir, I wish him to drive on " (Boswell's 'Life of Johnson' 1811, i. 113).
We cannot say, from this, that Johnson would have countenanced *cruelty:*
but we may, and perhaps do, infer that he was not scrupulous in his conduct towards the brutes.

gave me this explanation of the circumstance. "Why, the fact is, sir, I could not have got my 'oss to go without flogging him. Bless you, he's a lazy old 'oss he is, and a knowing one too; doesn't he just know well enough when he's got a gemman behind him, as don't like to see him flogged!"[1]

Carlyle tells us that his friend Sterling had not "much depth of real laughter, or sense of the ludicrous, but what he had was genuine, free, and continual." This little trait in his character is thus illustrated by his biographer. "We once got into a cab, about Charing Cross, I know not now whence, or well whitherward, nor that our haste was at all special—however, the cabman, sensible that his pace was slowish, took to whipping with a steady, passionless, business-like assiduity which, though the horse seemed rather lazy than weak, became afflictive,"—mind it was Carlyle, not the horse that was afflicted—"and I urged remonstrance with the savage fellow, 'Let him alone,' answered Sterling, 'he is kindling the enthusiasm of his horse; you perceive that is the first thing, then we shall do very well,'—as we accordingly did."

[1] "Charlotte [Brontë] was more than commonly tender in her treatment of all dumb creatures, and they, with that fine instinct so often noticed, were invariably attracted towards her" (Mrs. Gaskell's 'Life of C. Brontë,' 1867, p. 203). *Cf.* Shirley—"Do you know what soothsayers I would consult? . . . The little Irish beggar that comes barefoot to my door; the mouse that steals out of the cranny in my wainscot; the bird in frost and snow that pecks at my window for a crumb; the dog that licks my hand and sits beside my knee. . . . I know somebody to whose knee the black cat loves to climb, against whose shoulder and cheek it likes to purr. The old dog always comes out of his kennel and wags his tail, and whines affectionately when somebody passes."

Now I think Carlyle would have more wisely consulted his friend's memory by allowing this little incident to drop into oblivion: a joke at the expense of a persecuted horse is but a sorry one. Nor does Carlyle himself look to the best advantage "urging remonstrance," but not remonstrating. None of the parties to this little drama seem to have had the excuse of irritability of temper or thoughtlessness. The castigation, like Sterling's sense of the ludicrous, was "genuine, free, and continual:" it was genuine in its severity, and it was freely and continually administered. It was also coldly calculated and mechanically inflicted. By the two good men inside it was calmly discussed and deliberately permitted. What a contrast is this to the less blameworthy conduct of a small tradesman whom I suddenly and angrily arrested in the passionate infliction of the whip on a stubborn pony. "What a brute you are," I said, "to flog your little horse so. You are by far the greater brute of the two." "I can't help it," yelped the little man with the tears in his eyes, "he almost drives me mad!" The common practice of mercilessly beating the Esquimaux dogs met with no efficient check from Sir Leopold M'Clintock. Hear his account of the matter.

"Poor dogs! they have a hard life of it in these regions. Even Petersen, who is generally kind and humane, seems to fancy that they have little or no feeling: one of his theories is, that you may knock an Esquimaux dog about the head with any article, however heavy, with perfect impunity to the brutes.

x

One of us upbraided him the other day because he
broke his whip-handle over the head of a dog. 'That
was *nothing at all,*' he assured us: some friend of
his in Greenland found he could beat his dogs over
the head with a heavy hammer,—it stunned them
certainly,—but by laying them with their mouths
open to the wind, they soon revived, got up, and
ran about 'all right'" ('Narrative,' 1859, p. 321).
And this "assurance," which even if true amounted
but to this, that the dogs were only put in pain, not
vitally or even seriously hurt, was sufficient to insure
Captain M'Clintock's toleration of the cruelty uniformly
practised towards those hard-working, hard-lived, gentle
creatures.   Man shrinks from calling his vices by
their right names. Gaiety and gallantry are terms
that from the days of Ancient Rome until now have
served to dissemble very great wickedness :

> " Hœc eadem illi
> Omnia quum faciunt, hilares nitidique vocantur."[1]

Cleverness often stands for fraud, and embellishment
for lying. What is sharp practice but dishonesty?
So, likewise, have cruelty and other abominable acts
been designated, as if the lower animals were the
aggressors rather than the victims. Every kind of
contempt has been heaped upon the brutes in our
words and proverbs. In particular the dog has been
made, as it were, the type of all the vileness which

---

[1] "Whenever they do all these same things they are called *gay* and
gallant."—Juvenal, *Sat.* xi.

was conceived to belong to the lower animals. Both the Old and the New Testaments countenance this use in many places: and this, perhaps, because the dogs were the scavengers of the camp and the city. From that appellative we derive our verb *to dog* (a verb of a bad sense), and *dogged*, stupid or obstinate; and in times past there were few "bad names" so offensive in their application to the Jew, and indeed to men generally, as 'dog.' In '1 Henry IV.,' ii. 8, we have the phrase or proverb "as dank as a dog;" in 'The Silent Woman,' ii. 2, we have, "as melancholy as a dog;" and in one of Marlowe's plays we have a roll-call of such phrases :—

> "Thou say'st thou art as weary as a dog,
> As angry, sick, and hungry as a dog,
> As dull and melancholy as a dog,
> As lazy, sleepy, and as idle as a dog;
> But why dost thou compare thee to a dog
> In that for which all men despise a dog?"

[Marlowe's Works, ed. 1826, iii. 448 ; cited by Halliwell, Shak, Soc. Papers, iii. 36.]

And yet, of all the animals God has given for our use, which of them comes so near to man in the affections and emotions as the dog, whom all men, by their speech, despise? It is convenient to affect this contempt for the brutes. Our own natural cruelty towards them thus gets called *brutality:* and yet in this sense the brutes are not commonly "brutal." In conformity with this usage, that quality which is so rare in men we call their *humanity*, as if all that is "human" were "humane."

The simple fact is, that by such a use of words we point an indirect compliment to ourselves, and transfer to the innocent brute the odium of our own barbarity.

But we have lived to see a new and strangely horrible phase of cruelty grow up among us, which let us earnestly pray for the means to eradicate, ere it be naturalised here, and get the privilege of a colloquial name. Contradictory as it may appear, it is a species of cruelty which could hardly be perpetuated by men until they had attained to a high condition of mental enlightenment and social progress. The late M. Magendie, of the French *Académic du Médecin*, instituted a new school of surgery in which all dissections of the lower animals were made on the living subject. These operations, which pass under the learned name of *vivisections*, made no small sensation among French physicians, not so much on account of the sympathy which even a Frenchman must at times feel for the sufferings of the helpless brute, as by reason of the rich prospect of scientific progress held out to his pupils by that fiendish *savan;* and since M. Magendie's introduction of the new method of dissection, the school of Vivisection has been widely patronised, not only by French and Italian, but also by English, students. Horses have been purchased in great numbers for the use of the *Académic.* These wretched animals are made fast into frames of admirable workmanship, and are then slowly and securely dissected alive,[1] the art of the operator being propor-

---

[1] Not always "securely."

tional to the length of time during which he can keep
the horse "stretched on the rack of life." Besides
horses, numbers of apes, dogs, cats, and rabbits have
been subjected to vivisection: and all for what? I can
hardly say. I believe science has not benefited by it.
Sir Charles Bell expressed a strong opinion that science
could not benefit by it. For my part, I should have
expected Atheism to have become religion, if vivisection
had become science. M. Magendie's experiments were
deemed so inconclusive that they have been repeated
over and over again by his pupils, among whom M.
Claude Bernard at present occupies the foremost place.
I am not aware that any French voice was ever
efficiently raised against these strange barbarities,
which in malignant and unnatural cruelty throw everything I have spoken of into the shade.

Honour to England in that she first uttered public
protest against Vivisection. In the month of October
(1861), the "Royal Society for the Prevention of
Cruelty to Animals" sent a deputation, headed by the
eminent surgeon, Mr. Curling, to the Emperor of the
French. The deputation presented a memorial from
the Society to that potentate praying him to prohibit
Vivisection in the French *Académie*. Let us render
honour to Napoleon III. in that he immediately issued
an interim order for the suspension of Vivisection,
and nominated a committee of inquiry into the facts.
The *Académie* responded by nominating a committee
on their part. The reports of these committees have
not yet been made : but it cannot be doubted that sooner

or later the indefatigable exertions of Mr. Curling and his colleagues will be crowned with success.

Well may we say with St. Paul, "The whole creation groaneth and travaileth in pain together." Some men more sensitive than others have manfully done their share in the duty of sparing the brutes. Shelley, the immortal poet, would never touch animal food, simply because he thought it wrong to purchase a benefit or a pleasure which is obtainable only at the cost of suffering to an inferior animal. Many have followed his example. We must revere the motive; and though we might scruple to partake of a *pate*, *de foie gras*, or a *fricassée de grenouilles*, we shall probably think that Shelley was mistaken in his view of the duty of abstinence from animal food. He also believed in a future state of retribution for the lower animals. Dickens fancies the horses crying out against men, and glorying in the thought that even men die.

It is not for us to speculate rashly on the question whether there is an hereafter for creatures who have neither reason nor conscience. The preacher, indeed, and the psalmist give it against them : but so they do against man in more places than one. Bishop Butler with his hard head and his large heart allowed room for hope that they will live after death in a higher and happier state of existence : and his reverent speculation has been finely translated into painting by Sir Edwin Landseer in his "Dying Camel." "The kind star," says a contemporary writer (*All the Year Round*, June 25, 1859), "which shines forth over the half-prostrate animal, dimly suggests a hope that even 'the mute creation' are not excluded from a share in Heaven's eternal mercy. The minds of those who feel deeply will at times stretch forward thus in a strong sympathy with the sufferings of creation, and will strain to get a glimpse beyond that glass through which we see so darkly."

THE END.

PRINTED BY BALLANTYNE, HANSON AND CO.
EDINBURGH AND LONDON.